THE MAN FROM MESABI

THE MAN
FROM MESABI

by Sarah Lockwood

DOUBLEDAY & COMPANY, INC., GARDEN CITY, NEW YORK

*All of the characters in this book are fictitious,
and any resemblance to actual persons,
living or dead, is purely coincidental.*

THE MAN FROM MESABI

PART ONE

CHAPTER 1

On a June day in 1880 a man lay on a bunk in a log cabin dying of a bullet wound. The cabin was small, still, and stagnant with the smell of blood. A coffeepot and a greasy frying pan stood on the cookstove at one end of it, its stack disappearing through the low-pitched roof, ashes and wood chips scattered on the floor around it. Cooking pots, coats, fishing tackle—anything that would hang up—dangled from nails driven into the unpeeled logs. Dirty boots and socks lay in a heap in a corner. The only clean thing in the room was a shotgun laid carefully across the antlers of a deer.

Through the open door the sun, reflected from the surface of the lake, dappled the floor with patches of brilliant light that shifted nervously, as if impatient with the slow passing of the man on the bunk; the tall pines that overshadowed the tiny cabin sighed in the light breeze with more of weariness than regret.

And there was more of weariness than regret over the plight of the man on the bunk in the faces of the two lumberjacks who were listlessly playing pinochle at a deal table in the middle of the room. A few days ago they had walked out to the cabin from Haley, a little timber town eight miles away, broke, sodden with bad whiskey, to look up one of their kind who had failed to appear in the lumber camps that winter. Ignoring a marked lack of cordiality in their reception, they settled down to loaf through the summer until, on the previous day, their hopes had been shattered by the crack of a shot coming from the underbrush. At first, their interest in this event had been lively to a point just short of blows, little Matt vehemently defending the man on the bunk and Jake protesting that Steve had got what was coming to him.

"He didn't have no right to the old man's shack. Man move in on my shack I'd shoot him too."

"Hell! You ain't got no shack. What you talkin' about? Steve's filed on this claim, ain't he? What's Beemer got to do with it? He ain't been here for a couple of years; then he comes back dodgin' around in the bushes, yellin', and lets fly at Steve. He's crazy, shoot a man like that." Matt chuckled. "I bet he done somethin' once made him take to the woods. But they won't catch him no more than they could a weasel. He's over the border by now."

"What's Steve out here for, anyhow?" grumbled Jake. "Why can't he let the old cuss be? Ain't nothin' here worth a man's time outside of trappin' like Beemer done."

"That's right." Matt shook his head. "But he's here, and he's got a right to be."

But twenty-four hours had passed since they had lugged Steve into the cabin and dumped him on the bunk, and by this time neither of them cared who was in the right of it. They were tired of hanging around, waiting for the man to die. Supplies were low, and in the earlier excitement all the whiskey had been wasted on Steve.

For several hours now they had been playing pinochle for Steve's shotgun, shuffling and dealing mechanically, spitting through the open door, where the sun continued to advance until it touched their heavy boots, crept up to the bright colors in their checked shirts. From time to time they glanced at the long form on the bunk. The boots were off the big gray socks, the pants loosened at the belt, and on the naked torso, glistening with sweat, a wad of blood-soaked linen rose and fell as the long slow breaths entered the body and left it. After one such glance Jake threw down his cards, rasped back his chair, and stood up.

"Hell!" he burst out, glaring at the sick man. "What's keepin' him? A man bleed like he done ain't got no right to live as long as this. Why don't he git goin'?"

"Maybe he don't want to." Matt got to his feet. "Can't say as I blame him after what he's gone through out here."

They moved cautiously across the room to the bunk and stood looking down. "Looks bad, don't he?" muttered Jake. "If he'd quit breathin', he'd be dead right now. Beats me how he keeps it up."

"I don't know about that." Matt bent over the still face, ghastly in contrast to the rough black hair matted on the massive skull. "Strikes me he'd be gone by now if he was goin'. A man like him can lose a powerful lot of blood without kickin' off, providin' he wants to stay— and Steve sure wants to stay." He straightened up and turned to Jake. "I bet you two bits, right now, he ain't goin'."

Without warning the cold green eyes opened with startling suddenness, the sick man's pale lips twisted in a faint grin. "Collect, Matt," he muttered. "You win." The hard glance shifted to Jake. "Clear out, Jake. Now. I don't like what I've been hearing." The eye-

8

lids, weighted by the heavy lashes, slowly closed. "See that he gets going, Matt."

When Steve opened his eyes again, Jake was some distance in the woods on his way to town and Matt was hopping nimbly around the stove whistling and frying salt pork. "I got buckwheats and pork gravy but there ain't no coffee," he burst out when he saw Steve was awake. "How about it?"

"Fine," said Steve. "I can eat twenty of 'em." He pushed himself with considerable effort into a half-sitting position against the log wall at his back. The blood-soaked wad fell off and he peered down at the ugly wound beneath his left shoulder. "Fine," he repeated with satisfaction. "He couldn't have done better for me. This fixes it. Beemer can't make any trouble now."

Matt, a long fork upright in his hand, stared at him. "You mean he had a right here? You mean you jumped him?"

Steve frowned. "No," he said curtly. "If he had any rights here they didn't show up in the land office. He hasn't been near the place for a couple of years. What could he expect?" He stared steadily at Matt for a moment, then his face relaxed. "No need to worry about Beemer," he said. "He's fixed it fine with that shot. How long have I been here?"

"About this time yesterday," replied Matt cheerfully. "Been out cold ever since and, man, did you bleed! You wouldn't think a man could hold that much blood. Must have been a couple of barrels."

Steve watched the fresh red drops, started again by his effort to sit up, work their way through the black thatch on his chest. "Some still coming from somewhere," he commented, "but from the looks of things around here I guess you're right. He came damn near getting me, at that. Before I eat, go outside and cut some fresh boughs for this bunk. It stinks."

9

CHAPTER 2

The next morning, after fixing Steve up as well as he could with a jug of water and a plate of cold pancakes on a box beside the bunk, Matt set off for town for the much needed supplies. It would take him most of the day and he shuffled around, reluctant to leave the helpless man until Steve cussed him on his way.

After he had gone, Steve lay with his good arm beneath his head, staring at the rafters and thinking hard. Except for his remarkable eyes, there was nothing particularly distinguished about him as he lay there. The easy grace in his long muscular figure was common to most lumberjacks and there was nothing in his face to denote any outstanding intellectual activity. The head was well formed, the forehead high, the eyes comfortably cradled between thick black brows and solid cheekbones. The mouth was full and firm. It was a hard face, not one to encourage a man to take liberties with it, but there was still the flexibility of youth in it, for Steve was young— still in his twenties, as close as he could figure it.

With Matt out of the way his thoughts turned to the adventure that had landed him here with a bullet through his shoulder. It had started one day the previous spring when a wiry, long-legged man of middle age, dressed in well-worn woods clothes had dropped off the train at Haley looking for a man to tote for him on a fishing trip. He looked prosperous and was particular about the man he took with him. Finally he got around to Steve, gave him a keen look, and offered him the job. Steve took it.

They hadn't gone a mile into the woods before the stranger stopped—and Steve learned he was on no fishing trip. It was no surprise to him. The heft of the duffel he had lashed on the horse had convinced him of that. He waited to hear what was coming.

"My name is Cramer," began his employer abruptly, "and I hired you because you look like a man who can keep his mouth shut." He raised his hand as Steve started to speak. "I'm a mining man, prospecting for iron, but it will be to your advantage, as well as mine, if you continue to regard this as a fishing trip."

10

"That suits me," said Steve, and they pushed on.

Steve thought he knew the country after logging over it for six years, but Cramer headed south and east away from the familiar logging routes into a savage wilderness where streams ran red, flecked with orange foam, and a man's compass played queer tricks. It was tough, hard going, and Steve, assisting his employer in his borings and prowlings, knew Cramer was finding iron but the mining man, silent and preoccupied, moved on with quiet persistence.

Finally, after a week or more, they headed north again and camped one night in a stand of pine on the shore of a good-sized lake. It was dark when they got there and Steve busied himself with balsam boughs for Cramer's small tent.

"We're about back where we started from," he said. "About eight miles to Haley from that shore over there."

"You mean you've logged through here?"

"No. Nobody been in here that I know of. Few stands like this but not enough to come for. How about a bass for supper?"

"Not tonight," said Cramer. "I want to turn in."

The next morning they started on their customary prowl through the woods. They hadn't gone a hundred yards before they came upon a tiny tumbled-down shack almost hidden by the underbrush. Steve pushed open the sagging door and stepped in. A chipmunk scampered up the log wall and sat shrilling at him from a rafter.

"Guess this must be where old Beemer holes up," he said as he backed out to join Cramer.

"Who is he?" asked Cramer.

"Trapper," said Steve. "Comes to Haley once in a while to get drunk. Haven't seen him around this spring. Looks like he's cleared out."

They went on through the woods, climbed a ridge, and after about a mile, came down to another lake, twin to the one they were camped on. It was a big lake, with a tangle of dead tamaracks at the far end. They stood for a moment, looking across the forbidding sheet of water, rust-red where the morning sun thrust through it. As if to challenge its forbidding spell, Steve picked up a handful of gravel and hurled it far out. The sound as it struck the water was loud in the silence. Steve wiped his palm on his pants. He noticed it was smeared with red.

They spent a long slow day with the instruments, but Steve's hopes that the job was about to pay off were dashed when they

11

finally circled back to camp that night. After supper Cramer sat on a duffel bag deep in thought, his pipe glowing and fading as the smoke from his lips joined the smoke from the campfire drifting toward the stars. He roused when Steve threw more wood on the fire and sat down opposite.

"Yes," he said, as if continuing some argument with himself, "there's iron here, plenty of it, but it isn't worth a damn."

"Why not?" asked Steve.

Cramer glanced at him with a faint smile. "It isn't difficult to find iron," he said. "The trick is to turn it into steel at a profit. That can't be done here."

"Why not?" Steve asked again.

"For many reasons," replied Cramer. "This region is interesting geologically but worthless from a practical point of view." He leaned forward, the firelight flickering on his face. "There is, unquestionably, a considerable amount of surface iron scattered through this area. You've seen me bring it up; we ran into it again this afternoon. It is easy to work and fair in quality but"—he gave his knees a decisive slap—"to strip, lift, and transport the stuff is out of the question." He puffed on that thought for a moment. "But if it could be got out of this godforsaken wilderness," he went on, rousing again, "the smelters couldn't handle it. They don't want it. May never want it. Certainly not while deep, rich ore is available. No! I'm looking for a mine, not an experiment. We'll push on north in the morning." He stood up and knocked out his pipe. "Still, you can't tell in this business—it's a gamble any way you look at it." He gave Steve an odd, oblique glance. "You're a smart young fellow. When we get to Alturos, why don't you go to the land office and file on a piece around here? It might make you some money someday."

After that Cramer's long legs ate up the miles and they were soon back in familiar territory, where the streams ran clear again and logging roads let the sun through the trees. When they neared Alturos, Cramer circled the little town to a wooded ridge to the north of it. There he was overtaken by another of his prowling fits and, at the end of the day, announced that the job was over.

"I came to look this location over," he said. "It looks all right."

"You mean you were headed here all the time?" said Steve in disgust.

Cramer made no reply. His gray eyes studied Steve for a moment, then he took a notebook from his pocket, wrote a message, and handed it to Steve. "Get in to Alturos and send this off as soon as you can."

"You want me to come back?"

"No. On the contrary, I want you to forget this trip. Say nothing about it to anybody."

They walked through the woods some distance. Cramer stopped, pulled out a roll of greenbacks, and handed it to Steve. "This is more than we bargained for but you're a good man." Again he gave Steve that odd, oblique glance. "When you go to the land office you may need it." He smiled. "Good luck, Steve. We'll meet again." They shook hands and Steve swung down the hill to Alturos.

He didn't go far before he pulled Cramer's message from his pocket and read it. It was addressed to someone in Boston and advised immediate action. Steve pushed on rapidly, his mind turning over every mile of Cramer's curious trip through the south. The mining man's repeated advice to go to the land office stuck in his mind like a burr. For some reason he couldn't figure why Cramer wanted him back in that red country; paid him to go in there. Well, nothing to lose by looking into it.

As soon as the message was sent, he went to the land office. There he learned to his disgust that Beemer had filed on the piece he wanted and it took considerable argument and some of his pay to get Beemer off the record and himself on it.

"Why are you in such a sweat for that piece?" asked the agent irritably as they bent over the maps. "Beemer's been out there trappin' them lakes for years."

Steve grinned at him. "I want to do a little trapping myself," he said. "It's good game country and there's a nice little bunch of timber in there, too. I want that half section in there between those two lakes. I like it."

The agent shook his head. "I'm tellin' you. I can't let you in there. The old man's lived there pretty steady, off and on, for a long time."

"Has he proved up on it?"

"No, can't say he has. He don't show up often—but if he did show up he could make a strong fight for that claim. He's done his time and more."

Steve's grin vanished. He looked hard at the agent as he pulled his roll of greenbacks from his pocket. "What's the law on that?" he demanded coldly. "Can a man hold land till hell freezes over while he makes up his mind to prove up? If you haven't seen this old coot for a year he's probably cleared out. What's the law on it?"

13

The agent blinked, looking anywhere but at the roll of money. "That's a fact," he said. "Old fellow like that might be dead and nobody know it. How can I tell?" he exploded virtuously. "Man doesn't show up for a year I got to assume he's abandoned, ain't I? The proof is up to him, not me." He looked Steve squarely in the eye. "If you want that piece you can have it. Does that suit you?"

"Suits me fine," said Steve as he slid two tens under the blotter. "Get out your papers and I'll sign up."

CHAPTER 3

Back in Haley, Steve, uneasy about the sticking power of his twenty dollars, went to see Curtis, the only lawyer in the town. He found him in his office above Gottlieb's grocery store, an anemic, slender young man in a neat gray suit slick with wear, but pressed and clean. His white shirt was clean. Everything about Curtis was clean from his smooth brown hair, already receding from a pale high forehead, to his carefully polished black shoes. Steve, who had never seen him before, was so shocked by his antiseptic appearance in that polluted town that he asked him at once what he was doing in Haley. The lawyer gave him a warm, slow smile.

"I don't know yet," he said. "I've just opened up here. What can I do for you?"

Steve sat down and told him something of his adventure with the land agent. The lawyer listened attentively.

"Who did you say put you on to this?" he asked presently.

"Fellow by the name of Cramer."

"He was working for the Massachusetts Mining Company, wasn't he?"

Steve gave him a quick look. "I don't know about that," he replied. "Why? Do you know him?"

"No, but if he is the man I think he is, he works for Massachusetts." His quiet smile touched his lips again. "It would be funny if they were coming in here."

"What's funny about it?" asked Steve. "Do you know these mining people?"

"Everyone around Boston knows Massachusetts Mining. They're big people back there. I clerked in the office of one of their lawyers for a while and I think," he reflected, "that Cramer is one of their men. If he is, you'd better take his advice. On the other hand"—he shook his head—"if there is anything in it I don't see why Cramer gave it to you. It isn't like Massachusetts to give anything away."

"I don't know what he was after but it wasn't this piece," said Steve easily. "Fact is, he passed it up. I guess he was feeling a little

15

free with advice." He paused a moment. "You think I can prove up and get title out there, don't you?"

"It would seem so from what you tell me," replied the lawyer. His brown eyes looked earnestly at Steve. "You're sure that prior claim is out of the way? The agent was certain about that?"

"He was certain about it when I left him," said Steve, "but it might be a good idea to get it in writing." He leaned back. "Why don't you write him? Tell him you want a copy of the record. How about that?"

"Certainly," said Curtis. "I'm surprised he didn't give it to you. It's the customary thing to do."

"That's what I thought," said Steve as he stood up. "What do I owe you?"

"A couple of dollars ought to cover it," replied Curtis with a faint flush. "I haven't done anything for you."

"Don't be too sure about that," said Steve.

Downstairs in Gottlieb's grocery store he picked up a load of supplies and started east again through the woods, as he had done with Cramer. After about eight miles of it he came to the big lake, dropped his pack, and stood mopping his face as he looked across a mile of water to the stand of pines where they had camped. He wished he had a boat. If he had he'd be there in fifteen minutes but there was nothing for it but to tramp around the end of the lake. When he reached the log shack he had seen three weeks ago, he pushed open the sagging door and went in.

It was filthy, no doubt about that, but better than he had hoped. There was a rusty cookstove in it, a couple of boxes to sit on, a pail, and a frying pan; a bunk built into one corner was filled with balsam boughs brown with time. It was all right, but he needed a boat more than he needed a cookstove. Beemer must have crossed the lake in something, and he went out to look for it. He found it without any trouble—a charred-out, clumsy old dugout lying in the reeds along the shore. He pulled it out, dumped it, elated by his luck. Now that he could cross the lake, he could tote in the lumber and build a boat easy. Back in the shack he got a fire going, cut fresh boughs for his bunk, then walked out on a rocky point to pick up a bass for supper. It was evening by this time, the fading pink in the sky reflected in the silver mirror of the lake, and as he turned to go up the bank, his finger in the gill of a good bass, he saw smoke drifting above the pines around the cabin. He stopped short and, for the first time, asked himself what he was doing there.

He'd been there now for almost a year and Beemer hadn't turned

16

up with the answer to that until two days ago. Steve lay in his bunk thinking of these things. His heart warmed toward Beemer for shooting him. The old coot would never dare show up again, not with two witnesses to his attack, and with that hazard out of the way he was free to go ahead with the plan he'd been mulling over all winter. He'd never heard from Cramer but he was certain the mining man would buy him out now that he could make the offer. Sure he would. He'd put him in there for that. He'd sell Cramer this piece, file on another, sell that, move along with the country and get rich the way the lumbermen did. He'd seen it work. Look at Saunders, the way he'd cleaned up on timber. Steve had worked for him for six years, fifteen hours a day, up before dawn, thirty below zero, for twenty-six dollars a month, while Saunders sat back and got rich. A senator now, in Washington!

This galling injustice caused Steve to jerk with violence and he let out a yelp that could be heard across the lake. He had forgotten his wound, which throbbed steadily but without too much discomfort as long as he lay still, but now it had his full attention. Hot stabs of pain shot through his body as he tried to ease the injured shoulder. It didn't ease. He lifted the bandage and looked at it. It looked bad, puffed up, and the ugly red had run down his arm. The arm was stiff, helpless. Sweat ran off his stomach in big drops and his heart began to pound like a triphammer. Blood poison—that was it. He had blood poison! He'd seen a man die of it once, and all he'd done was cut his foot with an ax. He didn't have a bullet in him, but his leg had swelled up like that and he'd died. Steve's eyes strained open. Horror seized him and the plans, the hopes, the brash confidence of the morning disappeared in a swirling mist of terror.

He was so absorbed in misery that, for a moment, he didn't see the three people who came through the door; Matt, grinning and waving a whiskey bottle, Doc Pearson carrying a little black bag, and behind him a young woman. She stood hesitating in the doorway for a moment looking at Steve, then walked quietly to the stove and began making up the fire. Matt got busy with the whiskey bottle and the doctor walked over to the bunk.

"Well, how are you, Steve?" he asked cheerfully.

Steve looked at him. "Bad!" he muttered hollowly.

"Bad? What are you talking about? Matt said you were doing fine."

Steve shook his head. "I'm bad, awful bad," he insisted. "I've got blood poison. I know it."

17

"Nonsense!" The doctor peeled off his coat. "Here. Let's have a look at you." He bent down, looked keenly at the injured shoulder, then straightened up, his fists on his hips. "You're the luckiest young cuss ever walked," he pronounced. "Nicked a blood vessel, tore the shoulder muscles—and that's all. Nothing the matter with you but loss of blood and a little inflammation. I'll get the bullet and you'll be as good as ever in a week." He glanced over his shoulder. "I want some boiling water."

"It'll be ready in a minute," said the girl.

Matt came up with a tin cup full of whiskey and Steve grabbed it. "It's a good thing you got here, Doc," he said solemnly as the whiskey went down in big gulps. "Did Matt think of it?"

"Me?" Matt spat with disgust. "I knowed you was all right and Doc, here, he didn't want to walk no eight miles neither, but Kit over there, she made him. Said a man been shot needed a doctor, and she kept pesterin' till he got here."

The doctor rolled back his cuffs and pushed up his sleeves. "She may be right. You can't tell. That bullet in there might set up something. Let's go after it."

He moved the table near the bunk and began laying out gleaming knives while Steve's eyes widened again. Finally he turned, waving a rubber inhalator in one hand and a bottle in the other. "I'll just put you out with this," he explained with satisfaction. "You won't feel a thing. May burn your mouth a little and you'll be sick as a goat afterward, but you won't feel a thing now." He turned to the girl at the stove. "Bring me that boiling water." She brought it. "Is this pan clean?"

"It wasn't, but it is now," she said.

No one paid any further attention to her. She stood for a moment, watching, her hands clasped tight against her dress. Then she went out of the door.

It was hard work to put Steve out. He kicked and thrashed, tore the cone from his mouth and yelled, but the two men finally got him under and he went into a deep sleep. The doctor bloodied around for a while until he presently came up with the bullet in the tweezers and dropped it with a clank into the tin pan. "There!" he said. "He'll do now. I'll clean him up and be off. You know"—he turned to Matt after a cautious glance at the still figure on the bunk—"that wound wasn't as clean as I thought after I got in there. Damned if I don't think he might have developed blood poisoning if I hadn't come out here."

When the doctor was ready to leave, Matt went with him to row him across the lake. Both men had forgotten the girl until they stepped out of doors and saw her standing under a big pine, her back to the cabin, her head lifted, looking up. She turned quickly when she heard them come out.

"Hell!" said Matt. "There's Kit. She'll have to go with you. Come on," he called to her. "Get a move on. We're goin'."

She didn't move but her shoulders straightened a little. "I'm not going," she said quietly. "I'm staying here with Steve."

CHAPTER 4

For the next week Matt did everything he could think of to get rid of Kit but she stuck like the key log in a jam, sleeping in his bunk and cleaning the cabin until it wasn't fit for a man to live in. The morning after the doctor left, she handed him a list of supplies and asked him to go to town for them.

"I ain't goin'," he retorted. "I toted in plenty yesterday. If you want fancy fixin's like sheets you go for 'em yourself."

"Ask Burke for them," she persisted quietly, "and tell him I'll be back in a few days. Ask one of the girls to go up to my room for a couple of aprons and a clean dress. And don't forget the meat for the beef broth."

Steve spoke up. "Get along, Matt," he said. "Beef broth is what I need. Get plenty of it and put some under your own belt." Matt glared; then his white teeth flashed and he went off.

Steve lay propped up in the bunk in a clean shirt, his rough hair as smooth as it ever would be. His face was still pale but there was a healthy glint in his eyes as they left Matt's departing back to travel around the cabin. It was clean and fresh. The tin pots shone in the sun that entered through the bright window glass, the floor was scrubbed, and a bunch of blue flags stood in a tin can on the table.

"This place looks all right," he said to Kit. "Come over here and sit down."

She sat on a chair facing him, her hands in her lap, her eyes down, a faint smile on her lips. Steve had seen her, off and on, at Burke's Hotel for the past year but he'd never given her a second glance. She wasn't his type—too small and quiet, with those brown braids pinned around her head—but she looked all right to him now, sitting there with those blue flowers behind her.

"How long you been around Haley, Kit?" he asked.

"I was born there," she answered. "My father was blacksmith out to Saunders' camp. I was born out there."

Steve's glance sharpened. "You're not old Carlson's daughter?"

She nodded.

20

"Well, I'll be damned. I remember your pa and ma. Your ma used to slip doughnuts to me—but I don't remember you," he grinned.

Her shy smile deepened. "I remember you all right," she said.

Steve lay silent for a while, thinking of the half-grown boy working his heart out to hold down a man's job. No one but the old woman had suspected what it cost him, and she never let on, but sometimes when he threw himself on his bunk he'd feel her put an extra blanket over him. He remembered the Carlsons, all right. He brought his gaze down to their daughter.

"How is it you're working for Burke?" he asked.

"Pa got killed that time the sled skidded on him," she answered simply.

Steve nodded. "Yes. I remember that."

"Ma ran a boardinghouse in Haley after that," she went on. "She died a year ago and I went to work for Burke."

"So that's it. How old are you, Kit?"

A faint color crept into her cheeks. "Me? Almost seventeen."

Steve's hard face lit up with a warm smile. "I guess we're old friends, Kit," he said, and his memory quickened by this girl of Carlson's, he began yarning to her about the old days in the lumber camps until the talk drifted to still earlier days when he was a boy on the *Mississippi Belle* lugging satchels, running errands, cuffed and kicked around from morning to night by passengers and crew alike.

"They were a tough lot," he said. "All but old Sully. He was working the river pretty steady then, and when he came aboard, I used to hang around with him every chance I got. I learned a lot from Sully. He'd been all over the world, working the liners. He was an old man when I knew him, but he was smart, all right."

Old Sully! He could see him now as plain as day, the tall thin figure in an old Prince Albert, the battered silk hat cocked to one side, the long pale face and stained goatee, the faded eyes swimming with moisture, as flat and expressionless as those of a catfish. They were standing at the ship's rail late at night, watching the lights catch the ripples on the water. Sully was depressed. "I tell you, boy" —the whiskey-sheezy voice came faintly down the years—"it don't pay to cheat. It ought to—but it don't. No, sir! Not in the long run." He sagged over the rail, gazing dolefully at the crescent moon hanging over the trees along the riverbank. "Understand me, boy," he went on after a moment, "I ain't saying it never pays. There are times when it's a man's bounden duty to God, but the trouble is a man can't tell. No, sir, he can't. Take that stranger tonight; a sucker if I ever saw one, but he had a percentage on me from the start. He did, indeed." He sighed and laid his long flexible fingers on the young head at his elbow while the paddle wheels splashed softly in the dark. "Remember that, boy. It ain't being smart makes a man rich. No, sir. It's percentage. Percentage six hands out of ten will make a rich man out of a jackass . . ." The faint murmur drifted away on the bosom of the river.

Kit listened, her clear blue eyes fixed on Steve until he ran down. "Did he get rich?" she asked then.

Steve laughed. "No," he said. "He got shot for cheating. That's the night I went overboard in a hurry and swam for the timber raft that took me up here. He was a smart old fellow just the same and a lot in what he said. Getting rich is like any other game. Trouble with Sully, he wanted to win every hand."

"Ain't that the way to play—to win?"

"Sure," agreed Steve promptly. "That's what you're there for. But it's where you'll be if you don't that Sully forgot. He'd get a nice stake ahead and then get cleaned out, time after time. A man can't get solid rich that way."

"You want to get rich, don't you, Steve?"

The smile left Steve's face and his jaw set. "I sure do. I mean to." "Why?"

"Why? Any man worth his salt wants to get rich." The black brows drew together and he moved restlessly on his pillow. "You think I'm going to jump for men like Saunders the rest of my life? I fell forty logs a day for that cuss and every eight of those logs cut around a thousand feet of lumber. That's five thousand feet I dropped for him every day, all winter steady, year after year. Say it costs him ten dollars a thousand, overall, to finish that lumber and he sells it for twenty a thousand. He makes fifty dollars a day out of my work—and I get a dollar a day for it." He snorted with disgust, doubled up his good fist, and thumped his chest until it boomed like a drum. "You think I'm going to stand for that the rest of my life? Not me! Figure out for yourself how rich Saunders got on the work of a hundred men like me."

"I can't," she said.

"Well, I can," he said emphatically, "and I've had enough of it."

"You mean you want to be like Mr. Saunders? Ma always felt sorry for him. When he come to camp, he couldn't eat nothing, not even beans."

22

"What's that got to do with it? A man gets rich is no reason he's got to have cramps."

"No. But they seem to." She stood up and smoothed her apron, smiling. "I guess I don't have to worry about getting rich, but if I don't get supper Matt will give me something to worry about." Her face sobered. "Will you be happy if you get rich, Steve?"

"Happy? What's that got to do with it?"

She turned across the room to the stove. "I don't know," she said. But her voice was so low he didn't hear her.

The day Steve stamped into his boots, and helped himself up without sitting down again in a hurry, Kit went back to Haley. When she was ready to go, Steve took her hand. "It was fine of you to come out here, Kit," he smiled, "but you must be glad to go back after all the scrubbing you've done."

"No." She shook her head. "I liked it here but I don't see why you stay, Steve. When Matt goes back to work, you ought to go with him. It ain't good for you all alone in the woods."

Steve's face clouded. "I know what I'm doing," he said shortly. "So long, Kit. Take care of yourself."

Matt, his smile restored at the prospect of getting rid of her, rowed Kit across the lake and she took the long trail through the woods alone, her white dress moving through the patches of light and shade while her eyes picked up the blazes on the trees. It was good to be alone in the woods, where the sun fell in long rays through the deep green vistas of pine and hardwood, good to feel the spring of the soft pine needles beneath her feet, to trace the lichen patterns on the boulders and push aside the tall sweet bracken in the sun-drenched open places. It was good! A young doe bounded across the trail, stopped, gazing at her until Kit laughed and waved her hand.

The trail came out behind the town where the big stumps that peppered the hill still oozed in the sun. After the clean fragrance of the woods, the acrid smell of pitch was like the smell of blood in the cabin she had left, and Kit shivered as she hurried down the hill to Burke's Hotel.

23

CHAPTER 5

Now that Kit was finally out of the way, Steve and Matt settled down to live like men on the fat of the land. The lake teemed with bass, ducks went up with a whir, partridge strutted in the underbrush, and it was no trick to drop a yearling buck for the liver or a steak. Raspberries and blueberries hung thick in the open spaces and the brief, deceptive summer months slipped by.

As soon as he was able, Steve walked into Haley to see Curtis. On his trips to town during the past year he had usually dropped in for a talk with the lawyer. He liked the little cuss. He was short on muscle but there was a quality about him, new to Steve, that made a man think twice about pushing him too far—and he was as alert as a kingfisher at picking up useful information. Early in the year Steve had learned from him that the Massachusetts Mining Company had come into the country, and that Cramer was developing a big mine for them north of Alturos. Curtis' Boston newspapers were full of the new venture but their enthusiasm was fixed on the iron region thirty miles north of Steve's claim and none of it was wasted on surface ore. This lack of vision on the part of Boston disgusted Steve but Curtis was steady in his belief that the country was opening up, and that, in time, the spread of interest might include surface ore. It was on the basis of this encouragement that Steve had worked out his scheme to get rich on ore lands.

When he climbed the stairs to the little office this summer day, he had a letter to Cramer in his pocket and was impatient for Curtis' opinion on it. Curtis greeted him with warmth. "Steve!" he cried, jumping up with hands outstretched. "Lord! I'm glad to see you! How are you? You look all right. Sit down. Sit down." He urged Steve into a chair.

Steve was glad to sit down after his long tramp, and they talked for a while about Beemer's attempt at slaughter. "Awful," said Curtis, his worried brown eyes fixed on Steve. "Shoot down an unarmed man like that—he ought to be hung."

"Nothing awful about it," returned Steve. "Matter of fact, he did

24

me a good turn." He pulled his letter from his pocket and pushed it across the desk. "Think this will make any money for me?"

Curtis picked up the letter and read it. "It might," he said, looking up. "What makes you think Cramer wants that claim?"

"I never did think he put me on to it for nothing," said Steve. "I went in there because he liked that piece. I think he put me in there to hold it until he got around to it. I think he'll take it now."

"He may," agreed Curtis, "but you'd do better to wait for him to come to you."

Steve shook his head. "I don't think so," he said. "He turned up that red stuff for ten miles along that stretch. I know where it is and I can pick up half a dozen of 'em before that interest you talk about gets ahead of me. If I wait for Cramer it may be too late."

Curtis smiled. "Not a bad idea if you can get away with it," he said. He paused for a long moment. "But I don't know, Steve," he went on. "I have a feeling you ought to hang on to that piece for a while. Not for the ore on it," he added. "I've thought, myself, for some time, that Cramer put you in there—but not for that reason."

"What do you mean?" asked Steve, frowning. "What's on your mind?"

"Nothing." Curtis raised his hands. "Not a thing I can put my finger on." He paused. "I haven't a thing to go on," he said finally, cautiously, turning to Steve. "You must take it on that basis. It's merely an idea."

"Go ahead," said Steve.

"All right. Look at it this way." He leaned forward. "Cramer was headed for Alturos. He could have gone there by train. He didn't. He stopped off here and took you on a roundabout tramp for two weeks to the south and east. As a mining man he was interested in the surface ore he ran into but, in my opinion, he wasn't after it. He was looking for something else."

"What?"

"That's it," replied Curtis. "What? The only logical answer is a right of way through there for a railroad. He was looking for a possible way out in case Massachusetts Mining found themselves under freight pressure from the North Line after they got into operation up there. They're an extremely canny bunch of men. They must have had a franchise under cover somewhere and their right of way pretty well lined up. Cramer went in there to look it over. This piece was still unsecured. He couldn't go to the land office himself without leaving his trail there, so he induced you to go in to secure it until he had time to size up his new mine." He shrugged. "That may be the answer. I don't say it is, Steve. I haven't turned up a thing that remotely supports it."

"Well, I'll be damned!" said Steve.

Curtis smiled. "Sounds good, doesn't it? Trouble is, if there was a word of fact in it Cramer would have come to you long before this. What actually happened was that Massachusetts got an extremely liberal contract with the North Line and they're skimming along on it."

Steve's strange green eyes burned black. "You mean Cramer hung me up out there with that yarn about surface ore?"

"No." Curtis shook his head. "I told you this is merely an idea. He may have given you his advice in good faith. I think, myself, that ore may come through in time. If you send this letter, the chances are you'll make the deal. Still——"

"Still, you think I should hold on," Steve broke in.

Curtis paused again, his face worried and intent. "Damn it all, Steve," he burst out, "I do. Wait until spring, anyhow, and see how things shape up. Massachusetts got that easy contract to encourage them to develop. They've turned in a fine mine. When that contract runs out next spring, the North Line will want a big piece of its profits and will put on pressure to get it. It means another winter out there—but I'd wait."

Steve crushed his letter in his fist and tossed it in the waste-basket. "I think you're right, John," he said. "I remember a lot of things on that trip. They fit. How they fit!" He tilted back in his chair, his hands in his pockets, his jaw thrust forward, deep in thought. Suddenly the chair legs dropped with a thump and, to Curtis' astonishment, he yelped with laughter. "I hope to God this new line gets there before the North Line can plug it up," he declared with energy. "I sure do hope to God it does."

"Why, Steve?" asked Curtis. "What are you getting at?"

"You ought to see it, John." Steve hitched his chair forward. "You know as well as I do that the men who own the North Line run this state. If this showdown does break next spring, they can and will condemn me. The North Line will come around the end of the lake from their branch line here in Haley and go through me. I wouldn't make chicken feed out of it, and your smart Massachusetts men would be sewed up in Alturos tighter than a drum."

"Yes," agreed Curtis. "That's possible. In that case, you'd do better to go ahead with Cramer now."

Steve snorted. "Like hell I will!" He rasped his chair in closer.

"You don't get it yet, John," he said. "This state will never condemn me to let another railroad through in competition with the North Line. Right?" Curtis nodded. "This Massachusetts bunch has been on to that all along," he went on. "I'm certain of it, and I know the railroad they're working behind—a little two-cent timber line rusting in the woods down there. I saw it when I went through with Cramer. It's right where they need it, and if they are as smart as you say they are, they're all set to jump in fast before the North Line can get on to it and nip around the lake ahead of them. If Massachusetts can get past that point first, they're in."

He leaned back, stretched out his long legs, and looked hard at Curtis. "They're in, John," he repeated. "But when they get to me, where do they go from there? The state won't let them through. They can't get around me—I've got a big lake at each end. They'll have to deal with me—or quit."

Curtis stared at the big muscular figure sprawled in the chair across the desk. His gaze dropped as the implication in Steve's remark sank in. "This is all talk, Steve," he said sharply after a moment. "Nothing behind it. You can't assume a situation like that. You jump to conclusions too fast."

"If Massachusetts don't get that road through me, they'll jump to a conclusion faster than I will," replied Steve. He gave Curtis a quick grin. "They'd do a lot better dealing with me than with the North Line. I'm betting they've got that road and will get in with it."

He stood up and came around the desk to lay his hand on Curtis' shoulder. "You're as smart as they come, John," he said. "It's mighty lucky for me I didn't mail that letter."

"I'm not so sure about that." Curtis shook his head. "I wish I'd kept my mouth shut."

"Nonsense!" Steve gave him a clap on the back that jarred out a strangled cough. "I wouldn't have thought of this angle in a million years. My mind was set on that damn surface ore. Come on, let's go to Pete's Place and have a drink."

Curtis, who was leading the ladies of the Methodist Church in a crusade to erase that hellhole from the face of the earth, declined, and Steve set out alone.

CHAPTER 6

Steve sat around in Pete's Place rehearsing his encounter with Beemer to the point of pulling off his shirt, and the exhibition aroused satisfactory enthusiasm for a while, but when Pete finally refused to chalk up any more drinks, enthusiasm waned and Steve, angry, soured by this discourtesy, slammed out down the street to Burke's Hotel. If Burke was as unco-operative as Pete had been, it would cost him a dollar to spend the night there, but he was too tired to take the long walk home, and as he sat in moody silence under the moth-eaten moosehead in the lobby waiting for the dining-room door to open, the necessity that had prompted him to write to Cramer flooded back into his mind. He'd been crazy to talk himself out of that deal. Curtis wanted him to look at facts. Well, he was looking at one right now—the plain fact that in a month he wouldn't have money enough for as much as a sack of beans to see him through the next winter. He'd have to write that letter again. No! He'd be damned if he would!

The door opened and he went in to supper. There was a fair showing of customers in the dining room, painted a poisonous green, the color of arsenic, and Kit passed him a dozen times, her slight figure bent sidewise under the heavy trays she carried, but Steve didn't see her until she came up with her quiet smile to take his order. "I guess you forgot me," she said.

He started, glanced up. "Oh—hello, Kit. How are you?"

"I'm all right. I guess you are, too, if you walked in. I've been wonderin' when you'd come. You better take the corned beef and cabbage," she advised. "I'll get you a nice piece."

Steve felt better after a good meal. Kit was there picking up the empty dishes when he pushed back his chair, and before he could stop himself, he asked her to take a walk with him. The last thing on earth he wanted was to walk, and he tried to back out of it, but she was too quick for him, and he had scarcely lit the first cigar he'd had in two months before he saw her come out of the side door. He thought for a moment he'd let her stay there but, well, he owed her something. He got up and went to meet her.

She had on a neat little red-checked dress, the ruffle on the skirt swinging jauntily around her ankles, and there were red flowers on the straw hat she wore, pinned too far back because of her braids, and when he told her how nice she looked, she blushed as red as the poppies on her hat.

"I'm glad you like it," she said. "I got it from Greenburg's. I hadn't ought to of—but then I thought I would. I've been afraid you'd think it's too red."

"Not a bit," said Steve carelessly. "I like red."

They walked along the plank walk gouged by the spikes in the lumberjacks' boots, past the saloons, dance halls, eating places, past the bursts of raucous laughter, the clink of glasses that came through the open doors. Once or twice Steve hesitated, glancing at the men clustered around the bars, but Kit's face, confident and happy under the new hat, kept him walking.

When they got to the end of the street, the moon, full and golden, was rising above the black fringe of the pines and the trail wandering through the stumps on the hillside was easy to follow in its light. They went on a little distance to a cleared spot, where scattered mounds had taken the place of the stumps. A few of these mounds were marked. Kit turned in that direction. "There's a bench by Pat O'Connor," she said. "Let's sit there."

Steve was glad to stop walking. They sat down and he tossed the stub of his cigar on Pat O'Connor's chest, propped his elbows on his knees, and went on with his thoughts. After a while he began to mutter his opinion of himself to himself.

"It'll be all right, Steve."

He turned his head sharply, surprised at the sound of Kit's voice. She was sitting quietly, her hands in her lap, gazing at the moon. "What do you know about it?" he asked harshly.

"Nothing." She shook her head. "Only I know it will come out all right."

"What makes you think that?"

"Nothing," she said again, "but I know it will. You're that kind of a man."

Steve straightened up and looked at her. He knew what she meant. He felt that way about it himself but it was good to hear it at this moment. He slipped his arm around her waist and drew her to him. "You're not as dumb as you look, Kit," he said. "Here—let's have a kiss on it."

She turned her face at once, obediently, and he saw her eyes shining in the moonlight. Her lips were sweet and fresh and he held her close, but the kiss was unsatisfactory. No response, no protest, nothing came of it. It was like kissing a sleeping child. He tried again. This time she sighed and closed her eyes. Steve seldom failed to excite some kind of reaction with his kisses and it disgusted him to fail now. He let her go and stood up. "Come on," he said curtly. "Let's get out of here."

Kit had to hurry to keep up with him, and when they got back to the hotel, he told her to run along. She smiled shyly, happily, and went down the alley to the side door.

He stepped into the saloon next door and watched a poker game for a while. He could pick up a couple of dollars easy from what he saw of the play, but he couldn't bring himself to go after it that night. He chalked up a drink there, finished it, and went out. Talk broke out around the table.

"Never seen Steve pass up a game before. What's ailin' him?"

"Aw, you can't tell nothin' about that son of a bitch. He don't open up to nobody. Never did."

"Ain't he the feller got shot four, five weeks ago?"

"Yeah. Old Beemer tried to run him off his place."

"Whose place? Beemer's place?"

"Naw. Steve's."

"Like hell it was. Beemer done his time out there, and more."

"What's he doin' out there, anyhow? What's he livin' on? Ain't been in the camps for a year."

"He any good in the woods?"

"Sure. Plenty good. Get a job any time. Here, wait a minute. W-a-i-t a minute. I got queens."

Back in his room, Steve couldn't sleep. Again and again his mind went over his talk with Curtis, shifted to the fix he was in if he spent another winter in the shack, went back to the glowing picture of his big play in the spring. If it worked. Hell, it had to work! He'd never get a break like that again. But Pete had refused credit. Gottlieb would pull up next. There was no work within twenty miles of his claim, and the minute his back was turned Cramer might show up and take possession. Oh, he had his rights. Sure, he had his rights, but they'd be in there—trump up some flaw in his title—and he'd be out. He'd seen it happen a hundred times. Every drunk in town had had a timber title at some time—thought he had!

He tossed and turned. Money! Money was the answer, always was, always would be, and the lack of it now stung like a whip. He leaped out of bed, went to the window, and drew the night air deep into his lungs. The moon was high now, its light cold and withdrawn. Steve stood for a long time looking out, unable to sleep for the first time in his life. After a while he pulled on his pants and went out. A lamp burned feebly in the lobby, the saloons were closed, the little town lay dark and silent. A mongrel dog, hearing his footsteps, trotted from an alley to sniff at his heels.

Steve walked out of Haley and up the hill. The trail was dark when he took it but he went forward with steady step. He walked for three hours, and they were the decisive hours of his life. When he came out of the woods, the sun was rising behind the clump of pines above his cabin. He stood still, looking across the water. The morning sun track lay at his feet. He got in his boat and shoved off into it.

CHAPTER 7

August slipped by, and with September the finger of frost
crept through the night, touching the hardwoods with flaming color; here, a spot of red burned in its reflection in the lake;
there, a branch thrust forward, gleaming like a burnished sword until, as the cold increased, the brilliant pageantry of fall swept over
the forest, mocking the steadfast green of the pines.

Matt was worried. The easy days were over. Winter was coming.
He couldn't wake Steve up to it and the look on his face didn't
encourage a man to try. But one sharp morning when he came back
from the lake with his water bucket, he braced up to it.

"God, it's cold," he said, rattling the lid on the stove as he pushed
a stick in the fire. "It'll be snowin' in a couple of weeks." Steve, sitting on his bunk, his brows drawn, silent, unapproachable, as he
had been now for weeks, paid no attention. Matt swung on him. "It
ain't no use goin' on like this," he blurted. "We got to quit. Glenning's movin' in the woods right now. We got to get there. Quick."

"Sure," said Steve indifferently. "I've been expecting it. Get along
any time you feel like it, Matt."

"Ain't you goin' with me?"

"No."

"You figure on stayin' here all winter?"

"Sure. Why not?"

Matt shrugged and scratched his head. Steve hauled off easy
lately. "It's goin' to be tough," he said. "You got to eat, ain't you?
How you goin' to eat? You ain't got no more money than I got when
I come here last spring. You better quit and come along." Steve's
eyes fell on him. "All right, all right," Matt said hastily. "You're goin'
to stick. It ain't none of my business." He hesitated, then went on.
"You got somethin' on your mind, Steve. You want to stay with it.
I et plenty grub off you this summer. What you say I leave my pay in
the company office? You need it, you take it. I don't never have a
nickel left anyhow, come spring. You ain't askin' for it, and I don't
want no kick."

32

Steve stared at him for a long moment; then stood up. "Well, I'll be damned!" he said. "You son of a gun! I've been wondering where the hell I'd raise a stake." His hand came down on Matt's shoulder. "You know what you're doing, don't you, Matt?"

Matt's smile flashed in relief. "Me? Sure. What you think?" he swaggered. "Maybe you got something here."

"You're dead-right about that," said Steve soberly. "I'll use your pay, Matt. Got to. But if this thing pays off, you've done the best day's work for yourself you'll ever do in your life. Take my word for it."

Matt spat. "Hell," he said, "I ain't thinkin' of that."

For the first time in weeks Steve's face broke into a broad smile as he landed a poke on Matt's chest. "I know you're not, you little runt," he said, "but you can bet your life I am. Hustle up a batch of corn bread while I go after a bass."

After Matt had gone, Steve settled down to face another winter. He knew what it took and this time doubled his supply of firewood, stacking the dry windfalls of birch and pine within easy reach along the cabin wall. He stuffed moss into the chinks, set up a cross-pole for the buck he would string up when cold weather came along, and gun in hand for the game he might raise, took long tramps over his claim and to the south of it. Sometimes when he came to an outcropping of the red stuff, he kicked it loose and stood looking at it thoughtfully while the scarlet leaves, drifting through the still October woods, touched him lightly on their way to earth.

As long as the lake was open, he went frequently to Haley for Matt's pay and his winter's supplies, and to find out if Curtis had turned up any news on Massachusetts Mining. Curtis hadn't, and was inclined to avoid the subject. One day Steve, moving restlessly around the office, pulled a thick volume from the shelf. "How about my taking this along?" he asked.

"Certainly," said Curtis. "What is it?"

"Thorp *On Contracts.*"

"Why do you want that?" asked Curtis curiously. "I wouldn't take you for a man who liked to read law."

"I don't," protested Steve. "Damned if I can see why a man wants to make a living reading law, but I'm liable to be snowed in any time now and I want something hard to see me through the winter."

"Thorp certainly ought to do it," said Curtis.

That night when he came out of the trail onto the lake, Steve found his boat fast in a skim of ice. He kicked it loose and rowed across to the shack. The next morning the ice had advanced far out from shore, its lacy edge undulating on a patch of blue water. In a few hours the patch was closed. Steve pulled up his boat and turned it over; he wouldn't be using it again for six months.

Early in November the first big snowstorm whirled in, the soft flakes blotting out the opposite shore. They piled up on the branches of the pines, clung to the roof, to the woodpile, drove into his face and stuck there like leeches. When he turned in the door to shake the wet mess from his shoulders, he saw his footsteps, deep in the spotless white; by the time he got his coat off, they were erased.

He settled down to take it, content enough. His supplies were in —salt pork, beans, buckwheat flour, kerosene, plenty of coffee and plenty of tobacco to see him through until he could cross the lake again. This was the time for that book on contracts. He built a big fire, got his pipe going, braced his feet on the fender, and began to read.

It was hard going. Steve had done little reading in his life and he was astonished to find out how much there was in one book. He struggled with it, his head back, eyes on the rafters, thinking through every page he read until finally the squirming legal technicalities straightened out, and he read rapidly, with intense concentration, scribbling contracts of his own, playing them against each other. It was a fascinating game. Sometimes he was roused by the cold to find the fire out. Sometimes he had to eat. He kept a big pot of coffee on the stove and drank quarts of it. When the snow piled up in the windows, he lit the lamp and kept it going, oblivious of the storm and the passage of time. The snow fell steadily for three days, while he read the book through twice, from cover to cover. When he slammed it shut for the last time, stretched as if coming out of a long sleep, Thorp *On Contracts* was accurately stored away in an extraordinary and retentive memory. He never read a word on contracts again as long as he lived. He never had to.

He walked to the door and threw it open. The snow had stopped falling but the wind had piled it waist high across the sill, and he stood there yawning, blinking at an immaculate world glimmering under the hard blue sky. He turned back into the cabin, cut himself a slice of ham, stuck potatoes in the oven, and had a good meal; then threw himself on the bunk and slept as if he'd been hit with an ax.

Steve hadn't been to Haley for a month and supplies were low again, so the next day he strapped on his snowshoes and broke a fresh, straight trail across the lake, pushing hard to keep warm, and impatient to see Curtis.

The lawyer smiled when Steve laid Thorp *On Contracts* on his desk. "Had enough of it, have you? Did you get anything out of it?"

"A little," admitted Steve. "Enough to know what you're doing when you write a contract for me."

Curtis smiled. "How are you making out? Must be tough lugging a pack this time of year."

"Not bad on snowshoes. You ought to try it." Steve glanced at the Harvard diploma hanging on the wall. "That thing would look a lot better with a good deer head alongside. Come and get one and you'll know as much about deer hunting as I do about law."

"Good Lord, Steve!" Curtis shook his head. "I've never been on snowshoes in my life. Anyhow, I'm going back East in a week. There's nothing going on here and"—his shy smile touched his lips—"there's someone back home I want to see."

"That so? How long will you be gone?"

"Until after Christmas. I'll leave the key at Burke's so you can use this office when you feel like it."

"Fine," said Steve. "I'll read another book."

They talked for a few minutes, but there was no news of any interest. Steve stood up and gripped Curtis' hand. "So long," he said. "Have a good time. I won't be in again before you go. While you're there, see if you can get a line on Massachusetts."

He went out and swung down the street to Pete's Place, the heels of his boots squeaking on the trampled snow filthy with tobacco juice, ashes, and sawdust sweepings.

Pete was mopping up the bar with a damp rag, a mechanical gesture, for the only customer in the place was a soggy drunk asleep at a table with his head on his arms. The air behind the storm windows was rank. A dirty lantern, swinging from the ceiling, cast a dismal light on the bar and the assortment of glasses stacked against the mirror behind it, and a wood stove at the back of the room, a red spot on its belly, pulsed with heat. Steve put his foot on the rail.

"How are things, Pete?"

"Bad." The bartender's fat face oozed disgust as he shoved a bottle forward. "Bad. I'm tellin' you. There ain't enough life in this town to pull a cork for."

"What's the matter? Don't the boys come in? Seen anything of Matt?"

35

"Naw. Ain't seen any of 'em. Camp's too far out. I'm tellin' you. Drive last spring's the last this town will ever see. Timber's gone around here. This country's bust. I seen it happen in Michigan. Same thing. Timber gone."

"How are the girls making out? Where's Liz?"

Pete spat a graceful trajectory at a spittoon across the floor. "Quit," he said. "All of 'em. Back to Chicago. That's the answer. When them harpies clear out, there ain't no more pickin's on the carcass. They know, same as rats on a ship. Ain't one of 'em around—far as I know," he added significantly. "Might be a couple somewhere hanging round for the drummers."

Steve leaned against the bar. In the mirror he saw the reflection of a tall young lumberjack in a red and black mackinaw open at the throat, a whiskey glass in his hand. The face was stern and set and the eyes stared back at him as lonely as a wolf's. Behind this resolute figure the drunk lay muttering in his sleep. Steve knew the drunk; he'd been quite a fellow at one time—owned a timber claim. The figure in the mirror scowled, tossed off his whiskey, and started for the door. He stopped, stared down at the snoring drunk, then slammed out of the door and went on to Burke's Hotel.

Every time Steve had been in town overnight during the past fall, he had seen Kit. He didn't mean to and never anticipated it but it seemed to come out that way. While the weather was still warm enough, he'd take her for a walk up the hill and they'd sit on a windfall somewhere and she'd ask him how he was getting along out there. "I bet you live on flapjacks and coffee."

"You hit it right, Kit."

"Well, it ain't funny, you livin' out there alone. You'll get sick. You take out some canned tomatoes, cabbage, stuff like that."

"Too heavy to lug. I'm all right."

She was a good-natured girl, always ready with her smile, and he liked to see it after his lonely days in the shack. After it got too cold to be out of doors, she came to his room. That surprised him. She didn't look like that kind of a girl, but one night he saw her at the far end of the hall as he was going along to bed. He wondered if she'd been waiting for him. "Hey," he beckoned cautiously, "come along in and we'll have a talk."

He had expected her to shake her head and shy off but she didn't. She came in quietly, readily enough, and sat in a straight chair, her hands in her lap, while he threw himself on the bed and stuffed a pillow behind his head. She sat there, her blue eyes round and

36

fixed, just as she had out there in the shack when he was sick. But he wasn't sick now and he recognized an opportunity when he saw one. He turned it over in his mind—and dismissed it. It was there but he didn't want it. Something about her put him off. Definitely. So he began one of his yarns about the old days in the lumber camps. She never tired of these yarns, and it was some relief to get his troubles off his mind in the telling of them.

But this had been going on now, off and on, for several months and he was getting tired of it. She was always there, hanging over him while he ate and sliding into his room with a plate of sandwiches when he wanted to sleep. He wished she'd let him alone.

When he went to supper this night, after leaving Pete's, Kit came up with her smile, her starched dress rustling, and handed him the familiar greasy menu. "You'd better take——" she began.

"Oh, shut up," he snapped. "I know what I want. Let me alone, can't you?"

Her smile vanished and her eyes popped open as if he had slapped her, but when she came back with his meal there was a dish of pudding with it he hadn't ordered. He liked that pudding, and she knew it, but he deliberately shoved it aside, untasted. That would show her where she stood with him!

It didn't. When he got back from the Last Chance around midnight, where he'd picked up a few drinks and a few dollars and was feeling better, damned if she wasn't sitting there in his room, in her usual patient pose, on the straight-backed chair. "What are you doing here?" He scowled. "Run along. I want to go to bed."

"I will," she said, but she didn't move. "I just came in to find out what's the matter."

"Nothing's the matter. Go along."

"Yes, there is," she persisted. "You act sort of down, the way I feel sometimes. It ain't good for you out there in the woods all the time. You get to thinkin', and that ain't good for anybody."

Steve sat down on the bed and began to unlace his boots. She could sit there until hell froze over, but he was getting out of his clothes—all of them—and going to bed.

"It'll be Christmas pretty soon," she went on. "Rob's got the turkeys hung up already, great big ones. They'll be awful good, the way he makes the stuffing. He's making mincemeat, too, for hot mince pies."

Steve kicked off his boots and stood up to unbuckle his belt. "Well, what about it?"

"You'll come in for it, won't you?"

"No."

"Oh," she cried. "You must. You can't be alone on Christmas."

"Why not? Same as any other day."

"No, it ain't. You can't say that about Christmas."

Steve said no more about Christmas. He unbuttoned his shirt. After another pause he heard her say timidly, a little breathless, "Well, if you won't come in maybe I could go out there."

"What!" He looked at her, his shirt half over his head. Her eyes were pleading with him. "Where did you get that fool idea? No. Certainly not. What makes you think I want you out there? I don't. It's the last thing I want. You couldn't get out there if I did. Quit talking nonsense and go to bed."

She jumped up and clasped her hands like a child. "Yes, I could. Yes, I could, Steve. I know the trail. I only said that about the turkey dinner. I didn't mean it. I don't want Christmas in this hotel —honest, I don't. I want it in the woods like it used to be. Ma'd make cookies and Pa'd play his accordion and we'd have schnapps and we'd sing. I want to be in the woods for Christmas, Steve. Please let me come."

Steve was astonished at the change in the girl. He could scarcely believe this was Kit. There was nothing dumb about her now; her cheeks were flushed, her blue eyes dark with excitement, the small, work-worn hands trembling on her breast. But he was firm with her. "No," he said. "Get that nonsense out of your head. It won't do. I don't want you out there. I mean it. You understand?"

She seemed to wilt, her face went blank, empty again. Her hands dropped to her sides. "Yes," she said. She went dutifully toward the door, but with her hand on the knob she turned. "I could get the cabin all cleaned up for you again," she said with a wavering little smile. "I bet it's awful dirty."

There was not much hope behind that pitiful appeal, but it was the best she could do and, in spite of himself, Steve was touched. He went over and put his hand on her shoulder. "You're a good sport, Kit," he said. "You deserve to win but I can't let you do a fool thing like that. It wouldn't be right and you wouldn't find the Christmas you're looking for anyhow. No use looking for days that are past. Thing to do is forget 'em." He bent down and kissed her lightly. "Forget it. Christmas will be over before you know it. Run along now." He opened the door and gave her a little shove.

After she had gone, he pulled off the rest of his clothes, got into bed, and went to sleep.

38

CHAPTER 8

Back in his cabin Steve lost all track of the days, and had completely forgotten Kit when he looked out one morning and saw her trudging across the lake, loaded down with bundles, slipping, righting herself on the frozen trail. The damned little fool! He knew the trail and what the trip must have cost her, and he boiled with exasperation as he grabbed up his cap and coat and went to meet her.

The day was gray and sullen, with an ugly green fringe around the horizon. It looked like snow, but no snow was falling yet. When she saw him coming toward her, she tried at first to hurry faster; then she dropped the satchel she carried, raised her arm, and waved to him. Steve's eyes were cold and angry as the skies when he came up to her. "What are you doing here?" he demanded savagely. "I told you not to come, didn't I? What's the idea?"

She had on a red hood tied under her chin; her face was red with the cold but she radiated happiness like a stove radiates warmth. It was in the air all around her, but it didn't touch Steve. He glared at her.

"Yes, you did"—she nodded—"but I thought you'd be glad when you saw me."

"I'm not," he said curtly. "I'd like to turn you around and start you right back, but I can't with this storm coming. You're here and I'll have to put up with it." He picked up the satchel. "Come along."

She hurried behind him, trying to talk. "I brought some things for the tree," she said. "Candles and popcorn and some other things." He stopped. "What are you talking about? What tree?"

"The Christmas tree." She laughed. "Didn't you know it was Christmas? I brought a can of oysters, too."

"Oysters!"

"Yes," she said. "You like oyster stew. I hope you've got some canned milk. I couldn't carry that."

Steve looked at her for a moment, then turned toward the cabin again. "Come along," he said more gently. "I've got the milk."

39

When they got to the cabin, Kit hung up her coat and hood, kicked off her overshoes, peeled off her leggings as if she'd come home. She opened the satchel and pulled out an apron. "Mercy!" she said, "I never seen so much dirt in all my life. Look at that lamp chimney." She lifted the kettle and began to shove wood in the stove. "No water. You'd better get some."

Steve picked up the bucket and went to the lake to chop out the water hole. He knew he was beaten but when he got back he put in one last protest. "I tell you again you shouldn't have come out here. It was a damn-fool thing to do and you'll find it out when you get back. Half the town must have seen you take that trail."

"I guess they did," she said indifferently. "I'll get things scrubbed up while you get the tree. Get a real pretty one, Steve, with branches all the way down, and not too big. Don't hurry. I've got lots to do here first."

Steve went off to cut a Christmas tree. There were plenty of them around but he took his time in selecting it—a pretty one, with branches all the way down. He smiled as he swung his ax. Hell!

As he dragged the tree behind him through the snow, he saw the smoke pouring from the chimney and stopped to cut a roast from the young buck he'd strung up a few days before. It took him some time, for the animal was frozen so solid it turned the blade of his ax, but he finally got it hacked out and lugged it in with the tree.

The cabin looked as if a cleansing whirlwind had struck it. The tree was just right when he set it up, and as the warmth thawed the snow that clung to it, the acrid perfume of balsam filled the room with its cool and lovely fragrance. Kit gave Steve the candles to wire on the branches and he fussed around with them while she worked at the table with her scissors and the gold paper she had brought. Finally she turned to him. "Steve, can you make a star, a big star to go on top? I can't get it right."

Steve drew a handsome star, and when he had it fastened at the top of the tree, he stood back and looked at it. It was a fine-looking star, all right! He was proud of it.

The roast was thawed by this time and Kit stopped making gold streamers to put it in the oven, and soon the fragrance of roasting meat mingled with the fragrance of balsam. She set Steve to popping corn, and when he'd filled a big pan with it, threaded two needles with long, coarse thread and handed one to him.

"What's this for?"

40

"To string the popcorn. It's going on the tree."

"Not all of it isn't," he said, munching handfuls of it. He pricked his fingers and split more kernels than he strung while Kit laughed, but at last the long white festoons were on the tree and they stepped back to look at it.

"Ain't it lovely," cried Kit. "Ain't it the loveliest thing you ever see?"

"Looks all right," conceded Steve. "That star up there's the best thing on it. Let's light the candles."

"Oh, not yet," she pleaded. "It'll be over too soon. Let's have supper; then we can put out the lamp and light the tree. It will look prettier that way."

There was something in that. He was hungry. The oyster stew hit the spot; the roast with brown gravy, baked potatoes, and stewed tomatoes fit for a king. He'd never tasted better coffee, and while he smoked his pipe, Kit hustled the dishes out of the way—and they were ready to light the tree.

They sat down on Steve's bunk across the room to look at it. The candles glimmered with a soft, beseeching light, but outside the wind was howling, shrieking in from the north, the great trees above their heads tossing and moaning in the fury of the blast. From time to time the candles quivered as the wind took hold of the tiny cabin and shook it. Steve lifted his head, listening. "Looks as if we're in for it," he said. "Sounds like a good one."

"It doesn't matter," she murmured. "It doesn't matter."

He glanced around at her. She sat entranced, her mouth open, her eyes glued to the tree, and he wondered again why he wasn't attracted to her. He wasn't. On the contrary, he felt uncomfortable sitting beside her while she stared at the tree with that look on her face. The candles were burning low and he jumped up to put them out. "Don't want to get burned out on a night like this," he said as genially as he could. He blew out first one, then two or three, until finally only one was left. He lit the lamp by its light, then extinguished it. "Well," he said, "that's over. Better build up the fire and get to bed."

She didn't hear him. She sat blinking as if the lamplight hurt her eyes and he had to tell her again that it was over. "Yes," she said then, her voice so low he could scarcely hear it. "Yes, it's over." She stood up slowly and came to him. "You didn't see your present, Steve."

"Present!"

"Yes. Under the tree."

He saw it then, a package in red paper tied with ribbon, and stooped down to pick it up. "What's all this?"

"Open it," she said as he hesitated, turning the package in his hand. "Open it. It's a Christmas present."

He tore off the wrapper. Two pair of warm, gray socks with red bands around the tops! "Fine," he said without looking at her. "Fine. I haven't had a pair of socks without holes for three months. Did you knit 'em?"

"Yes," she said. "I thought maybe you wouldn't have any."

He put his arm around her and drew her to him. "It was mighty kind of you, Kit, mighty kind, but you shouldn't have done it. I haven't anything for you."

She laughed. "Of course not. You didn't even know it was Christmas."

"That's a fact," he said. "I didn't." He gave her a little squeeze. "You're a good little girl. Get to bed now. I'll step outside and see what's going on. Better hustle—I won't be out there long. Put on a pair of these socks. It's going to be cold before morning."

When he came back she was in Matt's old bunk, covered up to the chin, her eyes closed. Steve got into his bunk and blew out the lamp. He lay for a while listening to the wind, wondering how he was going to get this girl back to town. Christmas! That star up there was catching the light from somewhere. He fell asleep.

He had no idea how long he'd been asleep when he heard her stumbling around in the dark. "What's the matter?" he called out, reaching for the lamp.

"It's awful cold," he heard her say in a small, frightened voice. "I'm trying to make up the fire but I can't find it."

He got the lamp lit and saw her standing over by the door in her flannel nightgown, the big gray socks on her feet. Her eyes were wide and frightened and she was shuddering with the cold. "The fire's all right," he said shortly. "Come away from that door and get back in bed." She turned obediently, her clasped hands quivering on her breast. He watched her, frowning. "If you're as cold as all that," he said bluntly, "come in here."

She came without a second's hesitation, scuttling across the floor as fast as the big socks would let her, and snuggled down, shivering, as close to him as she could get. Steve blew out the lamp, turned on his side, and tried to go to sleep again. But sleep didn't come. The girl's soft body close to his own did the trick. He resisted for a while,

42

then turned and slipped his arm around her. "Kit," he whispered, "Kit, is it all right?"

She didn't answer. Her head turned weakly, helplessly, on the pillow once or twice, then settled against his shoulder, and she gave a long, deep sigh.

CHAPTER 9

That settled it. From then on every time he went to town Steve continued his relationship with Kit. He didn't intend to, didn't want to, for it had shocked him profoundly to find out that she was what he called a "good girl" when he took her. Such a possibility had never crossed his mind, never had to with the women he'd known, and it enraged him to be tricked into it. That's what it amounted to, and he told her so as she trudged along behind him on the way back to town.

"But I thought you knew it, Steve," she murmured once.

"Knew it? How in hell could I know a thing like that? You hopped in bed with me at the drop of the hat, didn't you? What was I to think?" he shouted. "What would any man think?"

"I don't know," she said.

He left her within a mile of town and turned back, fuming, determined to have nothing more to do with her.

Two weeks later he had to go to town again for supplies. He dreaded the sight of her but when she came up to him at the supper table he could see no change in her at all, no resentment in her eyes, and she came to his room that night as quietly and simply as she had always done. Well, it was too late to do anything about it now and she seemed to want it that way. After that he walked in many times when he was in no need of supplies.

Shortly after the New Year, Curtis came back from Boston and Steve, impatient to hear about the trip, tramped in to see him. He found the little lawyer sunk in gloom, and for a while had to listen with what patience he had to the details of Curtis' unhappy visit to the little New Hampshire town where he had been born. "The long and short of it is she won't have me," he said finally, miserably.

"Why not? What's the matter with her?"

"I don't know, Steve." Curtis ran his hand over his thin brown hair, his sensitive face as open as a book. "I thought it was all settled when I came out here but it looks now as if she's just too pure to entertain the idea."

44

Steve laughed. "She bluffed you, John. They all try it. Next time call her, fast. That's what she's asking for. Did you have any better luck in Boston?"

Curtis shook his head. "No," he said, with deepening gloom. "I hate to tell you, Steve, but it looks as if Massachusetts Mining is set to consolidate with the North Line this spring. I didn't see Mr. Stoddard but I know most of the men in his office and they all look on it as settled. They ought to know. They're working on it."

"Consolidate with the North Line at this juncture?" Steve frowned. "That don't make sense, John. They haven't been under any pressure so far. Why should they jump the gun like that at this time? I don't believe it. You say they're a smart bunch of men. What's their object?"

"The office seemed to think it was a good thing all around."

"A good thing?" Steve jumped up and began pacing the floor, his face black with anger. "Why, it's suicide. The North Line's got 'em over a barrel if they close now. I don't believe it," he repeated vigorously. "It's a stall for time. Can't be anything else. There's a hitch somewhere. Must be. Got to be. It stands to reason. They've got to work fast when they start and they're held up somewhere."

"I'd like to believe you're right," said Curtis, "but it didn't look that way in Boston. I wish now you'd gone ahead with Cramer."

"Nonsense. If they're actually tying in with the North Line, he wouldn't have bought anyhow. Listen, John!" He sat down and went on more quietly. "The crux of this thing is Cramer's trip through that country in the first place. The situation with the North Line was as plain then as it is now. Cramer wasn't interested in surface ore. He needed that mile and couldn't secure it himself without leaving his trail wide open. He worked that surface-ore racket on me to get me in there. Things are coming to a head this spring, and when it breaks it will break on that ridge. I'm positive of it."

Curtis shook his head. "I hope you're right," he repeated.

"I know damned well I'm right."

This was in January, with the worst of the winter still ahead. Blizzards howled in, burying the little cabin to the eaves, the sun shone without heat but with blinding intensity on the snow, and the bitter cold prowled around the cabin, snuffing at the cracks like a wolf. It was no time for a man to venture on the trail, and after his return from Haley, Steve was in no mood to risk it. There was nothing to do but wait. He kept the fire going and worried through the long, slow days, deliberately absorbed in filing away Curtis' *Laws of Minnesota* in the rapidly expanding archives of his mind.

Finally, toward the end of March, the snow took on the gray, sullen look of an old man reluctantly backing away from defeat. The icicles began to drip, slow tears that fell and froze again, and Steve found that he need no longer whang the woodpile with an ax to get a chunk loose. About the middle of April the bottom of his boat came through the snow and one morning in early May he looked out and saw open water sparkling in the sun.

It was a lovely morning, the great trees above his head whispering, lifting their branches to the sun. He got his boat in the water and rowed across the lake. Now that he had started, a curious urgency possessed him, and he swung over the soggy trail as fast as he could, as if to meet some definite appointment with Fate. He was right. He walked straight into it when he got to Curtis' office.

CHAPTER 10

As he opened the door, he saw Curtis talking to another man. He recognized Cramer at once but there was no sign in his face of the shock of excitement that raced through his nerves. "Hello, John." He nodded casually to the lawyer. "How are you, Mr. Cramer? You don't remember me. Steve Bradway. I toted for you a couple of years ago."

The mining engineer looked older than Steve remembered him, his face etched with worry but his smile was cordial enough. "Certainly I remember you, Steve." He held out his hand. "Oddly enough, I came here to see you. I've just been asking Mr. Curtis if he knew where I could find you."

Steve glanced at Curtis, sat down, crossed his legs, and thrust his hands in his pockets. "That so?" he said. "Why?"

Cramer's genial smile broadened. "I hear you followed my advice and have taken up a claim out here somewhere."

"That's right," said Steve. "I've got a half section."

"Just where is it?"

"You made it pretty clear where you wanted me to go in," said Steve easily. "I'm in there."

"Ah, yes." Cramer tilted his head in thought. "I believe I know where you are. Yes. We camped there on a lake." Steve nodded. "Good. Good. I remember considerable evidence of surface ore in that locality. I'm glad you went in there." He paused. "You have title there, I presume?"

"Close to it," said Steve. "I can close at any time. Why?"

"How would you feel about disposing of your equity out there?"

"I'd feel fine," replied Steve promptly. "I went in there on the chance of making a little money. But if you're interested, you must have changed your mind about surface ore, Mr. Cramer."

Cramer reddened as if Steve had touched a sore spot. "My opinion is beside the point," he said. "The Massachusetts Mining Company is already committed in this region and certain members of the board feel that if a limited amount of this ore-bearing land can be

47

had at a reasonable figure, they are willing to take the risk of a possible profit at some future time. I have been instructed to look into it." His manner eased. He beamed at Steve. "Naturally, in going over my experience in that country I remembered my advice to you. If you had acted on it, this might be the opportunity I promised you. I cannot, of course, be more definite until I've had a chance to look over your location again but I should say, offhand, that the prospect for a sale looks fairly favorable."

He leaned back and Steve met his benign smile with his own disarming grin. "That's mighty kind of you, Mr. Cramer," he said. "How about going out now? It's a fine day for a walk."

"Certainly," agreed Cramer at once. "I'd be glad to. But you understand I am making no promise to purchase."

"I understand, Mr. Cramer," said Steve. He stood up. "I'll get my pack filled and be back in half an hour." He turned to Curtis, who had been listening quietly. "You'd better come along, John. We might flush some game."

They reached the cabin in the early afternoon and Cramer set off at once through the soggy woods to look over Steve's claim. As soon as he was out of sight, Steve turned to Curtis. "We'd better go fishing, John," he said. "Let him go his own gait for a while."

"What's he up to, Steve?"

Steve laughed. "He's made a beeline for that second lake to figure out how he can get around it in case he runs into a snag with me. He's worried about that lake."

"You think he's after surface ore?"

"Hell, no. He's not after ore; he's after that right of way," said Steve with emphasis. "It's printed all over him. He gave us that yarn to build up a plausible excuse to buy fast before I get on to his real purpose. He's a damn good liar, I'll say that for him. Come on. Let's go fishing."

The bass rushed at the bait like dogs from behind a fence, and for a while the two men drifted along the rocky shore in silence. Finally Curtis came back to the subject that even fishing for bass could not erase from their minds. "What makes you so sure it's the right of way they're after?" he asked.

Steve let the oars drift in the oarlocks and leaned forward. "It's bound to be, John," he said. "Can't be anything else. I was certain of it the minute he jumped at the chance to come out here. He didn't come to look for ore. He knows this country like a book. No. It's worked out the way you saw it last fall. Massachusetts Mining has known all along they were over a barrel with the North Line and they've worked a slick scheme to get out. They'd like to slip around me if they can—they'd have me over the barrel then if this surface ore ever develops. But just about now Cramer's found out they can't —and he'll come back on fire to do me a good turn by buying me out."

Curtis sat in the stern of the boat, too deeply absorbed to be aware of the bass thrashing on his line. "I hope you're right, Steve," he said soberly. "If you are, it sets up an interesting situation. A very interesting situation from your point of view. You think Cramer will close with you tonight?"

"He's going to try almighty hard," said Steve, "but he's in the position of that bass you've got there. Pull him in. He looks like a good one." He waited until the fish was in the boat. "You're right about the setup here," he went on. "It's going to be tough from now on. That's why I wanted you out here."

Curtis' thin face flushed. "I'll do my best for you, Steve," he said simply. "But if you get into a jam with Massachusetts Mining, you'll need a bigger man than I am."

"I'll be the judge of that," said Steve shortly. "It's mighty lucky for me you're around." He glanced at the sun. "Time we got back."

He picked up the oars and rowed without hurry back to the cabin. Cramer was there, standing on the shore, slapping irritably at the black flies, but his look brightened as they pulled in. "Have any luck?" he called.

"Pretty good," replied Steve, tossing bass out of the boat. "How did you come out?"

"Very much as I expected," returned the mining man promptly. "You have a certain amount of surface ore here and I'm ready to make you a reasonable offer on it. I must say it gives me a certain satisfaction to be able to do so after advising you to come in here."

"That's a fact," said Steve. "You put me in here, Mr. Cramer. I'm not likely to forget that." He lifted the big bass Curtis had caught. "How about this for supper? Seems to me I remember you like your bass skinned."

49

CHAPTER 11

Steve went about the preparation of the meal without further reference to the matter of sale. He was in a genial mood, recalling incidents on his trip with Cramer, yarning about blizzards and deer hunting. This jovial behavior continued until the supper dishes were shoved aside and they sat around the table smoking. Finally Cramer, no longer able to control his nervous preoccupation, pulled his watch from his pocket.

"It is getting late, gentlemen," he interrupted with decision, "and I must make an early start in the morning to catch the train back to Alturos. If it is agreeable to you, I should like to get on with this matter of sale." He turned to Steve. "As a start, can you give me some idea of what you think this land is worth to you?"

"No." Steve puffed deliberately, took his pipe from his mouth. "But I have some idea of what it's worth to you, Mr. Cramer. You want it. Suppose you make the offer."

Cramer frowned and some of the benevolence faded from his manner. "Very well," he said crisply. "I can't haggle over a small matter like this. You have around three hundred and twenty acres here, I believe. I'll give you ten dollars an acre for it. I consider that, and I am sure Mr. Curtis will agree, an extremely generous offer."

"It is," said Steve with evident surprise. He leaned forward. "Why do you make such an offer, Mr. Cramer? I would have jumped at five dollars last spring."

Cramer sat back, twirling the watch chain that spanned his middle. He pursed his lips. "It looks as if I should have insisted on getting a price from you, Steve. I hope"—he smiled and shook his head—"I won't find myself in hot water over this small transaction. However, I shall have to stand by my guns now."

"You mean you're ready to close at that figure? Tonight?"

"I see no reason for delay—certainly not from your point of view," returned Cramer blandly, as he drew papers from his pocket and laid them on the table. "I've been instructed to purchase a sizable piece of this ore-bearing wilderness. This piece, in my opinion, fills

50

the bill and I'd like to get this commission off my hands and get back to my mine. I'm not in sympathy with the idea, but those were my instructions."

Steve's smile lost its genial expression. He sat back and shook his head. "You're wasting your time, Mr. Cramer," he interrupted. "I've heard enough."

Cramer's startled face flushed red. "What is the meaning of that remark?" he demanded sharply. "I've made you a generous offer of sale. I resent your reception of it."

Steve's face hardened. "Drop it, Cramer," he said. "Since your walk this afternoon you are as well aware of my position here as I am. I brought you out here so that you should be aware of it. I've not the slightest intention of closing with you until my advantage is openly acknowledged and your offer renewed on that basis." He smiled, not pleasantly. "You've tried to deceive me and I succeeded in deceiving you. That's the long and short of it." He raised his hand as Cramer attempted to speak and turned to Curtis. "Tell him, John, what you put me on to this spring."

Curtis looked across the table littered with greasy tin plates at the big man tilted back in his chair against the log wall, the lamp highlighting the winter's black beard, the strong features, catching the glimmer of the cold eyes, and the picture of a pirate in a book he had known as a child flashed through his mind. Except for the absence of hoops in the ears and a cutlass on the table, the likeness was too close for comfort. He pulled his eyes from Steve and turned to Cramer.

"Steve is referring to the idea that Massachusetts Mining was not likely to commit themselves to extensive operations in a locality where they could be dominated by the North Line," he said quietly. "He is inclined to think that another railroad is going through here."

Steve snorted. "Inclined to think!" The chair legs thumped on the floor. "Goddamn it, I know it. I've been down there. The little D. & W. that hasn't spun a wheel in ten years is all set to go. Ties and rails hid in the woods."

He raised his hand again as Cramer once more attempted to speak. "You put me here depending on purchase if and when your development warranted pushing the D. & W. through to Alturos. You took the risk of delay rather than alarm the North Line into action before you were ready for action yourself. You're ready now. In two weeks you can pass the point on the lake where the North Line would have to come in. In two months you can push through to

51

Alturos—*if* you can get through me. That is the situation. What are you going to do about it?"

The color drained from Cramer's face, and for a moment he sat motionless, meeting Steve's demanding stare. "It is plain that nothing can be gained by beating around the bush," he said at last. "I admit that my confirmation of your position this afternoon shocked me considerably. You are quite right. Except for minor details, your analysis of the situation is correct. Therefore it is obvious that I must come to terms with you. I am committed to that but"—he managed a smile—"in the interest of all concerned that should not be beyond adjustment."

There was a long silence in the cabin. The breath of night was chilly now that the sun was down, and Curtis got up to close the door. Steve, puzzled by Cramer's prompt acknowledgment of the hole he was in, leaned forward, his forearms crossed on the table, watching for some sign of the next move.

"What do you mean by adjustment?" he asked. "What's on your mind?"

"Frankly, I don't know," admitted Cramer slowly. "You are well enough informed to realize there is no time for delay." He moved uneasily. "I don't know," he repeated. "It looks as if my only course is to go to Boston at once and explain your position. Nothing short of that would induce the board to increase the terms I have offered you." He looked at Steve and shook his head. "It is difficult for me to adjust myself to the change in you," he said. "Let me repeat that I considered those terms extremely generous to the young man I remembered going through these woods with me, and I anticipated a considerable personal pleasure in your acceptance of them. I doubt" —he raised his hands and dropped them with an air of resigned patience—"that I can effect any substantial advance in those terms, but if you will give me some idea of what you want I will do my best for you."

Steve was beginning to admire Cramer. "I can tell you what I want," he said evenly. "I want stock in the Massachusetts Mining Company—a bunch of it."

Cramer jerked as if a missile had whizzed past his ear. "Stock?" he repeated. "Why should you want stock in Massachusetts?"

"Why not?"

"But Massachusetts is a private corporation," explained Cramer. "None of its stock is for sale without a two-thirds consent of the

52

board. Mr. Curtis can tell you they would not consider a transfer of stock to you under any circumstances."

"Is that right, John?"

"I believe it is," said Curtis thoughtfully. "It's good stock, and likely to go up when this road goes through, if that's what is on your mind, but I doubt that the board would consent to parting with any of it under any pressure you could bring. If they did, I doubt that you would make as much money out of it as you can make now by pressing your advantage. I think you ought to take a cash settlement, Steve."

"Stock is what I want," said Steve.

Cramer's patience came to an abrupt end. "This is ridiculous," he declared. "I know, and Mr. Curtis apparently knows, the attitude of the board in the matter of stock. It would be utterly useless for me to advance any such proposal and I refuse to do so. Any reasonable cash settlement will be met, but if you persist in a demand for stock, Massachusetts will drop the D. & W. and settle with the North Line. There is still considerable question in the mind of the board as to the advisability of doing so in any case. Your position, as you call it, is far from being as strong as you think it is."

There was another silence in the room. It lasted for some time. Both men turned sharply when Curtis finally spoke. "Mr. Cramer is right, Steve," he said quietly, disregarding Steve's quick frown. "There is no time to be lost, and in my opinion, it would result in nothing but delay for him to take any stock proposal to his board." His mild brown eyes behind his glasses rested for a moment on Steve's. "Why don't you go to Boston and take up this settlement yourself?"

For a moment Steve stared at him, then his set lips parted in a broad grin. "By God, you've hit it, John," he said. "That's the answer. Cramer is the last man to tackle this. It's between me and Massachusetts."

"It looks that way to me," said Curtis mildly.

Cramer flushed red. "I can't permit any such thing as that," he said sharply. "It's preposterous and unnecessary. I represent the company and I insist that you——" But Steve turned on him.

"You're not insisting on anything, Cramer," he interrupted. "You're out of it—well out of it. You're in no position to negotiate this." He shoved back his chair and strode around the room, his eyes cold and glittering. "Do these people know you put me in here?"

"No," said Cramer. "And I did not put you in here, as you call it. I suggested it in good faith and am here now to deal fairly with you. This matter can and should be adjusted here and now. I insist upon it. What possible reason is there for going before the board over my head? What position does it leave me in?"

Steve stood over him, his thumbs hooked in his belt. "In a damn sight better position than you'd be in if you went yourself," he said. "You can't handle this without explaining how I got in here. If you want to save your skin and see this deal go through, keep out of it. Give me a free hand. Tell them I refused to deal with you. Tell them that the last time you saw me I was headed for Boston. Leave the rest of it to me."

"You mean you are quite determined on this course?"

Steve grinned down at him. "I wouldn't miss it for a million," he declared. "This is the ninth. Tell them I will be in Boston on the fifteenth."

"Very well." Cramer leaned back, his face worried. Finally he sighed. "If you're determined to take this matter out of my hands, there is nothing I can do to stop you." He paused, then added dryly, "The board is quite capable of dealing with you without assistance from me." He was thinking of old Cyrus as he spoke, and looked up with a glint of amusement at the black-bearded, arrogant young man standing before him. "By all means go to Boston and state your case yourself."

Nothing more was said. After a few moments of thoughtful silence Cramer retired to his bunk and Steve and Curtis settled down to their contract with the Massachusetts Mining Company. They worked hard and long, Curtis, to Steve's surprise, agreeing to press for stock.

"I thought you were taking the cash angle on this," he said.

Curtis smiled. "Not after you got Cramer backed out of the picture," he explained after a cautious glance at the tired man gently snoring in the bunk. "You may get that stock, and if you do, it may be mighty useful in the future. Try for it, but take it easy. If you are forced back on to a cash basis, take all you can get, but," he added earnestly, "don't, under any circumstances—stock or cash—let them have your mining rights."

"Why not, if it means more stock? I want a thousand shares of that stock. I'm going down there to clean up."

Curtis shook his head. His brown eyes gazed steadily at Steve. "You may get it if you include your mining rights," he said after a pause. "You certainly won't if you don't. This may be your only

54

chance. It's a question of considerably more stock now or a big gamble on the future of surface ore—and I may be wrong about that." He stopped, reached for the coffeepot, and poured another cup. "I may be wrong," he repeated anxiously, "but it's a chance that won't come again if you clean up now. Take what you can get for the right of way but stay with your mining rights for a while anyhow, Steve."

Steve shoved back his chair. "John," he said, "the only smart thing I ever did in my life was tie up to you. I wouldn't have thought of this—not any of it—if you hadn't put me on to it."

Curtis' slow smile bent his lips. "You make too much of it, Steve. Wait until you see how it turns out. Now—about this stock . . ."

They worked until daybreak. When the sun came up, they blew out the lamp and stepped out into the limpid clarity of the new day. Neither man said anything, but Steve's arm lay across the narrow shoulders of the little man beside him.

When they went back into the cabin, Steve piled his clothes, maps, and papers into his packsack, and after breakfast the three men walked through the woods to Haley.

CHAPTER 12

Curtis gave Steve his Gladstone bag to take to Boston. "You can't show up there with that packsack," he said with disgust, "and you'd better get yourself another pair of pants."

"Why?" asked Steve. "These are the pants I wear."

"God knows they are," said Curtis fervently, and he looked at the big man with increasing concern. That massive, black-thatched head, the arresting bold green eyes, the arrogant swing of the shoulders were admirable in the woods but they would certainly fail to arouse admiration in Boston. He began to seriously question the wisdom of his advice. "And get that beard off your face before you meet the board," he cautioned nervously.

Steve grinned. "What you scared of, John? They're men, aren't they?"

"Yes," admitted Curtis, "but a different breed. You won't get anywhere with them if you go in there looking like this. You better take it easy, Steve."

"Men are the same the world over when they're stripped. No difference in 'em—except brains."

"You'll find these men have brains," said Curtis, sticking to his point.

Steve was in his room at Burke's, packing his grip, when Kit came in. He hadn't seen much of Kit lately, hadn't wanted to. Her quiet sparkle had faded and he had caught her sneaking funny looks at him at times, as if she had something on her mind. He wondered if she had picked up with some other man and was afraid to come out with it. He hoped she had.

She stood now with her back against the door, hesitating, looking at him. "Are you going away, Steve?" she asked after a moment, her voice faint.

"Yes," he said, and because he was so full of it, he told her briefly about his trip to Boston. He tossed a gray flannel shirt to her. "Think you can get that washed before train time?"

She caught the shirt and held it in her arms across her breast. The

56

color ran over her face. She was animated enough now. "Oh, Steve," she said, "I'm so glad of that. I knew everything would come out all right. I always said so. It will, won't it?"

"It sure will," he said emphatically. "What do you think I'm going for? When I get back, things will get a move on here. You can bet on that."

"Oh, I'm so glad," she breathed again. "Here. Give me those pants and I'll press them for you. I'll wash this shirt first so it will get dry and then I'll come back and pack for you."

Steve sat down in a rocking chair at the window, lit his pipe, glad enough to give up packing. Everything was all right. Sure. Everything except money. He twisted in his chair as if strapped into it. Money! He had Matt's pay in his pocket, and Curtis had come across with fifty dollars, but if they held him up down there for any length of time, he'd be in a fix. He was wondering, glumly, what kind of work he could find in Boston when Kit came back. He didn't speak and she stood at the bed, folding his rumpled clothes and packing them.

After a while she spoke gently. "If it's money you're worried about, I can give you some."

His head swung around. "What?"

"I've got a hundred dollars you can have if you want it."

"What?" He stared at her. "A hundred dollars! Where did you get a hundred dollars?"

"I've saved it," she said. "You can have it if you want it."

Steve turned away and looked out of the window. He didn't want it. Money from Kit was the last thing he wanted. He felt cheap. Lowdown cheap. But a hundred dollars would make a difference—a hell of a difference—when he faced that board in Boston.

"If you let me have it," he muttered, without looking at her, "I'll give it back to you, double, inside of two weeks."

Kit laughed a little unsteadily. "I didn't mean that, Steve," she said. "I don't want it back double. It ain't that. I want you to have it. It's only—only . . ." To his astonishment she began to cry. "I've got to iron that shirt," she said, and ran out of the room.

That night when Steve got on the train, he had Kit's hundred dollars in his pocket. It was in her father's old tobacco pouch, dimes and dollars and a few gold pieces, and he had felt so mean when she handed it to him it was all he could do to kiss her. But that was some time ago now and he felt better about it. Fact was, she'd done herself a good turn. He dismissed Kit from his mind, propped his feet up on the opposite seat, and let his thoughts run on what lay ahead while the train rumbled through the dark on its way to Chicago.

There was plenty to think about, and he went over his procedure step by step. He knew what he had to do, but a good deal would depend on the right start. Curtis was right about that. He'd buy those new pants. And thinking of pants reminded him of old Sully's remarks as they sat one night on a cotton bale.

Sully was depressed. "I tell you, boy," he said, shoving his battered silk hat back on his naked dome, "it ain't always what a man can figure on that wins. No, sir, it ain't. Don't ever underestimate a man in a new suit. He's got an edge on you from the start. Now, take that gent in the checked suit tonight. I had as pretty a pot rolled up as you'd wish to see, but," he sighed, "that suit gave him an unpredictable confidence in sixes. I knew he had 'em, but I overlooked that suit." He was silent awhile, his long fingers exploring the frayed edges of his old Prince Albert. "I took this suit off an Englishman on the *Empress,* out of Calcutta, years ago," he mumbled on, "and it has served me well on many occasions, but I must admit it has been failing recently to do so. I think," he said reflectively, "I shall be compelled to win that checked suit before we reach Louisville." He did win it, and Steve never forgot what he looked like in it, but it seemed to work. From that time on the old man won on every trip up the river until one customer became sufficiently incensed to shoot him dead.

When he got to Chicago in the morning, Steve went to the Palmer House and asked the clerk where he could get a new suit. The clerk swung the register to him with marked indifference. "I'm going out on the night train and I want a suit," repeated Steve curtly. "Where can I get one?"

The clerk eyed the old woods clothes deliberately. "How much can you pay for a suit?"

"How much will it cost me?"

"Thirty-five dollars ought to get you one," said the clerk. "How does that strike you?"

"Strikes me like a kick in the pants," admitted Steve, "but if you say so it's all right with me. Where is this pirate?"

He swung along the streets, his eyes alert, taking in the vibrant, noisy town. He liked Chicago, and made up his mind he'd do business there someday. After a shave and haircut he found the tailor and was persuaded into a medium gray cutaway that fitted his supple, muscular frame to perfection, but the high collar on the shirt that went with it galled his chin and he cussed it, tossing his head like a restive horse until he gave it up as a waste of good invective. He bought shoes, socks, more shirts, and a hard black hat that clung to his head like a turtle's shell. His purchases cut into his cash to an alarming extent, but when he surveyed the tall figure in the glass, saw the arrogant angle of the chin propped up on the stiff collar, the swagger in the tilted hat, the elegance of the black mustache that embraced his lips like a cant hook he decided the percentage was worth it. No question about it, he looked like a man from Chicago.

When he walked into the Palmer House again, the clerk hastily swung the register to him with a smile of welcome. "I'm still going out on the night train," Steve reminded him.

The clerk spread his palms on the desk and stared at him. "By God, I never would have known you."

"That's the idea," laughed Steve. "I'll be back in a few days and I'll want a room then. A good one."

CHAPTER 13

The Massachusetts Mining Company occupied offices in a forbidding red brick building that crouched on State Street within a stone's throw of the old State House. It was an old-fashioned dingy building and the most desirable business address in Boston. Getting into it was as socially and financially significant as getting into the Summerset Club, and no man once in there ever loosened his grip on his space until death took him out.

The Forsyth family, which now in its ramifications composed the Massachusetts Mining Company, had occupied large offices in the building for many years, but it was within the present generation that the clan had decided to dispose of the clipper ships that had been the foundation of the family fortune and turn to the more profitable and less obtrusive business of mining. Now that the tall ships no longer thrust their bowsprits into the drawing rooms, the source of income could be ignored and the Forsyth family, blessed by a perpetual financial dew from heaven, retired into an impregnable social sanctity that weighed on Boston like the hand of the Almighty.

On the thirteenth of May, Horace Forsyth issued from his house on Beacon Street and, as was his custom, started across the Common to his office. The route he took was unvarying. Having learned to walk on those particular paths some thirty years previously, it had never since occurred to him to change his course, and he proceeded now at a dignified pace, his long sharp nose tilted skyward to avoid, if possible, the irritation of having to speak to anyone.

When he reached his office, there was a letter from Cramer lying on his desk and his feeling of satisfaction at not having experienced, so far that morning, anything of an exasperating nature slightly increased. No doubt Cramer had secured the bit of property that was holding up the D. & W. and causing considerable irritation in certain members of the board. It was gratifying to be able to pacify them. He sat down, twitched the trousers of his new suit, picked up a silver paper cutter, eyed it severely for an instant, and deliberately slit the envelope.

There was no change of expression in his face as he read the letter, for it was a face incapable of change, but after a moment he got up and went through a door into the adjoining office.

Reginald was there, decked out in a dreadful tie with white spots on it, and again the question of where, in God's name, Reggie got his ties sped through his mind. He laid the letter on his brother's desk. "Read that," he said. "Confound it!"

Reggie plowed through the letter and looked up. "He says he's coming here," he said. "We can't have that."

"Of course we can't," snapped Horace. "I wish you would overcome your tendency to express the obvious, Reggie. Cramer must be out of his mind to let such a fellow come down on us. He'll have to stop him."

"He must have had some reason for it," said Reggie. "Cramer is usually good at that sort of thing." He picked up the letter. "He says he'll be here on the fifteenth," he squeaked. "He can't be stopped. He is on his way." He stared helplessly at Horace. "We better talk this over with Grandfather, don't you think?"

Old Cyrus Forsyth was the last of the "windjammer Forsyths," and although he had consented after considerable reluctance to the change of course in the Forsyth fortunes, he had never ceased to glory in his trips around the Horn, or to talk about them. He was eighty-five years old, and for the past ten years, his associates in the Massachusetts Mining Company had tried with every inducement they could think of to get him to retire, but, as he put it, he meant to keep his hand on the helm as long as the wind held. There was nothing to do about it. The helm he talked about was a majority of the stock.

The two brothers found him in his office, the dingy walls enlivened by dozens of colored prints of clipper ships, sitting at his desk playing solitaire. He lifted his untidy shock of white hair and slipped a troublesome ace out of the way while he looked at them. "Well, boys, what's the matter now?" he asked. He chuckled, and went on with his game. "I'll bet, from the look of you, Horace licked a two-cent stamp when a one would have done."

Horace, his pince-nez glittering with suppressed antagonism, laid the letter before him and the old man hunched over it, still chuckling. "Looks like this fellow's got a clove hitch on Cramer somehow," he remarked. "Cramer's scared of him. Must be quite a man. It'll be a change to see a man around here. When's he comin'?"

61

"If you'd take the trouble to read it, you'd see Cramer tells us to expect him on the fifteenth," said Horace acidly.

"I've read it. I've read it, son. Just findin' out if you had. The fifteenth, eh? That's day after tomorrow. We got a board meetin' that day, ain't we? We'll treat this cuss to that and see how he takes it. One look at Higgins ought to take the wind out of his sails, if anything can."

"That's out of the question," protested Horace. "We'll have to get rid of him some way. Cramer implies plainly enough what kind of a character he is. We can't subject the board to a brawl with a drunken lumberjack."

"Sure we can. Sure we can," interrupted the old man. "Why not?" His rugged, weatherworn countenance beamed with anticipation and he tapped the letter with the king of spades. "I've got a hunch we're goin' to get a lot of action out of this fellow. I want to see it. Been a long time since I've seen any action around here."

Steve was wearing his new suit when he strode into a full meeting of the board of the Massachusetts Mining Company three days later. Horace, confused by the appearance of this "lumberjack" in a suit almost exactly like his own, stood up slowly, and after a brief hesitation held out a limp hand. "We've been expecting you, Mr. Bradford," he said with a frosty smile. "Allow me to introduce you to these gentlemen."

Steve returned his look with his own warm, engaging smile. "We'll get off to a better start if you get my name right, Mr. Forsyth," he said easily. "It's not Bradford. It's Bradway. Steve Bradway."

Horace managed to correct his blunder with considerable dignity. "And now, Mr. Bradway," he concluded, "if you will sit down, the board will be interested in the purpose of your visit."

Steve hitched his chair around and sat down in a silence that hung in the room like a cold fog. Eleven men were seated around the long table and his glance traveled deliberately from face to face. Ten of these faces were turned to him with varying expressions of curiosity and suspicion, but the old man with the white hair and heavy shoulders at the far end of the table, tranquilly at work on his fingernails with a small knife, did not look up. Steve's eyes rested on him for several seconds before he spoke.

"Mr. Cramer must have explained my position," he said. "I'm here to talk about it."

Mr. Higgins, a stout, florid gentleman at some distance down the table, turned with pompous dignity and stared at Steve. "Mr. Cramer has not made your position, as you call it, clear to me," he said testily, "and I believe several members of this board are equally at a loss to understand your presence here. Mr. Cramer was authorized to deal with such matters, and fully capable of doing so."

"He wasn't capable of dealing with this one," said Steve.

"Why not?"

Steve shifted to an easier position and crossed his legs. "Let me put it this way, Mr. Higgins," he said. "Cramer came to me with an offer to buy my claim. He said he was buying additional ore properties for you. He thought there was ore on my place and was willing to give me a fair price for it. I knew Cramer wasn't looking for ore and refused to deal with him. What he was after was a right of way over my property." He paused to let that sink in. "You can take it for a fact," he went on, "that I know, and have known for some time, your purpose to put through a railroad to Alturos. To do that, you must go through me."

"What of it?" barked Higgins with increased irritation. "What of it? Cramer was there."

"Just a minute, J.D." A member with the benign expression of a clergyman raising funds leaned forward. "Was Mr. Cramer aware of your reason for refusing his offer, Mr. Bradway?"

"You are the lawyer here, Mr. Stoddard?" questioned Steve. At Stoddard's nod Steve proceeded. "He was aware of it after he'd been over my claim. Plenty aware of it. He admitted my position and renewed his offer on that basis."

"And you still refused to deal with him?"

"I did. For one thing, there is no time to lose if you want to get in there ahead of the North Line."

"I see." Stoddard paused. "Do you mean us to understand that you think we are in difficulty with the North Line, Mr. Bradway?"

Steve moved impatiently. "I don't think it; I know it. You're in a hell of a fix out there."

A chuckle from the far end of the table broke the silence that followed that remark. Horace, after an angry glance in that direction, turned to Steve. "You evade your reason for not closing with Mr. Cramer, Mr.-er-Bradway," he said icily. "The board has other business before it this morning. We would be pleased to have you come to the point of your visit."

A glint leaped to Steve's eyes but he continued to speak with

63

casual good humor. "I think you're right, Mr. Forsyth," he said. He pulled a map from his pocket, opened it, and shoved it across the mahogany to Horace. "This may clear it up. Pass it along. The portion marked in red, lying between those two lakes, is my property," he went on, as the map began its slow journey around the table. "Because of those lakes any railroad coming up east of the ridge must go through me. There's no getting around that."

When the map reached Stoddard, the lawyer fixed his glasses on his thin nose and studied it for some time. He sat back, a thoughtful expression on his face, and the map moved on. Every man at the table bent over it except the old man, who shoved it along without a glance. When the map reached Steve again, he folded it and put it in his pocket. Nobody said anything. Finally Stoddard cleared his throat. "I believe that you have made your visit entirely clear to the board, Mr. Bradway," he said dryly. "It appears that you are in a fortunate position and we must come to terms with you. But that should not be too difficult," he continued. "This is, after all, a simple matter of laying a half mile of track across your property, an advantage to you, as well as to us."

"That's right," conceded Steve.

"Ordinarily, it would be a matter of no financial importance, the sum being fixed by law on the value of the land; in this case, of little or no value," the lawyer went on. "As you, no doubt, are aware, if you were condemned by the state, you would get little, if anything, out of it. But since you are in a position with us to demand it, I believe I voice the opinion of the board in saying we will pay you a satisfactory sum for it."

"Within reason, Stoddard. Within reason." A sour voice spoke up.

"Certainly, within reason," Stoddard agreed promptly. "Mr. Bradway understands that. But we must, in our turn, face the fact that he is entitled to take advantage of his opportunity."

"That's right," said Steve again.

"But before we go into the matter of payment," continued Stoddard smoothly, "let me be as frank with you as you have been with us. We want the D. & W. to go through, but are not yet too deeply committed to it. If we find the going too difficult, it is still possible that we may consolidate with the North Line; in fact, there is some opinion among the board that we should do so. In that case your position would no longer be of any value to the North Line, or to us. The road would go through regardless of you, and you would be left with a worthless piece of wilderness on your hands." He stopped, frowned, rubbed his lean jaw as if struck by a sudden idea. "Mr. Bradway, you spoke of the possibility of ore on your property. Do you think there is anything in that?"

"I think there's some surface ore there."

Stoddard nodded. "That may be, but I doubt there is ore of any value in that region. If there was, we should have known it long since. But mining people pick up mining rights when they have a chance. It's a bad habit, apt to cost more than it's worth. But," he smiled, "since we are the victims of this weakness, it might be to your advantage to include your mining rights in this discussion."

"No." Steve shook his head. "I think I'll hang on to my rights for a while."

Stoddard gave him a close, keen look, entirely out of harmony with his genial expression. "Very well." He shrugged. "It's of no importance. Perhaps it is just as well not to complicate this simple matter. Now, Mr. Bradway, bearing in mind your position and what I have told you of ours, what do you consider a reasonable sum for this right of way?" His bland glance traveled around the table. "If you give us a reasonable figure, I believe the board will consent and the matter can be closed."

Steve pulled a paper from his pocket and slid it across. "These are my terms," he said.

Stoddard again fixed his glasses on his narrow nose. The paper was brief. After reading it through, his face changed, his lips set as he slowly took off his glasses, laid them down, and stared sternly at Steve. "What is the meaning of this, Mr. Bradway?" he demanded coldly. "We have been discussing a cash sale."

"You have. I haven't," said Steve.

"Certainly I have. What other possible basis is there for discussion? This is nonsense."

"That's what I want," said Steve.

"What is it, Stoddard? What's up?"

Stoddard pulled his harsh stare from Steve and turned to the board. "This man wants a thousand shares of Massachusetts stock for his right of way," he said.

"What? Stock?" An angry buzz went up. "That's out of the question. You know that, Stoddard. He can't have stock. Why does he want stock?"

"It may be a natural mistake." A conciliatory voice cut across. "No doubt Mr. Bradway is unaware that this is a closed corporation."

65

Steve squared around to the table and rested his forearms on it, his eyes narrowed and intent as he watched the agitation around the board. A faint smile twitched his lips as his glance slid over the old man, who, at that point, was taking a nap, but his face was grim and his voice clear when he raised it.

"There is no mistake about this," he said. "I want stock in this company." He turned to Stoddard. "Don't make any further attempt to bluff me about a deal with the North Line. They aren't going to deal with you and you know it. They've got you cold right now. Unless you go through me, and do it quick, they'll stand pat and take you over on their own terms. If you want that kind of consolidation, it's yours." He paused, then went on with less vehemence. "On the other hand, if you put this road through, you've got a profitable future in that country, possibly a great one. Surface ore is bound to develop sooner or later, millions of tons of it, and the North Line not within gunshot of it. I want the D. & W. through, and it will go through if I get a thousand shares of stock."

"But why do you insist on stock, Mr. Bradway?"

"Because I think it will make me a rich man," said Steve. "That," he added, "plus the fact that it may be useful when you get the whip hand in there and try to freeze me out."

Mr. Higgins, red in the face, his fat jowls quivering, had been on the verge of explosion since the first mention of stock. He exploded now. "Rank rubbish from beginning to end," he declared violently. "All we want is a strip of track across a worthless piece of property and this fellow has the impertinence to sit there and instruct us in our business. If he had a modicum of business sense himself he would accept a fair price and get out. Stock, indeed! I never heard such poppycock."

Stoddard raised his hand as the angry man gulped for breath. "Wait a minute, J.D.," he urged, but Higgins turned on Steve with renewed fury. "What you are attempting to do is to bully respectable men into accepting you as a stockholder in this company. It's a holdup. A barefaced holdup. I object to it, and to your impertinence in coming here, and I express the feelings of every member of this board in saying so. It's an outrage. As far as I am concerned, we will have no further dealings with you whatever."

Steve, leaning forward on his arms, listened to this tirade without apparent concern. "There's a good deal in what you say, Mr. Higgins," he said, "and if you express the opinion of this board, I am well pleased to have no further contact with it." He stood up

66

without haste and picked up his hat. "Gentlemen," he said, "you're at liberty to deal with the North Line from now on—and I'm inclined to think you will learn a good deal more about holdups before long."

Excited exclamations burst forth at this abrupt termination of the conference. Chairs scraped as men stood up hastily.

Steve started for the door, but it was a voice from the far end of the table that stopped him. "Just a minute, young man." Old Cyrus looked up casually. "Go along to my office down the hall. I'll be there in a minute. I want a word with you."

CHAPTER 14

Steve was wandering around, his hands in his pockets, look-ing at pictures of clipper ships when the old man came into the room. "Those are nice boats you've got there," he said.

"Ships," snapped Cyrus.

"What's the difference? They float, don't they? Anything that floats is a boat on the Mississippi."

"What do you know about the Mississippi? Thought you were a lumberjack. What's this about the Mississippi?" Cyrus sat down be-hind his desk and laid out his solitaire while Steve, slipped low in his chair, his long legs stretched out, yarned along for a while, glad to shift his thoughts from Massachusetts to the Mississippi. He was tired, tireder than he had ever been lugging a pack, and it was pleasant in the dingy, paneled room. Finally the old man chuckled.

"You don't say," he said. "Sully. I remember that sharper; tall, thin, black-haired feller. Out in the East somewhere—mighta been Calcutta. Smart, too. You learned a lot from him. Wondered where you got it. That was a good bluff you put up in there. Think it'll hold?"

"I've got my stake on it," said Steve. "It ought to."

Cyrus shoved the cards away and sat back, looking hard at Steve from under his shaggy white brows. "How'd you get in there, young man?"

"Toting for Cramer a couple of years ago."

"Cramer slipped up and you slipped in. That's it, ain't it?"

Steve met the shrewd eyes fixed on his. "Cramer's a good man," he said. "We can leave him out of it. I know that country. It was plain as print that any road coming up from the south would have to come along that ridge between those two lakes, so I got in there. That's all I had in mind at that time; that nobody could squeeze in on me without my knowing it."

"Not all you've got in mind now."

"No," Steve admitted promptly.

Cyrus studied Steve for several long seconds, his fingers drumming on the desk. "Higgins is the hitch in there," he said at last. "He's stubborn as a mule. Next to me, he's the biggest stockholder and he'd like to get me out. Been tryin' to get my berth for years. Crowdin' me pretty close, too. I'd like to see you get your stock, but they're goin' to work on you for cash. You'll get a lot of it if you play it right."

Steve straightened up. "I'm not playing this for cash," he said curtly. "I'll get that stock."

Wrinkles pulled up around the keen old eyes. "Think you're headed for port, don't you?" Cyrus chuckled. "That's the time to look out for shoals, young feller. You don't know a thing about deep water yet." His smile broadened. "At that, I like the cut of your jib. Come up to my house for dinner tonight. Where you livin'? . . . The Avery, eh? Cross the Common to Beacon Street. No. 49."

When Steve mounted the steps to Cyrus Forsyth's red brick Georgian house on Beacon Street that night, the glow from the delicate fanlight above the door fell full on him. He stood waiting, his hat cocked a little to one side, looking forward to seeing old Cyrus again and wondering if his money would hold out until he got back to Haley. As the door opened, the lace curtain at the window on his right moved slightly as it fell back into place, but as he stepped over the threshold no premonition told him that the course of his life had been changed because his new suit had already established a percentage in his favor.

A pale, impassive manservant took his hat, led him down the hall past a stairway curving gracefully to the upper floor, and opened a wide mahogany door. "Mr. Bradway," he announced.

Steve, tall, dark, muscular, and vibrant, stepped through the door. The large room, lit by a crystal chandelier that hung from the high ceiling, was cluttered with furniture—much of it gilt. Portraits of sour-looking men and meek women hung on the pale blue walls, and the rose color in the flowered rug was repeated in the heavy damask draperies. He hesitated, wondering how far he'd get before knocking some of those china dolls off the tables, when he heard Cyrus' voice. "Come along, young man. Steer your course," and Steve saw him sitting in a big wing chair beside the fire, his hands spread out on its arms. He looked old, old and tired. "Come along," he repeated grumpily. "Glad to see you. Meet my granddaughter, Mrs. Hamilton."

She was sitting in the curve of a blue satin sofa opposite Cyrus; a small, graceful woman dressed in pale gray shimmering silk. A wide purple velvet sash around the slender waist fell in long ends over her full skirt to the floor. There were a lot of diamonds glittering on her hands, and pearls around her neck. Her face was long and narrow, topped off by a tight, crisp fuzz of ash-blond hair, and she had her brother Horace's sharp nose and thin, pinched lips. When she raised her eyes briefly to acknowledge the introduction, they shone with the glossy opaque luster, gray blue and faintly light-streaked, of a pale star sapphire. She was not—definitely—Steve's idea of a pretty woman. She moved her hand toward the place beside her. "Sit down, Mr. Bradway," she said with languid indifference.

Steve got himself down on the sofa, feeling his bulk and wishing he'd left his fists with his hat in the hall. He liked women, and usually got off to an easy start with them, but he felt checked by this one, and a little shocked, as he sometimes did when he came unexpectedly on some small animal, hidden in the woods, watching, motionless and alert, for its prey to come by. He wished she'd move —say something, but she didn't. Old Cyrus' chin was on his chest, his eyes closed. The only sound in the room was the hiss of the gas in the chandelier. Steve, in desperation, was about to launch an expurgated edition of a funny story he had heard on the train when dinner was announced.

Cyrus heaved himself out of his chair and they crossed the hall to a white paneled dining room, where candles glimmered on the flowers, crystal, and silver on a long table covered with a white lace cloth. Steve hadn't seen such a display since the days on the old *Belle,* and he smiled as they sat down. Conversation here was somewhat more animated, Cyrus furnishing most of it, grumbling about the food and the lack of light. "I can't see this mess. Damn nonsense, eating in the dark."

"I'm sorry, Grandfather," murmured Mrs. Hamilton gently, "but you should be used to it by now. Candlelight is so attractive—don't you think so, Mr. Bradway?"

Steve didn't, but now that he had settled down to it, the lack of light did not interfere with his enjoyment of the meal. The oysters were fresh and cold on the half shell; the mushroom soup was good; the flat fish better than any bass he'd ever tasted, and a blood-warm red wine came along with the beef. By the time he'd finished the ice cream with chocolate sauce, his interest in conversation was as negative as Mrs. Hamilton's.

On the way back to the drawing room, Cyrus laid his hand on his guest's shoulder for a moment. "They're raisin' hell down there," he grumbled. "Looks like they're takin' this chance to hoist me out along with you. All this hullabaloo about reorganizin'—tyin' in with the North Line."

Steve laughed. "If they do that, the North Line would mop them up inside of a year."

"Sure they will. Damn fools, playin' right into their hands. Higgins is behind it—but he can't swing it—not with me around. I'll let 'em do a certain amount of palaverin' before I bring 'em into the wind. May delay you some."

Coffee was served in the drawing room in little cups that teetered. Cyrus swallowed his in one gulp, laced his fingers across his stomach, and promptly went to sleep while Steve and Mrs. Hamilton again sat on the sofa in silence. After a while she asked, "Do you play bezique, Mr. Bradway?"

"Never heard of it."

"Don't you play any games?"

"Well, yes," admitted Steve. "I play a little poker."

"Oh, splendid," she said brightly. "We can play cold hands. I play with Grandfather every evening. He loves it. It's his favorite game."

They played cold hands at a little gilt table. She played surprisingly well and with the luck of the devil, filling inside straights with baffling frequency. When he called her, she spread the cards down with a little ripple of satisfied laughter that exasperated him. "I seem to be lucky playing with you, Mr. Bradway." When she had most of the chips on her side, she laughed again. "You ought to learn to play bezique, Mr. Bradway."

By this time Steve detested her. When the game was over, she stacked the cards neatly, placed them in a silver box, and closed the lid with a decisive snap, then went to the piano and Steve, forced to follow her, leaned on the instrument while she ran her glittering fingers up and down the keyboard in a series of thumps, runs, and trills that finally amused him. He grinned down at her. "You don't have to keep that up," he said. "I know you can do it. How about some simple little thing that I can understand—like bezique?"

He liked her better when she glanced up with amusement that matched his own. "I imagine something sweet and simple like 'Jeanie' is what you like," she said, and the haunting little air came gently, slowly from the instrument to wander like a ghost through the silent room. When it was finished, she sat for a moment, her head lowered, her hands resting on the keyboard. Then she raised her head slowly, deliberately, and looked straight into Steve's eyes. It was a steady look, completely unveiled, and she gave Steve plenty of time to see what was behind it before the white lids lowered to conceal it. "It's a disturbing little air, isn't it?" she murmured. "I can't say I like it. Dreams are such lonely things, aren't they? But perhaps you don't dream, Mr. Bradway."

Steve stared at her. He couldn't believe what his senses were telling him. He leaned heavily on the piano, groggy with astonishment until, with a faint derisive smile, she swung around on the piano stool and moved gracefully back to the sofa. Steve followed her like a stunned ox, getting past the hassocks and tables by a miracle. But when she patted the place beside her on the sofa, he shook his head. "You're very kind," he stammered, "but I must be getting on."

"Oh, don't go yet, Mr. Bradway," she said with her former cool indifference. "Grandfather will be waking soon and will be disappointed not to find you here."

Steve muttered something about a pleasant evening, got out of the house, and strode rapidly across the Common. He was crazy! He must be crazy—but he knew damn well he wasn't. He was too familiar with that particular message not to recognize it when he got it. No mistake about it, that smooth little white-faced female back there had deliberately put it up to him—and she was Cyrus Forsyth's granddaughter!

After a considerable burst of speed he stopped, took off his hat, mopped his brow, and lifted his hot face to the cool night air. "By God!" he declared to the stars above Boston.

72

CHAPTER 15

The proposals, counterproposals, and objections that went on between the members of the board and Cyrus, stubbornly determined to inject new blood into the list of stockholders, dragged on for several days, and during that period Steve spent most of his time in the old man's office playing cold hands. For a while he enjoyed those hours in the dingy, pleasant room but time was running out and his money with it, for Cyrus was winning with an uncanny persistence that recalled Sully at his best. Finally the day came when Steve's patience came to an abrupt end. He shoved back his chair and thrust his hands in his pockets.

Cyrus stopped dealing. "What's the matter?" he asked. "Can't you take bein' licked?"

"No," said Steve. "I don't like it. When did you shift decks on me?"

Cyrus slid the deck into his desk drawer. "Why, Steve, what you talkin' about?" he inquired with injured innocence. "I've had a little streak of luck, that's all."

"Like hell you had," said Steve. "Let me see that deck."

He stood up and began pacing restlessly around the room. "I don't like it. I don't like any of it," he went on with increasing irritation. "What are they doing in there? What's all the bickering about? Can't they make up their minds? If this goes on, the North Line will be in there. May be now, for all we know."

"You're doin' all right, holdin' off," said Cyrus. "That was a whoppin' cash offer you got yesterday. Why didn't you take it? Sensible thing to do."

Steve swung on him. "I'm not holding off for more cash," he declared with considerable heat. "I'll need that stock when you start jacking up freight rates out there. There's an enormous future in that country. I know it. I'm positive of it, and I mean to ride in on it with your stock. But if those damn fools delay much longer, their precious stock won't be worth the paper it's written on."

"We've got a little time yet," said Cyrus easily.

"What makes you think so?"

Cyrus took out the cards again and riffled them with a practiced hand. "We got a good man out there watching it. The North Line can't ramp in there without condemning you first. They'll have to go to court for that—and if they do, we'll know it. In the meantime the D. & W. is going right ahead. Must be pretty close to that bunch of timber you've got by now."

"What do you mean by that?"

"Why, the D. & W.'s a timber road, son. You know that. It's in there haulin' timber. Has been for years. We let 'em through a few pieces we own down along there, and when they butted into you, we undertook to oblige them again. That's all. The North Line's got no interest in the little old D. & W. prowlin' around for more timber. They've got bigger troubles, all they can handle right now, tryin' to get through to the coast."

Steve shrugged. "Put it any way you like, it's a risk," he said. "A big risk—and I don't like it."

"Sure, it's a risk," agreed Cyrus, "but there's an angle to it can't be hurried. Got to let 'em ripen in there a few days more. You'll get your stock if you hold your course." Steve received this news with an impatient glance, and for a while the old man watched him closely. Then, "How much money you got?" he inquired abruptly.

"About ten dollars," replied Steve. "Why? What's that got to do with it?"

"I didn't ask how much you got in your pants," snapped Cyrus. "I asked how much you got."

Steve stopped his restless tour and glared at him. "What's that got to do with it?" he repeated harshly.

Cyrus leaned back and regarded the angry young man with amused satisfaction. "Ten dollars, eh," he chuckled. "I figured you for around a hundred. Sailin' mighty close to the wind, ain't you? Can't remember bein' quite that broke in a foreign port myself— well, yes, maybe. A couple of times. It pinches, but it ain't any use losing headway over it. Thing to do is figure how to get around it. Sit down."

Steve dropped into his chair and the old man continued to regard him calmly for a moment, his fingers laced across his vest. "Now, son," he said, "what you goin' to do with that stock when you get it? You can't sell it outside this board."

Steve gave him a quick look. "What are you getting at?"

"You can't sell it and don't want to," Cyrus went on, unruffled.

74

"It's good stock and pays nice dividends. But you can borrow on it, and being away out there in the woods, you'd probably want to vote it by proxy." He rummaged in his desk and hauled out a checkbook. "I'll advance you a thousand on that stock right now," he said with an air of benevolence. "How does that suit you?"

Steve's face beamed like the sun coming from behind a dark cloud. "Well, I'll be damned!" he exclaimed. "So that's what you're up to. Why didn't you let me in on it?" He grinned with affectionate admiration at the old man. "While you're at it, you'd better make that check for two thousand."

"Steve, how you talk," said Cyrus reproachfully. "Anybody'd think, to hear you, I could use that stock." He scribbled laboriously, tore a check from the book, and handed it across the desk. "Run downstairs to the bank and cash this so I can take some of it away from you."

They played cold hands contentedly the rest of the afternoon. Horace came in once with another proposal of agreement. He stood in the door, as decent a man as there was in Boston, and sharply aware of it, watching the pair of them toss cards and chips across the desk, silent, intent, and apparently unaware of his presence. The papers in his hand trembled, he seethed with disgust, but he backed out, unable to pluck up the courage to interrupt the game.

That night, on his way to his hotel, Steve went to the best florist in Boston and sent Mrs. Hamilton a huge bunch of violets. No card went with it.

During this interval of delay Steve had seen Mrs. Hamilton several times, the first time no later than the morning following the dinner party. He was strolling through the Common, telling himself he was there to see what Cyrus' house looked like in the daylight when he saw her sitting on a bench not far from the house, watching a small boy roll a hoop. She wore a black bonnet trimmed with violets, and the lapels of her tight-fitting black jacket were faced with silk of the same color. She seemed absorbed in watching the child but she looked up without surprise when he spoke.

"Good morning, Mrs. Hamilton," he said, lifting his hat with a flourish. "Well! I didn't expect to see you."

Her eyes had picked up some color from the flowers in her hat. "Didn't you?" she said calmly. "I was quite certain I would see you."

This hit the nail such a rap on the head that he was baffled for a moment. Then he laughed and sat down beside her. "You're right," he said. "I came because I wanted to see you. I didn't tell you how much I enjoyed that dinner. It was a good one."

She received this without interest and turned to the child. "Come here, Victor," she called gently. "I want you to meet Mr. Bradway."

The boy came at once, walking sedately with his hoop over his arm. He was a handsome child, tall for his age, but pale and shy, and his fair hair hung in ringlets over the lace collar of his black velvet jacket.

Mrs. Hamilton drew him to her. "This is my son," she said fondly. "Take off your cap, Victor, and shake hands with Mr. Bradway."

Steve took the limp little hand and smiled at the downcast face. "I didn't know you had a big son like this," he said genially. "How old are you, young man?"

"Seven," the boy murmured.

"Seven! That's fine. You're almost grown-up. What are you doing with those long curls, a big fellow like you?"

The boy's face flushed a painful red, the head dropped lower, and for an instant the mother's face set sharply; then cleared as quickly. "Victor is very fortunate in having such lovely curls, aren't you, darling?" she said gently, winding one of the tresses around her finger. "We want to keep them as long as we can." She kissed the child's flushed face. "Run along now, pet, and play—but not too hard. Remember, darling."

When they were alone again on the bench, there was silence for a few moments. "That's a fine little fellow," Steve managed at last.

"Yes," she sighed, "but he's so delicate I am fearful he may develop his father's heart ailment. It is so difficult to know just what is best for him. It worries me constantly."

The reason for the purple and black burst upon Steve. He had been wondering where Hamilton was. He knew now. "I'm sorry," he said. "I had no idea of this."

"I'm quite sure you hadn't," she said.

She turned her back on him, her eyes on the boy trying to roll his hoop at a walk. Steve, his antipathy roused again to the boiling point by her behavior, was about to get up and end the encounter when she spoke again. "Grandfather believes he is infallible in his judgment of character," she murmured. "It is his boast that he has never been mistaken in a man." She turned and her eyes rested on his. "Aren't you flattered that he so obviously approves of you?"

Steve looked hard at her. "No. His approval of me is based on something beside character. At that, he's a mighty shrewd old fellow."

She smiled faintly, and after a moment glanced at a tiny jeweled watch pinned on her jacket. "I must go," she said. "It is time for Victor's luncheon. Come, Victor," she called. "Good-by, Mr. Bradway."

Steve stood up with her and watched her walk slowly, gracefully, up the path, her arm around Victor. He shook his head. "Damned if I can make out what she's up to," he thought. "Damned if I can."

CHAPTER 16

After this Steve met her every morning. She was always there on the same bench, the fresh showers of golden forsythia a pleasing background for her slender figure, her eyes resting tranquilly on Victor while he pursued the light exercise scheduled for that hour. Steve couldn't understand why he came to this rendezvous but he did, urged on by a senseless but increasing determination to assert his ascendency over this woman, as if his manhood depended on it. She defeated him with ease, barbing her little pricks at his conceit with tantalizing, sly amusement until, satisfied that she had stung him sufficiently for one morning, she left him with a casual smile and went home with Victor.

Steve, smarting with humiliation, felt like breaking her neck. He detested her. She aroused a depth of emotion in him he had never experienced with any woman in his life—and it was not a satisfactory emotion. It tormented him, but he came back for more—and sent her violets.

During these sessions with her he kept his exasperation concealed and talked with what ease he could muster about his reasons for delay and his desire to get out of Boston.

"You don't care for Boston, do you, Mr. Bradway?"

"No," he said. "It's dead on its feet. Everything is over here, all in the past. This business of mine would have been settled in two hours in Chicago."

"What a pity you weren't there," she said. After a little silence she murmured, as if to herself, "I was born here and so was Victor. All our people for generations have been born in Boston but that, of course, would mean nothing to a man of your background. We must seem to you the withered branches of an old tree, but our roots mean a great deal to us."

"What?" demanded Steve. But she seemed to have no reply to that.

It was only when he spoke of his cabin in the woods and his life there that she showed any interest in anything he said. Then her eyes would slide around beneath their lids to rest somewhere on his coat, and he would see a glimmer through the colorless lowered lashes. "It must be stimulating to find such satisfaction in the size of a bass," she remarked at one time. "Your life must be very romantic, Mr. Bradway."

"Nothing romantic about it," protested Steve. "It's a hard, tough life, but a man knows he's alive out there."

"You mean you are not alive in Boston?"

"I am," retorted Steve, "but I see no evidence of it in anybody else."

At last, to his profound relief, the day came when he could tell her that his business with the Massachusetts Mining Company was settled and he would be pulling out for Chicago that night.

"Are you satisfied with the settlement?" she asked, without apparent interest.

"Yes. It was a foregone conclusion. I should have been out of here ten days ago."

"You don't seem particularly happy about it." She gave him one of her sly, amused smiles. "Is it possible you regret leaving Boston?"

"No," he said boldly, "but I regret leaving you, Mrs. Hamilton."

"Really? How very kind of you."

Steve looked straight at her. "It's not meant to be kind," he said. "Suppose we call it unfinished business. I like to clean up a job while I'm at it. Finish it one way or the other."

She thought that over for a moment, her hand on her cheek, the little finger across her lips. "I know nothing about business," she said at last, "but I should imagine yours here was finished. Would you care to come to tea this afternoon before you leave?"

He gave her a close look but could make nothing of that composed, pale mask. "Yes," he said.

He found her that afternoon, in a soft, long, lavender dress, sitting on the blue sofa, barricaded behind the tea table, her jeweled hands lightly busy with the silver and china. He sat down in her grandfather's chair, crossed his legs, and leaned back. For the first time in her presence he felt detached and at ease, and watched her graceful, accustomed affectations in the business of making tea with amusement. She lifted the lid of the silver kettle and peeped in. "How do you like your tea, Mr. Bradway?" she asked.

"Strong and straight—and preferably in a tin cup."

She served him a strong hot brew that would have aroused praise in a lumber camp, fed him thin sandwiches and tiny sweet cakes. He ate quantities of them and drank three cups of tea but made no attempt at conversation, his eyes deliberately watching her. Her cup clattered a little as she put it down. Steve's did not.

When it was no longer possible to prolong the tea ceremony, she sat back, one arm flung across the sofa, her head turned. Steve had sent her some long-stemmed American Beauty roses and they were on a table behind her. She looked charming in the half-light. Her chatter limped along for a few minutes and then died. Steve did nothing to save it. Suddenly, as if unable to endure his calm scrutiny any longer, she jumped up.

"Perhaps you would like me to play for you." She flushed, stopped, and tried to reseat herself.

"Sure." Steve smiled at her. "Let's have 'Jeanie' again."

She didn't play "Jeanie" but she played everything else she could think of while Steve leaned in the curve of the piano, looking down at her. Finally the music faltered and she stood up.

"I am sorry, Mr. Bradway," she said coldly, "but this is Victor's suppertime and I must leave you."

Steve stepped in front of her. "Just a minute," he said.

She drew back, glancing nervously for a way past his big bulk. "What is the meaning of this, Mr. Bradway?" she said. "Let me pass."

"Just a minute," he repeated. He threw back his head and laughed; then swung one arm around her and scooped her light figure from the floor. She struggled like a cat, beating his chest with her tiny fists, twisting her face from him, until with a little grunt of amusement, he took her chin in his free hand and kissed her thoroughly. He kept her there until he felt her submit, cling to him; then he held her from him, shook her lightly as he might a plaything, and set her back on her feet. She pulled away, blazing with anger.

"How dare you! Oh, how dare you," she gasped. "You—you—insufferable——"

"Drop it!" said Steve bluntly, no longer amused. "What are you kicking about? You've been asking for it for ten days. You asked me here this afternoon expecting me to beg for it. That was your mistake, not mine. I don't dabble in this pastime. It may work around Boston but it don't go down with me. At that"—he looked her over deliberately from head to foot—"you've got a lot of woman in that little body. Give it a chance sometime. You'd be quite an armful if you did."

He turned and walked to the door. There he looked back at her.

She was standing as he had left her, rigid, her head high, her eyes wide open, fixed on him. "That business I spoke about is finished," he said casually. "Accounts balanced and the books closed." He went out of the door and slammed it.

On the train going back to Chicago, Steve spent a good deal of time shoving Mrs. Hamilton out of his thoughts. He had other things to think about. One thousand shares of Massachusetts stock snuggled in an inside pocket against his breast, and this was, no doubt, the source of the glow around his heart. Old Cyrus had given it to him with a hearty thump on the back. "There you are, young feller. It's good stock and the dividends will keep you goin' for a while." The old eyes twinkled. "Might be smart to borrow money on it and pick up some D. & W. Goin' to jump now." Steve tried to thank him but the words stuck. "Pshaw!" the old man interrupted. "Good thing for you I had it in for Higgins. I needed that proxy. He'll sweat when he finds out about it." He chuckled, then a shadow fell across the tired face. "Don't like to see you go off," he said gruffly. "Ain't likely I'll see you again."

"No," said Steve as he gripped the big square hand, gnarled with age. "Not unless you come out there to look things over. I wish you would. We'd have a fine time."

Cyrus brightened at that. "Maybe I will, son. Maybe I will. Pull out now. The tide is with you. Make the most of it." And they parted with the affectionate understanding of two successful rogues.

Now Steve sat with his feet braced against the opposite seat while the landscape somewhere in central Ohio slid past his abstracted gaze. He was on his way back, and the future looked good; fair beyond any vision of his dreams. He had Cyrus to thank for that, and his heart warmed to the stubborn old man back there, battling to keep his supremacy in spite of the heavy years. Succeeding, too, except in the matter of candlelight on the dinner table. And again Mrs. Hamilton—Amelia—shuttled across the warp of his thoughts to spoil the pattern of his content.

Damn her! She'd made a fool of him, no question about that, and his final encounter with her had failed to erase the sting of it. Well, he couldn't expect to cope with the tricks of a woman like that. The women he knew came out with it. Flat. Over and done with. But they weren't as fragrant as she had been when she struggled in his arms, and again he felt the passionate resistance, the tremulous brief yielding of her soft body close to his. He moved uneasily. Well,

81

one thing was certain, he'd never see her again. Not if he could help it. He got up and went into the smoking car to pick up a game.

When he got to Chicago, he took the box the tailor had left for him at the Palmer House up to his room. He had been meaning to wear his new suit back to Haley, but when he opened the box and the familiar scent of his comfortable old woods clothes greeted him like a long-lost friend, he ripped off his high collar, hurled it across the room, and with it went all thought of Boston. By the time he had climbed into his old pants and buttoned his soft shirt around his neck, his eyes were sparkling with anticipation of the future and his thoughts were on his cabin in the woods.

CHAPTER 17

It was early evening when Steve jumped off the train at Haley. Len, the stationmaster, eyed him speculatively. "Where you been?" he asked. "Look's like you got your hair cut."

Steve laughed. "Took a trip," he said.

"Well, some people do," said Len.

The snow was gone, the street, littered with the winter's trash, revealed by the searching finger of the sun. More trash still lay gripped in ice in the narrow alleys between the saloons but the spring air was sweet with the lingering perfume of the pines, and as he swung along on his way to Burke's Hotel, Steve filled his chest with it. It was good to be back.

Kit wasn't in the dining room when he went in to supper but he didn't notice that until the waitress who brought him his meal told him she was sick.

"What's the matter with her?" asked Steve, launching into his corned beef and cabbage.

"I guess she's in love," replied the girl with a pert glance.

"That's a good way to be sick," grinned Steve.

"Well, yes, maybe. Sometimes," said the girl. "You had your hair cut, ain't you? Looks good."

After supper Steve hurried around to see Curtis. He found the lawyer still in his office working under the lamp on his desk. "Steve!" he exclaimed, jumping up, his face lit with pleasure. "Lord! I'm glad to see you. Didn't expect you for a couple of days. You got your hair cut, didn't you?"

"So they tell me." Steve roared with delight as he seized the narrow shoulders in a bone-crushing grip. "Got those new pants, too. Everything's in good shape. Sit down before I tell you. You've got quite a shock coming."

They sat down and Steve spread the papers on the table. Curtis opened them with fingers that trembled a little and Steve saw his face change from apprehension to bewilderment, saw him frown with disbelief, until finally he stared across the table in utter astonishment. "You mean you got the entire thousand shares—and kept your rights?" he asked. "We didn't expect a quarter of that, Steve. What—what happened?"

"Luck," said Steve, beaming with satisfaction. "The damnedest luck a man ever ran into, and we wouldn't have had a share of stock if I hadn't been there myself. I owe that to you, John." And he began his story about Cyrus and the board. "They had him pretty close to the edge when I got there," he concluded, "but he's got a proxy vote on a thousand shares now and we've got the shares."

"Funny Higgins didn't see that," said Curtis, still incredulous.

"He would have if Cyrus hadn't worked on him right. But he's a hot-tempered, pigheaded cuss and Cyrus got him so mad he couldn't see what he was up to. Old Cyrus is a grand old fellow, John, as slick as they come."

It took Curtis some time to grasp the significance of Steve's luck but they finally got down to practical talk. "When that road goes through, there'll be a rush in there," said Curtis at one point, "and you can cash in again on your mining rights." He smiled. "You'll be a rich man one of these days, Steve."

"That's the idea," said Steve, "but I'm going to ride with my mining rights awhile until I know what I've got in there." He grinned. "I'll sell 'em fast enough if there's nothing there."

It was midnight when he got back to his room in Burke's Hotel. He felt tired after the excitement of the past few days, and he had an early start ahead in the morning. He wasn't pleased to find Kit sitting there waiting for him, but he greeted her affectionately enough, and when she jumped up and came to him with eager timidity, gave her a light kiss and a pat on the back. "I hear you've been sick," he said. "What's the matter with you?"

"Nothing," she said. "I'm all right. I've just been waiting for you. You've been gone so long I was afraid something happened to you. You been all right?"

He threw off his hat and coat and sat down to unlace his boots. "I sure have," he said. "It was a great trip. Everything's squared away now, Kit. Things will get a move on from now on." Then, remembering, he stood up and hauled money from his pocket. "Here you are, Kit. Double. Much obliged to you. It was a great help."

She pulled away from his outstretched hand. "I don't want it," she said, shaking her head.

"Nonsense," he said impatiently. "Of course you want it. Don't be silly. Here, take it."

84

She took it, her eyes on his face, and slipped it in the bosom of her dress. "I'm glad you had a good trip," she said. She sat down and stretched her arms, hands clasped tight, on the table in front of her. "I'm glad of that," she repeated. "Everything will be all right now, like you said."

"It sure will. I'll tell you about it in the morning. Here"—he reached into his coat pocket and tossed a small box to her across the table—"something I got for you in Chicago."

She held the box in her hands a moment, staring at it, her face flushed with surprise and happiness. Then slowly, carefully, she unwrapped it until a pretty gold breastpin lay in her hand, glittering in the lamplight. "Oh, Steve," she breathed at last. "Oh, Steve, I never thought I'd have anything like this. Never. Why—it's a lover's knot—a true lover's knot. Did you think of that?"

"Is it?" Steve stood up and leaned over her shoulder to look at it. "It's some kind of a knot all right. Glad you like it. Run along now. I'll see you in the morning."

She didn't hear him. She sat there, her round blue eyes glued on the trifle in her hand. "It's gold," she murmured. "It's real gold and there's a blue stone in the center. Oh, Steve—I'd rather have it than a ring."

"A ring? I didn't know you wanted a ring. Why didn't you say so?"

"I did want it," she said absently, "but I don't any more. I'd rather have this. But I thought maybe you'd bring me a ring. I thought it would be a ring in the box."

"A ring!" He looked at her, puzzled. "What made you think that?"

She didn't answer for a moment, gazing at the pin in her hand. "Because I thought we'd get married when you got back," she said simply, "and maybe you'd bring me a ring."

"Married!" Steve sat down on the bed as if someone had hit him. "Married! I never said we'd get married. Where in God's name did you get that idea?"

"You said everything would be all right when you got back," she said, her voice low, a little frightened. "You said so, just now. I always thought you meant we'd get married. I always thought that. I was sure of it."

Steve stared at her, too thunderstruck to utter a word. Married! Finally, after what seemed a long time, he pulled himself together. "Look here, Kit," he said as reasonably as he could. "You've got this thing all balled up. I never said anything to you about getting married. It never crossed my mind. I'm not getting married. I've got

85

other things to think about. Right now it's the last thing on earth I'd do."

"That's all right," she said, her voice still lower. "It don't need to be right now. I can wait. Only—only—I thought we would."

He got up and put his hand over the one holding the pin. "Look here, Kit," he said again. "We'd better get this straight right now. I'm sorry it happened with you. You know that." She nodded, not looking at him. "But I'm damned if it was my fault," he went on more vigorously. "I never meant to do it, never made any play for you. To get it straight, I never wanted to. You're a nice girl, but you didn't mean that to me."

She gave him a furtive, frightened glance. "But you said it," she repeated. "You said everything would be all right when you got back."

Steve swore and walked to the window, his back to her. After a pause he spoke again over his shoulder, trying to keep his voice level. "I don't want to hurt you, Kit, but the truth of it is—I never wanted you that way. I never made a play for you when you came here night after night. You know that. But when you jumped in bed with me out there, what was I to think? You're not so damned innocent you didn't know what to expect. You did know, didn't you?"

She nodded again, tears beginning to roll down her cheeks. "But I thought we was going to get married," she persisted. "I always thought that. I never thought anything else."

"Hell!" Steve threw himself into a chair. "I can't help what goes on in your head," he said. "I didn't put it there and it never was in mine. And never will be," he added bluntly. "You better get this straight, Kit. I'm not going to marry you now, or any other time. It would be the worst thing in the world for both of us."

She raised her head and looked up at him then, as if hearing him clearly for the first time. "You won't never marry me, Steve?"

"No."

Her mouth fell open and she stared as if unable to comprehend what was happening to her. "Not ever?"

"Not ever, Kit."

For a moment she continued to stare, her hands stretched across the table, her wide eyes fixed on him. And beyond him, way beyond him, on something far in the distance. Then she dropped her head on her arms and bawled like a sick calf. She seemed to go to pieces under Steve's eyes. Her hair loosened, her face lay sideways on her arms, her eyes closed, tears pouring down her cheeks and into her open gasping mouth, rocking, ready to fall from her chair. Stripped of what little grace she had, she looked what she was—a common, stupid servant girl in broken shoes and a soiled, patched blue gingham dress.

Steve, shocked by her abandon, disgust and pity struggling in his breast, got up and stood again at the window, staring into the dark. After a long time the gulps and sobs slowly quieted and he turned to see her lying there, her face on her arms, the pin still clutched in her hand. He went to her and laid his hand on her shoulder. "I'm sorry as hell, Kit," he said gently, "but it's not as bad as all this. You'll feel better about it in the morning. Sure you will. Brace up and forget it." He patted her shoulder. "One of these days you'll settle down with some young fellow and be glad you got rid of me."

She jumped up and wrenched away from his hand as if it scorched her. "Don't touch me," she muttered, her voice so changed it startled him. "Let me alone. Oh, let me alone! I don't never want to see you again; never, never, as long as I live. Never. Never!" And she rushed past him out of the room.

"Here, Kit. Wait a minute," Steve called, hurrying after her.

But she was running down the long, dark hall toward the feeble light that burned at the foot of the stairs to the attic where she slept, and he saw her clamber blindly, frantically, up the stairs and disappear. He stood perplexed for a moment more, then went back into the room and closed the door.

"Goddamn it," he said irritably, as he settled down to sleep. "Why did she have to cut up like that the minute I get back?"

CHAPTER 18

The D. & W. Railroad that the Massachusetts Mining Company was using to relieve the freight situation at Alturos was an inconspicuous little carrier. For years it had served the timber interests along the shore of Lake Superior but those regions were now depleted, and for some time miles of its lightly laid track had been abandoned to rust and weeds.

Suddenly, however, it showed a spurt of new life by proposing to run some thirty miles of track from its main line on the lake shore to Alturos. The North Line, indignant at this audacity, hastily turned to plug it up, only to find that, in its meek way, the D. & W. had acquired its right of way and was going through.

It was no easy task. The wedge of land between the lake shore on the east and the North Line Railroad on the west was wild country, webbed by a network of lakes and streams. Pushing through this rugged country in haste and secrecy had proved an arduous undertaking, particularly troublesome at one point, where the course ran square between two lakes. On the shore of one of these lakes stood a small log cabin, and in it lived the man who owned the ridge from lake to lake—a lumberjack—said to be a tough character, opposed to letting the road through. He must have been eliminated, however, for Baker, chief engineer in charge of construction for the D. & W., had recently been told to go ahead in there.

The tough character, toting a heavy load of supplies, was on his way back to the cabin. He didn't look like a man who had been eliminated, but neither did he look like one returning in triumph. He walked with a strong free stride, but his face was grim, and the great day he had looked forward to so long had settled into a gloomy tramp through the woods. He was exasperated, and his irritation grew with every step he took.

It was all Kit's fault, coming up at this particular time with her idiotic idea of getting married. Married! He grunted with disgust. Again he went over every step of his relations with her and, except for the fact that she was innocent when he took her, he couldn't blame himself for any part of it. He couldn't blame himself for that, either. When he thought of the way she had tricked him into it with her damn Christmas tree, it riled him to the point of cussing out loud.

His heavy mood clung to him until he reached the cabin, and to his pleased surprise, little Matt was there. Steve hadn't seen him for more than six months and the sight of the lively, friendly fellow raised his spirits with a bound. "Matt," he shouted, raising his hand in greeting, "glad to see you. How've you been, you old polecat?"

Matt, his black eyes snapping, hurried to him and grabbed his hand. "Me?" He thumped his chest. "Had a little rheumatiz in camp but she's all gone. How's yourself?"

"Great," said Steve. "How long you been off the drive?"

"Week, maybe. I walk through from Clearwater. Been here two, three days."

"Drive didn't stop at Haley?"

"Naw. Went past. Saunders, he's through with that river. Camps closed. He's goin' in down below next winter."

Steve dropped his pack and Matt lugged it into the cabin. Coffee was bubbling on the stove, the fragrance of baked beans in the air. "Glad you're here, Matt," Steve repeated with feeling. "How about working for me from now on?" He pulled a wad of money from his pocket. "How's this for a start? Your winter's pay twice over. How about it?"

Matt hopped with excitement as he took the money. His eyes gleamed. "By gar, Steve, you fix 'em, eh? You boss around here now?"

"Sure," grinned Steve. "Why not? We'll have a railroad through here this summer. Fellow by the name of Baker will be along here in a few days to stake it out. We'll have to slick up for him."

"Sure. Sure, Steve. Anythin' you say." The little fellow gazed at him with the trustful devotion of a faithful dog.

Steve laughed. This was more like it.

Less than a week later he was on the ridge early one morning, looking things over, when he heard voices and presently saw a man working his way with accustomed ease through the woods with two men toting for him. He watched them for a moment, then strode forward, his hand outstretched. "You're Baker, I take it," he said cordially. "I'm Bradway. I've been expecting you. Where did you drop from at this hour?"

Baker was a rangy man with long legs and good shoulders, dressed

89

in woods clothes that had unquestionably been his for a long time. His face was lean, angular, and brown from exposure, and as he grasped Steve's hand, he gave him a steady appraising look from a pair of gray eyes as noncommittal as a slab of granite. Steve took to him at once.

"I've got a camp about five miles below here. Walked in," replied Baker.

"That so? Put in any work down there?"

"Yes. Quite a lot."

"Took a chance on it, did you?"

"Had to, to get through this summer. We didn't think it was much of a chance."

"Well, I'm glad to have you around," Steve said heartily. "I'd like to see where you're going through here."

"Come along."

The men picked up their tripods and they started through the woods. Baker, disregarding Steve, worked rapidly, shifting his tripod, squinting through the transit, waving his arms, making notes, placing his markers with the activity of a bee on its way home. Finally they picked up the markers on the other side of Steve's property and Baker stopped. "That's the way it goes," he said. He sat down on a windfall, shoved back his hat, and spread his blueprints on the ground. "There it is," and with a stick he traced the route from Merrill to Alturos. It suited Steve, and he said so.

"Think you'll get through this summer?"

"Ought to, unless we get a bad break," said Baker cautiously. "There's a bad curve down below here I'd like to get rid of and considerable blasting up above, but I think we'll get through."

"How you going to work it?"

"Both ways to the middle. Competing crews. I think we'll get through," he repeated.

"That will be fine until I dig a mine under you."

Baker's gray glance caught him. "What do you mean by that?"

Steve turned on him. "I'll make you a bet right now, Baker, that when you strip off this roadbed you'll find the red stuff right under the surface, ready to dish up."

"We find it all along this ridge," said Baker with chilling indifference. "Makes good ballast, but that's all it amounts to in my opinion." He folded his blueprints and stood up. "This gravel ain't diamonds you can pick up and drop in your pocket," he added.

They walked through the woods along the route to the point nearest Steve's cabin, a quarter of a mile away. Steve stopped. "My shack's in here," he said.

Baker nodded. "I know. I've been through here before. This was just a checkup."

"You son of a gun," laughed Steve. "I thought you were working mighty fast. By the way, I've got a man here—he's good with an ax. Can you use him?"

"Send him along," said Baker.

They parted, and Steve turned through the woods toward his cabin. He walked slowly, thinking, conscious of a deep content. It had been a fine day. He liked Baker. If any man could get thirty miles of track through that wilderness in time to beat the snow, he would. Things were coming along exactly as he wanted them. Exactly as he wanted them!

These pleasant thoughts were interrupted by the sight of Matt hurrying toward him through the woods. Neither he nor Matt had been to Haley since his return but Matt had gone in that day for supplies and wouldn't be back until night. Steve stopped short as Matt, sweating and excited, came up to him.

"What's the matter? Why are you back here?" he asked sharply. "Did Curtis send you? Anything wrong?"

"Kit," said Matt, his eyes on Steve's.

"Kit!" A wave of anger swept through Steve. "What's she got to do with it?"

"She's gone. Skipped. She skipped out a couple of nights ago. Len seen her. She took the train." Matt poured it out.

Steve's face hardened. "What of it?" he asked harshly. "You mean you came back to tell me that?"

"Sure." Matt nodded vigorously. "Burke don't know nothin' about her. She didn't leave no word nor nothin'. Just skipped out."

"What of it?" repeated Steve, his anger rising. "What's it got to do with me where she's gone? Why in hell did you come busting back here to tell me? It's none of my business."

Matt gave him a puzzled look. "Kit's your girl, ain't she? You been runnin' with her a year almost. You been livin' with her."

They had reached the cabin by this time and Steve went in and slammed the door. He pitched off his coat and crossed the room, trying to control himself. Kit again! He scowled as her face as he had last seen it under the lamplight rose vividly before him and again disgust surged through him. Damn her! He didn't want to hurt her—wouldn't have, if she hadn't forced it on him. He turned to Matt.

"Look here, Matt," he said. "Use your head. Sure, I've been living with her. She wanted it that way. She'd tell you so herself. But a man can't carry on a thing like that the rest of his life. She knew that, so she cleared out. She's got more sense than you have."

"You mean you quit her?"

Steve rounded on him, his eyes blazing. "I did not," he protested violently. "I played fair with Kit from the start. I never told her I'd marry her—never gave her any reason to think I would, but she came up with it the night I got back and we had it out. She quit the minute I told her. Hell, Matt, I never chased Kit. She'd tell you so herself. You can get that out of your head."

Matt stood his ground during this outburst, his black eyes fixed on Steve's. "She tell you she's havin' a baby?"

The sense of injustice that had sustained Steve's outraged feelings up to this point collapsed like a pricked balloon. His jaw sagged. He stared at Matt. "No, she did not," he said after a pause. "Certainly not. Why should she? Who told you that?"

"Nobody," admitted Matt. "Nobody told me—but I been thinkin'. Kit ain't got no reason to run—ain't got no place to run to. She ain't never been out of Haley. Take somethin' like that to scare her off. She'd run then. She ain't the kind to face it down."

Steve frowned, staring hard at Matt. "You're crazy," he said emphatically, after a moment. "I don't believe it for one second. There's nothing the matter with Kit. I haven't been with her for over two months and I know for a fact she was all right then."

Matt wagged his head. "She skipped out."

"That proves it," insisted Steve. "If she'd been in a fix, she'd have said so the other night to cinch it with me. First thing she'd do—first thing any woman does. You're all steamed up over nothing, Matt. I know it for a fact. I'm positive of it."

"Mebbe so, Steve. Mebbe not. You goin' after her?"

Steve turned on him. "No," he shouted. "No! Goddamn it! What do you take me for? Why should I chase after her? It was washed up months ago. Shut up about it. I've had enough."

Matt gave him an odd look, picked up his hat, and turned to the door.

Steve's manner eased. "It's all right, Matt," he said. "You made it once today. No hurry about that stuff. Wait till morning."

Matt shook his head. "I ain't comin' back. I'm quittin'."

92

"What?"

"Sure. Why not? I ain't got no railroad on my neck. I'm goin' to find out what makes Kit run off. Mebbe she needs somebody." He shrugged. "Mebbe not—but I find out."

Steve's face softened. "Matt, you're a damn fool," he said. "I got you a good job today. You better stay with it—and with me. Don't go off on a wild-goose chase like this. You'll be drunk before you get out of Haley. Unless," he added, "you're after Kit yourself. That it?"

"Me?" Matt shrugged again. "Ain't my style," he said. "But she's a nice little kid out to Saunders'. She ride on my sled sometimes." He turned at the door. "You get along fine, Steve. You big boss now. You don't need nobody. Kit—mebbe she does."

After Matt had gone, the cabin seemed very still. The evening sun through the open door lit up the drab interior, dancing away from the dirty floor, the greasy pots and pans, as if loath to touch them— and night was coming on. After some time Steve went to the door, hesitated, and walked out. Matt had gone the way he came, through the woods around the end of the lake. Steve got into his boat and rowed across. He was halfway to town on the dark trail before he stopped, shook his head—and turned back.

CHAPTER 19

The brief summer months flew by. Steve heard nothing from
Matt or Kit and gradually, under the battering of reason, his
uneasy conscience subsided and his duty toward Kit faded under the
pressure of more important problems.

Baker bunked in with him now, and every day both men were
with the construction crews, north and south, often spending the
night in the camps. The work went fast. As soon as the roadbed was
as good as haste could make it, a section of ties and rails was slapped
down and the engine, panting with impatience, crawled gingerly
over it, pushing ahead the flat car carrying the next ties and rails.
Steve often rode in the engine, sometimes took the throttle, and
when he stuck his head out of the cab window to cuss or shout encouragement, the men grinned and jumped to it, knowing that the
last spike would not be driven before he grabbed the whistle cord
and the car rolled forward to the next section. McCarthy, the construction boss, highly approved of Steve.

"Stick around," he said one night, his hand on Steve's shoulder.
"You're making me money on this contract. You got both crews
thinking they'll win that bonus you put up for being first at the
junction."

"That was the idea," laughed Steve.

Baker was the only man not pleased with the progress of the work.
Every day the track through the wild unconquered country ex-
tended its tentacles, and every day he grumbled at the speed with
which it grew.

"I'd like to get through as well as the next man," he said to Steve,
"but McCarthy isn't giving us a job. Look at that track," pointing to
the slithering ties that rose from the earth like the spokes of a fan
as the engine rounded a curve. "You call that a roadbed? When the
frost hits it this winter, it'll come up like an earthworm."

"That's right," agreed Steve, "but you'll have a train through and
in possession. We can't be held up after that, and McCarthy can go
back over it."

94

The work pushed ahead, and along in September, when the first frost lay heavy on the ground, the day came when the advancing crews were within shouting distance of each other, and catcalls, hoots, and yells mingled with the clang of steel on steel as the frantic crews approached the midway line marked by a keg of beer. Two flatcars, one from the north and one from the south, draped in bunting, and crowded with interested citizens, followed close on the heels of the crews. Cramer was there, ready to read a telegram of congratulation to the winning crew; Curtis, who during the summer had moved his office to Alturos, stood beside him, pale with excitement, and the cooks from both camps were on hand to serve a bang-up banquet of baked beans, doughnuts, and coffee. Baker looked on with no expression on his face, and Steve stood by the beer barrel, with his watch in one hand and a sack of silver dollars in the other.

The crew from the north won by a spike and the swarming men pitched into the beer and each other. A glorious free-for-all developed but bloody noses and black eyes did nothing to mar the hilarity of the occasion. Citizens descended from the flatcars to join the melee and Steve found himself surrounded by a group of well-dressed men, officials of the D. & W. Company, up from Duluth to celebrate the opening of their new railroad. They were young, vigorous men, undeterred in their behavior by their silk hats, and they expressed a lively enthusiasm for his activities in Boston by grabbing his hand and thumping him on the back. "By God, we ought to hang a medal on you."

"Get this road going," countered Steve. "I've got a little bunch of stock in it. I'd like to see it do something."

The track was laid. The grueling summer's work was over, and when the battle and the beans were cleaned up, citizens and crews swung aboard the flatcars, a hurrah went up and the two engines, one pulling, the other pushing, rolled the cars over the new railroad past the trail to Steve's shack, and on to Alturos, fifteen miles distant. Gradually the smoke against the blue sky faded, the toots and the cheers died away, and an immense silence succeeded the uproar of these men as the wilderness settled back, patient, inscrutable, indifferent to this feeble scratch across its vast domain.

Alturos, with two railroads now at its service, was growing fast and a good many enterprises had abandoned Haley to open up there. Pete's new place, gaudy in orange and blue paint, glittered with polish, glasses, and bottles. Burke, too, with the genius peculiar to some hotelkeepers, had repeated every discomfort in his old hotel at Haley in his new one here and the addition of several artificial palms, already worn out by a hard life in Chicago, added the last funereal touch to the familiar lobby.

That night a banquet was held in Burke's dining room to further celebrate the opening of the new road, and during the jostling, drinking, talking that preceded it Steve found himself next to Cramer. "Hello, Mr. Cramer," he said. "This is quite a blowout, isn't it?"

Cramer looked at him uncertainly for an instant; then a dry smile bent his lips. "It is. You must be feeling very proud of your achievement."

"It isn't my achievement," said Steve with unaccustomed modesty, "but I'm feeling proud all right. It's a great thing to have this road through."

Cramer moved to take his place as toastmaster at the big table. Speech followed speech, rehearsing the ambitions, promises, and future of the new railroad. Finally the toastmaster looked across the table and rapped again for attention. "And now," he said, "as a fitting climax to this occasion, I call upon Mr. Steve Bradway."

Steve, who had enjoyed himself up to that point, stared at Cramer with horrified surprise. He had never made a speech in his life—not that kind of speech. He shook his head, but the clapping continued until he was forced to stand up. Nothing happened. No words came. His eyes saw nothing but expectant, grinning faces, until his glance caught Curtis, cowering in misery. His charming, irresistible smile broke over his face, he raised his hand high in affectionate reassurance to the little man. "Hell!" he said—and sat down.

The table roared with delighted laughter, and even Cramer joined in the applause as he pronounced the occasion at an end.

Now that business was over, Steve took several of his new friends to Pete's Place, where the celebration became a reality. By the time he got back to Burke's Hotel at daybreak, he had increased his financial status by a considerable amount, and if vociferous protestations meant anything, he now had friends in the city of Duluth who loved him like a brother.

Unfortunately, Cramer had invited the officials of the D. & W. to visit his mine that morning. Steve was with them as they toiled up the hill to the shaft house straddling against the sky. It was going full blast. The hoisting engine throbbed, the bucket ascended, retched out its cargo again and again while the shuddering officials followed Cramer around, deaf to his explanations of the workings of his mine. When they reached the stock pile, Cramer picked up a slick specimen the color and shape of an unhealthy beef kidney.

"That," he said with satisfaction, "is ore! And we've got a world of it. This will be the biggest iron-producing mine in the country in another year. There is a profitable future ahead of us, gentlemen. A very profitable future."

The future was of little interest to his guests at the moment and the specimen moved from hand to hand with a marked lack of enthusiasm in its passage until it reached Steve, who turned it over, hefted it. "Even I can see this is ore, Mr. Cramer," he said with a quick smile at the older man. "Doesn't look much like the stuff I've got."

Cramer's irritation flared up. "Mr. Bradway is referring to the so-called surface ore found along the ridge," he explained testily. "He entertains the idea that it may, in time, be of profit to this railroad. Let me assure you, gentlemen, that the prosperity of the D. & W., now and in the future, lies in shaft ore of the abundance and quality mined here."

Steve laughed as he tossed the specimen back on the stock pile. "Maybe," he said.

In the cold light of morning one or two of his new friends looked Steve over with awakened interest. What was this talk about surface ore along the ridge? Why was Cramer hot under the collar about it? Anything in it? Did that big lumberjack have something up his sleeve?

That night when the city men started homeward on the new branch line, several earnest invitations to come to Duluth were renewed. "Sure. Sure thing," agreed Steve heartily, as the train reached the trail to his cabin and he swung off with Baker.

Baker was staying to see that McCarthy finished his job and McCarthy was raging-mad about it. "What you expect me to do?" he shouted. "Rebuild the whole goddamn road? I got that track laid according to contract. I'm through."

"Better read that contract again," said Baker quietly. "It says the road's got to be in workable condition by the spring. We expect a certain amount of natural damage this winter, but if frost pulls this track out of the ground, as it's bound to do in this condition, it won't be workable next spring, and we won't pay for it."

"It ain't my fault," bellowed the contractor. "I can't get a man to drive a spike home with that cuss Bradway waving that sack of dollars under their noses. You're gettin' six months' service out of this road you ain't entitled to. Ain't that worth something?"

"Get to work on that roadbed, Mac," insisted Baker. "If the weather holds, you've got a month to do it in. Get going."

McCarthy did, and Baker remained with Steve to keep an eye on him. Both men enjoyed the companionship, working on the winter's chores together, or tramping through the still October woods to flush a brace of partridge. Steve developed a lasting respect for the long-legged fellow who stuck to his job until it was finished. He wondered what was going on behind that lean, close-lipped countenance. One night he tried to find out.

"You know anything about this open-pit mining?" he asked as they sat by the fire.

"No."

"Ought to be right in your line," persisted Steve. "They haul it out on track, don't they?"

"Yeah." A pause. "They do."

"Ever seen any of it?"

"Yeah."

"Where?"

"Utah. Fellow name of Harding works a copper mine out there."

"Think it could be worked here?"

"Sure. Why not? A man can dig anywhere. Depends on why he digs. This stuff ain't worth it."

They smoked in silence for a while. "Question of time," said Steve.

"Maybe," said Baker.

And Steve let it go at that.

After Baker had gone, Steve settled down to wait through another winter. With a railroad to drop off supplies at the end of the trail it was a luxury prospect compared to the previous one, but after the activity of the summer the days were long, and Steve fell into the habit of walking to the track to watch the little ore cars from Alturos roll past.

Pat O'Brien, the engineer, usually pulled up to pass the time of day and once, on an impulse, Steve climbed into the cab with him.

"Where the hell do you think you're goin'?" demanded Pat as he eased the throttle.

"Going where this ore goes," answered Steve.

"Then you ain't goin' far," said Pat as they started to roll. "They been buckin' ice for two weeks now, tryin' to squeeze in another trip. I'll lay you a bet right now we'll find the harbor froze solid when we get there. Suits me. I don't like haulin' the stuff in this weather."

"Think you can keep the road open this winter?"

"Dunno. Depends," replied Pat. "We ain't had no real snow yet."

It was a long, slow trip to the docks at Duluth, sixty miles away, and bitter-cold, but the harbor was still open and Steve walked around, watching the laborious business of transferring the ore in cranky buckets on cables into the little blunt-bowed freighters that would carry it to some port on the lower lakes, there to be transferred again for shipment by rail to faraway Pittsburgh; a long, tedious, wasteful operation from beginning to end. If this was the mining business, Cramer was right. There might be profit in trundling solid ore around in this primitive fashion but surface ore, gravel, thousands of tons of it, couldn't be moved this way in a hundred years! Transportation was the answer to soft ore. The furnaces would come around if that problem could be licked; but until it was, all the scientific experiments on earth wouldn't get the stuff out of the ground.

When the last car was empty and Pat ready to start, Steve joined him. "You ain't goin' back, are you?" asked the engineer with surprise. "Why don't you stay and have a good time? This town's a daisy."

But Steve, dirty, cold, tired, was in no mood for a backslapping good time. He climbed into the cab, Pat opened her up wide, and they went careening back at a fast clip, the empties clattering behind.

It was black night when they got to the trail to Steve's cabin, and Pat slowed up. For a little distance the headlight picked up the meandering vista through the trees that led to a cold and empty cabin. Steve looked at it with distaste and turned back into the cab. "I'll go on to Alturos, get some supplies, and come down with you in the morning," he said.

"Gettin' soft on city life, ain't you?" snickered Pat as he opened up the throttle. "Snow ain't more than up to your crotch yet, and you back out."

Steve hadn't been in Alturos since Curtis had gone East two weeks before. When he got to the hotel, Burke handed him a telegram. "Where you been?" he said. "This has been hanging round here for a week."

The message was brief. "Come immediately. Forsyth." Steve frowned, thrust the message in his pocket, and walked out at once

99

to see Cramer. He found him still at his desk, working hard at being the superintendent of a big mine. He cut short Cramer's remarks of surprise at his visit at this hour and laid the telegram on the desk.

"Know anything about this?"

Cramer glanced at the message and shook his head. "No," he said. "Nothing specific. They've had some trouble back there. You know the old man had a stroke."

"No," said Steve. "Bad?"

"No. He seems to be doing all right, but of course he's laid up." Cramer's eyebrows went up. "I can't understand why he should send for you."

"Neither can I," said Steve. "But I'm going to find out."

The next morning Pat held up the train while Steve plunged through the snow to his cabin to get his grip. Four days later he was in Boston.

CHAPTER 20

Steve found old Cyrus propped up on pillows in an enormous black walnut bed with a headboard carved in an emphasized Gothic design soaring behind his head and a patchwork quilt made of bits of brilliant colored silks across his knees. The white collar of his nightshirt was buttoned around his neck and his hands were folded piously on his chest. He looked like a dissolute bishop in a stained-glass window, and he was swearing steadily at an agitated female dressed in starched white.

"Get out!" he bellowed. "Stop neighing at me. Take your damn doses. Get out and stay out."

Steve, who had been shown directly to the old man's room, stood in the door, greatly relieved by this normal behavior. The old man was all right. He stepped forward. "What's the matter with you?" he asked, his face warm with affection. "Quit bullying this woman." He pulled up a chair and laid his hand over the big feeble one stretched across the coverlet toward him. "I'd have been here long ago if I'd known I had a chance like this. Got you where I want you now."

The sick man's eyes, blue and sharp with malice, clung to the back of the hastily departing nurse. "Keep her out of here. Keep 'em all out," he barked. "Pestering damn ninnies. Can't do this; can't do that! Who do they think they are, giving me orders?" His eyes came back to Steve and the bushy white brows drew together in a truculent frown. "And where have you been?" he demanded. "Kept me hung up while you went your own course. You're a damned ungrateful cub like all the rest of 'em. Where you been?"

Steve told him about the road going through and the ore cars rolling past his trail, and the old man listened for a while with keen interest. "There'll be a town there someday," said Steve, "and I'll call it Forsyth."

"I'd like that," said Cyrus. "Forsyth, eh? On the map. That would last. You see to it." Then, weary, he turned away. "Yes," he muttered, as if to himself. "Yes, Forsyth." He gave a faint, derisive grunt and was silent, while the winter sun through the window fell with cold clarity on the bright colors of the patchwork quilt and the pale, veined hand moving restlessly over them. A patch of yellow caught the old man's eye. "Shanghai," he said, pointing to it. "My wife made this quilt at sea. Worked in the name of every port we made. She was a good woman—but sharp." For a moment longer his abstraction held; then he pulled himself up on his pilows. "Get the cards out of that chest over there," he said.

Cyrus was feeble but there was nothing the matter with his mind, as Steve discovered before a dozen hands had been played. They played all afternoon, the old man chuckling, his spirits restored, as the chips piled up on his side. From time to time the nurse peeked through the door, but when she finally entered with an authoritative rustle and lit the gas, Steve pulled the cards together and stood up. "We'll have to quit," he said with a glance at the nurse, "but I'll be back in the morning and break your luck."

"All right," agreed Cyrus grumpily. "Come early and keep 'em out. This is the first good day I've had since they got me in here. It's been hell. How long you goin' to stay?"

"Until I get my carfare back," grinned Steve.

"You'll be round quite some time, then."

Steve went down the heavily carpeted stairs with the caution of a man who expects an explosion on the next step. He was hoping to get out of the place without seeing Amelia, but when he was half-way down he saw her standing in the double door to the drawing room. He had been conscious of Amelia all afternoon, wondering how she would accept his presence in the house, and when she didn't come to her grandfather's room, decided she meant to avoid him. He was doing his best to assist her in that when he saw her. There was no further caution in his tread as he continued down the stairs and went toward her.

Hamilton, at any rate, was now obviously out of the picture. She wore a blue wool dress, the tight bodice and long gored skirt trimmed with elaborate swirls of white braid. The positive color was becoming to her; she looked younger, more alert. She was still no sparkling beauty but she was one hundred per cent better-looking than Steve remembered her in the twilight colors of her mourning garb. She greeted him with composure but without offering her hand.

"Come in, Mr. Bradway," she said. Steve smiled as he followed her into the familiar room with the crimson draperies, the hassocks, the clutter of ornaments on the small tables. She seated herself on the

102

sofa and he sat down once more in Cyrus' big chair across the hearth. "How do you find Grandfather?" she asked politely as she busied herself at the tea table.

Steve eased back in his chair. "I think he's all right," he said. "He's had a bad jolt, but it's being confined and bossed around by doctors that's getting him down. If he could have his own way, he'd probably pull out of it for some time."

To his surprise she agreed with him. "I think so too," she said. "There is nothing more trying for a man of his disposition than to be tied down." She raised her eyes and looked at him calmly over the teacups. "That is why I sent for you."

"You sent for me!"

"Yes. He kept insisting on it, poor man, but Horace and the doctors wouldn't agree to it. Finally I decided to send for you myself." She dropped her eyes. "I thought you wouldn't mind coming East at this time of year, and it seemed to mean so much to him. I do hope he will find the pleasure in it he has looked forward to so long."

Steve smiled across at her. "He did—to the tune of seven dollars this afternoon," he said.

She nodded with faint amusement. "I know. I tried to play with him and it made him perfectly furious to have me win, but perhaps you won't be as lucky as I am."

Steve looked at her. If she had any recollection—as he had—of the last time they had been together in this room, she showed not the slightest trace of it. She was perfectly at ease; apparently as open as a book. He knew she wasn't. He wondered what she was up to now. He thought he knew.

"How's Victor?" he asked.

"He's away at school," she sighed. "It's much too soon, but with Grandfather ill it seemed best for him."

"Did you cut off those curls?"

She flushed a little at that. "Yes. And it changed him dreadfully. He looks almost grown-up now."

"That's fine."

"It isn't fine at all," she retorted with a trace of sharpness. "I don't want him changed. I want my little boy to stay just as he is."

"That's a little tough on him, isn't it?"

She poured herself a second cup of tea and sipped it. "I wouldn't expect you to understand," she said. After a moment she gave him the first of her sidelong glances. "How is your cabin in the woods?"

Steve laughed. "Up to its ears in snow right now. I've had enough

103

of it for the time being; at that, it's not so bad, with the railroad through there."

"Tell me about the railroad. That was your business here last spring, wasn't it?"

"Some of it," Steve smiled. He talked to her for a while about getting the road through but she listened with an abstracted air, as if her thoughts were on something of more interest to her, and soon the familiar, pregnant silence grew up between them. To his amusement, she had remembered how he liked his tea, and after a third cup of the strong, hot brew he stood up. "I'll be around tomorrow," he said.

She looked up without rising. "I wonder . . ." She hesitated. "I know Grandfather would be pleased if you stayed with us. We can make you quite comfortable and——"

"No. No, thanks," Steve interrupted bluntly. "I'll see plenty of your grandfather. We'll let it go at that."

"Very well," she said quietly. "It was kind of you to come."

As he started across the Common, Steve came to the bench, forlorn now in the trampled snow, where he and that woman had had their meetings in the spring, and he sat down to think this thing through. Amelia hadn't sent for him to play cards with her grandfather; that much was certain. She wasn't through with him, and he wondered how far she meant to go. He took it as a matter of course that she was attracted to him; that was no new experience and usually he had no difficulty in handling such situations. But this was different. He wanted no mix-up with Amelia Hamilton! It could come to nothing and the last thing he wanted was a blowup with Cyrus. He stood up, determined to avoid Amelia.

He succeeded with surprising ease. In fact, for the next week he caught no glimpse of her whatever and it was beginning to irritate him a good deal, keyed up as he was, to find his presence in the house regarded by everyone but Cyrus as a matter of no interest. It annoyed him, and he showed it one afternoon when he was playing cards with the old man.

Cyrus was sitting up in a high-backed chair near the window, dressed in a bright yellow brocade dressing gown, embroidered in blue chrysanthemums. He looked horrible in it and Steve told him so. "Trouble with you is you don't know a handsome thing when you see it," retorted Cyrus. "Two jacks."

Steve swore and threw down his hand. "Take it away," he snapped.

104

Cyrus placidly pulled in the chips. "It's a fact," he repeated. "You don't know a good thing when you see it, and if you had the sense of a cod, you'd know what I'm talkin' about." Steve stared at him and the old fellow went on. "What's the matter with you? Take her. She knows what she wants—shows it plain as a hen. Be a good thing all round. Ain't a man jack comin' up in this family amounts to a hill of beans. We need new blood in here. Go ahead with her." He chuckled. "If you do, there'll be a lot more strokes in this family. Mine won't be a patch on it."

Steve grinned in spite of himself. "That's an inducement." Then his face clouded again. "What are you driving at?" He scowled. "Did you get me here to marry Amelia?"

"Sure," replied Cyrus promptly. "Ain't you caught on to that yet? She needs it and a man's got to come to it sooner or later. If he's got any sense, he'll make a good thing of it. Fact is, it's the women in this family put us where we are. Man's got to use his head. If he don't, he's likely to get worked up over the wrong woman and make a mess of it. You ever been in that fix?"

"No," said Steve.

"Got it comin' to you, eh?" The old fellow chuckled. "It's a bad business but a man can lick it if he's got a wife to pull him through."

"You seem to speak from experience."

"I do." The blue eyes twinkled at him. "Fell into it a dozen times all over the map, and it was hell every time." His hand strayed over the silk quilt across his knees. "But I got over it. In the end I wouldn't have traded my wife for the lot of 'em."

"How did your wife take it?"

Cyrus shook his head. "Tough," he said. "Tough—but she hung on, and after a while it was plain sailing. I ain't wastin' my breath," he added.

Steve jumped up and began prowling around the room. "I know you're not," he said. "I see it—but I don't like it. I don't like it at all."

"Why not?" The old man gave him a close, sharp look. "Afraid of bein' hog-tied, ain't you? Afraid of her money. Better men than you have swallowed that, and it goes down easier than you think. Hell!" He snorted. "Deal the cards and stop talkin' like a jackass."

It was snowing when Steve crossed the Common that afternoon, a damp, melancholy drizzle unlike the crisp, clear cold he was accustomed to, and he was conscious of a penetrating chill as he tramped through the slush, his collar turned up, his hands in his pockets, going over in his mind Cyrus' extraordinary proposal of marriage. He didn't like it. He resented with considerable vigor the old man's obvious attempt to maneuver him into taking that woman off his hands. Amelia was all right in her way; smart enough, and she had a lot of money. It didn't disturb him to admit that if he married her it would be for her money. Any man who took her would be tarred with that brush, and he could use her money as well as the next man. It wasn't that. It went deeper than that. The more he thought of it, the more his spirit seethed at the old man's bland assumption that he could use him as he pleased to further his own ends. Well, he wouldn't work it this time. What did Cyrus take him for? A stallion ready for a fee? Led up to it with a halter round his neck? He'd be damned if he'd play that role. When he married a woman, he'd take care of that business himself. Disgusted, angry, he threw up his head and looked around to see where he was. Then, with the free resolute stride of a man with his mind made up, he started for his hotel.

Curtis was there, waiting for him. He hadn't seen Curtis since the day after his arrival when Curtis had brought his girl to Boston to meet him. He was glad to see him now and Curtis beamed on him with evident joy. When they got to his room, Steve took off his damp coat and collar and went to the washstand to clean up while Curtis moved nervously around the room.

"It's grand to have you here, Steve. Grand. What a piece of luck!" He repeated this so often that finally Steve took his face out of the towel.

"What's so lucky about it?" he asked. "You haven't been around for over a week. Only lucky thing about it is you got here before I pull out."

"Pull out?"

"Yes," said Steve. "I've had enough of Boston. I'm getting out tonight."

"Steve!" Curtis cried, anguished. "Steve! You can't do that. I'm getting married!"

Married! Since it came so quickly on the heels of his own meditations on that subject Steve, for a second, couldn't be sure who was the victim. He realized with relief that it was Curtis. "Well," he said. "Well, you son of a gun. That's fine."

"Fine?" Curtis' joy burst through his trouble. "It's a miracle, an absolute miracle. She's the most wonderful girl in the world and—" his voice dropped in solemn awe—"if nothing happens, in another week she'll be mine. Think of it, Steve. A wonderful girl like that. I can't understand why she's doing it."

Steve looked at the shining eyes, the radiance that beamed in the face of his poor friend. "I think she'll manage to put up with you," he said.

"But you can't leave me, Steve." Curtis clutched his arm. "You've got to stand by me. I'm absolutely depending on you to see me through. You will, won't you? You don't have to go?"

"No," admitted Steve. "I can put up with it another week or so." He threw down the towel with some irritation and buttoned on a clean collar. "I need a drink, and so do you. It's high time you got drunk, John, and this is the occasion for it. Come along."

"I can't, Steve," said Curtis plaintively. "I'd like to stay with you but I've got to catch the five thirty-two." He pulled his watch from his pocket. "They're having a church concert out home tonight and Mary's going to sing. I'll have to be there. You can understand that."

Steve looked at Curtis with the pity, tinged with disgust, of a free man for one in bondage. Married! Well, Curtis was the kind to fall into a thing like that. "I can understand it all right," he said. "Run along if you have to."

The next day Steve walked again across the Common to see Cyrus. If he stayed in Boston, he had no excuse for not seeing the old man, but he went with reluctance and anticipated no pleasure in it. And he had no pleasure in it. Nothing further was said about the scheme to hog-tie Steve but the old man was grumpy, irritable, making frequent use of the word jackass, until Steve got up and left him. As he reached the foot of the stairs, the front door opened and Amelia came in.

She had on a tight-fitting sealskin jacket with a bit of blue under her chin, a small fur cap with a touch of the same blue set jauntily on her fair hair, and the elusive, delicate scent she wore was in the cold air she brought in around her. She looked charming as she took her gloved hand from her muff and offered it to him. It was small and warm in his grasp.

"I'm so glad I didn't miss you, Mr. Bradway," she said pleasantly. "I want to thank you for my opportunity to be with Victor. We had a holiday together. I knew Grandfather would be quite happy with you here, so I ran away for a few days."

Steve received this news with some confusion of mind. She hadn't been avoiding him. She'd been with Victor. "How is Victor?" he asked.

107

"Wonderfully well. We had such a good time together. He's learning to skate and he wants a hockey stick." She moved away and started up the stairs. "Go into the drawing room and wait for me. I'll be only a moment. We'll have tea and you can tell me how Grandfather has been."

"Why don't you ask him?" said Steve.

She leaned gracefully over the bannister. "I'd so much rather hear it from you." She smiled.

CHAPTER 21

During the next few days Steve began to wonder if he wasn't the jackass Cyrus took him for. Amelia was all right. She was always charming when he saw her, fragrant and graceful, barricaded behind the tea table, chatting fondly about her grandfather, while her femininity tugged at his imagination. Sometimes, seeing her surrounded by her familiar luxuries, he was convinced that Cyrus was crazy and she wouldn't have him at any price. At other times he got out of the house in a cold sweat, sure that she was on the verge of it.

While he was in this state of mind, he saw a good deal of Curtis, trying to help the distracted man in the selection of ties, socks, and other items of his wardrobe, and had learned to dread the sound of the Wonder Girl's name. "Sure, she'll like it," he said a thousand times. "Go ahead and buy it. They like green. Color of hope." But when it came to nightshirts, Curtis was beyond reason. He blushed and paled.

"I can't let her see me in one of those things," he whimpered. "She'd never take me."

"Go without it, then."

"Oh, God, Steve, don't talk like that! If you knew what I look like in a nightshirt."

"Most men do," said Steve cheerfully, "but they seem to get away with it. She'll like it," he added.

On the day of the wedding Steve took the train to the little village where Curtis had been born. John, green around the gills, met him at the station and, sleigh bells jingling, they drove some distance through the snow-covered hills to the town. "How you feeling, John?" asked Steve.

"Awful," groaned Curtis. "This is a terrible thing to go through, Steve. I wish I'd never got into it. Awful!"

"What's the matter with you? You know what you're headed for, don't you?"

"Of course I do—in a way," snapped John. "It's the uncertainty

109

I can't stand. I've been sick all night," he added miserably. "I'm going to throw up as sure as we sit here."

"Nonsense," said Steve heartily. But Curtis was beyond help and they drove in silence through the village street, the neat white houses sagging beneath the weight of snow on their sloping shoulders.

"There's the church," said Curtis with a desperate glance at the sacred structure, its delicate steeple outlined against the hard, blue sky. They pulled up at the house next to it and John's father opened the door; a man of resolute dignity, with a tuft of white hair standing upright above a pale, intellectual forehead.

"Come in, sir," he said. "We are glad to have you here. If you will step into my study . . ."

"You'll have to excuse me," muttered John, bolting up the narrow boxed-in stairway.

The room was snug and warm and smelled of rose petals and old books. John's father sat down and lit a pipe with an air of committing a major dissipation. "I don't smoke, as a rule, during the day," he explained as Steve lit his cigar, "but this is an exceptional occasion. I have baptized, married, and buried the people of this village for the past thirty years but I find marrying my own son a new, and I must say, a trying experience."

The door opened and a little woman, who looked as if the waters of life had washed her clean and now left her in the sun to dry, came in with a glass of milk and some cookies on a plate. "You haven't much time, Father," she said. "You'd better leave Mr. Bradway to his refreshments and get dressed." She gave Steve a quiet smile. "They'll be ready, both of them," she said, "but you must excuse me while I see to it."

Steve had never been in a church before, never heard the marriage ceremony in his life, and as he stood beside Curtis looking at the kindly interest in the faces of the people who filled the boxed-in pews, he felt conspicuously alone, not only in this church, but in the world. So far as he knew, he hadn't a relative on the face of the earth, no knowledge whatever of the family network that cushioned the lives of most men. He wondered about these people, dependent upon each other. He wondered how a man must feel with these various strands tugging at his life. He didn't think he'd like it.

He glanced at Curtis. There was a light film of sweat on his brow but his face was lifted as he listened with his whole soul to

110

the majestic, cabalistic words that fell from his father's lips. "I do," he said in a clear, firm voice.

". . . I pronounce you man and wife."

The congregation bowed in prayer; Steve, upright, lifted his head and shook it as if in answer to a challenge. Then Curtis, with his bride billowing in white on his arm, walked down the aisle, the pews burst their bonds, and the people poured out behind them. The minister, with a kindly but abstracted smile, beckoned to Steve as he hurried to join them, and for a moment Steve was alone in the austere purity of the little church.

The happy pair had driven away by the time Steve reached the crowded vestibule. He found his coat and stepped out into the cold. A white rose, fallen from the bouquet he had sent the bride, lay in the path. He stopped as if to pick it up, changed his mind, and stepped over it on his way up the street to find a cutter to take him to the station.

The next day, back in Boston, Steve played cards with Cyrus most of the afternoon. It was not a satisfactory game, and after a while, to relieve the silence between them, Steve talked about the wedding and concluded by saying that now, with Curtis out of the way, there was no reason that he could see for his remaining any longer in Boston. Cyrus promptly agreed with him.

"Might as well get goin' if that's what's been keepin' you," he said. "Married a Wentworth, did he?"

"Yes."

"It's good stock. Wonder what branch she comes from. He did a good thing for himself, pickin' a girl like that."

"What makes you think so? She's as plain as a fence post."

"What's that got to do with it?" snapped Cyrus. "Man that marries for looks is a jackass. Humans breed same as any other animals and good stock produces good stock. That's what a sensible man's after when he marries. Stock." He snorted. "Looks? Buy 'em by the bushel." He stopped and peered at Steve with the cunning of an old possum. "Weddin' give you any ideas on the subject?" he asked.

"If it did, it's my own business," snapped Steve.

The old possum gave him an injured look, curled up, and played dead the rest of the afternoon.

When the sun faded and the nurse came in to light the gas, Steve stood up to say good night, but the old man, already at dagger's

111

point with the nurse, paid no attention to him so he started briskly down the stairs. At the top of the stairs he would have bet his life that he was on his way out; at the foot of the stairs he turned abruptly and went into the drawing room.

Amelia was sitting on the blue sofa, sipping tea. She looked dainty as a doll in yellow silk shot with amber that brought out the gold lights in her hair. Her eyes were darker than usual and a faint color stained her cheeks, but she showed no other sign of being aware of the tension that, to Steve, seemed to shake the crystal drops on the chandelier as he stepped into the room. He stood at the end of the sofa and looked down at her. "You know why I came in here, don't you?" he said.

The teacup clattered as she set it down. She raised her eyes briefly to his and lowered them. "Yes," she said simply.

"Yes," he repeated. "Of course you do. It's been hanging in the air like a bombshell since the day I got here, and it's got to be settled now, one way or the other." He turned away, crossed the room and back again, kicking hassocks out of his way, and braced his big hands on the arm of the sofa. "But before we go into it, I want you to know exactly what it means. If you come with me, you will be going straight from here to a one-room log shack in the woods, buried in six feet of snow, with not another house or human being within fifteen miles of it."

"But you don't have to live there, do you, Steve?" she murmured.

His jaw set. "That is exactly the point I'm trying to make," he said bluntly. "I do, and will, for some time to come. You must understand that now. I won't be coming into your life; you'll be coming into mine, and you'll be there to stay. It's not the life for you and you'd better think twice before you let any romantic ideas get you into it."

She leaned back on the sofa and looked up at him. He stood before her, firm as a rock on his feet, without a trace of pleading in his face, the remarkable eyes behind their thick black lashes as gray green as the sea and as relentless. She dropped her gaze to avoid the challenge in them and the vitality flowing from him was like the wind at sea, sweeping through her. She shivered a little, her eyes on her clasped hands.

"I am not a romantic person, Steve," she said presently. "I've thought about this a great deal and I believe I have some idea of what my life with you would be like. You're a hard man and you don't love me. I'm glad you don't pretend you do. It isn't that. I'm

112

not afraid of that. It's—I . . ." Suddenly her calm deserted her, the red rushed over her face, mounting to the fringe of her pale, fair hair. She jumped up and grasped his arm in both of her small ringed hands. "Take me, Steve," she whispered, her trembling voice low and vibrant. "Oh, take me with you! Don't you see? Can't you understand? I can't live without you, I've found that out. I love you! I love you!" And as Steve put his arms around her quivering body, she dropped her head on his breast and clung to him in a passion of tears.

Steve thought this was the damnedest proposal he had ever heard of, and as he held her close, trying to soothe her, it occurred to him that it must be tough to be in this state and unable to do anything about it. He was touched, too, by her honesty and pluck and, for the first time, his heart warmed with tenderness for her.

"There, there," he said, caressing her, "it's not as bad as all that. What do you think I'm going to do? Throw you to the chipmunks?" He straightened her up and smiled at her as he helped her mop her eyes with a tiny lace handkerchief. The tip of her sharp nose was red and her face less dewy than drenched when she raised it and he was a little startled at the ardor of her response when he kissed her, but decided he could take care of that in time. "Just the same," he insisted, sobering, "you'd better think this over. Take your time."

She shook her head, still sniffling. "I have," she said. "I have. I know."

"You think you do," he said. "Come along, we'll talk this over with your grandfather. He'll put it straight to you." He put his arm around her and they went up the stairs.

Cyrus, propped up in bed playing solitaire, eyed them sharply when they came in. "Fixed it up, have you?" he said. "It's about time. Got around him, eh? Now you've got him, you sure you want him, Amelia?"

She stood at the foot of the bed and faced him straight. "You know perfectly well I want to marry Steve—and you want me to marry him. You planned it the first night you brought him here."

"Now, now," said Cyrus. "I wouldn't go as far as that. Just wanted you to look him over. Didn't think he was the tough customer he turned out to be. Think you can put up with him?"

"Grandmother put up with you—and my mother was born on a clipper ship," she retorted. "That wasn't easy."

"It wasn't, for a fact"—Cyrus nodded—"with a sixty-mile gale blowin' the canvas out of the bits. But what's that got to do with it? You've had it easy all your life."

"That's just it," she cried passionately, striking the footboard with her tiny fist. "Easy! So easy I've never lived at all! If I stay here I'll wither and die like everybody else in Boston. I won't do it, I tell you! I can't stand any more of it. I don't care where Steve goes, or what he does. I'll be with him, living the way I want to live, a full, big life like other women live."

"Here. Wait a minute." Cyrus rolled his eyes on Steve. "I guess you better do a little more thinkin', Amelia. You ain't goin' to live the life you want with this feller. You're goin' to live the way he tells you to. Better quit now if you think you can boss him round the way you did that ass, Hamilton."

Anger flashed in her eyes. "How unkind you are," she said. "Both of you. Steve has already made it quite clear what he expects of me but neither of you seems to understand that it's Steve's life I want, not my own. You've said, yourself, a hundred times, Grandfather, that Steve will do big things. I can't do them. I can't have them—sitting around Boston with all this wretched money—but if Steve has it and I'm with him, I'll have the life I want. Can't you see that? Either of you?"

Cyrus turned to Steve. "How do you feel about this, young feller?"

Steve slipped his arm around Amelia and she wilted against him. "I'm proud of her," he said. "We'll make out fine together with this start." He grinned at Cyrus over her head. "A chip off the old block if I ever saw one."

"She is that," nodded Cyrus. "She don't quit when she's once set her course." He folded his hands with pontifical dignity over his stomach. "You'll make out as well as the next pair, but this big life you're both after ain't the point. I want to see a couple of strappin' males come out of this. If we get 'em, it's a good deal all round. How about that part of the bargain, Amelia?"

To Steve's astonishment she flushed scarlet and pulled out of his arm as if to bolt from the room. "Grandfather!" she exclaimed. "How can I——"

The old man chuckled. "That's right. You can't," he said. "It's up to Steve. And speakin' of strappin' males," he went on, "you goin' to lug Victor round on this safari?"

Amelia dropped into a chair and began to cry, dashing the tears from her cheeks with her lace handkerchief. "I do wish you men

114

would let me alone," she wept. "I know just what to do. Of course I can't take Victor with me. His grandmother would never leave him a penny if I took him away from her, and I can't bring him up in a —a shack in the woods. He couldn't stand it. He belongs here in Boston." She jumped up, agitated. "You don't know, you can't know, either of you, what it means to me to leave Victor," she cried dramatically, "but if I can do it for his sake, it must show even you how deeply I——"

"It does," interrupted Cyrus cryptically. "Ten fathoms deep." He hunched back on his pillows for more comfort. "All right. If your sails are set, get it over with quick before the wind changes." He cocked a weather eye at Steve. "It ain't goin' to hold too long and I don't want to miss it. I want it right here in this room so I can see Horace's face." His laugh rumbled like the approach of a summer storm. "After that I'll be willin' to cross the bar."

"He won't come. Catherine won't let him," declared Amelia. "None of them will come."

"They will so," pronounced the old man. "The whole kit and caboodle of 'em will come if I tell 'em to. Have it next week."

"Next week?" Amelia looked at Steve. "Is that all right? I'll have to get some clothes and pack."

Steve took the long, deep breath recommended as the quickest way to get under ether. "All right with me," he said. "Won't take you long to pack what you need out there."

Her pale blue eyes, fixed on his face, widened and she looked frightened. Then she gave him the first spontaneous, happy smile he had ever seen on her face as she ran to him and threw her arms around his neck. "Oh, Steve," she cried. "I'm so happy. It's going to be wonderful. Wonderful."

Steve held her tight as he looked across at Cyrus. The old man's eyes were twinkling with satisfaction. "She's got a lot of ballast," he said. "She'll sail well."

115

CHAPTER 22

Amelia fussed incessantly over her packing and Steve went
over the lists with her a dozen times. "You can't use all that
stuff out there," he protested repeatedly. "The whole place isn't any
bigger than this rug," he said, glancing at the magnificent Oriental
at his feet. "Might be a good thing to take a rug like this, and you'll
need a bed, a bureau, a couple of easy chairs—and that's all. Plain
wool dresses; none of this rustling business like you've got on now.
Leave everything else here until I can get a house built."

"But we've got to live decently, Steve," persisted Amelia.

"All right," he said impatiently. "Send the whole works and we'll
stack it in the woods."

The goods were shipped, the wedding day approached, and
Amelia went off to bring Victor from school. While she was away,
Steve and old Cyrus had a long talk. Cyrus began it by handing
Steve an envelope containing a thousand shares of D. & W. stock.
"Don't amount to much now," he said, "but it will give you a little
headway in there sometime."

Steve laid the envelope on the patch quilt over the Port of
Tsingtao and looked steadily into the blue eyes, bright beneath the
shaggy white brows. "That's first-rate of you," he said soberly.

"Might as well get our cards on the table while we've got a
chance," the old skipper went on. "You'll have the handling of
Amelia's money. I fixed that up with Stoddard a few days ago. You
can't get along with her unless you have control, and she'll be safe
with you—I figure on that. Fixed up my will at the same time." He
stopped and breathed heavily for a moment. "I ain't leavin' you any
Massachusetts, son," he went on. "They'd sue you for undue in-
fluence if I did. It ain't any use to you, anyhow. Better get rid of
what you've got, too. It's done its work." He chuckled. "Unload on
Higgins and buy more D. & W. Outside of that I got a million or so
lyin' round, and it'll be yours before long. You'll probably drop it in
that hole in the ground you're thinkin' about, but I ain't got any
further use for it."

116

Steve said nothing; there was no need for it. He knew—and he knew Cyrus knew—that this was, in all probability, their last long talk together, and his heart was heavy. Cyrus studied him for a long moment. "No use gettin' worked up about it, son," he said finally. "I ain't." Then his chuckle came again. "You swallow money easier than any cuss I ever saw. What you goin' to do with it? I'd like to hear."

For a long time Steve had been wanting to talk to the old man about his hopes for surface ore but the moment had never seemed right. It did now.

"I'd like to mine that ore," he said. "Somebody's going to do it. There's a mountain of it and it's bound to come out sometime—and not too far off, either. They're experimenting with it right now in Pittsburgh; some kind of a new furnace."

"What does Cramer think of it?"

"He doesn't think much of it. He likes operating the deep stuff."

"Better talk to somebody else, then. Feller name of Harding out in Utah. Good man. Used to work for us."

"I've heard of him. I'll get hold of him, but I'm not thinking of the mining angle yet. Transportation's got to be licked first." He leaned forward, frowning. "We've got the stuff but no sense in going after it until we can move it. It's got to go down the lakes, a thousand tons at a clip to make it pay and there's nothing of that tonnage around now. What we need is a new type of freighter altogether," he went on vigorously. "An ore freighter that will take all we can pile into her and ride off with it, fast, under her own power." He fixed his intent gaze on the old man. "You know all about ships and cargo. Think anything like that could be worked out?"

Cyrus' eyes glistened with interest. He put his head back and squinted at the ceiling. "An ore freighter, eh? Kind of a barge under her own power. Nothing like that afloat that I know of." He reached for a pad on his bedside table and scribbled on it. "Here," he said. "When you get around to it, go and see this feller. Used to build for us. Tell him I sent you. He might think of something." He looked at Steve. "You got your work cut out, young feller. You don't know a thing about ships. Know anything about mining?"

Steve thrust the paper in his pocket. "Less than I do about ships," he said. "But other men do, and they're for hire."

Cyrus nodded. "You're right. I got the credit for it but it was my first mate got us round the Horn. If he'd washed overboard, we'd have piled up. A man don't need to know a thing in the world but how to use other men."

117

Dusk was coming on, shadows creeping into the quiet room. Steve leaned back, looking at his old friend. The fading light seemed to gather around the pillow and the massive white head that lay on it. "I wonder how things would have turned out if I hadn't come to Boston," he said quietly, after a while. "My luck began then."

"It did for a fact," agreed Cyrus, "but it was your own doin'. You've got nothin' to thank me for—not that I hear any out of you," he grunted. Steve laughed. "At that, I think you're one to come out on top," the old man went on, "but a man can't tell. Luck's got a lot to do with it. A dozen times in my life I'd have lost every nickel I owned if my luck hadn't held. Makes a man wonder, sometimes, just how good he is." He turned away, his keen eyes narrowed as if he glimpsed the landfall of an unfamiliar country. "No," he muttered. "A man can't tell. No sense in it any way you look at it." He turned back to Steve. "May be luck, may be just plain horse sense, but you've got a good head start now. Go ahead. I'd like to be here to see what you make of it."

Steve had no reply to that and they sat silent while darkness filled the room. When the nurse rustled in, Steve stood up. The hand that for so long had gripped the helm lay lax in his own, and for a moment Steve didn't speak. Then, "So long," he said briskly, "I'll see you tomorrow."

"Sure, son, sure. Gettin' married, ain't you?" Cyrus chuckled, his spirits restored. "That's a thing don't come under the headin' of luck. It's a dead certainty."

The next day Amelia, distracted, ran Steve ragged over last-minute details. One of her major inspirations was to have a large screen moved into her grandfather's bedroom. "What's that for?" demanded the bridegroom.

"To keep you out of sight," she said, shoving him behind it, while Cyrus eyed them with derisive glee. "You mustn't be seen until I come in and there's no other place."

And there Steve crouched on a piano stool, like a guilty secret, while the Forsyth clan assembled for his wedding. They entered in grim silence, spoke to Cyrus in hollow whispers, then crept into corners among the massive furniture that already filled the room, as if in horror of a catastrophe worse than death.

At last, Horace, pale with fury, stalked in with a bottle-shaped woman in purple silk who clamped her thin lips shut and settled her clasped hands on her waistline with the air of a martyr at the stake and, as if this were the signal to put a match to the fagots,

118

Reggie, twitching nervously at his tie, hurried to the spare room to bring the minister to his task.

Steve stepped from behind the screen and Amelia, her head and color high, swept in, with Victor lagging on her hand. She wore a new blue traveling costume with a flaring gored skirt and a tight-fitting jacket with high puffed sleeves and a ripple at the back. A dark mink scarf was around her neck, an elaborate hat trimmed with mink and blue ostrich feathers perched on her head. One finger of the white glove on her left hand was slit ready for the ring, and she wore Steve's orchids pinned on her breast. She was evidently prepared to depart in a hurry, which pleased Steve, and in the face of that company, she looked a beauty.

They lined up at the side of the huge bed. Victor, with marked indifference, traced the carving on the bedpost with his finger, the minister opened the prayerbook, and the ceremony began.

It was made to order for Cyrus. Propped up on his pillows, his white hair a rakehell's halo around his head, the bright silk quilt over his knees, the old man was having the time of his life. Satisfaction beamed from him like a headlight as he urged the minister to get under way. He produced the ring at the wrong moment, then lost it in the bedclothes, cursing cheerfully as he searched for it, winked lewdly at Steve at certain points in the service, and in general, behaved abominably. Steve was so delighted with him that he was scarcely aware of what was happening until Amelia nudged him and he floundered badly in his hurry to get to his feet from the hassock he'd been kneeling on. Amelia rose gracefully from hers and faced her relatives across the room.

"You will find refreshments in the dining room," she said in a clear, cool voice, "but we cannot join you there because we have so little time to catch our train. I feel sure you will understand that I want these last few moments with my grandfather and"—her voice wavered a little—"my son. Thank you for coming, and good-by, all of you."

Brief words and nods accompanied the prompt departure of the guests and Victor went to the window. "Halsey's out there with the carriage," he said. "Grandmother told me not to keep him waiting."

"Oh, Victor," cried Amelia, clutching him. She fondled his curly gold head. "But it won't be long before I come for you and we'll have a wonderful time in the—in the woods. Remember that. Think of it every day, darling, and I will too."

"I don't want to be in the woods. I want to go to Marblehead this

119

summer," said Victor firmly. "You can come there, can't you?"
He turned to Steve and held out his hand politely. "Thank you for
marrying my mother," he said, "and I'd like those Indian moccasins
you said you'd send me."

Steve laughed. "You'll get 'em," he said. "Run along now. I'll take
care of your mother." He put his arm around his weeping bride.
"Let him go, Amelia. Get it over."

"Good idea," grumbled Cyrus. "Get going, all of you. No need for
any more." He looked at Steve. "Take over, young feller, and don't
palaver about it. I'm tired." He chuckled feebly. "I've had my fun.
Horace's face will keep me goin' through eternity, if anythin' will."

After Victor had raced away, Amelia braced up, got into her long
mink coat, and they started down the stairs. Horace, coming up,
looked ready to leap the bannister to avoid them, but Amelia continued calmly down until she reached him. "I am so glad for a last
word with you, Horace," she said sweetly. "Do tell Catherine how
much I appreciate her wearing that old purple silk she always wears
to funerals."

No rice or laughter followed the big family brougham as it
clopped down Beacon Street to the station, and nobody watched it
go.

Horace, who had awakened Cyrus from a peaceful nap, paced his
grandfather's room with angry strides. "It's an outrage," he stormed.
"Utterly incredible. That abominable bounder marrying Amelia for
her money, and you put up with it. Not only put up with it but
force this humiliation down our throats. We'll never recover from
it. Never! It's scandalous. Preposterous. You must be out of your
mind to countenance such a thing."

Cyrus listened with satisfaction until he got tired of it. "Shut up!"
he said. "I ain't out of my mind, and you ain't got one to go out of.
Clear out of here. I've had enough. Obey me," he snapped with a
ferocious glare as Horace hesitated. "Get out, and try to behave
like a man. You've just seen one."

But Horace was right. Amelia had not stopped sniffling before the
scandal of her behavior burst on Boston like a bombshell. Teacups
clattered, false teeth clacked, and set lips whispered long-buried,
unsavory incidents of the Forsyth clipper-ship days. Men in their
clubs didn't bother to go into detail; they merely shrugged and
looked pleased.

CHAPTER 23

By the time they got to Chicago, Steve was enchanted with Amelia. "By God," he said to himself, "she's one in a million." And she was. Sparkling with gaiety, her cheeks flushed, she clung to his arm as they strolled the streets or entered fashionable shops and restaurants. Steve was proudly conscious of the amount of money he was spending and of the admiration his wife excited. Added to that, she had the prettiest legs he had ever seen in his life.

Amelia didn't think much of Chicago. "This awful wind, and these dreadful people," she complained, adjusting her hat. "That man nearly knocked me down and he didn't even apologize. Why are they all in such a hurry?"

"Hustling to get rich," laughed Steve.

He wanted to stay in Chicago and repeat the good time they had had in New York but Amelia wouldn't hear of it. "I want to get to our little home," she pleaded wistfully. Steve gave her an amused glance but she wasn't joking. He was beginning to realize that Amelia never made or saw a joke. That evening they took the train to the north.

When they got to the junction where they changed cars, Steve walked up the track to see Pat, who was getting up steam. Pat was out of his cab, tinkering with the snowplow. "Well," he said as Steve came up, "where'd you come from? You look like a damn dude. Climb in. We'll be off in a minute. Where you been?"

Steve shook his head. "Can't. Where's the passenger car?"

"Passenger car! Hell! I don't haul no passenger car through this snow. What's the matter with the caboose? You so soft you got to squat on plush?"

"I don't, but my wife does," grinned Steve.

"Wife!" Pat stared at him, then sent a long stream of tobacco juice into the snow. "Well, I'll be damned! Go along back there. I'll give her a ride."

He did. The little train bucked and jerked, snow whirling from the plow, sparks spinning from the frozen rails while Amelia, in the caboose, sat huddled on a chair, her feet braced on the box stove, and Steve played pinochle on the top of her trunk with the crew. When they finally got to the trail to the cabin, Pat pulled up and leaned out to watch Steve lift his bride from the platform; her trunks—three of them—went after her into the snow. Then with a derisive toot, the train pulled away up the track.

Amelia, in her mink coat, her hands in her muff, stood in the snowbank by the track where Steve had planted her, shivering with the cold. The great trees around her were black and still against the glistening white, particles of frost glittered in the pure, transparent air, and silence weighed heavy on the ear, but she was unaffected by the menace of the solitude around her; her eyes were on the peaks and planes of the crates strewn along the track, buried in the snow. "Our things have come but they must be soaking-wet," she said. "How awful."

"They're all right," Steve assured her. "Snow doesn't melt at twenty below."

Up the trail he was relieved to see what looked like elephant tracks leading to and from the cabin. Cramer must have sent the bohunk woman down there on a handcar that morning, for it had snowed in the night and the tracks were fresh. At any rate, the trail was broken and he was glad of that. He picked up his wife's dressing bag. "Come along," he said as he started ahead, scuffing the snow to make the going as easy as he could for her.

Amelia was warm enough and breathing hard when they reached the tiny cabin. A thick white blanket lay on the roof, long icicles fringed the eaves, and a plume of smoke rose lazily above it. "Oh, how pretty it is, Steve," she exclaimed happily. "Like a Christmas card."

Steve kicked open the door. The floor was scrubbed, the windows shone, and through the half-open door of the oven he saw a pan of baked beans. Three loaves of fresh bread lay on the table under a white cloth. His heart warmed to the bohunk woman.

Amelia stood in the middle of the room, looking around uncertainly. "It isn't very pretty inside, is it?" she said after a moment. "Is this the way you've always lived, Steve?"

"It is not," he said. "Nothing like it. This is in fine shape." He took off her coat and hung it on a nail. "Get your hat off and we'll have a go at those beans."

She took off her hat and, after holding it uncertainly a moment, found another nail and hung it up. When she turned around, she was smiling. "I thought something smelled like Sunday morning at home," she said. "How nice of the cook to think of beans." She ran to the oven and peeped in. "But they're in a tin pan!" she exclaimed. "Why aren't they in a brown pot? We can't eat them this way."

"I guess you'll have to." And perched on Steve's knee, she did. "They're good, Steve!" she exclaimed. "I do believe they're better than Fawcett's." Steve, delighted by her pluck, gave her a hug that sent her tin plate rattling to the floor. After that she clung to him and it was some time before he got into his woods clothes and started up the trail with his sled to bring in the goods.

Her trunks were easy but he was cussing with everything he had by the time he lugged in the mattress. The four-poster came crated in sections, and when he got it set up, he took the ax and started to knock out his bunk in the corner. "Don't do that, Steve," protested Amelia. "I can cover it with a rug and it will make a nice couch."

"I want it out," said Steve bluntly, and swung the ax.

By the end of the next day everything was in place; the rich rug glowed on the floor, the four-poster, gay with chintz, filled one corner, and Amelia's bureau, with a gilt mirror above it, stood against the wall. She pushed the old table under the supply shelves and a handsome mahogany one took its place, with chintz-covered easy chairs on either side. The transformation was complete and the cabin in the woods was as cozy as a nest in the trees.

The honeymoon continued without a flaw for almost a month. Amelia was a surprisingly good housekeeper; she kept a broom outside the door and made Steve brush the snow from his boots; she made him hang up his clothes and change his coat before sitting down to the candlelit table, carefully set with pretty china. He was amused at first, but after a while her perpetual insistence on these things began to irritate him. He put up with it cheerfully enough until she refused to have venison in the house.

"I don't like it, Steve. I don't like game."

He looked at her. "I do," he said shortly.

"But why should you want it when I don't?" she persisted. She tried another tack. "I don't know how to cook it."

"I'll show you. I've cooked plenty of it." But when she gave in meekly, he kissed her and let it go at that. He was conscious of a slight rift in the lute but he still found her an exciting and dainty bundle in his arms.

So far the weather had been comparatively mild but now, as

123

March approached, winter lashed out with all its pent-up reserves; the temperature dropped to thirty below, blizzards howled in, blowing the snow in swirling, impenetrable clouds. Trees, lashed by the wind, groaned and tossed and split with the cold with a sound like the crack of a pistol. It was nothing new to Steve but Amelia was terrified. When the train was held up by the drifts, the fear of starvation added to her horror and she clung to Steve, not letting him out of her sight long enough to keep the water hole chopped open. He did all he could to quiet her but with little success. In spite of the stove going full blast, her thin lips and long nose were blue with the cold, her pale eyes glassy with despair and she wore her mink coat most of the time, and sometimes slept in it. And Steve's untidy habits, now that he was in the house most of the time, drove her frantic. She followed him about, sweeping up the snow he tracked in, the chips he dropped when he filled the wood box, the ashes he spilled when he replenished the stove, twitched back in place the chairs he sat in and complained constantly about the smoke from his pipe. For a time Steve pitied her, but finally he clamped his lips tight on his cold pipe and joined her in exasperated misery.

Unable to leave his wife for an hour to tramp off his restlessness in the woods, Steve paced the little room waiting for the toot that would tell him the track was open again. When at last he heard it, he strapped on his snowshoes and hurried up the trail. Pat was waiting for him, his red face peering from the cab. "How you been makin' out?" he asked cheerfully.

"Fine," said Steve grimly, as he handed him a letter to Cyrus and a long list of supplies. "Ask Curtis for some books and bring me the newspapers as far back as you can get 'em."

"Ain't you comin' along?"

"No."

"Aw, come on. Do you good. I'll bring you back early. Ain't no schedule this time of year. I'll get you back before dark."

Steve longed to climb into the cab more than he had ever longed for anything in his life. "No," he said harshly. "Get those supplies down here this afternoon if you have to make a special trip for 'em —and the newspapers."

CHAPTER 24

With supplies coming in, Amelia, reassured, stitched on a
piece of canvas with colored wools while Steve read the
books Curtis sent to him. Time passed more pleasantly and they
got back to something like their former enjoyment of each other.
Steve tried once or twice to interest Amelia in the plans that were
constantly seething in his mind but he soon gave that up. The only
plans of any interest to Amelia were those for a house, and she began to work on them. Finally, one night, she spread several neat
little sketches under the lamp on the table. "Here's the house, Steve.
At last I've got it just the way I want it."

Steve, puffing on his pipe, looked over the plans with considerable
interest. "Looks all right," he said after a moment, "but it's too big.
You'll have to cut out some of those rooms. How about that one?"

"Oh, no, Steve," she protested. "That's the den off the dining room.
It's going to be draped like a Turkish tent, with divans all around
the walls. It's the latest thing for coffee drinking after dinner. I
couldn't possibly cut that out."

"A Turkish tent!" exclaimed Steve. "I'm not putting up a tent for
the Turks in Alturos. It don't make sense. If you've got to have a
den, fill it with books and put a fine deer's head on the wall."

"Oh, Steve," she pouted. "What a dreadful idea. A deer's head! I
don't want one in the house—not anywhere."

She resisted every suggestion he made, until finally Steve pulled
the plans together and handed them to her. "Go ahead," he said.
"Have it your own way. It's your house."

"Yes," she said. "And we must get it started. We can't go on living like this. How long will it be before this horrible snow is gone?"

"Another month. Six weeks, perhaps. I'll look up a lot for you the
next time I go to Alturos."

"Don't buy it until I can go with you," she insisted promptly. "I
want to be sure my house is where I want it."

Some days later they took the train to Alturos to buy a lot. It took
a man a good four hours to walk the fifteen miles to Alturos but Pat

whizzed them through in twenty-three minutes by Steve's watch and Amelia had scarcely settled down to the trip before she was off the train. This was her first visit to Alturos and during the lonely winter months the charms of her future home had multiplied in her imagination until she could hardly wait to see them—the pretty white houses, the tree-lined streets.

Now she stood on the platform looking up the main street. Two long ridges of filthy melting snow piled between the sidewalk and the roadway carried her eye past the flimsy, ugly buildings, most of them with a square false front. Here and there among them saloons and eating places blazed with color but, with the exception of the red brick bank on the corner and the flat yellow face of Burke's Hotel at the far end of the street, there wasn't a substantial structure to be seen. Some distance away, on the crest of a hill, straddled the ugly shaft house of a big mine, its steady thump beating like the heart of the sordid town.

Amelia stood perfectly still for a long moment, one gloved hand in her muff, the other lifting her skirts from the trampled snow.

"What's the matter?" asked Steve.

"Matter!" She raised her eyes to his. "You can't expect me to live in a place like this! Why didn't you tell me it was like this? I've never seen anything so awful in my life. What is that horrible thing like a guillotine up there on the hill?"

"That ought to make you feel at home," said Steve. "It's the Forsyth mine. A good deal of your income comes out of it. I've asked Cramer to have dinner with us. You know him, don't you? He's worked for Massachusetts for years."

"Of course I don't know him," she retorted icily. "I'm not accustomed to dining with employees."

A quick frown gathered on Steve's brow. "And I've asked Curtis and his wife. I had an idea you'd like to meet some people for a change."

"People!" Her voice quivered on the edge of hysteria. "In a place like this? Look at them. Look at that creature over there. Are those your friends—the kind of people you expect me to meet?"

Steve was not an easy man to face when he was angry, and he was angry now. He stepped back and looked full at her. "All right, Amelia," he said. "Have it your way. This thing comes to a showdown here and now. If you can't put up with this town and these people, get back there in the waiting room, take the first train down, and keep going till you get to Boston. If you've had enough,

126

face it and say so. I got you into this and I can let you out, but I'll be damned if I'll put up with any more of this nonsense. Understand, once and for all, you'll live my life and like it—or quit now."

Amelia hesitated, staring at him. Then she slipped her arm through his. "Oh, Steve," she pouted. "How silly you are! Just because I didn't like your horrid little town! It is horrid, and you know it—but that doesn't mean I want to rush back to Boston. How can you suggest such a thing?"

"That's better," said Steve. "Keep it up."

"Don't be so mean," she went on. "How could you think——" At that instant a shrill, piercing blast rent the air. "What's that?" she gasped as she clung to him.

"Noon whistle at the mine. Goes off at six in the morning, too. You'll like that. Come along. I understand it isn't polite to keep guests waiting."

In the dining room at Burke's Hotel, Mr. Cramer, in an extreme state of social uncertainty and conscious of his Harvard tie, immediately engaged Amelia in a flood of gossip from "home" and Curtis, in his quiet way, beamed his approval of Steve's fetching bride. But Mary, to Steve's delighted amusement, was unimpressed, pursuing her way through a meal of milk and vegetables with the calm detachment of a Wentworth. Finally, as the vapid bandying of names went on between Amelia and Cramer, she apparently wearied of being ignored, and a certain resolution gathered in her plain face. She finished her cole slaw and leaned forward. "You were a Forsyth, were you not?" she asked Amelia. "I don't believe I have ever before met a member of your family."

"Really?" smiled Amelia. "It would be rather surprising if you had, would it not?"

"Very," agreed Mary calmly, sipping her milk. "But I do recall that our families had some association in the past. One of my ancestors—he was Governor of Massachusetts at the time—once hanged one of yours. It created quite a sensation at the time. The Forsyths were beginning to be rather prominent in trade with China, and the Chinese objected to their practice of killing them at sea. The case was about that. I have often wondered," she went on, "if it wasn't that story that first aroused my sympathy for the Chinese. Have you any interest in missionary work, Mrs. Bradway?"

Amelia said frigidly that she had not. Mary said that was a pity because there was plenty of missionary work to be done in Alturos —and with that the party broke up.

127

"What an impossible woman!" exclaimed Amelia as Mary's straight back disappeared through the door. "Your lawyer friend is rather sweet, but she's impossible. I've never seen such airs."

"Airs?" Steve grinned. "I'd put on airs myself if I'd hung certain members of your family. Come on. Let's go and look for that lot."

Amelia chose a site on the slope of the hill some distance from the dwellings clustered around Alturos. It was rough land but there were several fine trees on it and the elevation gave it a view across the town to the undulating distant ridge.

"I think you're right," said Steve. "When this town moves, it will come in this direction. But it's too close to the mine."

"I know it is, but at least I have my back to it, and there is no excuse for all that racket," replied Amelia firmly. "Mr. Cramer will have to run his mine more quietly. I've already told him to stop that whistle."

"You have? What did he say?"

Amelia looked up, surprised. "He said he would, of course."

Steve bought several lots on the hill and, before he left town that night, had received an offer on one of them which pleased him. "You're a smart woman, Amelia," he said. "We'll make money on those lots."

Amelia was glad to get back to the cabin that night. The banked stove was still warm, the cheerful colors glowed in the lamplight, and as she took off her hat, she looked around with deep satisfaction. How pretty it was! How charming she had made this miserable little shack. How much more charming she would make her new house on the hill, and her mind leaped to the colors and furniture she would use.

Steve came in with an armful of wood, dribbling chips on the floor, and she started impulsively to scold him, but remembered in time his face as she had seen it that morning. Steve could and would send her from him without a moment's hesitation if it pleased him. She wasn't necessary to him, but every fiber in her body cried out his necessity to her. With a little shiver, she tied an apron around her waist and began to get supper.

Steve went to Alturos every day now on the morning train, back at night. He had an office next to Curtis above the bank and spent his time there, fretting with impatience for spring. One night when he came home he showed Amelia a letter from Cyrus.

"Considerable interest in that truck you've got out there," it read. "Looks like Hamby is working it up. If so, they'll be swarming for

128

it this spring, but hold back. It ain't ripe yet. You say Amelia's doing all right. Keep her at it. She needs a strong hand. Tell her I said so. Thing for us to do is hook up with you out there but Horace won't hear of it. You're better off without him. Lie low until the scum boils off. I don't get around any. This female wants to wash me in bed but I ain't come to that yet. Yours truly, Cyrus Forsyth."

"He might have said something kinder about me," commented Amelia.

Steve frowned. "I think he's having a tough time," he said. "You ought to go back and stay with him awhile. You'll have to go anyhow pretty soon to get Victor."

"I don't want to go yet," she objected. "Victor's school won't be over for another two months and I want to get my house started."

"I'll get the house started," said Steve impatiently. "The contractor knows what you want. I'll go myself if you want to stay here," he added as he saw her hesitate.

"Perhaps I ought to go," she said after a moment's thought. "It would give me a chance to buy the things I need. I've been wondering how I'd manage that."

"Yes," said Steve with an odd smile, "and you could see the old man, too."

When he put her on the train in Chicago, she stood on the steps reminding him again and again not to let the contractor make any change in her plans—not to unpack any crates or boxes until she got back. She was insisting on these instructions when the train began to move. Steve raised his hat. "So long, Amelia," he called. "Tell the old man I'd like to be with him."

"And remember," she called back, "white on the outside—two coats. . . ."

CHAPTER 25

After Amelia had gone, the dreary, soggy weeks dragged by and Steve, restless with the uncertainty of impending crisis, fretted through the long days. He got the house started before the frost was out of the ground, and under his impatient urging, it shot up like a geyser, sprouting turrets and balconies flounced with jigsaw trim. "Do the plans call for all that rigging?" he asked the contractor one morning.

"Sure do," replied the man. "She wants every inch of it. Told me so herself. And she don't want no changes, either," he added significantly.

"Looks like a Mississippi showboat hung up on a sand bar," commented Steve. "Well, go ahead with it if that's what she wants."

The house took up some of the slack, but spring was slow in coming. The disorder in the cabin lacked the familiar comfort of the old days when he was alone; he felt a fool in the chintz-covered bed and wished he had his bunk back in the corner. When the ice went out and he caught his first bass, he threw it back, too disgusted to dress and cook it.

Amelia wrote frequently, repeating at length her instructions about the house, but he heard nothing further from Cyrus about the activity in surface iron and Curtis, dazed by the miracle of his wife's pregnancy, was less than no help. Days were slow to pass, and for the first time in his life Steve's spirit failed to rise with the sap in the spring. He felt tired and drank a good deal.

The break came one morning when a man rode out of the woods and pulled up at the cabin. Steve, down at the shore fussing with his boat, glanced at the burly figure with the square-cut black beard and wide-brimmed black hat who sat his horse like a block of granite, the skirts of his closely buttoned frock coat spread over the saddle flaps. That dramatic figure was familiar from one end of the country to the other. It was Hamby, all right; the spectacular gambler whose operations in mining stocks were a constant source of jitters on the stock market. Steve walked up the bank.

130

"You Bradway?"

"Yes. Why?"

"I'm buying land around here," said the rider bluntly. "What will you take for your piece?"

Steve, spring mud on his boots, his blue shirt open at the neck, set his fists on his hips. "You're making the offer, Mr. Hamby," he said casually. "Go ahead."

The bleak, hooded eyes looked Steve over. "You know who I am?"

"Yes."

"Then you know I don't make an offer twice. You take it or leave it."

"That suits me."

"You've got a half section here. I'll give you two hundred dollars an acre for it."

Steve had heard tall stories of Hamby's sensational gambling habits and he had some of his own, but he didn't expect the play to be as fast as this. He managed to keep his look steady. "That's a big offer, Mr. Hamby," he said. "What's your reason for it?"

"That's my business. You selling?"

"You calling me?"

"Yes."

It was all Steve could do to shake his head, but he managed it. "I drop," he said, "but I'm damned glad you're not making that offer twice."

For what seemed a long time the cold eyes remained fixed on him; then the big man's teeth bared behind the black beard as he spat contemptuously into the underbrush. "Think you're smart, don't you? You'll regret it." With a savage wrench Hamby spun his horse around. Steve checked the yell on his lips and let him go.

After the speculator had disappeared, Steve sat down on a stump to think. For years he had waited for this break and now, when it came, he had rejected it. He had let a pile of money ride away on that horse—more money than he had ever dreamed of in the old days. He wondered why he had done it. It made him sweat to think of it. Well, if the bet looked good for that amount to Hamby, it looked good to him, but before he turned down any more offers like that, he'd better get Harding in here. Long ago, at old Cyrus' suggestion, he had written the mining expert and received a highly interested reply. The time was ripe to put that interest to the test.

With this thought in mind he looked at his watch. The up train was about due and he decided to catch it and send a telegram to

Harding in Utah. As he started up the trail, he stopped and looked down at the soggy red muck that clung to his boots as if it meant to hold him fast, and with a surge of emotion that surprised him he lifted his head and thanked God Hamby had ridden away.

Old Cyrus was right. Hamby's visit to the country was a signal for a rush in that direction. It came within a month. With a sudden, extravagant burst of violence, the boom in surface ore blazed up on the wind of frenzied speculation with the rapidity of a forest fire. Men on horseback, men on foot, lugging tripods and drills, swarmed in the woods like black flies. Trains jammed with men poured into Alturos, and within forty-eight hours there wasn't a bed to be had in the town. Burke, slick as a weasel behind his desk, shook his head a hundred times a day. "Can't do a thing for you at any price. Tables, chairs, floors all taken. Try that tent over there on the hill. They might have a blanket for you." Food ran out, but a man could live on whiskey if he could get to a bar.

Steve, in the jostling, shouting crowd that blocked the street, raised his hand and his voice a dozen times in as many steps. Everybody knew the big man. "Bradway? Yeah. Son of a bitch got a strip a mile long down there on the ridge. Shot a man to get it." "Bradway? Sure. I know him. Comes from Haley. Worked in the lumber camps four, five years ago. Used to be pretty handy with his fists."

Bums and chiselers whined at his elbow. McCarthy hustled up looking for another stripping contract. He thought he saw Jake and wondered if Matt was there. Funny he'd never heard from Matt. And Kit? Kit, with that red hood tied under her chin! In spite of himself his glance searched the tinsel-tawdry slatterns posing in the doors of the saloons; then, frowning, his face black with anger at this betrayal of his conscience, he pivoted his broad shoulders and forced his way through the crowd to climb the stairs to Curtis' office.

The room, crowded with disheveled men, reeked of whiskey and tobacco smoke. Curtis, his thin hair on end, looked up from the mass of papers on his desk. "Hello, Steve," he said feebly.

"How you making it, John?"

"I'm swamped. Sunk. They won't give me time."

"Make these crooks pay in advance and you won't have so much work." Some of the men laughed and Steve picked up one of the papers. "What's this? The northwest quarter of the southeast quarter of the—— Hell! That piece has been out of circulation over a year."

"Yeah? Who says so?" an angry voice demanded

"I do. I own it."

Roars of laughter followed the man as he snatched the paper from Steve's hand and bolted from the room. Steve grinned after him. "Someone will be stuck before night and there'll be one less crook in town tomorrow," he commented. "Watch your step, John."

"I can't look up everything they bring in here," said Curtis irritably. "I have to take their word for it."

"Sure." Steve nodded. "It's a lawyer's business to believe his clients. Just see that you don't get hooked yourself."

He sat down, lit a cigar, and watched Curtis' clients come and go. A tough lot. This was the scum that Cyrus had talked about but it wouldn't be long before the unwary were broke and the quick-change artists had skipped town; all but the suave, high-hatted operators waiting for the big game. He thought of Sully with a pang of regret.

In two weeks the frantic scramble was over; the crowd thinned out and the situation began to jell. Businessmen in well-cut suits came in, brief cases under their arms and figures on their tongues. One morning a private car slid into the siding with an air of opulence as solid as a stone wall. Word flew around that Douglas had come in, and all day long men, spruced up in their best, trekked to the siding at the beck of the mighty steel magnate.

Steve was one of them. As he approached the shining walnut palace on wheels, its sides decorated with large landscape paintings and gilt flourishes, he looked it over with an appraising eye. Must be a nice way to travel. A dignified colored man in immaculate white led him to a large compartment at the end of the car where four men were sitting in upholstered chairs on a thick flowered carpet, backed up by red curtains at the windows; men in fine clothes, with heavy gold chains looped across their waistcoats; all of them with the wooden expression familiar to Steve of men with aces up their sleeves. The host, a bristling and decisive little man, introduced himself and his companions, and a thin, white-haired man in a neat gray suit cleared his throat.

"Sit down, Mr. Bradway," he said pleasantly. "Our reason for sending for you must be obvious." Steve nodded and sat down. "As you know, we've been experimenting in Pittsburgh with the smelting of surface ore, and we now believe we have a furnace that can handle it in considerable quantity." The dry, persuasive voice went on. "Naturally, we are interested in the future production of ore in this region. Would you have any objection to telling us the possible extent of surface ore on your property?"

133

"None at all," replied Steve genially. "But I have no idea, myself."

"You mean no one has gone over it for you?"

"That's right. But I expect a man along soon—man by the name of Harding, from Utah."

The little steel king kept his shrewd, bright eyes on Steve. "Dave's a good man," he broke in, "but there's no necessity to wait for his report. What we want is a blanket contract on any ore you may have, terms left open depending on what you turn up. It would be to your advantage as well as ours to be in position to negotiate. We're out in front with this furnace and we want the ore."

Steve eased forward in his chair. He looked young, strong, vigorous; out of place in that cramped space. "I appreciate your interest, Mr. Douglas," he said with his quick smile, "but I'm not making any commitments until I know what I've got. The ore will keep."

To his surprise a faint twinkle appeared in the eyes fixed on him. "I see you are in no hurry to jump in, young man," said Douglas. "You're not obliged to accept at this time." He stopped and rubbed his hands on the knees of his tweed suit while the twinkle brightened. "But would you do us the favor of keeping us in mind when you get around to it?" he asked with amiable sarcasm.

"Sure," said Steve. He stood up and held out his hand. His smile broadened. "There's no telling. We might make a good team, Mr. Douglas."

CHAPTER 26

That was not the only private car that slid into the siding nor the only offer of contract, lease, or sale that Steve rejected. Under this rush to get aboard the surface-ore bandwagon, Alturos grew with the rapidity of a hothouse plant, throwing out new streets into the void from the parent stem of the old town, and the air resounded with the pounding of hammers. Steve sold his lots at huge profit, and several substantial houses were under construction on the hillside where Amelia's house, almost completed, glistened like a wedding cake in the June sunshine. The sight of it never failed to amuse Steve.

One morning when he walked up there to see how things were coming along, he stopped short at sight of a life-sized, cast-iron stag standing in an attitude of startled astonishment in the middle of the flat skim of new grass that surrounded the house. For an instant he, too, froze with astonishment, then skirted the figure warily to find the contractor. He found him unpacking another stag.

"What's all this?" he demanded. "Must be some mistake. Mrs. Bradway doesn't want anything resembling a deer around the place."

"Well, these don't resemble 'em," returned the contractor. "But she wants 'em all right. I got my instructions and she don't want no changes. That settles it."

"You mean I've got to look at these things?"

"You sure have. Right past 'em every time you go down the path." The contractor nodded. "What's the matter with you? Don't you like art?"

Steve shook his head and gave up. This must be close to the finish; he couldn't imagine anything more she could do and Amelia was bound to arrive any day now in pursuit of those stags.

But on the day he expected her, he received instead a letter with a wide black border addressed in Amelia's neat hand. He knew what it meant before he tore it open.

"Dear Steve," he read, "Grandfather died in his sleep last night. I was all ready to leave this morning with Victor, so you can imagine what a shock it was. I'm too tired to write much except to tell you he left me the contents of this house, and the house to Horace. Catherine wants to move right in here but Mr. Stoddard says she can't until I have removed the furniture, and I mean to take my time about that. He left you, of all things, that old silk quilt, and something called the residue. Horace is furious. It's been an awful day. The funeral will be on Wednesday. Poor Grandfather! He looked so tired yesterday, and after the room got dark, he seemed to think he was talking to you. But I don't believe that means he was out of his mind, the way Horace says he was. I'll write again soon and tell you my plans but I'm too tired now."

Steve thrust the letter in his pocket. After some time he got up heavily and walked down the hall to see Curtis. The lawyer glanced up with a pleased smile that vanished when he saw Steve's face. "What's the matter?" he asked quickly. "What's happened?"

Steve stood at the window looking out, his back to Curtis, his hands deep in his pockets. "Old Cyrus is dead," he said after a silence. "Died four or five days ago. I've just had a letter from Amelia."

"I'm sorry, Steve," said Curtis gently. "He meant a lot to you. Are you going?"

Steve came back to the desk and sat down. "I don't think so. I wish I'd gone earlier, but there's no point in it now."

"How about Amelia? Won't she need you?"

Steve shook his head. "No. She'll get along better without me." He sat silent for some time. "The old man left me the residue of his estate," he continued, "and it looks as if Horace is raising a row about it. He certainly would if I showed up there."

"You think he'd take it to court?"

"He might try to and I don't want that to happen. I think," he went on thoughtfully, "this is the time to get rid of my Massachusetts stock. They've got a piece along the railroad to the south of me. I'd like to trade for that."

Curtis looked at him, astounded. "Steve, you can't mean that! You don't need any more land, and Massachusetts is booming. Look at the dividends it's paying. Why, that's giving it away."

"Looks that way to you, does it? Then Horace may see it that way —take his mind off the will at any rate." Steve's face hardened. "I don't want that stock now the old man's gone," he declared bluntly. "It's done its work and I want no further connection with Massachu-

136

setts Mining. If I can I want to make that trade. I want you to go to Boston and handle it for me. Keep an eye on Amelia's interests at the same time. If the trip is worth a thousand dollars to you it is to me."

"A thousand dollars!" ejaculated Curtis. "Good God, Steve. Now I know you're crazy."

Steve smiled. "Not so you'd notice it. Get off tomorrow if you can make it. Now"—he reached for a pad and pencil—"this is the situation you'll find back there."

The next morning Curtis was on his way to Boston.

A few days after his departure Steve was sitting in his office when a man he'd never seen before came in. "I'm looking for Mr. Bradway," he said as Steve glanced up. "Can you tell me where I'll find him?"

Steve's look sharpened. "I'm Bradway," he said. "Sit down. What can I do for you?"

The stranger tossed his soft hat on the desk and sat down. He was a lean, clean-cut man of medium height, with a well-set head topped by close-cropped brown hair, his face weathered except for the band of white across his forehead where his hat protected it. Unusually long brows curved far down the square temples, framing a pair of steady eyes with a hint of amusement in them. "I'm Harding," he said. "Dave Harding."

"Harding!" Steve's face broke into a smile as their hands met. "I've been expecting to hear from you. Thought you were in Utah."

"Your letter caught me as I was starting East," explained Harding, "and I'm delighted to get this chance to see your country. Cyrus Forsyth wrote me some time ago that you might be out my way but I understand you were delayed." Harding's amused look deepened. "You married Amelia Hamilton, didn't you?"

"You know Amelia?"

"I knew Hamilton. In fact, I was an usher at his wedding. But I doubt that Amelia would remember me. I haven't seen her for a good many years."

"She's been in Boston for some time but I expect her back in a week or two," replied Steve. "You know old Cyrus died last week?"

"No." Harding's face sobered. "I'm sorry to hear it. He was a splendid old fellow."

"He was all of that," agreed Steve.

They talked awhile about Cyrus and the Forsyths, until finally Harding swung the conversation around to the purpose of his visit.

137

"I'll be interested to see what you've got out there," he said. "Matter of fact, that boom you've had here has stirred up the steel industry to a considerable extent. I hear Douglas came out here. Did anything come of it?"

"Not with me," said Steve. "He was looking for contracts but it seemed a little early for that."

Harding nodded, and Steve told him of Hamby's earlier visit.

"Hamby himself showed up at your place?" Harding asked with quick interest. "That means Reisburg has been over it. He's got the sharpest nose for mineral in the country—finds it where there isn't any. He and Hamby make a great team. You didn't tie up with Hamby, did you?"

"No. I'm not tying up with anybody until I know where this thing's going."

Harding again nodded his approval. "That makes sense," he said. "No rush about it. It'll be a year or more before the furnaces can handle it in any quantity."

"When would you like to go out to my place?" asked Steve.

"As soon as possible," replied Harding. "I can't spend more than three or four days here. I'll need a man to tote for me."

Steve smiled. "I'll tote for you. Toting for Cramer is what put me on to this."

"That so?" said Harding. "How is Cramer? I'd like to see him."

Steve pulled out his watch. "There's a down train in an hour. Why don't you run out there now?" he suggested. "He's got a good mine. Putting in another shaft. I'll clean up here, pick up some supplies, and meet you at the station."

That evening they dropped off the train at the trail with their supplies and Harding's gear and walked through the woods to the cabin.

CHAPTER 27

The sun was setting across the lake as Steve shoved open the door of the cabin, and as its bright revealing light poured in, he remembered with relief that he had sent a woman down to clean up the place on the chance that Amelia might come back before the house was finished. He was glad of it when he saw Harding's astonished look.

"I scarcely expected to find a setup like this," exclaimed his guest. "This must be Amelia's doing. Do you mean to say she spent the winter here?"

Steve dumped the supplies on the floor and got busy with the cook stove. "Five months of it," he replied, "and it was a tough winter."

"I never would have believed it of her. She was a spoiled little thing as I remember her." Harding looked at the rugged features lit by the fresh blaze in the stove. "She probably thought she had good reason for it," he said dryly. "It must have pleased Cyrus to see the old buccaneer spirit show up in her. Not much of it left in the family."

"She showed it, all right," said Steve.

The next morning they set off through the woods. The black flies were a torment, the June day hot and still, but Harding tramped tirelessly over Steve's holdings, silent, intent, casting over the surface like a hound on the scent. Steve, lugging his instruments, watched him with growing satisfaction. "You seem to feel your way through the earth like a mole," he commented at one time.

"Yes. Something like that," replied Harding, slapping at the black flies. "A man has to sense it blind, more or less."

When descending night put an end to their work, they tramped home and, after a refreshing plunge in the lake, went fishing for their supper until a star or two twinkled above the pines. Then, a good meal out of the way, they relaxed in the easy chairs, pipes going, conscious of the deep accord that had grown between them during the day. Harding got two or three small volumes out of his grip. "Ever read Voltaire?" he asked, handing one to Steve.

139

"No," said Steve. "Let's have a look at it." Presently he said, "This old fellow had some good ideas."

Harding looked up. "Yes, but he got most of them from men further back. He's comparatively recent."

"Recent? It says here he lived more than a hundred years ago."

Harding smiled. "That's recent to a man who plays around the earth's surface as I do. It's yesterday. Are you interested in what's gone on in the past on this little planet?"

"No," replied Steve promptly. "A man has no time to think of the past—not any of it, even his own—if he means to get anywhere."

"Depends on what he's after. What are you after, Steve?"

"Money. I want it."

Harding glanced across the table at the big man sitting in the lamplight. "It looks as if you may get what you're after," he said. "I've known a good many men who've made money and been satisfied with it. I wonder if you'd be."

Steve frowned. "Why not? Money's the answer to everything a man wants."

"Not always," returned Harding quietly. "Depends on the man, of course," and he went on with his book.

They spent four days together in the woods. In the middle of the afternoon on the last day, after an exhausting tramp, Harding stopped abruptly, shook himself like a dog coming out of water, and dropped down wearily under a tree. "That's it," he said, getting out his pipe. "Want to hear it now, or wait for my written report?"

Steve, seated on a windfall opposite, lit his pipe with more composure than he felt. "Now," he said.

Harding settled himself, drew up his knees, puffed vigorously for a moment to drive off the flies. "This is, of course, a superficial survey," he began, "but it has shown up a few facts. The ore is here, no question about that, and it's a good grade—better than I expected— and, unless I've struck only the high spots, you've got a world of it. It lies something like this." He picked up a stick and drew a rough outline on the ground. "If Reisburg found what I've found, it's no wonder Hamby was after it at any price." He stopped and looked at Steve. "In all my experience I've never run into anything remotely like it," he went on. "It's a stupendous freak. If Reisburg hadn't been through here, damned if I wouldn't think I was off my chump. And I may be, Steve. There's no telling, with certainty. Never is. Now, as I understand it, you're thinking of developing here yourself."

"That's right," said Steve.

140

Harding shook his head. "You want my advice. Here it is. If you try it, you'll be sunk before you get a pick into it."

"What are you getting at?"

"You ought to lease this thing, Steve," Harding answered bluntly. "Do it now before you're forced into it. Even if I'm fifty-per-cent wrong, it's too big for you. Turn it over to men with the resources and experience to take the risk. It's the sensible thing to do."

Steve frowned. "You mean play safe, sit back and take what I can get."

"Exactly," agreed Harding earnestly. "I understand how you feel about it but I've never yet seen the original owner of a mine succeed in operating it. They sink the last dollar they've got, and when they're helpless, the big money takes over. I've seen it happen over and over again. I'd hate to see it happen here, and in a venture of this size"—he waved his arms—"it's inevitable. I know what it takes. I know what I'm talking about, Steve."

"I appreciate that." Steve stood up and began pacing back and forth. "I've thought a lot about it myself," he said soberly. "But damned if I'm ready to give up without making a try for it. If I lease I'll be out of it—piddling around cashing another man's checks the rest of my life." He swung on Harding. "I've hung on here for years, Dave. I've made up my mind. I'll swing it myself or go under with it. What do you expect me to do?" he demanded. "Knuckle down now and let the big fellows hand me the small end of the stick? I'm damned if I will! They've got the capital but, by God, I've got the stuff they're after."

"I was under the impression you wanted to make money," remarked Harding mildly.

"Hell! Not that way."

Harding shrugged, stood up, and brushed off the seat of his pants. "If you want to monkey with that buzz saw, go ahead. I've said my say. At any rate, the ore is here." He smiled. "You're capable of changing your mind, aren't you?"

Steve cooled off. "It's possible."

They picked up the gear and walked back through the quiet woods in the waning light. Nothing more was said until they neared the cabin, then Steve laid his hand on his companion's shoulder. "Just one thing more I want to clear up with you, Dave," he said. "If I do get this thing going, will you undertake the development here?"

141

Harding looked into the steady eyes, the whole set of the man before him. "How old are you, Steve?" he asked.

"Around thirty," replied Steve with some surprise. "Why?"

"I've worked for a good many of the so-called giants of industry this country is producing just now. Something about you makes a man wonder if the last of them has shown up yet."

"That's not answering my question."

"I'm not answering it. But if you're fool enough to try to swing this thing, you'll have the pick of any mining man in the country."

"I've got him picked," said Steve.

That night they walked up the trail to flag the down train. They had little to say as they waited for the headlight to pierce the long avenue of pines, but the wires were up between them and humming strong. Pat pulled up with a toot. A hand clasp, a steady look, "So long," and Harding got aboard. Steve stood in the right of way watching the red taillight flicker and disappear. Then he turned and walked down the dark trail to the light shining in the cabin window.

Now that he had Harding's opinion, Steve waited with impatience for Curtis to get back from Boston, and the day the lawyer arrived, pinned him down to report on his negotiations with the Massachusetts Mining Company.

"There was a little difficulty at first over the stock," admitted Curtis. "Horace wanted all of it on the ground it had belonged to his father. The board was willing enough to make the transfer but they wouldn't put up with that. I wanted to back out, Steve. I honestly did. I hated to see you give up that stock, but when Horace saw how I felt, he quit." Curtis smiled. "I think he detested having you on the board more than he did sharing the stock. At any rate, here is the deed."

Steve laughed as he slapped the paper on the desk. "Wanted to back out, did you? What would you think if I told you Harding found the richest single deposit down there on that forty? I'll bet you right now a half million dollars will come out of it before we're through. That's the best piece of work you'll ever do in your life." He slipped the deed in his pocket. "How did you find Amelia?"

"Fine. I couldn't do much for her. She's busy clearing out the house. Didn't seem to be in a hurry about it but she ought to be home in a week or two."

Steve thought a minute, rubbing his jaw. "How much do you make a year, John?" he asked abruptly.

142

"Don't worry about me, Steve. There's plenty of work in Alturos now. I do pretty well."

"How much?"

"Around three thousand. Why?"

"I'd like to double that on an annual basis if you'll come in with me."

"Six thousand a year?" exclaimed Curtis. "Nonsense. You can't do that. I'm not worth it to you."

"You earned twice that in the last three weeks," said Steve impatiently. "I need you with me. How about it?"

Curtis shook his head. "I'll be around when you need me," he said, "but this isn't the time for it. Steve, you go too fast," he burst out with unaccustomed vigor. "You've just paid me a big fee for getting rid of the only good investment you've got. You aren't earning anything. You're riding on air. It may be years before this ore comes through—if it ever does. And if it does, you'll need every nickel the old man left you." He shook his head again. "No. You don't need me. What you need is sound investments for every dollar you've got."

Steve frowned. "You're as bad as Harding," he said. "He gave me the same line of talk."

"Any man with sense would," interrupted Curtis.

"All right. Have it your own way. You've just turned down six thousand a year. If that makes sense I'm a Chinaman." He stood up and laid his hand on Curtis' shoulder. "At that, it may make sense in the long run—for both of us. Go ahead with those investments. That's your job. If I'm riding on air, no telling when I'll need a cushion under me." He started for the door. Turned. "You're a bigger man than I am, John," he said soberly. "I know what six thousand means to you just now, with that boy coming on."

Curtis flushed. "That's not the point," he said.

"It's the point with me," said Steve as he went out.

CHAPTER 28

Not long after this Amelia came home. One hot July day she ran lightly down the steps of the train and into Steve's arms. She was dressed in black, which was not becoming to her, and her face was pale and tired, but she was soft and fragrant when he held her to him, and he was glad to have her there. "Oh, Steve," she wept, "it's been so long. I'm so glad to be back."

"I'm glad to have you," he confessed, kissing her.

She clung to him for a moment before turning to the tall, handsome boy coming slowly down the steps. "Come along, Victor. Shake hands with Uncle Steve. You remember him."

Victor looked up, dark eyes in a pale, sensitive face. "He isn't my uncle," he said. "I don't like my uncles."

Steve smiled as he took the limp hand in his. "Right, Victor," he said. "I'm not your uncle by a long shot. Grown a lot, haven't you?" He turned to the waiting hack. "Come along. Get in."

"We'll need another for Fawcett," said Amelia. She glanced toward a kind-faced old woman standing in the background, her arms filled with bundles, a black string bag, stuffed full, hanging from her wrist. "Follow on, Fawcett. Make sure you have all the pieces."

"Who's that?" asked Steve as they drove away.

"Fawcett? She's Grandfather's old housekeeper. She begged to come so I brought her along. I thought it was a good idea to have one trained servant in the house. Mercy! How this town has grown!" she exclaimed, peering from the window. "It looks quite attractive. What's that big building?"

"Opera House. We had a good minstrel show there the other night."

They reached the corner where her house stood, flounced and glistening in the sun. "Oh, Steve," she cried. "Look, Victor! That is Mama's house. Oh, it's exactly what I planned." She threw open the door, jumped from the carriage. "How pretty and gay it is. Aren't

144

those stags charming with the petunias around them! They really are the finishing touch, aren't they, Steve?"

"No doubt about that."

Amelia drew Victor to her. "Isn't it a pretty little house, darling? You like it, don't you?"

"No," said Victor. "It's a silly house."

"Oh, Victor, don't say that," Amelia cried. "You must like it. Mama wants you to."

She hurried up the path, calling to Fawcett to follow, her eyes darting over the boxes and crates piled on the long veranda, and ran up the steps into the house.

The interior was unpainted and the sun shone on the few pieces of scattered furniture with harsh brilliance. "I hope the wallpapers have come," she worried. "They must be here somewhere. I must get the painters tomorrow. Nothing can be unpacked until they're out of the way. What's that, Fawcett? Oh, don't bother me. I'll look at the kitchen presently." She hurried from room to room, Victor lagging, heavy-footed, in the rear, and Steve went into the kitchen.

"Well, Fawcett, what do you think of it?" he asked genially.

Fawcett, her black bonnet still on her head, was tying an apron around her thick waist. She looked him respectfully in the eye. "It's like the lad said, sir," she replied, "but we'll make out to live in it."

Steve laughed. "How do you like that stove?"

"It's a fine stove, thank you, sir. I'll have it going in a minute. That boy needs something to eat. It's a good thing you got in them supplies."

"I'm used to that." He paused. "How was the old man toward the last, Fawcett? I thought a lot of him."

The faded blue eyes filled with quick tears. "I know you did, sir, and him of you. He was never the same after you left. It was a sad time for him. He played them cards from morning to night; wouldn't let nobody near him hardly, except me. We had some talks when that nurse wasn't around. I've got that old silk quilt kept safe—for you, like he said. And the cards."

Steve laid his hand on the old shoulder. "We'll get along all right, Fawcett."

"I know that, sir. That's one reason I come. I didn't have to," with a touch of pride. "The old gentleman gave me a good bit before he died, God bless him."

Steve went off to look for Amelia. On the way up the stairs he

145

heard her shrill voice. "Don't be so exasperating, Victor. It is, too! It's just the way you like it, all those shelves for your books, and that nice big window. And it's going to be blue—your favorite color."

"Blue is not my favorite color," came Victor's voice. "It's yours. I don't like blue and I don't like this house, and you can't make me say I do."

Steve turned quietly and went down the stairs. It was time to get back to his office.

Summer, during her brief stay in Alturos, did nothing to ease the temper of the already hysterical town, and in the days that followed this was nowhere more evident than in the glistening, blistering white house on the hill. Amelia, in a black lawn dress, mopping the sweat from her pinched lips, ran incessantly from room to room on the heels of the painters, who swarmed all over the place. "Nonsense! Don't tell me that's the color I wanted. I told you to put in a touch of chrome. You know what chrome is, don't you?"

Steve came in from the office. "Oh, Steve, do try to help a little. This man is driving me distracted. He knows absolutely nothing about color. He's never heard of chrome."

"That so, Charlie?" Steve glanced at the painter kneeling on the floor, tamping the lids onto his cans. "Charlie's a pretty good billiard player, Amelia. Better hang on to him. How about this chrome, Charlie? Think you can shoot it?"

The painter looked up. "Hell! A drop of this and a touch of that! I'll give her what she wants if she'll let me alone." He shrugged, prying the covers off the cans again. "All right, Steve, I'll stick."

Steve turned to Amelia. "How about my taking Victor down to the cabin for a few days, out of your way?"

"If you think that's being helpful," she began; then hesitated. "Perhaps it's a good idea. If this paint makes Victor sick I don't know what I'll do. But you'll be careful with him, won't you, Steve?"

"Sure," said Steve. She cautioned him again as he went up the stairs not to let Victor get his feet wet.

He found the boy standing at the window of his room. He looked as if he had been there a long time. The thin, young figure drooped against the light and Steve thought he was crying until he saw the face turned unwillingly to his. "I think we'd better get out of here until your mother's through painting," he said casually. "How about a few days' fishing down at the cabin?"

"All right," said Victor indifferently.

146

"Good. Get into some old clothes and I'll meet you at the depot in half an hour."

"How do I get there?"

"Get there? Walk. Run, if you feel like it. You can see it from here. Get going."

A freight was going down that evening and Steve helped Victor into the engine cab, showed him how to toot the whistle, pull the bell, but the boy's apathy remained unbroken. He sat, a dead weight in Steve's arms, flicking cinders off his clothes.

"First kid I ever see didn't wake up to an engine ride," commented the engineer. "He yours?"

"No," said Steve.

"I wouldn't think so. You can't tell, though. I got one picks flowers."

On the trail Victor carried the bundles he was told to carry. When they got to the cabin, he put them on the table. The unfamiliar surroundings, the deer's head, the log walls, the shotgun, failed to awaken any interest in him. He simply stood.

Steve was beginning to wonder what he'd do to Victor before the week was over. A number of things occurred to him. He took down the rod, dug some worms, and handed the can to Victor, who promptly dropped it. "Pick 'em up," ordered Steve. "Pick 'em up, fast."

Victor shrank back. "I don't want to."

"Do as I tell you. Pick 'em up. You dropped 'em, didn't you?"

Victor looked up into the tall man's face and something he saw there made him act. He grabbed a stick and hastily scraped the worms back into the can. Steve smiled. "Good boy. Used your head, didn't you? Come along."

They got in the boat and Steve put some of the exasperation he felt into the oars. It was a lovely evening. The rosy sunset colors reflected on the placid surface of the lake glowed like an opal in the dark setting of the pines; silver ripples undulating from the oars gleamed for a brief moment and died away; a heron loafed home across the sky; from far away the yearning plaint of a loon pulsed faintly in the silence—and Victor sat in the stern of the boat, his chin on his hand, staring at his feet.

Steve dropped the anchor and threaded worms on the hook. "Have to still-fish this time of year," he explained. "They're down deep, where it's cold. Drop it until you feel bottom, then pull up about a foot."

147

Victor, the rod limp in his hand, let the line down until loops of it lay on the surface, but Steve, his pipe going, made no further effort to instruct in the art of fishing, his apathy by this time fully equal to that of his small guest. He sat back wondering what was the matter with this boy. He looked healthy enough in a pallid sort of way. There was nothing sullen about him, no sign of antagonism. "He just don't give a damn," he thought, and compassion for the young one began to soften his exasperation. But not much, and it increased again as the end of the rod followed the line into the water.

A deer came out of the woods not far away and waded in to munch the lily pads but he didn't bother to mention it. Neither spoke. Nothing happened. Steve knocked out his pipe and pulled up anchor. "Might as well go back," he said. "They're not biting."

Then, with a rush that took the slack, a bass grabbed the bait. "Hang on to that rod!" yelled Steve. "Hang on to it now." And Victor, electrified, hung on, his back arched, his face red, his eyes popping, while Steve maneuvered the boat to play the fish. "Take it easy. He's a whopper. Bring the line around to me now. That's right. Easy. Easy, now." Steve grabbed the line, flipped the tired fish into the boat, and lifted it for the trembling boy to see. "As fine a bass as ever came out of this lake," he declared. "Good for you, Victor. I'm proud of you." Steve's laugh rang out across the silent lake and Victor's excited treble joined it.

Steve dressed the fish and Victor cooked it, hopping with excitement when Steve helped him turn it in the pan. Victor ate his fish and washed his plate. That night, in bed, he crept close to the big man beside him and went to sleep with his head on Steve's shoulder.

The days that followed were the happiest in Steve's life and he never forgot them. They fished, or tramped the woods, the man's long stride shortened to match the efforts of the plunging boy, and sometimes Steve stopped abruptly to ruffle the blond head at his elbow or look down at the eager face raised to his. At night he told stories of old Cyrus' trips around the Horn, or of giant trees crashing in a thunder of snow in the logging camps, until Victor fell asleep and he carried him to bed. After the lamp was out, he lay beside the boy, listening to his quiet breathing while his thoughts went forward to a new horizon and his heart filled with a yearning sharp as pain.

In Alturos the paint had been dry for a week and Steve had not yet come home with Victor. Every morning when the train came in,

Amelia, tired, nervous, hurried to the window until at last she saw them coming slowly, indolently, up the hill. Victor, dirty, sunburned, his hair on end, laughing as he clung to Steve's hand.

Amelia's exasperation boiled over. Her lips parted and, for an instant, the figures of her husband and her son disappeared in a whirling mist of anger; then she flew from the house, down the path and fell on her knees to gather her boy in her arms. "Oh, Victor!" she cried. "Oh, my darling, what has happened to you?" She raised her head and blazed at Steve. "Oh, how could you? Look at him! Look at his poor little arms and legs—and his face! How could you abuse him so?" Half dragging, half carrying Victor, calling shrilly for Fawcett, she hurried into the house.

Victor cast one startled look at Steve, who shook his head. "Go along, son," he said. "It's all right."

Steve followed, undisturbed. Amelia was behaving like a fool quail over her chick but she'd get over it. He saw the familiar blue sofa in place against the wall in the living room and sat down on it to wait for her. She was gone some time and he was about to leave for the office when she came running down the stairs, her face flushed with fury. She faced him. "Now," she demanded, "I want an explanation of this."

Steve stood up. "Explanation? What are you talking about, Amelia?"

"About your behavior in keeping my son away from me all this time and bringing him back in this condition. He's covered with bruises from head to foot. I never saw anything like it in all my life. What did you do to him?"

"Do to him? Nothing. He got mussed up a little, but it did him good. We had a fine time together." He started for the door to get away from this silly scene, but she rushed ahead of him.

"You can't run away from me," she blazed. "I won't let you. A fine time together—you and my son! I thought as much from what he told me—those awful stories about lumber camps and barrooms. You taught him to play poker—a little boy. You ought to be ashamed of yourself." She began to tremble, her voice rose, thinned. "He's my child—my son; not yours, as you had the effrontery to call him a few minutes ago. I won't have him brutalized and coarsened by you. He's my son! Mine! Not yours! I won't have it, I tell you!"

Steve took her wrists and held them gently enough, looking down at her congested face. "Get hold of yourself, Amelia," he said quietly. "You're acting like a fool over nothing. Victor's a fine little

149

fellow; I'd like to help him make a man of himself, but I'm not going to quarrel with you over him—he's had enough of that between you and his grandmother." His face hardened. "But let me tell you, my girl, it's going to be different with my son."

"Your son!" Amelia, beside herself, threw back her head and laughed in his face. "Your son! Your son! Don't you know yet, you fool, you'll never have a son?" She stopped, gasped, frightened by what she saw. "Let me go!" she cried, wrenching to get away from him. "Let me go—you're hurting me."

Steve's grip tightened. "Say that again," he said quietly. "Say it again." He shook her gently back and forth. "Out with it. What did you mean by that?"

"No. No, Steve." She struggled, twisted, averting her face from his relentless look, but he held her easily, watching her, a thin smile on his lips. "Let me go! You're killing me," she whimpered. "Let me go. I didn't—I didn't mean to tell you. It's not my fault. Let me go."

"Didn't mean to tell me? That's the point, you little cheat. You've had plenty of time to make it straight with me. Why didn't you? You knew I'd take it—knew I'd have to. A man can put up with a thing like that if he's got an honest woman. But you got more satisfaction out of it this way. Didn't you? Didn't you?" He shook her hard this time. "But you'll come out with it now if I have to break your neck to get it."

But she cheated him again. Her head drooped and she wilted against his chest. Steve, seething with disgust, carried her to the blue sofa and went to find Fawcett. "Your mistress thinks she's fainted," he said harshly. "You'd better go to her."

The old woman searched his face. "I been afraid of this, sir."

Steve threw back his head and laughed. "So, you were in on it too, Fawcett? Well, well, everybody in on the big joke! That's the way of it, was it?"

"I was with her when the boy was born, sir. I couldn't help but know. When she couldn't have no more, she took a hate for men in a way. In another way, she didn't—that's bad for a woman." She started for the door. "Don't be too hard on her, sir. She's a pitiful woman."

"The old man knew it too, didn't he? Of course he did. That explains a lot that's puzzled me. Get rid of damaged cargo."

Fawcett turned in the door, her face stern. "Shame on you, sir, for such a thought. Him? No, sir, he did not. He died in hopes, poor man."

150

It was almost daylight when Steve got home that night. He had learned to hold his liquor before he was fifteen but he swayed now as he gripped the footboard and stared at the woman in the bed. The pink-frilled lamp cast a soft, deceiving light on the fair, crisply curling hair, on the white arms and bosom lightly covered with lace. While he watched, the thin lips fluttered and Amelia gently snored. Steve was drunk enough to go to bed anywhere, but it was some time before he got into bed with his wife.

Steve was not the first or the last man to face the fact that he would have no son, but he took it hard. Until his companionship with Victor in the woods, he had given the matter little thought, confident that time would take care of it, but Victor had aroused an impatient desire for a boy of his own and it had shocked him profoundly to have his hope so abruptly shattered. He yearned for a son. He looked at Curtis, jittery with impending crisis, with bitter envy, and for several days prowled around with no appetite for the future.

But he was too vigorous a man to be dominated very long by an emotion that got him nowhere. The yearning burned like a coal in his vitals but he gave up blowing on it and it gradually subsided. To his surprised relief he found that with it went all feeling for Amelia; she ceased to exist for him emotionally. Her presence in his life meant nothing one way or another. Well, not quite that. He finally decided with considerable satisfaction that she meant about as much to him now as a good steak, and on that basis it was no effort to continue his relations with her.

Amelia, deceived by his casual behavior, quickly resumed the feminine, artless ways that had once so charmed him. She dressed carefully, her pretty, perfumed silks whispering around her as she devoted herself to his comfort.

Steve, who had known some cunning vixens in his time, was amused to watch this one getting out of the trap she had sprung. "You're so good, Steve," she murmured pensively one evening as she sat near him, bent over her needlework. "So generous and kind. I might have known you would be, but I was so frightened, so terribly afraid you'd be angry with me. It would have been so easy if I'd realized how little men care about those things. You do understand, don't you, darling?"

Steve raised his eyes and looked at the submissive head. "It took me some time to get around to it," he said dryly, "but you can bank on my understanding from now on," and went back to his book.

151

It was different with Victor. For a long time the boy's hurt, bewildered eyes caused him considerable pain, but he managed to ignore the child until the look faded with the tan on the young cheeks and Victor's apathy engulfed him again. The last chink in Steve's armor was closed. In September, when Amelia took her son back to Boston, Steve watched them go—mother and son. Secure behind the barrier of his indifference, he sighed with relief. Neither of them could ever bruise him again. He was wrong about that.

CHAPTER 29

Steve never knew where he came from. Sometimes he thought he remembered running away from a woman who was always crying into the suds in a washtub. He wasn't sure about that, but his memory of scrambling around on the *Mississippi Belle,* dodging blows for nickels and dimes, was as clear as crystal, and it hadn't been long before he learned that the passengers who knocked him around the hardest were those with the most money. Old Sully helped him along with that idea. "Why, boy, it stands to reason," he declared. "Man with the chips calls the turn. Bound to. Thing to do is figure out his play and take 'em away from him." This advice took root in fertile soil, and the struggle to survive hardened into a lasting obsession to get rich, but it was not until after his trip through the woods with Cramer that his eyes had opened to new horizons that glowed with increasing promise as he pursued them.

After his marriage to Amelia his pursuit changed somewhat. For the first time in his life he was in no immediate need. He could afford to wait, and it was in this arrogant mood that he had rejected Hamby's offer. At the time this act of independence had given him deep satisfaction, but his brief domestic felicity at an end, his pride curdled at the thought of owing it to a woman who had tricked him out of his manhood with her money. The fact that it was his own fault did nothing to erase that humiliation. Now, with the violence born of disgust, the full tide of his energy rushed back into the familiar channel. He had no further interest, no time, no thought for anything but money. The answer to that lay in the development of his mine.

All around him men were slashing through the woods, rushing in equipment in a frenzy to ship ore, but impatient as he was to get started, the bottleneck in Duluth loomed in Steve's imagination. He saw ore, pulled out of the ground in haste, piled up there at the mercy of outgoing rails greedy to absorb the D. & W. and dominate the ridge. To forestall that certainty another means of transportation had to be found and found fast. A vision of a continuous operation from mine to smelter under interlocking control by way of the Great Lakes took hold of his mind to plague him day and night. A thousand tons at a clip by water would knock the spots off rail rates. But where were the freighters of that capacity? Could he find them? Charter them? Could they be built?

With these questions seething in his mind, Steve, during that fall, visited every shipyard and harbor on the Great Lakes. Some ore in small quantities was dribbling down the Lakes in small freighters, but there was nothing, neither freighters nor docks, to handle the tonnage he needed, and no man, shipper or builder, would admit for a minute that such shipping could be either possible or profitable. For one thing, the harbor in Duluth froze up solid four months in the year. What would a man do with that tonnage then? "You don't know what tonnage you've got yet. Come back when you do. Sure, I'm interested, but looks to me you're going off half-cocked." Steve, gaunt, tired, persistent, his coattails flapping in the breeze, became a joke, then a nuisance around the docks.

Back in his office after one of these trips, weary, depressed, he was standing at the window one day wishing he could talk to old Cyrus about the tonnage he had taken around the Horn. The old man would know what he was after. He knew ships. Ships! A quick frown gathered on his brow. He hurried to his desk, still frowning, rummaged around, found what he wanted. The frown vanished and he went down the hall to Curtis' office. "I'm going out on the night train, John," he said abruptly.

Curtis looked up. He worried a lot about Steve lately. "You just got back this morning. What's taking you off again?"

"Nothing definite. A hunch, that's all; but it's big as a barrel. Old Cyrus put me on to it over a year ago. Damned if I can understand why I didn't think of it before. I'll need Harding's report and a statement of my holdings—everything I've got. Get it out for me, will you? Dress it up as much as you can while I go to the house for my grip."

"Where are you going, Steve?"

"East somewhere."

"How long will you be gone this time?"

"No idea." He went out.

Amelia got the same answers to the same inquiries. "Oh, Steve," she wailed. "I've seen so little of you lately. Must you go? Why are you taking your dress suit?" she asked with quick suspicion as she saw it go into the Gladstone.

154

"Because I expect to wear it."

Four days later Steve walked into McCrea's Shipyard, at Newburyport. It was a clear October day, with a light breeze riffling the blue waters of the harbor. The tide was high and the air brisk with the salt tang of the sea. Various craft moored offshore lifted and dipped in the sunshine, and as he walked toward the office, he saw men working on a large yacht cradled on the stocks, her lovely lines as free and graceful as the wings of the sea gulls wheeling above her.

He found Donald McCrea in a small room flooded with light from the wide windows that faced the sea; a spare old man, his steel-rimmed spectacles pushed up into his thin white hair, a sharp-pointed pencil behind his ear. He took his time about looking up from his drawing board. When he did, Steve met the steadiest gaze he had encountered in a long time. "And who may you be?" he asked.

Steve took Cyrus' letter from his pocket and handed it over. "Cyrus Forsyth told me to come to you if I ever needed help in the shipping business," he explained. "I need it now."

The keen eyes looked him over. "Cyrus Forsyth was a good man—the last of a fine line." McCrea handed the letter back to Steve. "But he's dead now and I'll soon be following. I'm taking no more work here."

Steve put the letter in his pocket. "I'm sorry, Mr. McCrea," he said evenly. "I've an idea you'd be interested in this craft I have in mind." He glanced through the open door. "That's a lovely hull you've got out there."

A glint showed in the old man's eyes. "She is. My best and my last. I'll rest with her." They were at the door before the old fellow cocked his head like an inquisitive bird. "And what's this new craft you've got in mind?"

Steve kept a sober face. He looked straight at the designer of yachts. "An ore freighter," he said.

"An ore freighter! Man, are you daft? You come to me for an ore freighter?"

"Yes. And if you'd listen to me for five minutes, you'd know why."

The old man snickered. "A freighter," he repeated. "There's no freighter gone out of this yard since freighters were noble ships under sail, but 'twill cost me nothing to listen to you."

They turned back into the room and Steve told the full story of the situation he was in and his idea for its solution. He pulled a cigar from his pocket. "What I need is something like this," he explained,

155

exhibiting the long black shape, blunt at one end. "A hull that will take anywhere from seven hundred to a thousand tons, move under her own power, cheap to build—and won't roll over," he added.

"A beauty that won't turn in her bed," said McCrea with sarcasm. " 'Tis a novel idea. And where would you build such a contraption?"

"On the Lakes somewhere. There's a man in Duluth, name of Jackson."

McCrea nodded. "William Jackson is a good man for such a craft. I'd like well to see him tackle this one. And have you the cost in mind, young man?"

"I don't care what it costs," returned Steve. "What I want is the ship."

McCrea snickered again with vast enjoyment. "The very words of the man whose yacht that is, and he'll soon be regretting them, I'm thinking."

"Whose yacht is it?"

" 'Tis none of your business, young man," replied McCrea, "but since you've such a love for fine craft, I'll put you at ease. She belongs to Mr. Morrison, a banker—but a good man in spite of it—and with ideas of what he wants as daft as your own."

"So I've heard," said Steve dryly, "but there seems to be an opinion that Morrison gets what he goes after. Will you consider designing this freighter, Mr. McCrea?"

The old man wagged his head. " 'Tis a novel idea," he repeated. "I'll not say I'll consider it, but since Cyrus Forsyth sent you here, I'll give it a wee bit thought. You'll be leaving the cigar for inspiration?"

Steve laughed and laid the cigar on the drawing board. "If you can let me have your decision in a week's time, I'd appreciate it. I'll be at the Waldorf in New York."

On his way out of the shipyard he stopped, and for some time looked thoughtfully at Morrison's big yacht.

Back in New York, while he waited to hear from McCrea, Steve spent a good deal of time in brokers' offices watching the market, took in a couple of shows, and saw several enticing opportunities parading in Peacock Alley that he was too preoccupied to pursue.

One day he went to Pittsburgh to look over Douglas' great steel plant. Douglas, the glint of contract in his eyes, received him cordially and, after a few minutes' chat about the ridge, sent him off with an enthusiastic young man to be properly impressed by the magnitude of his steel business. But after a couple of noisy, bewildering hours watching the dramatic "blow" of molten steel while the complications of the process were yelled in his ear, Steve departed without making any commitment. Not that he was unimpressed. His first glimpse of an enormous enterprise in action sobered him considerably, and on the train to New York he was of two minds about turning back to talk to the little giant who had created this monster. But Pittsburgh was a long way from the ridge. There were other steel mills along the lake shore. Some of them must be getting ready to handle surface ore. He decided to think it over.

CHAPTER 30

McCrea's summons came, and once more Steve walked through the ordered litter of the shipyard. This time a heavy fog hung above the surface of the water and the silence was unbroken save for the muffled sound of a hammer somewhere and the gentle slapping of a halyard on some invisible craft. As Steve made his way to the office, his eye sought and found Morrison's yacht, her lovely nudity veiled in a shroud of mist.

McCrea was standing at his drawing board, his back to the door, his suspenders over the shoulders of his white shirt, exactly as Steve had first seen him, and again he took his time about looking up. "There's the monstrous ugly thing," he said at last, without greeting, pointing to the blueprints pinned to the board. "The most loveless craft ever devised by man—but she's economical to make up for it."

Steve bent over the board, his heart pounding. Broadside on, the ship looked indeed like a long cigar, the sides curving to a blunt point, the long hull as free of obstruction as a barrel. "Going to be difficult to get fore and aft in bad weather, isn't it?" he asked finally, to cover his excitement.

The old man looked pleased. "It is that," he said. "She's a cranky, uncomfortable wench but I'll not clutter up cargo space to please the hands. She's got to be free, man, to swallow her cargo and discharge it. She's no pleasure craft, but she'll do the dirty work."

"She looks capable of it," agreed Steve. "She's what I want." He took one of his big black cigars from his pocket and handed it to McCrea. "That's what she'll look like," he said as he lit one himself. "That's the way I pictured her."

"She'll look more like the back of a whale when she's in ballast," corrected the old man, "but except for that coincidence, she's like nothing ever seen on the face of the deep. 'Tis an insult to the Almighty to float her."

Steve laughed. "She's a whale of a ship for loose cargo. We'd better get her patented before the grain people get on to her."

The old man shook his head. "I'm loath to admit she's a creation

158

of my doing," he said, "but if I make a penny on the patent 'twill ease my shame."

He unpinned the blueprints and rolled them up. "You'll be taking these to Jackson?" Steve nodded. "He'll tell you she'll roll like a bottle," McCrea snickered. "Let him. A little device on Plan Four will teach him not to jump to conclusions. Will's a good man, but impulsive. He'll do well by you."

Steve took the blueprints and looked at the frail old man. "I'll let you know how I make out with Jackson," he said, trying to make light of his emotion. "If he can pull off this 'whaleback,' I'll want one of those yachts someday."

"I'll not be here, lad," said McCrea.

Steve looked a moment longer into the faded, steady eyes, the color of the misty sea beyond the window. "You'll be here and I'll find you," he said. "You can bet on that. Let me know what I owe you—I mean in money. I can pay that. I'm in debt to you for the rest of it. So long, Mr. McCrea. Good luck." He went out, hesitated for a second to get his bearings, then plunged ahead into the fog.

The next day Steve took the step that determined the rest of his life. This was the period when the tired old century gave birth to the last of its lusty offspring; a red-faced infant whose yells would soon be heard all over the face of the earth. Its name was the Age of Steel.

Up to that time most of the iron in the country had come from deep shafts in the south, Michigan and Wisconsin, but the demand for steel far outstripped production and the eyes of the industry were on the alert for more ore. Deep shafts had been put down in northern Minnesota with good results, but so far, there had been little substance to the rumors of surface ore there, and less faith in the stuff, until Hamby's spectacular figure appeared in the region to focus attention on it. Steel men were now interested in surface ore but not yet fully convinced beyond the point of cautious experiment and watchful waiting.

If there was some interest in the rugged iron ridge in northern Minnesota, there was none whatever in the rugged individual who mounted the steps of an impressive building on Wall Street that day and pushed open the heavy bronze door. A neat young man on duty there asked him what he wanted. He wanted to see Mr. Morrison. "I'm sorry, sir," said the young man with a glance at the roll of blueprints. "No one sees Mr. Morrison except by appointment. Perhaps someone else . . ." But something in Steve's eye stopped

159

him and he led the way to an oak-paneled waiting room, where several men were sitting in easy chairs, reading newspapers.

Steve sat down on a leather sofa, laid the blueprints beside him and his hat on the blueprints. Through the door he saw a large, high-ceilinged room where clean-cut young men, as alike as the desks they sat at, worked in hushed activity. At the far end of the room a glass partition spanned the space from wall to wall, and behind it, in plain sight, sat Morrison at an immense mahogany desk. The door was wide open. Occasionally the banker made a brief note on the pad before him. Occasionally he received a visitor or rapped a bell for one of the brisk young men. After an hour or so he pulled out his watch, got up abruptly, and walked out; a heavy, solid block of a man moving with the deliberation of conscious power, without a glance to right or left. That was the last Steve saw of Morrison that day.

Steve waited in that room for three days. The first day he was approached several times with suggestions that he see someone else. He said he was waiting to see Mr. Morrison. After that no one paid any further attention to him, and Steve sat quietly, his hat and the blueprints on the leather seat beside him, watching men come and go in the outer office. During most of this time Morrison sat as stolidly as he did, behind his desk, alone.

In the middle of the fourth morning Steve picked up his blueprints and before any of the astonished men could reach him walked through the open door of the glass partition. Morrison glanced up and Steve found himself looking into black eyes that blazed at him like a pair of headlights. "Get out of here," snapped Morrison.

Steve laid the blueprints on the desk. "These are McCrea's designs for a new freighter to carry iron ore from the ridge in Minnesota to the steel mills," he said.

The eyes bored into him. "If you mean Don McCrea, he never designed a freighter in his life. Get out!"

"He designed this one," insisted Steve, holding his ground. "And it's a better craft than that yacht you've got down there. This one will revolutionize the shipment of ore."

"That's of no interest to me. Get out."

"Thousands of miles of steel rails will come out of the ore shipped in these freighters," said Steve.

There was no change in the expression of the black eyes, but the hand reaching for the bell hesitated. "What's your interest in it?"

"I've got the ore. Here is Dave Harding's report on it. Hamby's

160

been after it, and a few days ago Douglas offered me an option on it."

"If that's a fact, what are you here for?"

"I'm not after an option from anybody. I want a dependable way to ship from the mine to the smelters."

"What's the matter with the rails? They want freight."

"The D. & W. can't get out of Duluth without kowtowing to the North Line. If they do that, the North Line will absorb them. I'm against that—I've reason to think you would be. If I'm mistaken, I'll go elsewhere."

"Have you been elsewhere?"

"No."

"Where do you come from?"

"Out there."

"What's your business?"

"I was a lumberjack until I took up this piece."

"You believe in this surface ore?"

"I've got all my chips on it," said Steve.

For a moment longer the black eyes bored through Steve but he took it, putting up a pretty good imitation of it himself. Then, "Talk this over with Mr. Allison," said Morrison bluntly. "You'll find him in the second office on the left. Tell him I sent you. Good day."

The cold, smooth, steel-gray mathematical machine known as Mr. Allison received Steve without enthusiasm, caressing his jaw with long white fingers while he listened to the details of Steve's problem. Steve poured them out. When he finally ran down, the pale fingers reached for Harding's report, the cold eyes read it, then looked thoughtfully at McCrea's plans. "You have an idea that if you don't put in these freighters the North Line will?"

"They're bound to in the long run," said Steve with conviction. "When these mines get into production the rails, anybody's rails, won't be able to move a quarter of the ore that pours out of there. If we're in there first, we'll be in control. If we're not, the North Line will mop up and build their own freighters. It boils down to that."

He leaned forward in his chair, his arms crossed on the desk. "My future depends on this, Mr. Allison," he said soberly, "but that's not the consideration here. In Harding's opinion the ore coming out of that region will change the future of the steel industry, of the railroads—and of the entire country. Control will mean either orderly expansion or ruthless manipulation by men like Hamby and, in my opinion"—he laid his hand on the blueprints—

161

"the answer lies largely in what happens to these designs of McCrea's."

There was a pause. Allison swung a little in his swivel chair. "All I can say is that I'll look into it, Mr. Bradway," he said at last, coldly. "I presume you have no objection to my getting in touch with the D. & W.?"

"None whatever," said Steve promptly, "but you'd better do it fast before they're committed to the North Line."

"Do you think they already are?"

"Possibly. To some extent. But there's no development to amount to anything out there yet and they're not eager to play in with the North Line if they can avoid it. They went in there in the first place to get Massachusetts Mining out from under." Allison nodded. "If you take over there's still time——"

"I'm not suggesting that," interrupted Allison, sharply.

"I understand that, Mr. Allison." Steve stood up and put on his hat. "But if you uncover the facts out there, I'll lay a bet with you right now Mr. Morrison will come in with both feet."

He walked out of the building into Wall Street. The austere citadels of finance that lined the narrow crooked alley frowned down on another man who had the audacity to dream.

CHAPTER 31

Steve stayed in New York a month while the nebulous vision of a mining-shipping combine slowly hardened into fact. Harding came and made an impressive report; members of the D. & W. sped like needles to a magnet at the beck of Morrison; facts and figures were assembled until finally the picture was clear enough for the bankers to see and the Street began to whisper that Morrison was up to something big.

Steve took an aggressive part in the earlier meetings, but when Allison had wrung every dribble of information out of him, he was hung up to dry while the financial powers took over the making, baking, and serving of the big new financial pie. He was content with that, knowing he held the apples that made this pie and that any time the applecart threatened to run off without him, his Iron Queen was the spoke that would stop it. He was surprised that Douglas wasn't in on these conferences, and one evening he got the answer to that.

"We ought to get this ore," insisted a rotund, bald-headed banker by the name of Babcock. "Bonanza's right there in the toe of the lake and Chicago's at the hub east and west. It's a short haul and we can use every ton of ore we get—and we're ready for it. Douglas has been trying to convert but our plant has been built for this ore." He turned to Steve. "You've seen Douglas' plant, Mr. Bradway. I'd like you to take a look at Bonanza on your way back. It's a new plant but I think you'll agree its advantage lies in that."

The new Midland Mining and Shipping combine was finally formed; the new Eureka Shipping Company underwritten, and the D. & W. Railroad financed for expansion. Morrison, satisfied that the enterprise was under way, agreed to promote the bonds and stock, and Steve went back to the ridge president of the Iron Queen Mining Company. On paper he came away from New York potentially a rich man, but enormous loans from the bankers at high interest had gone into the development of his mine and it would have to move fast to get, and keep, ahead of these commitments. He had

163

pledged every nickel of his own resources to development and he was under no delusion as to the action of these bighearted financiers if he failed in production within the given time. Meanwhile, he could dig his own pit without interference.

On the way back he visited the new Bonanza steel plant on the lake shore south of Chicago. It was, as Babcock said, a new plant, but there was an air of progressive activity about it that contrasted favorably with the ponderous operations in the big plant in Pittsburgh.

"You think you can handle surface ore in quantity?" Steve asked the young engineer who was piloting him through the maze of half-finished structures.

"That's what we're here for," replied his guide. "We believe the future of steel lies in that stuff you've got up there. We're putting everything we've got into it. We think we've got the capacity in that big blast furnace you saw back there."

"When will you know?"

The young man stopped and turned to Steve. "We know now," he said. "In a year—two at most—if we get the ore, we'll have rails radiating out of here like a spider's web, all over the West."

"It looks like a deal," said Steve, and with that gleaming, silvery spider's web flickering in his thoughts he went on to Duluth to see Jackson.

"Sure, I can build her. Half a dozen, if you want 'em," declared the shipbuilder. "McCrea told you that, didn't he? But it'll take time. A year, anyhow. If I get my plates through fast, I ought to be able to give you a trial run down the Lakes before the freeze-up next fall. That suit you?"

"Fine!" Steve nodded. "We'll have a load ready to ship by that time. See if you can't jack it up to a thousand tons."

Jackson shook his head. "Like I told you. Better stick to seven—eight hundred on this first one till we see how she handles. That's a big load," he cautioned. "Where they going to put her dock?"

"That's up to the D. & W. Keep in touch with them. Fellow by the name of Baker will be working it. He's a good man." Steve held out his hand. "Go ahead, Jackson. Get your plates started."

When he got back to Alturos the next morning, he went straight to the office to find Curtis going over the terms of a clearing contract with McCarthy. "You got my letter, John? Good," he said, cutting short the greetings. "Glad to find you here, Mac. Saves a day if we can clean up now. How far along are you?"

They went over details of the clearing job—payments, equipment, crew, camp supplies—McCarthy protesting, laboring with a pencil until finally Steve shoved back his chair. "It boils down to this, McCarthy," he said, circling a spot on the blueprint. "You'll have a spur in from the main line at this point. Get ready for that first so we won't waste time hauling in by team. Then log off the timber and clear this area here by May fifteenth, ready for Harding to take over. You've got six months to do it. That's the gist of it. If you can't do it, say so. I'll get Cooper up from Duluth. He wants it and he's a good man. And don't give me any more talk about advance payment. Your credit's good and the job is your lookout. We're not paying for it until it's delivered."

McCarthy, red in the face, squirmed in his chair. "That's tough on me," he blustered. "I got a big camp to construct and stock, let alone keepin' it goin'. Take every dollar I've got, and how do I know I'll get paid? I don't trust you no further than you trust me and that ain't a rod."

Steve nodded. "Right," he said. "We'll put payment in escrow if a boost in credit is what you're after. Think it over. If you want the job on these terms, start tomorrow morning."

McCarthy got to his feet and reached for his battered hat. "You puttin' up any more of them bonuses?" he asked slyly.

Steve's sober look didn't relax. "You're not working for the D. & W. this time, McCarthy; you're working for me. Remember that when you start chiseling nickels and dimes. So long."

After the contractor had gone, trying to hide the satisfaction that shone through him like a light, Curtis settled back to hear the details of the negotiations in New York, but Steve asked him first about the boy born while he was away. "What's he like, John?" he asked, leaning forward, as if the subject was the only one of any interest to him. "How did Mary get along?"

Curtis' sensitive face turned pink. "That's kind of you, Steve. She had a hard time. I never want to go through that again, but we got the boy." Then parental fervor took over. "It's incredible! Seven and a half pounds and with a yell you can hear across the street!" A shy smile touched his lips. "He's like you in some ways—hangs on to anything he grabs." He hesitated. "I—we'd like to call him Steve if that's all right with you."

"Nothing I'd like better," agreed Steve heartily. "Give Mary my congratulations and tell her I'll be over tomorrow. Now, about this

165

New York business." He piled papers on the desk. "They're a lusty bunch there too, if we can raise 'em."

It was late that night when Steve walked up the path to his home, past the outline of the stags against the brilliant, metallic glitter of the stars. The night was cold and still. Not much snow had yet fallen but the relentless approach of winter hung in the thin, clear air like the sound of a bell, not heard but felt. Steve felt it. McCarthy would have to hustle to get the spur through and his camp in before the heavy snow held him up. It was a close job, at best. He went up the steps and into Amelia's emotional embrace.

"Oh, Steve," she cried, clinging to him. "It's been so long and so lonely without you. Why didn't you come home when you got here? I've been waiting all afternoon and it's after eleven. What kept you, darling?"

"Business." He kissed her lightly, picked up his grip, and started up the stairs. Amelia followed, the long crimson sash of her blue dressing gown trailing behind her.

"But I can't see why you didn't come home first," she persisted. "Most men would after being away so long."

"Most men would, but I didn't."

"That's a nice way to talk after keeping me waiting all these hours," she began sharply, but checked herself. When they got to the bedroom, she sat down at her shining bird's-eye maple dressing table and picked up her hairbrush. "Did you have a good time in New York?" she asked, her voice bright with suspicion.

"You might call it that. Yes." Steve unhitched his watch chain and unbuttoned his waistcoat. "I got what I went for."

"Oh, darling, how wonderful!" Amelia spun around. "Tell me about it. I'm so glad. Then you did make a lot of money?"

"Money? No. It will be some time before I make any money. On the contrary, I'm short of it. You'll have to take it easy for a while. Cut down where you can."

"What?" The quick red ran over her neck and face. "Cut down? You mean you've actually lost money on this trip?"

"No, but I've put everything I've got behind the work I'm doing. It won't pay for a couple of years, perhaps longer. In the meantime we'll have to go easy."

The hairbrush went down with a clatter. Amelia jumped up. "I've never heard anything so ridiculous in my life!" she cried. "After all your big talk do you mean to tell me you've come back worse off than when you went—that you expect me to go on living like this—

166

cut down on what few comforts I have? I won't do it, I tell you! I can't stand it! This life is killing me! Oh, I was so in hopes it was over. It's too cruel of you after all I've put up with."

Steve pulled his shirt out of his pants and over his head. His voice came muffled through its folds. "You'll put up with it and behave, if you stay with me." The shirt came off, revealing a stern and tired face. "I've told you before you can quit any time you feel like it. I mean it. In the meantime, hold your tongue. I've had enough of it."

For a moment Amelia stared at him while the angry color drained out of her face. She sat down slowly and turned to her mirror, her pale eyes darkening as she covertly watched her husband's strong, male body emerge from his undershirt and pants. "Oh, Steve," she coaxed presently, "don't fly up so over every little thing I say. Of course, I'm disappointed. You must be, too. I understand that. It's hard to fail when you expected so much but I didn't mean to reproach you." The dressing gown slipped from her shoulders, disclosing her pretty rounded figure in a dainty, lacy nightgown and she raised her white arms, brushing her hair that shone like a curling nimbus around her head. "Don't look so gloomy, darling." She smiled at him over her shoulder. "You're home now and it can't be as bad as all that. Everything will come out all right. I'm sure of it."

Steve grunted and got into bed. Soon his wife's soft body snuggled close to his own, and for a moment it was a comfort to feel her there. But Amelia had been too liberal with the bath salts, and the cloying fragrance, musty-sweet in the warmth of the bedclothes, touched off the wrong response. The familiar trick disgusted him. Tired, repelled, he turned on his side, gave a long deep sigh, and in two minutes was fast asleep.

CHAPTER 32

The winter that followed Steve's return from New York was remarkable for two reasons; it was the coldest winter in the history of the Northwest and it saw the first activities of the Midland Mining and Shipping Company. Its stock, promoted by Morrison and underwritten by a group of powerful financial interests, was now on the market, where it sat fluttering feebly while waiting for results in the West. These results, for better or worse, largely depended on what happened at the Iron Queen mine.

The Iron Queen was not the only iron mine in that region but it was, potentially, by far the largest and it lay now under a blanket of seven feet of snow in a temperature of thirty degrees below zero. McCarthy was frantic. "I tell you I can't work no faster," he shouted at Steve as they stood watching teams and men floundering through the drifts. "We ain't had snow like this in twenty years. Men can't make time in weather like this. You can't expect it."

Steve, who spent a good deal of time at the camp lending a hand where he could, gazed at the scene with a heart as cold as the frost that clawed at his face. He knew from experience that clearing under these conditions was next to impossible. He straightened up. "It's got to be done, Mac," he said. "No getting around it. Get in more men."

"Yeah? Who's goin' to pay 'em? I'm figured close on this contract. I got that spur in. What more do you want?"

Steve looked hard at him through eyelids rimmed with frost. "You know damn well what I want. You figured on it. Don't try any of that talk on me. If you don't deliver this job by May, when Harding comes in, you lose every nickel you put into it. That's final."

The harassed contractor snatched his cap from his head and hurled it in the snow. "By God," he exploded. "I'll quit now if you say so. What's got in you, Steve? A couple of weeks one way or the other ain't goin' to make such a hell of a difference. You got to give a man a little leeway on a job like this. Look at that snow. I'm behind a month now. I can't make up all that time and you know it."

"You can if any man can." Steve laid his hand on the angry man's shoulder. "There's no leeway for anybody on this job, Mac. Get in more men." McCarthy started to protest again. "Hold on, wait a minute. Tell you what I'll do. Get in the men you need to make up this lost time and I'll give you my written agreement to pay for them if you deliver this job when Harding steps off the train. How does that suit you?"

McCarthy leaned down to pick up his cap and hide the greed that leaped to his eyes. "I'll take a shot at it," he grumbled. He gave Steve a quick look. "I'll need twice the crew I've got now to make it."

"Get 'em," said Steve.

He left the camp, assured that the contractor's cupidity would pull him through more than seven feet of snow. But clearing the land for Harding was merely the first step. During those winter months far more important steps harried his imagination and sapped his energy day after day and night after night. Things were not pulling together as he had been confident they would on that triumphant return from New York the previous fall. His trips to Duluth depressed him. Jackson couldn't get started on his ore freighter. "I can't get my plates out of those sons of bitches," he fumed as they sat huddled over the stove in his office one day in February. "If this goes on, we'll be froze up next fall before I can get her off the stocks. That's the hell of it. I could save time on the next one if I could take a load down and see how she handles. She's a new craft. No telling how she'll take to it at first."

"I know." Steve nodded. "I've been thinking about that myself. We can't have any experiments after we begin regular service. That ship has got to move and keep moving, Jackson."

The shipbuilder drew a long breath. "I'm not too worried about that," he protested. "She's sound, as far as that goes. McCrea couldn't go wrong on that. It's those damn plates not coming through. Well, I guess we'll make out all right. I'll do my best—you can bet on that. How's the D. & W. coming along with that dock? That young fellow, Baker, was in here the other day. He seems to have things lined up pretty well."

"He would," agreed Steve. "He's a good man. If we had more like him, we'd pull through."

But the D. & W. showed no such spirit. Bred in Massachusetts Mining and dominated by conservative stockholders, the board hung back. Days and weeks were spent in angry dispute over details while the broad aspect of a united endeavor was lost in wrangling for individual advantage. Steve's persistent efforts to come to some decision were met with frigid resistance. "There's no sense in committing ourselves to all that rolling stock until we know what you've got to haul," they protested sourly. "You haven't sunk a pick in there yet. When you've got anything to haul, we'll be there to haul it."

"Like hell you will." Steve's voice rasped with angry impatience. "You know the potential tonnage I've got up there. You've been financed to haul it. Every ton of ore I've contracted for will be on the surface a year from this spring whether you're there to haul it or not. Gentlemen"—he paused, leaning forward, his eyes intent as he searched the faces of the men around the table—"we have a chance to participate in the biggest industrial development this country has ever seen, and our success as individuals, as well as that of the combine, depends on co-operation. Any link that fails to hold a year from now will be thrown out and another forged without mercy. There is no possible question about that. The only question is whether we survive as we stand now. We will if we prepare to meet our several obligations. I intend to meet mine. The shipping company will meet its schedule. The only weak spot likely to develop is lack of rolling stock for this railroad." He stood up, his tall, powerful frame dominating the table. "What you do with this railroad is your business until it affects mine. This lack of rolling stock does affect mine. Unless you contract for those ore cars within a month, I shall report it to Morrison as inexcusable negligence." He slammed out of there, sweating.

Steve aged during that winter. The flesh left his bones, the thick, black thatch on his head looked as if the frost had touched it, and his step slowed to the persistent plodding of a man with a pack on his back. When, on a fair spring day in May, Harding swung off the train where the spur to the mine went in from the main line, he was shocked by the look of the gaunt man there to meet him, but after a quick glance, greeted him casually enough. "Well, Steve, here we are. I'm glad to see you."

For a full moment Steve gripped the firm hand thrust into his without speaking. "Glad to see me!" he repeated with difficulty. "Glad to see me! Dave—I can't——" He stopped, straightened. "We're ready for you. Everything's in good shape."

Harding turned away to give him a chance. "It looks like it," he said easily. "You've got quite a settlement here." His eye caught .

the sign FORSYTH, MINN. beside the track. "That's nice, Steve." He smiled. "We'll have a town here one of these days. Has the steam shovel come through?"

Steve was all right now. The ten years picked up in the last six months dropped away. "It's here and set up," he replied. "McCarthy has been using it for stripping. It works fine." He waved his arm, and McCarthy, who had been watching from a handcar on the spur, came forward. "Here's the man who pulled it off, Dave."

McCarthy, swelling with pride, shook hands. "That's a fact, Mr. Harding," he swaggered. "It was a tough job but all you've got to do now is go ahead."

They piled Harding's gear on the handcar and trundled through the woods, where the snow still lingered in the shadows, to the clearing, where men and teams were slithering in a sea of sticky muck already colored by the rich red gravel mingled with the top- soil in the scrapers. The squat, low-pitched log cabins of the camp were set back some distance from this area, and after looking at the clanking, active scene for some moments Steve and Harding made their way to the shack, where the engineer's gear had been dumped, and Harding got into his woods clothes.

"You've been through hell here, Steve," he remarked gravely as he laced up his boots.

Steve, relaxed on the bunk in a sweet stupor of relief, didn't reply for a moment. "Well, not exactly," he said finally. "As I under- stand it, there's no snow in hell. If you're satisfied, we can forget it."

"I'm more than satisfied. You say this man McCarthy wants to stay on. How many men has he got now?"

"About fifty. Most of them have their wives and children in those shacks down by the track. They're set to stay."

"Couldn't ask for a better start. We'll see how this crew works out and increase as we need it. By the way, Tom Baker put that spur in, didn't he? He worked for me for a time in Utah. He's a good man. I'd like to have him in here. Do you think he'd consider it?"

"I don't know. He's building a dock for the D. & W. now but I don't believe he's under contract with them. I'll have a talk with him and find out."

Under Harding's energetic management the chaos in the woods rapidly took on the shape and function of a mine. McCarthy, puffing with importance, drove his men with the relentless savagery of a Pharaoh building a pyramid, and by the end of July enough covering had been stripped from the Iron Queen to see what she looked like.

171

"Well, Dave, what do you think?" asked Steve one day as they stood on the rim of the scoop-out pit, gazing down at the dusky red gravel.

"There's not the slightest doubt of it now," replied Harding emphatically. "It's there. A world of it. It's a damn big mine. From what I know now, I'm convinced of at least twenty years of life for it—perhaps more." He turned and looked at Steve. "I can't understand it," he went on. "I don't mean the mine—that's astonishing enough—but why you hung on to this godforsaken piece of wilderness. There was no sense in it. What made you do it?"

"Damned if I know, Dave," confessed Steve. "I don't know and never will—but from the day I went through here with Cramer, I've been seeing this spot exactly as we see it now. I knew there was no sense in it. You told me so yourself, but I couldn't cut loose from it. Call it luck—I don't know." He paused, his eyes on the sullen red mass at his feet. "The Iron Queen!" he muttered. "For better or for worse." He turned, a strange expression on his face. "You know, Dave," he said, "I've got a funny feeling about this thing. I'd like to bet that if any other man went into that old girl she'd be barren as a barrel."

They turned and walked back slowly to Harding's office. "By the way," said Harding as Steve was about to leave, "there's a man around here wants a job. Says he knows you. Fellow by the name of Matt. Do you know him?"

Steve hesitated for a fraction of a second. Matt here! Was Kit with him somewhere in one of those shacks clustered around the siding? "Yes," he said, "I know him. He's a good worker. Give him a job if you can."

"He wants to live in that old cabin of yours down by the lake," Harding went on. "I told him I'd speak to you about it."

"Sure. Let him have it. He lived with me there years ago when this thing started. Tell him I'd like to see him."

But several days went by before he saw Matt. Finally one evening he walked down to the cabin and looked through the open door. Amelia's things had long since been removed and the look and smell of the little room jarred awake sleeping memories better left undisturbed. He stood for a moment watching Matt; not as spry as he once was, busy at the old stove frying salt pork. "Hey, what you doing there?"

Matt, fork in hand, spun around and his swarthy face lit up with a quick grin. "What you standin' out there for?" he shouted. "I got buckwheats. Come an' get it."

172

Something stuck in Steve's throat as he clapped the little man on the back. "You took your time about showing up, you old polecat," he grumbled. "Where've you been? Why haven't I heard from you?"

"Me?" Matt's grin broadened. "What you think? I ain't chasin' no big boss. You come; not me. You got a bottle?" Steve thrust one in his hand. "Good! We get drunk, eh—like old times?" He knocked the top off the bottle with a practiced whack, filled two tin cups with whiskey, poured his down his throat on a single breath, and began beating the pancakes while Steve sat on the bunk and let the walls speak to him. They ate and drank and talked until long after dark. Finally Steve pulled out his watch, a heavy gold one Amelia had given him when they were married. It took him a minute to read it. "I've got to get going, Matt. Almost train time." He heaved himself up. "Got to be in the office tomorrow, early. Important," he added with disgust.

They started up the trail to the track. From some distance away through the trees the glimmer of flares and the thump of machinery came from the mine working on the night shift, but it was dark and silent where they were, and at last Steve came out with it. "Matt," he said, "did you ever find Kit?"

"Kit? Naw." Steve caught the flash of Matt's grin in the dark. "Never went after her. Time I got to Haley I seen you was right. Ain't none of my business what she done."

"Why didn't you come back?"

"What you think? I got money you give me in my pants. I go on down to Clearwater, where the bunch is. We bust up Clearwater fine that year but I ain't no good when I get in camp, and I get fired. I get two, three jobs—sawmill, raftin' downriver like you done. Then I get the rheumatiz bad last winter and I think, by gar, I find Steve now."

Steve laughed. "Harding made you a timekeeper, didn't he? That's a good job for a man with the rheumatiz. Better hang on to it. You got a watch?"

"Me? Naw. I don't need no watch. I got the sun."

The headlight of the train pierced the long, dark lane up the track. Steve unhitched his watch and pressed it into Matt's hand. "Here, take this. Take it," he insisted as Matt pulled back. "If Harding finds out you haven't got a watch on that gang, you'll get fired here, too. I want you around, Matt."

He climbed aboard and watched the lights of the mine slide past.

173

Then with his head on the back of the seat, his eyes closed, his body satiated with Matt's buckwheats, Steve fell asleep. The last thought that drifted through his mind was that he hadn't felt as fine as this since he walked out of Morrison's office almost a year ago. That thought stayed with him through his dreams.

CHAPTER 33

That fall another move was made that considerably affected Steve's future. He moved to Duluth. During the previous winter the coquettish little house on the hill in Alturos had been a spectacular failure in its contest with the cold and Amelia had been anything but silent in her suffering. All that summer she continued to harass Steve with her demands for a house in Duluth until finally he bought a substantial stone mansion from a lumber king who was stepping out for Chicago and glad to get rid of it at a fraction of its cost.

It proved to be a good move. The appearance in Duluth of Amelia, daughter of Massachusetts Mining, boosted his credit when he needed it most, and when the handsome, massive furniture, the rugs, and crimson draperies from Beacon Street had been installed, the meetings of the Browning Club in Amelia's drawing room, her teas, and euchre parties became the object of intense social rivalry in the lively young city. These ladies did, indeed, labor under the handicap of not having been born in Boston, but what they lacked in accent they made up in energy. They studied French, waved checks at opera and concert managers, dined and danced all winter, and in summer, armed with the winter's crop of irregular French verbs, a heavy money pocket dangling from a belt around the corset, sailed for Europe. Amelia, who thoroughly enjoyed her supremacy among these ladies, joined the exodus, and Steve joined the other husbands in enthusiastic support of it.

This solved the problem of Victor's vacations. Amelia now took him with her on these trips, and Mr. Stoddard, who brought the tall, handsome youth to New York to meet his mother, listened with flattering consideration to her plans for his future. It was agreed that Victor should continue his education in Boston, go to Harvard, and then to Oxford. By that time his mother would have a home for him in New York. Victor, his dark eyes lowered, his hands thrust in the pockets of his first long trousers, listened to these discussions without a ray of expression on his face.

175

Amelia never went to Boston on these trips to the East. If Stoddard knew the reason for this, her sharp eyes saw no sign of it but she, herself, was keenly aware of it, and the memory of her last visit to the city of her birth burned with intense and increasing bitterness.

It had occurred in the spring after that dreadful, cold winter in Alturos, not long after Harding's arrival at the mine. Harding had been a disappointment to Amelia. She seldom saw him but it was a satisfaction to have a man of his social background working for her husband and she looked forward to spreading the news among her friends in Boston when she went there that spring to bring Victor back with her.

It never occurred to her not to go to her grandfather's house. Except for the brief, unhappy years of her marriage to Hamilton, she had always lived there. It was her home, and she returned to it as automatically as a horse to its stall. Catherine wouldn't like it, but that merely increased her pleasure in the visit, and as she mounted the steps to the familiar front door, she smiled behind her veil at the discomfort she was about to cause. A servant she had never seen before preceded her to the drawing room. "Mrs. Bradway," he announced.

Catherine, in a gray silk dress trimmed with black velvet bands, her seed-pearl choker around her scrawny neck, her liver-spotted face as cold as a tombstone in December, was seated behind the tea table. She turned her head. "Ah, Amelia," she said calmly. "I've been expecting you this last half hour. Let me give you a cup of tea. You look exhausted. Do sit down—no, not there—in the yellow chair if you don't mind." Her thin, ring-laden hands moved over the teacups. "I've forgotten how you like your tea. Ah, yes, lemon, of course." She passed the cup and tea plate. "I'm sorry I can't give you your old room; it is my upstairs sitting room now," she droned on placidly, "but you will be quite comfortable in the pink room. Such a pretty room since I've done it over." She sipped her tea. "May I ask you, Amelia, how long you expect to be with us?"

Amelia picked up her teacup. "I'm sure I don't know," she answered deliberately. "I'll be doing a good bit of shopping for my new house and seeing my friends, so there's no telling how long I may stay. Does it matter?"

"Your friends? Really? I'm very much afraid Horace will not approve of that."

"Approve of it!" Amelia's cup clattered as she put it down. "What has Horace to do with it? What concern is it of his?"

Catherine sighed. "It is very much his concern, Amelia. Since we are on this unpleasant subject, I must tell you your telegram was a severe shock to him."

"Shock to him? He knew I was coming for Victor."

"Oh, dear, dear!" Catherine shook her head. "This is most unfortunate. We supposed you knew it. I understand from Horace that his grandmother means to keep Victor with her this summer. She seems to feel that the poor child came back in a dreadful state of nerves last fall and she is unwilling to risk it again. I cannot understand why you were not informed of it."

"I never heard of anything so ridiculous in my life," Amelia declared, a shrill edge in her voice. "State of nerves, indeed! Victor was perfectly well last summer and I certainly intend to take him back with me now. This is just another scheme to keep him from me and I don't mean to put up with it. It was agreed that he should spend his vacations with me."

"I know nothing of your affairs, Amelia." Catherine's cold eyes rested placidly on her guest's flushed face. "But I do know that Mrs. Hamilton is in Saratoga Springs, and that Victor is with her. However, that is your affair. Your tea is cold. Let me give you another cup. . . . No? Perhaps you would like to go to your room to rest awhile before Horace comes home. He will be here shortly."

Amelia's knees shook as she stood up. "How kind you are, Catherine," she said with bitter sarcasm. "The pink room, isn't it? I believe I know where it is although I'm not very familiar with the servants' quarters."

Catherine poured herself another cup of tea, carefully adding the sugar and cream before she spoke. "Don't be tiresome, Amelia. You know perfectly well I mean the old sewing room. It's a pretty room now although, of course, pink is not your color." She looked up. "And do try to show Horace some consideration. He is so upset, poor man. The scandal of your marriage has only just begun to die down, and now it will be stirred up again if you appear socially." She shook her head. "Really, Amelia, it is too much to ask. You must think of your brother's feelings. After all the humiliation he has suffered, to come back here and expect——"

"Humiliation!" Amelia's face flamed with anger. "How dare you speak to me like this? You, of all people! Horace should be well accustomed to humiliation since his marriage to you. How dare you sit in my own home, behind my mother's tea set, and speak to me like this? Even Horace——"

177

Catherine covered her ears with her ringed hands. "Amelia, do control yourself. I've said nothing to cause such an exhibition of bad manners. This is no longer your home. You know that. But since you have chosen to come here, Horace does insist that you behave with some consideration for him. That is not too much to ask, surely."

Amelia, blazing with rage, rushed to the bellpull and yanked it. "This is intolerable," she gasped. "Intolerable! Nothing would induce me to stay under this roof. Call a cab and put my bags into it at once," she ordered when the servant appeared. She turned and pointed dramatically to the tea table. "And pack that tea set. It belongs to me."

"Do nothing of the kind, Herbert," said Catherine with composure. "Mrs. Bradway is mistaken, but you may call a cab for her if she insists."

The startled servant advanced into the room as Amelia, blind with fury, rushed toward Catherine. "How dare you lie like that?" she shrilled. "That tea set is mine! It belonged to my mother and I've used it all my life. I supposed it was in storage until you had the effrontery to use it in my presence. How much more have you appropriated while my back was turned? We'll see about that! I shall have this house searched. That man will pack that tea set or I swear I'll smash every piece of it."

Two red spots burned on Catherine's high cheekbones but she kept her composure. "Very well, Herbert; you may pack the tea set." She stood up. "And bring Mrs. Bradway a glass of wine. I fear she is not well." She inclined her head courteously and crossed the room. At the door she turned, her thin hands clasped at her waist, and regarded her guest with calm detachment. "If you change your mind, Amelia, you are quite welcome to stay here, but apparently Horace was right; we could expect nothing but unpleasantness from your visit." She left the room.

Amelia flew out of the house and down the steps, but the instant the front door closed behind her, she realized her mistake and turned swiftly to re-enter—but it was too late. For a moment she stood shivering, wondering where she could go, more frightened than she had ever been in her life, while the stern, hostile façades of the familiar old houses on Beacon Street looked down upon her. The cab drove up. Herbert, with her bags and the tea set, helped her into it. "Where to, madam?"

Amelia started. "What did you say? Where? I . . ." Her mind

raced, trying to think. A hotel? Impossible! "To the station," she said. "Hurry."

In less than two hours after her arrival in Boston Amelia was back on a train for New York, her head throbbing, too ill to know or care why she was there; but finally the monotonous rhythm of the wheels penetrated the emotional tumult in her mind, and her thoughts settled into a passionate hatred of Boston. "They'll pay for this," she whispered with the wheels. "They'll pay for this! They'll pay for this!"

By the time she got to New York, Amelia was really ill, and for two days she lay in her bed in the Waldorf, too weak to move. On the morning of the third day she went to the window, parted the lace curtains, and stood looking down at the glittering procession of carriages on Fifth Avenue. The sunshine of a clear June day seemed to gild everything it touched; the dresses of the ladies, the tin cup of the organ-grinder across the street. She stood for a long time gazing at the opulence of the bright scene, and when she turned away, her mind was made up. It would take time, but from this day forward every act of her life had one objective; she was determined to live in New York. Her first act was to start packing to go home.

If Steve was surprised by his wife's early return without Victor, he gave no sign of it and Amelia made no explanation. She spent that summer planning the move into the new house in Duluth.

CHAPTER 34

During the winter that followed the Bradways' move to Duluth, the members of the Midland Mining and Shipping corporation worked energetically toward the fulfillment of their first commitments that would come due the following spring. The prospect looked good. Ore in sufficient quantity was coming out of the Iron Queen; the D. & W. had the rolling stock to move it, and Jackson's big freighter lay gripped in the ice of the harbor receiving her last few bolts. No question about it, Midland would come through, but there was considerable question in the minds of certain financiers who were watching him with the patience of a cat at a mousehole whether Steve Bradway would be with it when it did.

More than once during that winter Steve had been within an ace of defeat, and defeat was never closer than on that spring day when Harding's first shipment of ore poured down the chutes into the new freighter. The big ship grunted as she took the heavy red mass; then she settled to it, and with flags flying, whistles blowing, she thrust her blunt nose into the ice still heaving in the harbor and started on her maiden voyage down the Lakes to her consort squatting on the shore hundreds of miles away and roaring with impatience for her arrival. The band blared, the crowd on the dock cheered and waved, and the frock-coated group of officials on the end of the dock solemnly raised their silk hats.

Amelia, standing a little to one side with Harding, looked charming in a delicate dove-gray costume, but she didn't feel it. She was certain her dress would be stained by that horrible red stuff, and the wind was wrenching at her hat. "What?" she asked.

"He's a great man, isn't he?" repeated Harding, his eyes on Steve, who stood at the end of the dock, tall, gaunt, his hat lifted high, as if he had forgotten to replace it. "There's not a man among them to approach him."

"How kind of you to say that," she smiled. "Steve is wonderful, of course, but this is your day, really. All that ore! You must be feeling very proud."

180

Harding turned and looked at her. Years ago, at dancing school in Boston, he had detested this particular female, and renewed acquaintance with her had done nothing to dispel the feeling. "I've done nothing to be proud of," he said coldly. "Any mining man could have done my job, but not one man in a million could have done Steve's. He has carried, and is carrying, an incredible load, with no help from anyone that I am aware of."

"Really? Then you must be unaware of what I've been through," she retorted acidly. "And as for having no help, if it hadn't been for my family——"

"Damn your family!" said Harding, under cover of the cheering.

The *Cyrus* was down the harbor by now, and the crowd began to move away. Some of the more daring citizens approached the official group with loud congratulations. One man among them stood silent, his black gaze fixed on Steve. "You son of a bitch," he muttered. His glare raked Steve from head to foot, then he spat contemptuously and lumbered off through the crowd.

The rosy-cheeked little banker, there from New York to watch Bonanza's angle of this affair, turned to Steve. "That was Hamby, wasn't it?" he inquired genially.

"Yes."

"What's the matter? You having trouble with him?"

Steve grinned. "Trouble? No. He's had a little trouble with me. I turned him down and he doesn't like it. He's a poor loser."

"I thought he was a pretty big operator."

"He makes that impression on some people," said Steve dryly. "My wife's over there. I'd like you to meet her."

As he ambled across the dock to meet old Forsyth's granddaughter, the banker's jovial expression didn't change, but his mind did. He liked Steve. Better ease him along a little more. Wouldn't do to have Hamby mixing in here.

And defeat backed away for a while.

The sailing of the *Cyrus* marked the beginning of Midland Mining and Shipping as a going concern. It was not perfect; various hitches of one sort or another had to be ironed out, but by the end of another year the departure of a "whaleback" headed for the smelters caused no further comment, and the big ships plowed the Lakes with monotonous regularity. In the meantime, Midland stock, largely dependent on the Iron Queen, bubbled nervously at the bottom of the list, waiting for the great mine to get into her stride. Production rose steadily with the inevitability of the tide until profits finally

181

lapped quietly over costs, and with that the simmering stock began to boil as the heat of speculation took hold.

Gradually pressure on Steve lessened, and with Curtis' cautious guidance behind him he began to liquidate his loans. It took him five years and the major part of his other holdings to do it but, by the end of that time, he owned outright, free and clear, a solid majority of stock in the Iron Queen. He stood alone one day in the heavy silence of a bank vault, staring at a bundle of papers in his hand. Slowly he closed his fist hard and the certificates crackled in his hand with the dry rustle of dead leaves on a trail. He thrust them into a steel box, slammed it shut, and walked out.

By this time the Bradways were the accepted leaders of the lively little city of Duluth and the dinners they gave were the outstanding events of the social season. These dinners were served with all, and a little more, of the formality of Beacon Street, and civic pride watched with satisfaction as guests from New York, Pittsburgh, and Chicago became acutely aware of Amelia's charm and of Steve, immaculate and genial, standing above the roast at the end of the long table vigorously whetting a long, sharp knife.

But after the guests had departed and Steve had hauled off his stiff shirt and gone to bed, Amelia, her charm replaced by a speculative frown, sat at her desk busily writing in a little black book. This book went with her everywhere, on her visits to New York, on her trips to Europe. It was a tired-looking volume, but Amelia cherished it, for as time went on it contained a long and serviceable list of names and addresses.

Steve, too, went frequently to New York but he didn't bother with any list, and when on occasion he found himself in the position of the feted guest, he smiled with amusement, wondering what notes were being taken about him. But his work was in Duluth. Plenty of it; his desk piled high with it. Paper work. Board meetings. Conferences. Contracts. Trips to the mine. He enjoyed his trips to the mine, tramping around in his old woods clothes, listening while Harding explained what was going on. But lately he had begun to wonder what he was doing there. Try as he would, he could no longer identify himself with what he saw, or recognize himself as the man who had brought it about. He felt ill at ease, a stranger there.

This feeling came to a head one day as he stood with Harding watching the panting steam shovels gouging tons from the red earth, men swarming like flies in the great open pit. Both men were silent, preoccupied, until Harding finally spoke. "Steve," he hesitated, went on. "You know what the old Queen means to me, don't you?"

Steve knew at once what was coming. He'd been dreading it for some time and a curious sadness, almost of foreboding, filled his heart. "Well, Dave?" he said.

"It's this, Steve. There's a tough job coming up in South America. Copper. They want me down there. I don't mean tomorrow," he went on hastily, "but it's on the way, and I'd like a crack at it. I wouldn't think of it if I were needed here, but I'm not. I'm through here. You know that. What you need now is a good production man. Any one of a dozen men I know could make a better job of that than I can. To tell the truth"—he tried to smile—"I lose interest in the stuff once it's on the table."

Steve was silent for a long moment. "I know how you feel, Dave," he said at last. "I wouldn't hold you if I could. Get some man you can depend on in here as soon as you feel like it." He paused again, looking across the big pit at the spot where his cabin had once stood. The little shack was gone and old Matt had died in it two winters ago. The tall trees were gone, and the lake shone like a reproachful eye in the raw landscape. The challenge, the pursuit, the schemes, and dreams that had started that night more than fifteen years ago by the campfire with Cramer were gone. What he saw now, sprawling at his feet, was a mine making money. Beyond that it had no significance for him. Well, that's what he wanted—money. He had it. He ought to be satisfied, but the load didn't lift from his heart. He turned to Harding. "You're right, Dave," he said. "We've done all we can for the old Queen. Both of us. She has no further use for either of us. She's on her feet now."

They turned and walked slowly toward Harding's office. Steve held out his hand. "All right, Dave," he said. "Get squared away with this new man as soon as you feel like it. The fact is," he added thoughtfully, "I've been thinking of pulling out for New York myself."

PART TWO

CHAPTER 1

Steve Bradway's growth paralleled the development of his mine, which in turn paralleled the growth of the Steel Age, which, from 1888 to 1905, grew with incredible rapidity. Its branches spread, its roots sought greedily for more iron, and large numbers of ambitious men hastened to promote its growth and gather its fruits. The production of surface ore developed into a wild stampede to find the stuff and hustle it out of the ground, and a large part of these efforts centered around the iron ridge in northern Minnesota, where some fifteen miles south of Alturos the ugly, serrated open pit of the Iron Queen continued to increase in depth and area, pouring forth a steady, turgid flood of red ore, day and night, without sign of exhaustion or diminishing quality. Year after year the great heart of the mine pulsed on. It is pulsing yet.

When Steve moved to New York in 1900 he was as vigorous as his mine, a mature man with a weathered face, strong and clean-cut in the planes and angles of the bone structure, a drooping black mustache that concealed a hard mouth, a pair of steady green eyes of unusual intensity, and a thick, rough thatch of black hair sprinkled with gray to top it off. He was handsome in his strength, dressed well, and carried himself with confidence.

Curtis was with him in his office on Wall Street. The space was modest but the address was excellent. Steve's own room was small and sparsely furnished. The only embellishment in it were an enlarged photograph of the Iron Queen, a rugged scene of steam shovels manned by savage-looking characters, and another of the *Cyrus,* deep-laden and awash in the waves of an ugly sea. A chunk of ore held down the papers on the big, flat-topped desk and two windows looked across at Morrison's building on Wall Street. Curtis' office adjoined his, and there were the old books, the Harvard certificate, and photographs of Mary and the two boys. They were snug enough for the time being and settled down to get acquainted with the big town.

Babcock, as head of the bank behind Bonanza Steel, had taken considerable interest in Steve's arrival in New York. One night, over their weekly game of chess, he spoke to Morrison about it. "Another one," growled Morrison. "Why do they come here? Damn fools. Kept his grip on that mine out there, didn't he?"

"He did, indeed," Bert chuckled. "He's been satisfactory to us so far."

"So far isn't far enough." Morrison shoved his bishop forward but kept his finger on it. "Keep an eye on him. We may need him."

It was easy to keep an eye on Steve but for several months there was nothing to report. Like a boy who had somehow wriggled into a circus tent, he seemed content merely to be there, his eyes on the daring and skillful acts of the acrobats under the big top.

Steve was not the only newcomer taking in the show. During these years a good many western millionaires were wading in, roiling the social waters by building mansions along Fifth Avenue to the disgust of established New Yorkers, who, alarmed at this threat to their social barriers, hastened to reform their battle lines to exclude these intruders.

Amelia, born in Boston, recognized at once the familiar antagonism, and was far too skilled in social warfare to make the mistakes of these plunging outlanders. To Steve's surprise she urged him to buy a tiny house, a stone's throw from Fifth Avenue on east Fifty-seventh Street. It was the smallest of the brownstone, high-stooped houses welded together along both sides of the street, but when Amelia had replaced its homely face with mellow red brick and white trim and filled her window boxes with flowers, it stood out from its neighbors like a tiny jewel box in a row of crates. Amelia was the jewel in it.

It was not long before lace curtains across the street began to twitch as carriages drove up and ladies rustled out of them. These acquaintances, made on her trips to Europe, and now encountered again at the Bagby Concerts or at Sherry's, greeted Amelia with chirps of recognition and were delighted to call. When they did, they found their hostess seated behind the tea table in an exquisite little drawing room; the gilt furniture, the porcelains, and flowers a perfect setting for Amelia's dainty figure. Charming, poised, and as wary as they were to avoid mistakes that might be difficult to rectify later, she received her guests graciously but with a hint of indifference.

One day a woman from Boston whom Amelia had known since childhood appeared with one of these groups. Amelia, immediately aware of the titillating gossip in the carriage on the way to her house, received her old friend's effusions with an air of puzzled condescension that sent the lady home to her husband seething with indignation.

"You should have seen her," she declared bitterly. "There she sat in a 'Worth' that must have cost a fortune, cool as a cucumber, pretending she scarcely knew me. Amelia Forsyth, of all people! Why, she left her son and literally ran off with that awful man. Heaven knows where she's been since, and now, to behave like that . . ."

"Who did you say he was? Bradway? I've met him downtown. Big fellow. Quite the best of the new lot, I should say. Might be a good idea to dine there."

Amelia, undisturbed by the fear that the opinions of Boston would be of any interest in New York, quietly continued her strategic maneuvers. Charity, the weak spot in all social barriers, was her first point of attack. Seated at her desk with her little black book at hand, she wrote not too generous checks to a carefully selected list of charitable organizations. Gradually some warmth crept into the acceptance of her generosity, but when, finally, she was invited to join in the good works, she refused the gambit with regret—but continued her checks.

On those mornings when she was not engaged in this charitable work, she joined the stream of carriages moving at a smart pace down Fifth Avenue to the shops on Twenty-third Street. Amelia loved the shops, offspring of the glittering city, and spent hours in them fingering, pricing, criticizing the abundance of tempting merchandise, but she seldom bought anything of importance in them, reserving those decisions for her visits Chez Suzanne.

Suzanne was an old friend. Years ago, on one of her first visits to New York, Amelia had drifted into a modest little shop on a side street looking for a hat. Nothing pleased her. Hats were strewn around the shop like the debris of a carnival when the saleswoman again pressed a small brown straw bonnet, trimmed with green ostrich tips, on her customer's ash-blond head.

"Yes, it's pretty," admitted Amelia, turning from side to side in the triple mirror, "but blue is my color. I can't wear green. Perhaps if you changed the feathers . . ."

"*Ah, mais non!*" cried the Frenchwoman. "Do not demand it change, madame. It is *parfait*. Pairfect. Always the ladies of America wish to match the eye! *Evidemment*, madame, too much *le bleu*, it kill the eye. It becomes dead as the fish eye. *Mais*"—she tossed a

186

kiss from her finger tips—"the little green ostrich make the eye of Madame to jump out. It catch the *regard. Ce petit chapeau est ravissant pour Madame.* It give *le chic. Mais*"—she shrugged, "if Madame demand *le bleu* I cannot give it. I am *artiste.* I cannot revolt myself . . ."

Suzanne, not entirely by chance, had hit upon the major misery of Amelia's life; her pale, lackluster eyes. "I wonder," she murmured, beguiled by the charming image in the glass. "You French are so clever. I wonder if you are right. It does seem to do something for me." She lifted the hat from her head. "I'll take it, and if it turns out well, I'll be back."

"*Mille remerciements,* madame," Suzanne, exhausted, smiled. "*Mais,* it is Madame who is clever. She recognize. If Madame trust Suzanne, she will never regret. *A bientot, madame.*"

Amelia never did regret, and now that she was settled in New York, spent many mornings Chez Suzanne in that caustic communion, more intimate than love and more enduring than sorrow, that can exist only between an ambitious dressmaker and her wealthy client. Both women understood each other as no one else on earth understood either of them.

When Amelia drove through the park in her pretty maroon victoria, her skirts foaming over the carriage step, her chiffon parasol discreetly tilted in her white-gloved hand, Suzanne's beautiful clothes caught the *regard* of other ladies without any trouble. Inquisitive glances followed her when she lunched at Sherry's, peeked at her from behind curtains in the beauty parlor, and when she swept down the aisle at the opera in shimmering white and silver brocade, the Diamond Horseshoe glittered with movement as glasses were focused on her. Mrs. Stephen Bradway was anything but inconspicuous during this time. Gossip swirled around her. She was wooed and shunned, with no apparent effect, while she coolly and skillfully pursued the stony path to the upper reaches of society.

CHAPTER 2

While Amelia was pursuing her sapping operations with the unobtrusive but implacable persistence of a mole, Steve had gradually inched into the big ring. Curtis watched him with growing concern. "Keep out of it, Steve," he cautioned. "You don't know this game. You've got plenty. Keep out of it."

"Nonsense," Steve countered impatiently. "Any fool can see rails are going up. If I'd grabbed Santa Fe last week, I'd be up there with it now. I'm not taking any chances."

He didn't, for a while. The bitter taste of risk was still in his mouth and the fear of jeopardizing the Iron Queen checked and steadied him. But as his vision cleared and he began to know the ropes, his grip tightened and he swung higher while his restless appetite for money grew with every swing he made. He was lucky, lucky and shrewd. He was soon swinging high, money was pouring into his hands, and more eyes than Babcock's were on him.

Far above him, under the big top, a highly skilled group of acrobats was busy trying out a new combination of grips and holds. These men were experts, and any performer who attempted to interfere with their tricks was ruthlessly jerked loose, to fall with a crash that occasionally shook the tent. One day these men were sitting around a long table planning a new and spectacular act. E. C. Shaw, at the head of the table, spoke up. "That fellow Bradway don't shake down easy," he said thoughtfully, shifting his cigar to the other side of his hard mouth. "He's got too good a grip on that mine. He's strong. Looks as if we'll have to cut him in."

An emaciated, sallow-looking member down the table objected. "What's that got to do with it? He wants too much. No necessity to drag in every Tom, Dick, and Harry who owns an iron mine. He's not a steel man."

"No." E.C. puffed on his cigar, smoke trickling through his set lips. "But the hell of it is Morrison wants him in. He made that plain the other night up at his place. If Bonanza comes in, this fellow comes in with it." His eyes swiveled to another face. "That's the idea, isn't it, Bert?"

Babcock's round, rosy countenance beamed with innocent good nature. "Yes, I should say so. Mr. Bradway is satisfactory to Bonanza and we don't want any disturbance out there. We're doing all right. If we come in, you'll have to take us as things stand now. That's understood."

E.C. gave him a sour look and his gaze labored on to a young man who was there because an enormous fortune, several generations old, was at his back. "How do you feel about it, Schuy? You've got a big stake in this."

The young man shrugged. "I don't know anything about these matters from your point of view, E.C." He smiled pleasantly. "You'll have to take it up with my people. But I've no personal objection to Mr. Bradway. I rather like him. I've played poker with him a few times——"

"Gambler! I thought so," muttered the sallow member. "I don't like it. Risky. Risky."

"—and he's a hard man to beat. He may not want to come in. As I understand it, he's producing about seven tenths of the ore out there. I should imagine," the young man added with a smile, "that Mr. Bradway is well aware of that. Fact is, he's in a position to develop a good-sized hornet's nest in the steel industry. That's your idea, isn't it, Mr. Babcock?"

After the pause that followed these remarks, a stolid, gray-haired man spoke up. "Let's leave this hornet out of it for the time being and get down to brass tacks," he rumbled. "If the object of this merger is to eliminate competition, it's idiotic to antagonize Morrison. He put over Midland years ago. This mine is at one end of it, Bonanza at the other. It's going strong, and the old man's satisfied. That's the long and short of it. Get this fellow in here and find out how much sting he's got. Chances are he hasn't any. The sting we've got to look out for is Morrison's. He's got one."

The question of Steve's participation in the steel combine was dropped, and the meeting went on to other business. After it was over, Babcock found the disgruntled dyspeptic in the washroom examining his tongue in the mirror.

"What's the matter, John?" he inquired genially. "Don't you feel well?"

"No," snapped the other. "These meetings upset my stomach. What are you and Morrison trying to put over on us with that fellow? I don't like it."

"Don't worry about Bradway, John. He's a good pawn."

189

"A what?"

Bert beamed over the towel he was using. "You don't play chess, do you, John? You ought to. A pawn is the smallest piece in the game, but useful. It can checkmate a king if it's played right."

Several weeks after this, after numerous meetings with the big boys, Steve found himself a member of the board of the new Independent Steel Corporation. He was an inconspicuous member among the mighty heads of the steel industry, and the only reason he was there was because he controlled the Iron Queen and this was the safest place to put him.

Steve was well aware of this, and of the opportunities it offered, and as he walked home from Wall Street that night, he turned them over in his mind. They were great. The power and scope of the new organization were beyond anything ever dreamed of in the industrial world—and he was in on it. There were millions in this deal. Millions! All he had to do now was stay with it—he and the old Queen. Suddenly he stopped short and cocked his head as if listening to the thump and rumble of his mine. The Queen had done this for him; the sultry, dusky witch that for twenty years had dominated every thought and act of his life. He started walking again, his stride longer, firmer. This was what he was after—what he'd always been after. Every step on the trail, every pound on his back had been headed for it. He thought of Harding, still down in Peru. He hadn't heard from Harding in a long time. He'd write him tomorrow, tell him the great news.

He climbed the stairs to his wife's sitting room and found her lying on the chaise longue, her bare arms flung above her head, her eyes on the ceiling. She turned her head languidly as he came in. "I've got rid of old Fawcett at last," she said at once.

Steve stopped, frowned, took it in. "Got rid of Fawcett? She's been with you since you were born, hasn't she?"

Amelia's eyes went back to the ceiling. "Oh, Steve, don't be tiresome. What's that got to do with it? She's utterly useless, and I need her room for a new maid. You've no idea what a burden she's been lately. I've packed her off to her daughter. She'll be perfectly all right."

Steve went off to wash for dinner. Presently they trailed down to the candlelit table, sat in silence, and trailed back again. Amelia threw herself on the chaise longue and Steve opened his paper to the financial page. After a while he tossed it away. "Get into some clothes and we'll go to a show," he said.

"Oh, Steve, no. Not at this hour. I'm tired. You never seem to realize how much I do all day."

"Come on," he insisted. "I feel like celebrating."

"Celebrating?" She sat up. "Is there anything to celebrate?"

"Nothing much." He tried to speak casually. "I'm in Independent Steel, that's all."

"Independent Steel? What does that mean?"

"It means a pile of money."

She jumped up then, lithe as a cat, her silks and laces and ribbons fluttering as she rushed toward him. "Tell me! Tell me! Do you mean it? Do you really mean a great deal this time? Oh, Steve, I've waited so long. So long." She made a passionate thrusting, grasping gesture. "Oh, I hope it's a barrelful this time. I've always wanted that—a barrel filled with gold so I could plunge my arms down into it like this—like this! A pile of money! You do mean it's a great deal, don't you? It really is this time?"

She went on at this rate for some time while Steve watched her with astonishment. He had considerable regard for money himself but he had no desire to plunge his arms into the stuff. The idea disgusted him. "Hold on, Amelia," he said when he had seen enough of it. "Calm down. Yes. I can give you a barrelful of gold to play with, if that's what you want. Have it carted up here tomorrow morning. I made around a million this——"

She wheeled on him, her face flaming, eyes and mouth wide with shock. "A million! Is that all? Why, that's nothing! Nothing at all! Hundreds of people in this town have a million dollars. Why, Grandfather gave you more than that years ago and you've had mine, too. And now you talk about a million dollars! Bosh!"

"That's the way you feel about it, is it?"

"Yes," she cried, striking her hands together. "That's exactly how I feel about it. Why, it's ridiculous! Grandfather had ten times that much and he wasn't a rich man. Not what I call rich."

"Cyrus never saw ten million in his life."

"He did! He did!" She shrieked, beside herself. "Oh, I'm sick of your big talk, sick of living in this little hole in the wall—sick of your common ways. Why, you don't even change for dinner! I can't stand it, I tell you. I can't stand any more of it. I want to live properly, the way I'm entitled to live. I want a big house. I want——"

"Stop it!" Steve's voice cut across like a whip. He stood up, his eyes black with anger. "All right. We know where we stand. If you'd held that tongue of yours I'd have told you I made that million this morn-

191

ing. It's not all I've got, not by a damn sight. Get your house. Spend this million on it. And while you're at it, get a divorce."

Amelia's rages were violent and genuine, but deep inside, behind them, there was always a core of cold, watchful calm. She gave him a quick, frightened look and dropped down on the chaise longue as if too weak to stand. "Oh, Steve," she whimpered, mopping her eyes, "don't be so hard on me. It's your fault, really. You should have told me instead of pretending like that. I know I've been silly, but it's only because I was so bitterly disappointed for your sake." She gave him a faint, wistful smile. "A divorce? Really, Steve! Where did you get such an idea? It's the last thing in the world I want. But I'll look for another house if you'd like me to."

Steve looked at her, sitting there, the picture of injured innocence. He shook his head. "You couldn't make a straight play to save your life, Amelia," he said, "but you're damn smart, at that. Hang on if you want to. We're quits from now out as far as the marriage angle of this thing is concerned, but you're an asset to me in other ways. Go ahead and get your house. I like the idea."

He walked out of the room, down the stairs, out of the house. He stood uncertainly looking up and down the street. A cab came by. He hailed it and drove to the Liberty Theatre.

CHAPTER 3

Steve was late getting to the theater. The second act was on and Florette was up there prancing around, switching her short skirts, coyly refusing another encore until she saw him coming down the aisle; then her saucy face lit up and she leaned forward over the footlights and sang her naughty song again straight at him while the audience laughed and craned their necks to see who the big man was. Steve, who hadn't expected to laugh again for a month, grinned at Florette as he settled into his usual seat.

It was a good show. The music was gay, the girls pretty and nimble in their scanty costumes, and when Florette leaned forward as she was doing now and put over her song in her intimate, husky voice, it wasn't hard for a tired man to forget his troubles for a while. From the time the curtain went up and the acrid perfume of grease paint and banana oil billowed out over the audience, until the final curtain went down—and up again, while dates were made with little nods across the footlights—it was a good show, and Steve enjoyed it again as he had a dozen times. He knew by this time where most of the dates tied up but none of them was with Florette when he was there.

When the show was over, he made his way backstage, to the confusion of stagehands hustling scenery back against the wall. Some of the chorus girls, scattering to their dressing rooms, pulling mascara from their lashes, had a smile for Steve, but most of them clattered unheeding up the steep iron stairway, unhooking as they went the spangled dresses sticking to their backs with the sweat of the last hard dance.

Steve stopped for a moment at Lew Bender's dressing room to give Florette a chance to get the make-up off her face. The tall, lanky comedian, a drip of taffy-colored hair over one eye, was sitting in his underwear drinking milk and trying to console a fellow comedian out of a job. "Hello, Steve," he drawled. "Sit down. Have a drink." Steve poured one and sat down on a trunk. "Chappy, here, is just telling me . . ." Lew went on, "Go ahead, Chappy."

193

Chappy, a wizened little man with enough skin for two faces draped on his melancholy countenance, glanced at Steve over his glass and burst out again. "Like I'm tellin' you, Lew, they got a jinx on me," he repeated excitedly. "Don't nothin' break right. I been in Shubert's office every day for three months, so help me God, and where am I that day he's lookin' for me? I'm at the track, that's where I am, watchin' 'em drop dead on me. So I miss it. Same thing all the time. Just missin'. Been goin' on two seasons. I tell you, Lew, a man's human nature can't stand it." He looked dolefully into his empty glass, as if ready to cry into it, but poured another drink instead.

"Why don't you try something else?" asked Steve. "Must be lots of jobs outside of show business."

Chappy looked up, his jaw dropped. "Who? Me?" he asked indignantly.

Lew stood up and started to pull on his pants. "Steve don't mean it that way, Chappy," he said good-naturedly. "He don't understand." He turned to Steve. "You ever know anybody in show business get out of it?" He shook his head. "Not show people like Chappy here. They don't get out. Ask Florette. She'll tell you. I was a shoe clerk myself, once," he added as if that explained everything. "Come on, Chappy, let's get something to eat."

As Steve crossed the empty stage, dark now where an hour ago music and laughter had created for a little while the illusion that life was a gay adventure with rounds of applause at the final curtain he thought that the illusion didn't last very long. The audience blinked when the lights went up—and it was gone. "Pretty good show, wasn't it?" . . . "I suppose so. But I can't see why you think that man's jokes are funny." . . . "Well, you've got to laugh some time. Come along; get in. I've got a hard day tomorrow. Home, James."

Steve found Florette at her cluttered dressing table busy with her make-up. A gaudy soiled Japanese kimono hung from the star's shoulders revealing a surprisingly immaculate white linen corset cover and full drawers gathered at the knee in a frill of embroidery. Her pretty legs, in black silk stockings, were crossed and black satin slippers with large rhinestone buckles dangled from her feet. In the light of the electric bulbs around the big mirror she looked ten years older than she did on the stage and she didn't bother to smile when she raised the hare's foot she was using in salute when she saw Steve.

"Hallo, Steve," she said. "I won't be a minute. How did the show go tonight?"

"Fine."

She shook her head, looking at him in the mirror while she dabbed at her face. "I didn't think so," she said. "Lew got off a good crack in the first act and there wasn't a ripple. Well"—she shrugged—"it's like that some nights. You give 'em everything you've got but you can't get 'em. Where are we going?"

"Anywhere you like," said Steve. "How about Rector's?"

"All right. I'll wear that pink satin," she said to her maid. She turned to Steve, her hands on her knees. "You know, sometimes I think I'll quit the lousy show business. Honest to God I do. Where does it get you?"

Steve laughed. "I've just been talking to Lew about that," he said as he stretched out in a sagging wicker chair. "I don't think there's much chance you'll quit."

"Don't be too sure about that," she said darkly. "I can quit any time I want."

Steve enjoyed sitting in the crowded stuffy little room, the air thick with the perfume of fading flowers, paints, and powders. Giddy costumes billowed against the wall; notes, flower boxes, slippers, littered the floor. He watched Florette's white arms and graceful hands moving over the untidy jumble of boxes and cans on the long, powder-filmed shelf beneath her mirror. He liked and admired Florette but he was not in love with her. Like many virile, vigorous men Steve was less interested in women than they were in him; they came too easy, too often, and too soon amounted to the same thing. One of the things he liked about Florette was that she seemed as content as he was to go out and let it go at that. "No," she'd say, "put me in a cab and I'll go home by myself. I've done my night's work." Then her pert little face would poke out of the cab window. "Pay him, you big slob!" And Steve would laugh. He liked Florette a lot.

Her make-up finished, Florette unbuttoned her corset cover, dragged out a key, opened a trunk, and pulled out a long black silk stocking, heavy in the toe. She tipped it up over the dressing table and out tumbled a mass of diamond jewelry, the stones making up in size what they lacked in quality. While the maid hooked the frivolous pink satin around her pretty figure, she slipped rings on her fingers, pendants in her ears, and pinned as many brooches as she could crowd into the lace of the low, square-cut neck of her dress.

195

Steve watched with amusement. "You're going to lose that junk one of these days," he said.

She shrugged as she tested a safety catch. "I got 'em insured. Honest, Steve," she said, "these rocks are the best investment in the world. Good anywhere, any time, and you can wear 'em to show what you've got. You tell me another investment can do that."

Steve laughed. She perched a wide pink hat with long ostrich plumes on her blond curls, slipped into a white fur coat, picked up a little jeweled purse—and there she was again—Florette, the pert, naughty, dashing little darling of the college men and Wall Street boys. "Come on," she said. "Let's go."

When Florette swept into Rector's dining room, pausing for effect at the top of the steps, the orchestra launched into her song. Heads turned and the little soubrette, nodding and smiling with the nonchalance of a reigning queen, tripped gracefully toward Steve's table.

"Who's that with her?"

"Bradway. I hear he's in on Independent Steel."

"That Bradway? Good-looking chap. She'll cost him something but I guess he can take it."

"Sure, she's cute, but I don't see why you've got to sit and stare at her like that for. She ain't the only one in this room. If you don't approve of my society you can stay in New Haven."

Interrupted a dozen times by the impetuous behavior of Florette's admirers, they were finally seated at the table and Florette, who was as hungry as a shark, began picking at a large broiled lobster. Her face never lost its impish, provocative expression, but her conversation was in another key.

"I hate wrastling with one of these damn things," she said. "The man that tackled the first one must have died of starvation."

"Why did you order it?" asked Steve, busy with an English mutton chop. "How about a nice steak with onions?"

"God! Don't talk like that," she breathed, clutching her champagne glass. "If this bunch was to see me eating onions I might as well cut my throat. No," she sighed, "I got to eat lobster or they'll think I'm slipping. I can scramble me a couple of eggs when I get home."

"Where is that, Florette? Where do you live?" he asked, pouring more champagne.

"Say, you don't know where I live yet?"

"No." He shook his head. "Probably in a frilly flat somewhere."

"Not me. I've had a few of 'em but I'm through with that kind of work. I live like I like and no frills about it. Say, mister"—she cocked her pretty head—"what are you getting at? A proposition?"

"No. Not unless you want it that way. I think we'd get along fine."

"Well, yes—maybe—but . . ." She hesitated. "Here comes Dick Barnum," she murmured while her face lit up with a radiant smile for the pompous man who approached and leaned with confident intimacy over the table.

"I'm having a little party upstairs in my private room," he whispered, eying Florette's white bosom. "We're having a hell of a good time. Like to have you join us. You know the way—through that red velvet curtain at the back."

Florette raised her innocent blue eyes. "Oh, Dicky," she mourned, her jeweled hand softly over his, "I'm so sorry. You always have such wonderful parties, but we're going on to Max's studio." She patted his hand. "Perhaps some other time. You know, darling, you can't get me at the last moment—but it was sweet of you to try."

Dicky, somewhat deflated, moved on, and Florette got out her mirror to see if her face was all right. "That's one of them," she said, touching her curls. "God, how I hate rich men. Just because they've got money they think they can whistle any time they feel like it. I don't mean you," she added with a glance around the mirror.

"Why not?" grinned Steve.

"You?" She lowered the mirror and looked at him. "You don't belong with that bunch," she said bluntly. "You didn't have it handed to you. That's why I like you. You've got a lot of money, I guess, but you don't think you're God Almighty yet. You're the same fellow you used to be before you hit the jackpot. When was that, Steve? Tell me about it."

"You don't look it but you are a smart woman, Florette," said Steve. "I wonder how many men know it."

"A few of them learned." She twinkled at him. "How do you think I got where I am if I can't size up a man? Go on. Tell me how you hit the jackpot."

Steve leaned back against the cushioned wall. The hurt Amelia had dealt to his pride earlier in the evening was still there, deep down and rankling. Somehow Florette had sensed his need and was trying to ease it. In spite of himself he yielded to the comfort she offered.

"What would you say if I told you I'd made a million dollars today?" he asked soberly.

"I'd say it was fine," she said promptly. "How did you do it?"

"That's the end of the story," he said.

"Oh, come on, Steve," she urged. "Loosen up. I want to hear."

He was silent for some time, his big fists stretched forward on the white cloth. Finally, as if talking to himself, he told her about the Iron Queen and some of the adventures that had landed him at a corner table at Rector's talking, until two o'clock in the morning, to New York's prettiest soubrette. He pulled up at last, a little ashamed of himself. He hadn't talked like that to anyone since . . . He looked up at Florette. She was leaning forward, her mouth slightly open, and her blue eyes, fixed on his face, were shining in the candle-light. Kit! She looked like Kit, back there in the moonlight. He hadn't thought of Kit for years. He moved restlessly. "That's it," he said abruptly.

"You're a grand fellow, Steve," said Florette after a moment. "I thought it would be something like that. You know, I think I could fall for you right now if it wasn't for Charlie, and I've never said that to a man since they picked him up."

"Who's that?" asked Steve, idly.

"Charlie Woods. My husband. You've heard of Charlie." Steve shook his head. "Oh, yes, you have," she insisted. "Everybody's heard of Charlie. He was in all the papers. He got away with close to two hundred thousand before they caught up with him. He was a wonderful man. That's why I believe in these rocks." She touched the brooches on her breast. "When I think of what Charlie could do to a bank . . ."

She sighed and got out her mirror again, running her fingers through the long soft feathers at her shoulder. Rector's was almost empty by this time, but here and there a couple lingered, leaning close, bemused, carrying on a communication deeper than words, and much more satisfactory. One such was now going on between Steve and Florette. "You still interested in where I live?" she asked finally, without turning her head.

"Sure," said Steve. "Sure," he repeated, smiling.

"You don't seem burning up about it," she said, still playing with the feather, "but I'll scramble you a couple of eggs if you want to come along."

In the hansom, Steve put his arm around her and Florette dropped her head against his shoulder, but neither spoke until they got to the modest little flat on Riverside Drive. Florette switched on the light under a pink shade, very like the one he had sat beneath reading his paper earlier in the evening but its glow seemed warmer in this homely room with its sagging easy chairs and gaudy pillows. He walked to the window and pushed aside the curtain. A ship was drifting slowly down the Hudson, its lights steady and peaceful in the night.

"Light the gas logs while I get out of this dress," Florette said briskly. She was back in a moment in a pink wrapper, tying an apron around her waist. "Come on. You beat the eggs while I get the coffee going."

The little meal by the fire was haphazard but delicious; coffee hot and strong, eggs light, salad crisp. Steve poured himself a drink but Florette wouldn't have one. "No," she said, "I don't drink much except for show, like at Rector's. Ain't it funny what the public wants of show people? Now you take Lew," she went on. "That poor guy has got the rheumatism so bad he can't hardly get out there some nights, but if he was to walk straight he couldn't get a laugh out of any of 'em. They like to think he's drunk. Can you beat it?" She chattered away, eating heartily while Steve, sitting on the sofa beside her, watched her over his glass, eased and contented. Finally she threw herself back and wrinkled her nose at him. "Well," she said, "where do we go from here?"

Steve set down his glass and pulled her close. "You know where we go from here," he said, kissing her. "You're a sweet little bundle, Flo, but you're more than that. You're a damn fine woman—and God knows I need you."

"God knows I know you do," she said, drawing away from him a little and looking in his face. "You're a good guy yourself, Steve, and I like you a lot, but don't go getting any ideas after this about a frilly flat like you talked about. I ain't having any. All I ask is you should act like a man should act."

Steve threw back his head and laughed as his arms went around her. "We'll see about that," he said.

CHAPTER 4

While Steve was living in occasional sin with Florette, Amelia had found the house she wanted on Fifth Avenue. She had been considerably upset at first when Steve insisted on moving his bed to his study on the third floor, but now, busy with plans for her new house, she gave it little thought. No doubt a man of his age was beyond the exigencies of youth and it was, after all, a comfort not to find those ugly shaving things in the bathroom. There were times, of course, when his avoidance of her room was trying but, on the whole, she was well content. He made no objection to any of her plans, and turned her contracts over to Curtis. When Curtis complained of the huge sums she was spending, he shrugged. "Let her have anything she wants," he said.

All that winter Amelia watched the renovation of her house on Fifth Avenue while architects and contractors struggled to find a loophole where they could make a dollar before she plugged it up. Finally, in May, the decorators came in with their brocades and taffetas and anxious Orientals spread bales of rugs in the rooms. One morning a magnificent Aubusson lay on the floor of the drawing room and Amelia knew at once she wanted it. "I don't care for that one," she said. "The medallion is too large."

The merchant, his dark eyes watching her with the alert intensity of a mongoose, clapped his hands. "Quick. Roll up this rug," he shouted to his crawling attendants. He bowed to Amelia. "I make a mistake," he explained. "I should not show this rug. It is a document from a cartoon by Adam for the Duke of Devonshire. A museum piece—I have papers to show. From Adam comes also this beautiful room but"—he wagged his head with regret—"Madam sees herself the medallion is too big. Quick. Quick. The Farahan. A very fine rug, madam. Not to compare by Adam, but very fine."

One after another the heavy bales were unrolled, spread, and rolled up again under Amelia's indifferent eye. "I'm sorry," she said at last, rising from her chair. "I don't care for any of them."

"Ah, madam," cried the dealer, "the blue one. Sam, again the blue."

"No." Amelia shook her head. "It is lovely but it spoils my color scheme." She turned on her way to the door. "Let me see the one with the medallion again."

"Certainly. A work of art from the cartoon of Adam, guaranteed. Sam, the Aubusson."

Amelia hesitated in the door. "It's not bad from here," she said. "How much do you want for it?"

"I lose money—but for Madam, twenty-five thousand dollars."

"Oh, ridiculous! I'll give you ten."

His fez fell off with the abruptness of the merchant's bow. "Madam has a great bargain. The finest rug from England in fifteen years."

"You've had it fifteen years, haven't you? I thought so. You're glad to get rid of it." They both smiled, satisfied.

Thus the house, a large old-fashioned brownstone structure, was gradually transformed. A wide, delicately wrought bronze door opened into a generous entrance hall, with a graceful curved stairway soaring to the upper floors. There was no particular character dominant in the hall, but gentle Queen Anne reigned in the library, Chippendale's hearty exuberance overflowed in the dining room, and sophisticated Sheraton slyly played with pretty chintz in the bedrooms. Sometimes Amelia, looking across her Aubusson rug to the chaste white marble mantel at the end of the drawing room, wondered if Adam himself had done as well for the Duke of Devonshire.

But it was the ballroom that gave the final distinction to the house. It was the largest private ballroom in New York, but now that the stage was so nearly set Amelia was uneasy. She would be obliged to ring up the curtain when the season opened that fall, but so far her committees had remained unimpressed by her hinted offers of her ballroom. She must wait, wait again, for a gesture from some impeccable source. The last thing she expected was that Steve would provide it.

It came about quite simply and with anything but charity behind it, because a man with something on his mind spoke to his wife one night as they sat in the drawing room in an old-fashioned brick house on lower Fifth Avenue. "Ruth," he said, "there's a man by the name of Bradway I'd like to ask to dinner before we go to Newport. Do you happen to know his wife?"

The lady, seated in a wing chair, was playing solitaire on a small table. She continued to lay out the cards with delicate precision until the rows were complete. "No," she replied then, placing a red jack on a black queen. "Why?"

The rosy little man opposite smiled amiably. "No particular reason, my dear. I'd like to show him a little special attention."

"Why not take him to your club? You know, Bertie, we never use the house for those things."

"I know, my dear. I've already put him up at the club. I wouldn't suggest this if I didn't think it advisable. He's a bit rough around the edges but I think you'd find him entertaining. I do."

"Who did you say he is?"

"Bradway. Stephen Bradway. I hear he's bought the old Farrington house on the Avenue and is doing it over. Silly thing to do, I should say. I believe they're on Fifty-seventh Street now."

"Ah, yes." A slight frown appeared beneath the Alexandra fringe on the lady's calm brow. "Bradway," she repeated thoughtfully. "She must be the woman who arrested Carrie."

"Arrested Carrie! What are you talking about?"

"She did. Carrie used to walk that dreadful little Peke of hers to this woman's door and stop him there. A horrid thing to do; just like Carrie. Finally this Mrs. Bradway—I'm sure that was the name—called a policeman and had Carrie arrested. It was in all the papers about a year ago."

"Are you sure, Ruth? If that's a fact, we can't ask people of that sort to the house," declared the old gentleman emphatically.

"On the contrary," replied his wife quietly. "I'd like to meet a woman with gumption enough to arrest Carrie. I've often wanted to do it myself. I'll call on her tomorrow."

When Amelia told Steve that Mrs. Cuthbert Babcock had called and asked them to dinner, he grinned with exasperating amusement. "So Bert got around to it, did he?" he said. "I've been expecting it."

"Oh, Steve." Amelia shook her head. "Don't take that superior attitude. You can't possibly know these people. I'm talking about the Cuthbert Babcocks."

"I've known Bert Babcock for years. You met him out there when the *Cyrus* sailed. What's so important about it?"

"Important? Important!" Amelia's voice rose. "I couldn't possibly have met him. You don't know who I'm talking about. This Mrs. Babcock is the most exclusive social leader in this town. It's ridiculous to pretend that's not important. Fortunately I was at home alone and we had a most delightful chat about the new house. She seemed to think her committee might want to use the ballroom next fall. She was charming. Really charming. I took to her at once."

"It's Bert, all right, and if she asked us to dinner, Bert put her up to it." Steve sat down and opened his paper. "Well, we're not going."

"Not going?" For a moment Amelia stared at him, too shocked to speak; then the telltale red flooded her face. "Oh, Steve, you can't mean that. Of course we're going. I've accepted. We must go. We must. This means everything to me. I've been wondering, and now . . ." She pleaded, she wept until finally, to put a stop to it, Steve said he'd go.

"Might not be a bad idea. Bert's all right. He'll have Norcross there from Chicago," he prophesied. "I'd like to see them try to work it that way. Might be interesting."

Amelia threw herself on his chest and, for the first time in months, he felt her lips on his own. He pulled away.

The next morning as her smart bays trotted briskly down the Avenue to the Chez Suzanne, Amelia's thoughts were glowing at the prospect of Mrs. Babcock's dinner. In this complacent mood she swept into the discreetly lit velvet-hung salon, to be greeted by shrieks of murderous rage from Suzanne, who was screaming at the top of her voice at a pretty little model shivering in chiffon on the platform. "Imbecile! *Va t'en! Va t'en. C'est impossible. Va t'en.* Out of my sight. You want I kill you? Quick! Out!" The dressmaker swung around, caught sight of Amelia, and surged forward, wreathed in smiles. "Ah, Madame Bradway, *comme c'est charmant de vous voir. Comment vous portez-vous, chère madame?*"

"*Oh, très bien,*" replied Amelia coldly, "but I must say I've heard enough French for one morning. Do calm yourself, Suzanne, and listen to me." She sank down on a small sofa and patted the place beside her. Suzanne, with a fluid gesture of appreciation, sat down on one hip.

"*Eh, bien, madame,* I am calm. What will you desire?"

While Amelia explained her desire, the dressmaker listened with complete understanding. "Aha!" she breathed. "Madame Babcock. *Enfin!*"

Her client didn't particularly like the implication but chose to ignore it. "I want something really right, Suzanne. You mustn't fail me."

"*Moi?* Fail Madame?" cried Suzanne reproachfully. "Madame is my best friend. I owe all—all to Madame since the little green feather so long ago." She spread her hand and struck her black taffeta bosom a violent blow. "Never will I fail Madame. Trust Suzanne. She fail only when she wish." The black eyes rolled heavenward. "I have the model from Worth," she murmured in the voice of a medium in a trance. "When I am in Paris, I buy it for Madame. It is perfect. Perfect. I rejoice but"—the shoulders sagged, the eyes dropped in despair—"alas, it will not do for the affair Babcock."

"Why not?" asked Amelia. "Have you sold it?"

"*Mais non,* but Madame Babcock detest the green. Never must she see green. No—no—*c'est impossible.* We must do something—something . . ." Inspiration seized her. "*Mais oui,*" she cried. "We copy in the color Madame Babcock like. Gabrielle! Gabrielle! Approach with the robe of Worth *en vert.* Green. Green," she screamed.

"I thought you never copied models," said Amelia sharply.

"Never I do," protested the dressmaker. "Never—but for Madame I do." She spread her arms dramatically. "I destroy this model if Madame wish—unless Madame permit me to sell it to Chicago? Ah! *Voilà!*"

The girl appeared in an exquisite soft green taffeta gown, the modest square neck trimmed with delicate lace, the flounce repeated at the edge of the tight elbow-length sleeves, the tight-fitting gored skirt flaring to the floor in lustrous folds. "Oh," exclaimed Amelia, "how lovely! I must have that dress. It is perfect for me."

"*Oui.* It is perfect for Madame," agreed Suzanne with regret, "but not for Madame Babcock." She turned to the attendant. "Bring at once the café-au-lait taffeta. We shall see."

"Oh, don't put me in brown, Suzanne," cried Amelia. "I can't bear it. It makes me think of Boston."

"*Exactement!*" said Suzanne firmly. "It makes Madame Babcock also think of Boston. She adore Boston. It is something, *n'est-ce pas,* that she shall think of Boston?" She jumped up, seized the shimmering silk, and flung it around the shoulders of the girl. "*Regardez!*" she cried. "*La couleur si subtile—si chic.* We dip the lace to look old for generations, we wear the pearls—only the pearls, and we allow the rose at the bosom. *Ah, madame, c'est un vrai chef d'oeuvre.* Madame Babcock, she adore this robe. Trust Suzanne. She know."

"She may like it," sighed Amelia, "but I can't say I do. It's much lovelier in green but I see what you mean. You really are clever, Suzanne." She gathered up her gloves and furs. "When shall I come for a fitting? And be sure to have the bodice tight and well boned."

"Trust me! Trust me!" cried Suzanne ecstatically, as she conducted her client to the door. "Madame will be most charming of her life in this robe. *Il faut avoir du tact, n'est-ce pas, madame? Mais—evidemment!*"

When, on the all-important tenth, Amelia, with her hand slipped under Steve's impatient arm, stepped from the carriage before the stately old mansion on lower Fifth Avenue, her heart lifted in gratitude to Suzanne for the charming, modest, richly rustling dress she wore. It was, as that clever woman had predicted, perfect. She was sure of herself; she wished she could be as sure of Steve. "Do be careful, Steve," she urged again. "Try not to laugh too much and don't tell any jokes."

"I'll leave you now if that suits you better," he muttered savagely as the door opened.

"Oh, Steve!" And as Amelia stepped into the quiet house, the mingled perfume of potpourri and furniture polish met her like the breath of Boston.

A number of people were gathered about in the cluttered, lofty drawing room, but the only face Amelia recognized as she moved into the familiar hostile atmosphere was that of the marble Psyche shrinking between the Nottingham lace curtains. There was no shrinking in her own attitude, however, and as her hostess introduced her, she met the level appraising stares with cold composure.

She had been seated for some time chatting, prettily at ease, with an austere old lady who all but fingered the quality of the silk in her gown when she heard, to her horror, Steve's laugh ring out and glanced up to see him clap his host on the back with a blow that staggered him. Every eye in the room was on them when old Bertie, his round face beaming with amusement, piloted Steve to his hostess, who took his arm as dinner was announced.

The dinner was an agony to Amelia and she wished with a furious despair that she had never come. She might have known that Steve would ruin everything. There he was at the far end of the table beside Mrs. Babcock behaving as she had so feared he would; sitting slewed around with his back to the woman next to him, his elbow on the table, laughing, actually leaning forward to pick nuts from a silver dish. It was horrible. She tried her best to keep her eyes from him and to make up for his behavior by her own sparkling charm, but it was no use. Mr. Babcock was not amused by her; he was amused by Steve.

"Extraordinary fellow, that husband of yours," he remarked at one point.

"Yes, isn't he?" Amelia turned her eyes, warm with affection for Steve, full on her host. "I am so glad he is having such a good time. He detests large dinners as a rule. He surprised me by wanting to come to this one."

205

"Did he, indeed?" remarked Bertie pleasantly. "Very flattering, I must say. Why did he want to come? Very boring for him, I should say."

"I don't know." Amelia shook her head with an innocence equaled only by Bertie's own. "Perhaps it was to please me—or because he has so much admiration for you."

"Has he, indeed?" said Bertie, his face beaming. "Believe me, dear lady, the feeling is mutual. There is no man of my acquaintance I respect as I do your husband. A remarkable man, in my opinion."

"Steve will be so pleased when I tell him that," she said with an artless smile.

She told him in the carriage on the way home. Steve, sitting in the corner, his shirt front buckled, silk hat tilted over his eye, was half asleep. "What's that?" he said. "Bosh! Bertie respects me about as much as I do him."

"Oh, Steve, how can you? You didn't antagonize him, did you?"

"Antagonize him? No. Bertie took particular pains not to antagonize me. I've got Bertie in my pocket, if that's any satisfaction to you."

Upstairs in the old Fifth Avenue mansion Bertie, already in bed in his nightshirt, lay watching his wife at her dressing table as she disposed of the Alexandra fringe and the switch that augmented her gray hair. "Well, my dear," he asked in his gentle voice, "what did you think of them?"

"It was amusing, wasn't it?" she said, her fingers busy with her scant braid. "She is definitely well bred. Boston, all over. But she's a mean-tempered little piece. I don't believe I'd bother with her if it weren't for him." She slipped off her clean, old-fashioned diamond rings and dropped them in a silver tray. "You were quite right, Bertie. He is a most unusual man. I like him. There's a refreshing zest about him. He told me one story about the Mississippi . . . Well"—a frosty smile touched her thin lips—"it was as good as some of yours."

Bertie chuckled. "He's a good-looking rascal. He told me a little story, too, tonight. I rather think he believed I didn't see the point. At any rate, my dear, if it is agreeable to you, it will please me if you take on the Bradways."

He patted the place beside him in the big four-poster. "Come along now, Ruth. It is time we got to sleep."

206

CHAPTER 5

In the meantime, during these years Victor, with the insouciance of a camel on the way to a certain oasis, had been approaching his inheritance. When he was seventeen, his grandmother died, leaving him a considerable fortune and, as he was about to enter Harvard, he continued to live in Boston. When he was twenty-one he came into the trust fund established by his father and, with Harvard behind him, decided to continue the family tradition by moving onward and upward to Oxford. Amelia highly approved of the idea. "Of course, darling," she encouraged him on one of his brief visits to the Fifty-seventh Street house. "You have plenty of money now and it will be lovely for you in England— you've already met so many delightful people on our trips there." She sighed. "I wish I might go with you, but perhaps by the time you get back, I'll have a proper house so we can live comfortably together here. You'd like that, wouldn't you, darling?"

Victor had been in England almost two years when one morning, not long after Mrs. Babcock's dinner, Amelia was seated at her desk, deep in plans for moving into the new house, when the butler came to her with a cablegram. It was from Victor, bluntly asking for money for his passage home. Everything about the message exasperated Amelia. It was rude and demanding. It was also most inconvenient. She didn't want Victor hanging about now. She wanted to introduce him in the fall at the ball she was giving for Mrs. Babcock's charity. That was part of her plan, an important part, and she had no intention of having it upset by Victor's premature arrival. He must stay where he was until she was ready for him.

All day long as she plodded back and forth in the brougham between the old house and the new, the carriage filled with bric-a-brac, she couldn't trust to the packers, she fumed with self-pity, and when Steve got home that night, she burst out with it. "Have you ever known anything more inconsiderate?" she complained, thrusting the cable into his hand. "I've told Victor I'm in the midst of moving. He knows I'm expecting him in the fall and yet he quite

207

calmly announces he's coming now and asks me to pay for it. I declare I never heard of such arrogance. The idea!"

"Well, did you?"

"Did I what?"

"Send him the money?"

"Of course I didn't. I cannot, I simply cannot have Victor here while I'm moving. I'm exhausted as it is. You've no idea how tiring it is—how much there is to do. All of you—all of you expect too much of me," and she began to weep.

"But there must be some reason for this," said Steve. "He's never done it before, has he?"

"No—but what reason . . ." Amelia mopped her eyes and read the cable again. "Why, it's from Mumpton-Mawbury," she said slowly. "I didn't notice that. He's been staying there with Lady Colchester. Steve!" she cried. "Of course! I understand now. He means Inez has taken him. Oh, how wonderful! I can't believe it! I pretended, of course, but I never dreamed she would—not really. Victor's not that rich. But he is terribly attractive and since the duchess had him down . . . Oh, I can scarcely believe it. It's too, too wonderful!"

"Better hold your horses until you know more about this, Amelia. Looks to me as if he's in some kind of scrape."

"Oh, Steve." She flared away from him. "Why must you always spoil everything. He couldn't mention it in a cable but it's perfectly obvious he's coming home to arrange the settlement so they can be married before the season opens next fall. That means I'll have to be in England. What a pity I'm committed to this ball—but that can be arranged. I do wish I'd sent the money this morning. Is it too late to send it now?"

Some days after this Amelia, looking the picture of sweet motherhood in a charming frock, a flower-laden hat on her head, the brougham glistening in the background, stood on the dock gaily waving a white-gloved hand. She wasn't as gay as she looked. She was a desperately tired woman but she had managed somehow, by heroic effort, to be comparatively settled in the new house, ready to receive her son. And there he was, handsome as a prince, coming down the gangway. He saw her, hurried toward her, tossed his bag to the footman, and urged her into the carriage. "Victor," she protested, "what is the matter with you? Give Martin your checks and trunk keys, darling."

"I haven't any trunks," muttered her son savagely. "Please, Mater, do let us get away from here."

208

"No trunks? What nonsense." Amelia laughed. "You act as if you were running from the police."

Victor shuddered.

The long drive through the city seemed interminable. Victor, silent, glum, stared out of the window while his mother, after a few abortive attempts to rouse him, retired in silence to her corner of the carriage. Finally, with a smart twirl of his whip, the coachman drew up before the palatial new house on Fifth Avenue. The footman leaped from the box, the butler swung open the big bronze doors, and Amelia swept across the pavement. Victor followed her, the footman followed Victor, and the doors clanged shut behind them.

"Take Mr. Victor's bag to his room," Amelia ordered coldly, "and bring tea to the library."

In the library she took off her hat and sank into a Queen Anne needlepoint chair while Victor moved restlessly to the bookcases. "Victor, what in the world is the matter with you?" she asked again, sharply. "Do sit down. You've scarcely spoken to me. Are you ill?"

Victor sat down, his eyes on the Oriental rug. "No," he said. "No. I don't suppose you'd call it illness. It's worse than that. I . . . ." He looked up, down again, hesitated, plunged. "The fact is I'm absolutely flat, Mater. I haven't a bean in the world." And with that, the wretched young man poured out the whole story. "When Inez and I——" He gulped, tried again. "I hadn't the faintest idea until his solicitors wrote to mine—I supposed everything was all right. They came back with some rot about having warned me. They may have. I don't know. Of course, Lord Monty sent me packing—and my creditors got wind of it . . ." Victor put his face in his hands and wept.

"But this is incredible!" exclaimed Amelia after a stunned silence. "Impossible! You had plenty of money, Victor. Do you mean to say you've squandered your entire fortune in two years? I can't believe it. I know you've been spoiled by your grandmother, but that you could actually squander——"

"I didn't squander it," interrupted Victor, roused by indignation. "I'd be all right if I wasn't loaded up with Massachusetts stock. It isn't paying dividends now."

"I know it isn't," said Amelia, "but what's that got to do with it? You had no Massachusetts stock. Your father didn't believe in mines and certainly your grandmother didn't have it. Where did you get it?"

"I've got it," repeated Victor miserably. "Plenty of it."

Amelia's patience was at an end. "I don't believe it," she declared bluntly. "This is just a story to cover up some mess you got into over there. Horace is the only one——" She stopped, her mouth open. "Victor! Where did you get that stock?"

"I don't know." Victor shook his head. "Old Stoddy said something about it before I left for England. He wanted me to see Uncle Horace. I remember that, but I didn't bother about it. Everything seemed all right."

Amelia jumped to her feet, her face flaming. "If Horace made Mr. Stoddard buy in my Massachusetts stock for you, I'll have him put in jail. It's downright criminal. I can't believe it, even of Horace, and yet how else can you be loaded up with it? It's not for sale except to members of the family. Of course Horace did it. He knew . . ."

At this point Steve walked in.

Steve was feeling fine. He had had a good day and had just left Bert Babcock at the club. They were dining there that night with several other congenial pirates and he'd come home for a clean shirt.

"Well, Victor," he said heartily, "glad to see you back. Did you have a good trip?"

Victor glanced at the big man and walked to the window. Amelia took over. "A good trip!" she cried. "Steve, you've never heard anything like this in your life. Victor hasn't a penny left, and now he's back here . . ." And she poured out her own version of the catastrophe.

Steve listened with no sign of emotion until she came to the perfidy of Horace; then he threw back his head and roared with laughter. "Well, I'll be damned," he said. "Unloaded on Victor, did he? I didn't think Horace was as smart as that. Well, it doesn't amount to anything. May be a good thing in the long run."

"A good thing!" Amelia's eyes, red with angry tears, blazed at him. "A good thing! How can you say that? I can't support Victor. I'm not going to. Why should I? He inherited his father's money—I didn't . . . And if he's wasted it, it's his own fault. He'll have to go to work—Victor, of all people—and I depended on him so much. Oh, it's so cruel, so unfair!" She threw herself on a chair and the tears rolled down her cheeks.

Steve went to the window and laid his hand on Victor's shoulder. Victor at once stepped back. "Don't let this worry you, Victor," he said easily. "I'll give you a job in my office tomorrow morning. I've got a fine bunch of young men down there. You'll like them. You won't make much at the start but you'll advance fast enough if you show ability." He gave Victor a genial smile. "I can't say you've shown much head for figures so far, but you'll catch on in time."

Victor gave him a look that surprised him; a deep, bitter look, burning with contempt. "Thanks most awfully," he drawled, "but if you don't mind, I'll make my own plans." He turned his back on Steve and walked out of the room.

Some time later, after Steve had gone back to his club, Amelia dragged herself downstairs for dinner with Victor. She dreaded it. Her head was splitting and she longed for a tray in her room but the servants would talk if Victor dined alone on his first night at home and she couldn't allow that. But she meant him to know what the effort cost her.

Victor was not in the library. She waited for some time with growing impatience, then rang the bell. "Tell Mr. Victor I'm waiting for him in the library," she said when the butler appeared.

"I'm sorry, madam, but Mr. Victor is not in."

"Not in? What nonsense! Of course he's in. Go to his room at once."

"Very good, madam," said the butler, "but Mr. Victor left the house some time ago. He took his bag with him."

Victor disappeared for three months. At first Amelia was deeply incensed, and blamed Steve for the collapse of the home-coming. "It's because you insulted him," she complained, "telling him he must show ability, that he had no head for figures. Why, you talked as if he were an office boy. No wonder his pride was hurt. And now," she wailed, "he's gone to Boston and I've lost him. My son! Oh, Steve, how could you?"

"Don't worry about that," said Steve. "If he's in Boston, he'll come back fast enough after he tackles Horace about that stock. He'll show up in a week or two."

Amelia's opinion of him had long since ceased to interest Steve. She and her young cub would have to work this out without him. He was going on a business trip, planned some time ago. Several men he liked, Bert Babcock among them, were going in a private car to look over the smelters, docks, and shipping that composed the Midland Mining Company, taking in the old Iron Queen on the way to a fishing trip in the north woods. He looked forward to the trip and it wouldn't hurt the boys to see that big hole in the ground. He lovingly packed his old woods clothes and told his wife he'd be gone for a month or more.

Amelia, not daring to leave the city while Victor's absence remained unsolved, stayed alone in the big house with the blinds pulled down. At first she bitterly resented both her husband's and her son's desertion, but when Curtis, instructed by Steve, found out that Victor was not in Boston, that his relatives were not even aware of his return to America, her resentment gave way to acute anxiety. Where was Victor? What dreadful publicity might be shaping up? Had he thrown himself in the river? Might she be called upon to identify his dripping body? Worse still, had he gone to California? Wretched, worried, Amelia spent hours weeping over her intolerable misfortune.

There was no rain for weeks that summer. Day after day, the steady intense eye of the sun glared at the prostrate city as if through a burning glass. Heat waves shimmered on the pavement, dust rose wearily on any fickle current of air and settled again; the grass in the park was worn and faded and the trees drooped with the tired resignation of martyrs clothed in dusty brown.

Every day another martyr drove through the park, her sunshade tilted as she scanned the faces of the people lolling on the benches or sprawled on the litter-strewn grass. The park swarmed with these awful people; men in sweat-stained shirts with the sleeves rolled up; women, straggling hair sticking to their tired faces, opening paper packages to feed half-naked, screaming children. Of course, Victor wasn't among these people. He couldn't be. And yet her eyes searched for him there.

And then, one September day, Victor came home. Herbert, seeing the shabby, hatless figure on the step, opened the door cautiously, then threw it wide. "Mr. Victor," he gasped. "I wouldn't have known you, sir."

"Wouldn't you?" Victor smiled easily. "You surprise me, Herbert." He came in with an air of giving his hat and stick to the servant. "Is my mother in?"

"No, sir. She is out driving, but I expect her in for tea, sir."

Victor crossed the hall and started up the stairs. "When she comes, tell her I'm in, will you? And you might bring a whiskey and sandwiches to my room."

Victor found his room, closed the door, and stood for a moment with his back against it. His silver was gleaming on the dressing table. He crossed to the closets, where his suits and boots were

212

neatly arranged; the chest of drawers filled with fresh linen, ties, and socks in the smaller drawers. These things were there because Steve had cabled his bank in London to pay the young man's debts and forward his effects—but Victor accepted the appearance of his clothes, as he had learned to accept many things, without question. He selected what he needed, went into the bathroom, kicked the filthy clothes he wore into a corner, and got into the tub.

He lay in the warm caressing water a long time, turning the sweet-smelling soap in his hands, his eyes wandering idly over the immaculate appointments of the bathroom. Then, with voluptuous deliberation, he soaped and lathered his body, scrubbed, washed, scrubbed again. A wave of nausea swept through him when he saw the tiny red bites on his stomach and legs, but he made his mind go blank again, and the sickness passed. After he had rubbed down vigorously and put on fresh linen, he stood before the mirror to shave.

It was a difficult moment. The face in the mirror stared at him with dark accusing eyes but he stared back steadily. His fingers touched the lump on his jaw. It was still painful but the color had faded to a dirty yellow that would pass unnoticed by a casual glance —but it was a lump Victor would feel for the rest of his life. His eyes wavered and fell, and for an instant he was flat on his back again, those massive legs straddled above him, hearing the contemptuous, bawling voice. "Get up, you good-for-nothing spalpeen. Let's have some more of your lip. I'd turn you over to the cops if you wasn't more fool than man. Get up. You heard me! Beat it! And don't try for no job around here if you know what's good for you." Then the insolent shove with the foot, the laugh as the legs walked away.

When Victor raised his eyes again, the face in the mirror smiled. It was not a pleasant smile. The shoulders shrugged. Victor picked up his razor, shaved, put on a handsome silk dressing gown, stretched out on the bed, and went to sleep.

He was aroused by Amelia's dramatic entrance. She rushed to him, arms outstretched. "Oh, Victor, my darling!" she began, but something in her son's look checked her. She stopped, and for a moment the gaze of the mother and the son met and held; then Amelia began drawing off her gloves, relief and anger contending in her face. Victor stood up and took her elbows in his hands, smiling down at her.

"You look charming, Mater." His eyes traveled over her dainty summer dress, the wide brim of her lacy hat dipping under the

213

weight of a large pink rose. "Charming. Very well turned out, I must say."

Amelia flushed. "Is that all you have to say to me after all this dreadful anxiety? After all I've been through, all I've suffered . . . ?"

"Come, come, Mater. We'll skip the histrionics, if you don't mind." Victor dropped his hands and sat down on the bed again. "Sit down and we'll talk this over. I know exactly what you've been through. Most inconsiderate of me to upset your plans, wasn't it? But, as you see, I've come back." He lit a cigarette and let the smoke curl past his face for a moment before he added casually, "I've come back to talk business with you."

"Business!" Amelia sank into a chair and took off her hat. "Business! Victor! I want to know where you've been, what you've been doing. I want some explanation for this extraordinary behavior. I expect it and I insist on having it."

Victor shook his head. "Sorry, but we'll not discuss that now or at any other time," he said pleasantly. "I've come back solely to talk business. At the moment I have an avid desire for money, and it occurred to me it might be to your advantage as well as mine to discuss it."

"Nonsense," Amelia interrupted sharply. "Don't take that high-handed tone with me, Victor. I've had quite enough of it. Evidently you failed in whatever you attempted to do and have come back depending on me to support you. Is that what you call business? If it is, I will, of course, make you a proper allowance but I expect, in return, more consideration than I've had from you so far."

Victor laughed. "How right you are, Mater. One must get *quid pro quo*, mustn't one? And by that same token, surely you can't expect—as I'm sure you do, by the way—to get my services while you hold the purse strings." He sobered. "To put it bluntly, I'm looking for work, the only work my upbringing has fitted me to do. I'm experienced in it and guarantee satisfaction. You need the services of a social escort, Mater. Very well. I'll take you about to boring dinners, dull operas, snare the best people for you, and marry any rich girl you fancy—but I mean to be well paid for it."

"Victor!" Amelia stared at him in shocked amazement. "How can you speak like this to me, your mother? I've told you I'll give you an allowance, but this talk of pay for services, like a—well, like a servant, is unthinkable. I couldn't possibly live with you in that relationship, not possibly. After all, you're my son!"

214

Victor sighed and got up. "Very well," he said quietly. "I see I must take myself elsewhere."

"Victor, are you mad? You mean you would go to someone else with this hideous idea?"

Her son looked at her. "Without a moment's hesitation, and I'd have the job before night. A first-class dancing man with an Oxford accent is always in demand. I knew several of them in London. Charming bastards." An expression of profound disgust swept his face and was gone. "You fail to realize, Mater, that you raised one of them. It is not, I grant you, a pleasant occupation," he went on lightly, "but at any rate, it's a cut above hanging to your purse strings."

Amelia could scarcely believe that this cool young stranger was her gentle Victor. He didn't even look like the son she knew. He was taller, thinner, his hands were coarse and roughened, but something deeper lay coiled behind the physical change, something better left unaroused. She found that she was a little afraid of Victor. She stood up.

"I can't understand you, Victor," she said, trying to speak as lightly as he had done. "You twist things so. But after all, it is merely a question of money no matter how you put it, isn't it? And that can be arranged."

"It's not merely a question of money," replied Victor. "It's a question of services rendered for pay. Quite a different matter, and quite clear."

"Oh well, do let it go for the time being, Victor. I'm tired. It's been upsetting to find you in this frame of mind. I believe I'll lie down before dinner." She turned at the door. "You're staying, aren't you?"

"Oh. Quite. If you wish it. Are we dining in?"

"Yes." She paused uncertainly. "Yes, we are, and I think—I hope—Steve will be in."

Steve, brown, vigorous, home from his fishing trip in the north woods, gave Victor a keen look when they met in the library before dinner. He was not surprised to see the boy there. Curtis had located him easily enough and reported his drift from job to job through the summer, and Steve, who believed a spell of hard work wouldn't hurt him, had decided not to interfere. Now he was not sure he'd been right. There was a difference in Victor, a big difference, and that lump on the jaw was back of it. "He's been licked and he can't take it," he told himself. "It went too far and he's gone sour—sour as hell." But he gave no indication of his thoughts, asked no questions, waiting for Victor to make the advances.

There were none. In that same moment of meeting Victor had conceived a burning, unreasoning hatred of Steve. The penetration in the big man's level look, the tolerance and compassion he saw there roused his stifled conscience and stung him to a fury of rebellion. All through dinner he was acutely aware of that strong, complacent presence at the other end of the table listening, undeceived, to his affected chatter with his mother. He couldn't look at the man, couldn't speak to him; he ignored him with the masterly technique he had acquired at Oxford, and yet the steady pressure on his soul went on.

But before the meal was over, Victor found release. It came as he toyed with his dessert. If he could find some way to defeat that man, shatter his pride as his own had been shattered, then his humiliation would be canceled and they would meet on equal terms. He didn't ask himself why he desired this so passionately; he simply seized upon it in the welter of his frustrations and clung to it. There must be some way, some weakness in Steve's armor. His life was worthless until he found it. He would find it!

As they left the dining room Victor, for the first time, looked full at Steve and smiled. Steve didn't see that smile. If he had, it might have warned him of what lay ahead.

216

CHAPTER 6

As the weeks went by and the city began to stir once more with social activity, Steve was glad Victor was in the house. He approved of the glitter his wife was making with his money but her persistent nagging on the formal obligations it involved depressed him to the point of actually wondering if the money was worth it. Now that Victor was there, the succession of stiff shirts was over, and he headed for Broadway like a man released from bondage.

Amelia, as relieved as he was to be rid of the burden of pulling Steve through social pitfalls, settled down with Victor to plan the winter's campaign. It was important; her first winter in the new house must be successful, and she was now secretly delighted that her handsome son was dependent on her. Call it what he liked, he was.

They met every morning in her sitting room, Amelia in a lacy negligee, her breakfast tray beside her, her son in an easy chair opposite, pencil and notebook at hand. The charming scene looked the picture of felicity; it was anything but that. Victor sat there, a polite smile on his lips, opening his mother's mail, listening to her comments with the detachment of a professional secretary giving satisfaction to a tiresome employer. Her endearments, her playful little intimacies met with no response and Amelia, baffled and exasperated, felt like shaking him. She jumped up and attempted it once. Victor quietly set her back on the chaise longue and walked out of the room. She rushed after him, chiffons and ribbons fluttering; finally, tears and a raise in salary brought him back and the conferences settled into a regular routine. Names and social occasions were selected or rejected with the delicate scrutiny of a merchant weighing gems. Amelia's knowledge was decisive there, but when it came to the setting for these gems, Victor took the lead.

"This is a rather good room," he said one morning as they stood looking at the drawing room, "but, of course, pure Adam is impossible. We shall have to break it up a bit."

217

"Oh, Victor, no. It cost so much. It's perfect."

"That's the trouble with it," agreed Victor. "It needs a bit of Great-Grandfather's old furniture here and there. Where is that furniture, by the way?"

"In storage—and don't ask me to get it out. It would ruin this house. I won't have it. After the way I've worked——"

"Only too evidently. And suceeded in erasing all trace of your own excellent background. It's ridiculous, really. This house needs a heavy dose of pure Beacon Street. Cling to the horrors of family tradition as they do in England, dear Mater, and leave exhibitions to museums. We'll bring in your grandfather's sturdy mahogany tomorrow."

By the end of the month Amelia had to admit that she was enchanted with the result of Victor's work. The dose of Beacon Street had mellowed the house, unified it without in the least detracting from the beauty of her period pieces. She was so pleased that for one fleeting moment she felt like raising Victor's pay, but controlled the impulse and said instead, "It really is a great improvement. I don't see how I could have missed it."

Yellow roses gleamed against the walnut-paneled walls of the library, the Forsyth portraits scowled in their gilt frames, hot water bubbled in the silver kettle on the tea table when Mrs. Babcock, back from Newport, came to discuss the coming charity ball. Amelia, seated behind her grandmother's Royal Worcester, jumped to her feet with a little cry of surprise as she was announced. "Mrs. Babcock!" she exclaimed. "How kind of you to come. I scarcely expected you so soon after your return. Have you had a pleasant summer? You look very well."

Mrs. Babcock slightly loosened her sable scarf. "I'm very well," she said, "but you must have had a trying summer. However, you seem comfortably settled now. You have quite transformed this house. It was a dreadful barn of a place when the Farringtons had it. I wouldn't have recognized it."

"Wasn't it?" agreed Amelia as she busied herself with the tea things, "but I'm quite happy about it now. It's such a comfort to be in a proper house with my own things around me. I feel at home again."

Mrs. Babcock bit into a tiny biscuit. "Ah"—she gave Amelia a frosty little smile—"I see you have Annie with you. Her puff paste is unmistakable. I've been trying to get her for years. How did you manage it?"

218

Amelia's guileless gaze rested on her guest. "I've no idea where she came from. She simply appeared one day, and she reminded me so much of Fawcett—Grandfather's dear old cook—that I took her without reference. She's so good I've been fearful something dreadful might turn up—drink, or something of that sort—but she's been excellent so far."

Mrs. Babcock, who had lived with Bertie's guilelessness for years, looked at Amelia with appreciation. "Annie is the best cook in New York," she said dryly. "She has no faults that I am aware of except, possibly, greed. She's been with Delia Witherspoon for twenty years, but, no doubt, tired of her. I should, myself, long before that."

"Mrs. Witherspoon?" Amelia was aghast. "Oh, how dreadful. Surely she can't think that I had anything to do with her losing her cook."

"Of course not. Why should she?" Mrs. Babcock bit into another little biscuit. "Annie has a mind of her own. You must try to keep her; she'll be invaluable to you."

The talk had drifted to the charity ball when Victor, immaculately groomed, came into the room. He greeted his mother lightly but with obvious affection, and smiled charmingly when presented to Mrs. Babcock. "Am I intruding?" he asked.

"Of course not, darling." Amelia beamed at her son. "Do sit down and have your tea. We were just discussing the ball."

"Ah, yes." Victor accepted his cup and draped himself in a chair. "I believe you said something about it. A charity affair, isn't it?"

Mrs. Babcock's cold gray eyes, as inscrutable as those of a horse trader, rested on him. "Yes," she said. "We usually open the season with a costume charity ball and your mother has kindly offered us her ballroom. This is the first time we have held it in a private house. We want to make something exceptional of it but we seem to have run out of ideas." She smiled at Victor. "Perhaps you could help us."

"I?" Victor's eyebrows went up. "I should be delighted, of course, but I can't think I'd be of much use to you."

"On the contrary," protested Mrs. Babcock mildly, "unless I'm mistaken you are a very clever young man. I feel quite sure you can help us. How many could we manage in your ballroom, Mrs. Bradway?"

"I really can't say," replied Amelia. "I've scarcely been in it. Would you like to look at it?"

Mrs. Babcock gazed in silence for a moment at the enormous expanse of satin-like floor, the mirrored walls, the gilt festoons glittering in the light of three huge crystal chandeliers. "It didn't occur to me you had a room of this size," she said at last. "It should easily accommodate two hundred couples, don't you think? I—it is really an amazing room." She turned to Victor. "Does it give you any ideas, Mr. Hamilton?"

Victor shrugged and smiled. "Louis Rampant, I should say, Versailles at its worst. Obviously any costumes but those of the period would be absurd in this room. It's incomprehensible how anyone could conceive such an exhibition of bad taste."

"Don't say that, Victor," protested Amelia. "It isn't my fault. I wanted a little music room but Steve kept insisting . . ."

At that moment Steve came in, bringing the cold air like a mantle around his shoulders. "Well, hello, Mrs. Babcock," he said heartily, seizing her hand. "That fellow out there said you were here. I'm glad to see you. What do you think of this outfit?"

Mrs. Babcock allowed her hand to linger in his firm grasp. "You must be pleased with it," she said, returning his smile.

"Pleased? Well, that depends on how you look at it. I can't say I think much of this, but I've got a good room upstairs. Want to see it?"

"Oh, Steve——" began Amelia.

"I'd like very much to see it," interrupted Mrs. Babcock. They started up the stairs, all but Victor, who had quietly withdrawn the instant Steve appeared.

It was a small room, paneled in pine, with plain leaf-green curtains at the windows that overlooked the park. An old silk patchwork quilt covered the bunk built against the wall in one corner and a sagging wing chair stood beside the fireplace. The opposite wall was filled with books, and a large pine table littered with papers beneath a green glass lampshade stood before them. Above the mantel the slick head of a young buck hung on the wall. Steve laughed when he saw Mrs. Babcock looking at it. "He's a long way from home," he said, "but I like him around."

"Of course you do," she said heartily. "This is a most interesting room. I'm glad I've seen it. I must tell Bertie about it. He'll envy you that deer head."

"I'll get him one," said Steve promptly. They moved into the hall. "I hope you've forgiven me for taking him off on that fishing trip," he went on as they descended the stairs, "but I wanted him along and I think he enjoyed it."

"I've never known Bertie to enjoy himself more." A little smile

220

of amused understanding softened her thin lips as she gave Steve her hand in parting. "And I believe I enjoyed his absence quite as much as he did. It is rather a good thing to get away from time to time." She turned to Amelia. "Good-by, Mrs. Bradway. You have been most kind. I am sure the committee will be delighted with your son's suggestion. Will you give him my thanks for his interest? And you might tell Annie I recognized her puff paste," she added.

That evening Mrs. Babcock laid out her solitaire with unusual deliberation. "Bertie," she asked after a time, "have you met that son of Mrs. Bradway's?"

"No, I have not. Why?"

"He's an extraordinary young man," she said. "Extremely good-looking and he has delightful manners. He'll create a sensation when he gets about this winter."

"And you don't like him. Is that it, Ruth?"

"I detest him," she said quietly, "and I don't know why. Nothing one can put one's finger on. Perhaps it's because he hates his step-father."

"Steve? Nonsense, Ruth. Most young men dislike their stepfathers. Nothing unusual about that."

"I know. But this was different. The moment Mr. Bradway came in that young man's face changed in a most startling manner. It was most unpleasant; alarming, really. I felt the way I do when there's a cat in the room, and you know, Bertie, when I feel that curdling sensation, something disagreeable always happens."

Bertie chuckled. "I wouldn't worry about Steve," he said. "He's one man I know who can take care of himself."

Mrs. Babcock swept her cards together as if the game no longer amused her. "I wonder," she murmured thoughtfully.

CHAPTER 7

The charity ball that would open the season of 1904–5 was society's bugle call to action; summer feuds were laid away with summer finery and winter feuds brought out with winter furs. Militant ladies, each armed with an idea she was determined to defend to the last ditch, hastened to committee meetings only to have Victor, with devastating charm, calmly discard all ideas but his own. Under the spell of his bronze curls, his youthful figure, his aloof impartial courtesy, the ladies capitulated without a murmur of protest and went violently to work to win his approving smile. He insisted that subscriptions be doubled, that court costumes be mandatory and, in spite of Amelia's shocked disapproval, ruthlessly slashed the invitations to a scant four hundred.

"But we can't leave out the Osgoods," she protested. "I'm not giving this ball to make enemies, Victor."

"No one will be particularly flattered to be here unless some people of importance are left out," observed her son. "Mrs. Osgood is a malicious gossip. If she's dropped, she'll keep the memory of this ball alive for years. She is far more useful as an enemy than as a friend. Mrs. Osgood is out, Mater."

He was equally adamant over his mother's costume, and when she showed him Suzanne's sketch he tossed it aside. "It won't do," he said. "There will be a dozen Pompadours in the room." A little smile touched his lips. "Tell Mlle. Suzanne to sell this costume to Mrs. Winthrop Carrington. The headdress will, for once, conceal those disgusting dun-colored locks. No, Mater. Leave the desecration of Pompadour to Mrs. Carrington." He leaned back and closed his eyes. "Your waist and your legs are your best points," he went on after a moment. "I want you as a Boucher shepherdess, in flowered *mousseline*, with a blue ribbon around your hair."

"Oh, no, Victor," cried Amelia. "Perhaps not Pompadour, but a shepherdess! I'd look ridiculous. I wouldn't think of it."

"You would look charming, conspicuously simple, and beyond criticism," insisted her son. "Give Mlle. Suzanne my compliments on her sketch and ask her opinion of my idea."

222

To Amelia's disappointment, Suzanne agreed enthusiastically with Victor. "*Ah, mais oui,*" she cried, smiting her forehead with the heel of her hand. "I, Suzanne, am idiot! Oui. *La petite Boucher!* It is perfect. Perfect. *Ce jeune monsieur* is smart, eh?" She squinted meaningly at Amelia. "Ver-ry smart. He show the legs."

She rushed around, screaming for silks, muslins, ribbons; threw them over the shoulders of the model, tore them off again, cursing the model when she winced at a pinprick. Amelia kept shaking her head. "I don't like it, Suzanne," she protested. "That skirt is at least twelve inches off the floor. I cannot appear like that. I—it isn't decent. And it's too simple. There is no use going on with it; I will not be a shepherdess."

Suzanne plunged instantly into an abysmal calm. "*Très bien,*" she said coldly. "Madame will tell me what she want. She does not approve the exquisite Marie Antoinette when she play with her ladies she is a shepherdess. Madame deceive herself if she think this costume is simple."

"Marie Antoinette never wore anything like that, Suzanne," declared Amelia.

"She do." The modiste nodded. "When she wish to be most charming, most gay, she dress herself and make milk. She become the shepherdess." She heaved a sigh. "But Madame wish to be La Pompadour? That is simple."

"Well . . ." Amelia hesitated. "I do like that blue silk puffed at the sides, and the tight pointed bodice; it might be becoming. Perhaps if you could make the muslin skirt not quite so full and a little longer . . ."

Elaborate entertainment by newcomers to Fifth Avenue was not unusual in New York at this time, but as a rule, these lush exhibitions were of little interest to entrenched society. The charity ball, however, clothed in anonymity, could be, and was, attended by the most exclusive members of society wherever it was given. Those who drove to this one did so with curiosity already tinged with boredom.

"Do you know anything about these people, Albert?"

"No. He's pretty well known on the Street."

"Is that all?"

"I'd like to run this sword through him for getting me into these breeches. They itch."

"Don't be so impatient, Albert. As soon as we've put in an appearance, we'll leave. I'm quite as uncomfortable as you are."

But at three o'clock in the morning Albert's breeches were still cavorting around the ballroom, and by that time the charity ball at the Bradway mansion was written in history.

Before the guests arrived, Victor, dressed in white satin breeches and a heavily embroidered white satin coat, snug at the waist, a foamy jabot of lace at his throat, and a light sword at his side, stepped into the ballroom for a last look at his work. It was good. The huge room was transformed into a salon of sophisticated elegance. Groups of easy chairs and sofas were arranged along the walls for those who gossiped and sipped champagne while watching the dancers; tall urns filled with flowers in the formal French fashion separated these groups; garlands subdued the harsh glare of mirrors, and candles in the crystal chandeliers twinkled with intimate gaiety. It was good, and as he set his hand on his sword and crossed the polished floor for a last word to the musicians, he saw, with satisfaction, the elegance of his figure reflected in the mirrors. It would not be long now before Evelyn Schultz, an ardent committee worker, buxom daughter of the soup king, would be in his arms. Victor's experience had not, so far, included soup in tins, but he had decided to curb his instinctive repugnance and learn more of this source of nourishment.

By ten o'clock the street was jammed with carriages, and Antoinettes, Pompadours, Du Barrys, Robespierres, and Louis' poured into the ballroom. They came in, New Yorkers—curious, nervous, or bored—but the moment they stepped into the fairyland of make-believe they assumed the character of their dress; the Du Barrys, released from inhibition, flirted, the Dianes began their pursuits, and the Antoinettes, fearful of their wobbling wigs, looked ready for the guillotine. The mirrors picked up the shimmer of the magnificent costumes, the flash of jewels, the music sighed into a beseeching waltz, and the charity ball was on.

Steve opened it with the exquisite little shepherdess. He had consented to wearing a blue ribbon stretched across his broad shirt bosom and the Order of the Garter around his neck. The Order looked as if it belonged there and the thick, iron-gray thatch on the massive head, the strong features, and the penetrating glance made the English Ambassador the dominating figure in the room. And Steve was a beautiful dancer, as light and free on his feet as he had been when he rode the logs down the river on the spring drive.

"Don't whirl me so much, Steve," begged Amelia, clinging to him. "I'm afraid my legs will show."

Steve laughed. "The more they show, the better," he whispered. "That's a pretty dress you've got on. Makes you look about sixteen."

Amelia, feeling his strength lifting, guiding her, looked up at him. "Steve," she said, a puzzled tenderness in her voice, "Steve . . ." Then, "Don't forget to dance with that woman in red over there. She's Mrs. Worthington. And tell Herbert to be sure that champagne is passed constantly."

The floor was soon crowded with circling couples, and after shoving a heavy woman in red around the floor a few times, Steve decided he had done his duty and could join the renegades playing poker in the library. On the way to the door he encountered Victor with a wholesome, good-natured-looking girl in his arms. "This is a good show you've put on, Victor," he said genially. "I congratulate you." Victor, the familiar surge of resentment clouding his eyes, moved on with his Diane, who peered around his white satin sleeve to follow Steve with her eyes.

"My goodness, he's a handsome man, isn't he?" she said. "I think he's the best-looking man I ever saw. I do wish he would dance with me."

Victor's arm was around the waist of millions but it loosened perceptibly. "I imagine he would be your type," he said coldly. "Let me get you some champagne."

Supper was served at small tables in the dining room, in the hall, and in the drawing room, and young couples sat in dozens on the curving stairway, laughing over the novelty of balancing plates on their knees. Annie's puff paste, filled with rich creamed chicken laced with sherry, was hot and delicate, the vintage champagne cold and sparkling, the ices in the shape of fleur-de-lis did not, thank God, melt around the edge. Steve drank whiskey and munched roast beef sandwiches in the smoke-filled library behind closed doors, where another party was in full swing without benefit of charity or court ceremony.

After supper dancing was resumed until, at about three in the morning, Herbert tapped on the door of the library to inform the gentlemen within that the queens and concubines desired their consorts. Satin coats were sorted out, chips dumped on the table, scores settled, and the Louis on the sofa woke up, yawned, looked at his watch, and swore.

Steve had helped his last guest to negotiate the course to the carriage door and was crossing the ballroom when he saw Amelia and Victor standing at the foot of the stairs. He was feeling fine, proud of this party in his home, and had started toward them to say so when he stopped short. Amelia, in her dainty dress, looked tired but her face was glowing with triumph and satisfaction. "Wasn't it wonderful, Victor?" he heard her say. "You did it magnificently. I am so happy about it, darling. It was marvelous. It will be a long time before anyone in this city will give a ball to equal this one. There wasn't a flaw anywhere."

Victor, cool, graceful, immaculate in his white satin, shrugged. "Aren't you overlooking the disgusting spectacle of Steve staggering across the room with that drunk? If the newspapers get hold of that they'll turn this affair into another western barroom debauch. They're waiting for just such a chance—your husband gave it to them."

"Oh, no, no, Victor!" Amelia's anguished protest came clear and shrill to Steve. "Don't say that. Oh, how awful! I'll die if that happens. I couldn't bear it. But it won't happen. It can't. They didn't see it, and if they did they can't blame me if a guest gets drunk. It would be different if Steve was drunk but he wasn't. I watched him. He behaved all right most of the time. He wasn't drunk; it was the other man."

Steve saw Victor look down at the agitated shepherdess and shake his head. "Are you quite sure, Mater?" he heard him say. "To my eye there was little to choose between them—except that one of them was a gentleman."

They went up the stairs, the shepherdess clinging to the gallant's arm.

Steve stood where he was, alone in the empty ballroom. The musicians had gone. The fading flowers filled the room with a lingering fragrance and the wide floor, littered with petals, programs, bits of tinsel, was as silent as an abandoned wreck on a forgotten shore. The only figure remaining in that hollow scene was that of the Ambassador from England. He stood rigid, motionless for a moment, his face flushed a deep and dangerous red. Then his fist yanked the Order of the Garter from his neck and sent it spinning to join the other trash. Steve, who seldom thought of money spent, thought of it now.

"Goddamn it!" he shouted, and his voice boomed through the empty room. "Who's running this outfit? Who paid for this damn puppet show, anyhow?"

226

CHAPTER 8

Nothing came of Victor's dire prediction. The morning papers came out in extravagant praise of the charity ball. Amelia leaned back on her pillows and wept with relief.

And Victor was not long in reaping his reward. The godlike young man soared on the social horizon like Phoebus in his golden chariot, his mother floating like a nymph at his side, her hand on the reins of social triumph.

Nothing like this happened to Steve. He continued to plod back and forth from his house to his office with the monotonous regularity of a horse pulling a plow. He had no fault to find with that. He liked the feeling of weight on his shoulders and his furrows were rich and deep. His work was all right, but he never entered the huge silent symbol of his wealth without feeling that he was in the wrong house, and he often hesitated like a stranger before climbing the curving stairway to his room. Once there in the familiar litter of books and papers, the deer head on the wall staring with fixed gaze into the past they both knew, he stretched out in Cyrus' chair, lit his pipe, and felt better. But this was thin comfort, and as the weeks went by, he climbed the repellent stairs less often.

He seldom caught a glimpse of Victor but occasionally came across Amelia as she rushed past, planning some entertainment or going to one. Since the ball he had curtly refused to attend her large dinners, and as they were frequent, he dined more often at his club.

But Steve was far from lonely for the society of Amelia and Victor. In fact, he welcomed the freedom to get back to the life he enjoyed. His days in the office were filled with the perpetual come and go of a large and active organization and for his after-business hours he had a wide choice of companions. Whether he wanted them or not, Steve picked up friends with the ease of a magnet picking up steel filings, and once within his orbit they stuck to him. Financiers who made money, society playboys who got rid of it, theater people, politicians, sportsmen, gamblers; all of them, all over town, welcomed a nod from Steve as the signal for a good time, a good game, or an easy touch. Not the least entertaining of these friends was Florette's Charlie.

Steve's affair with Florette had long since petered out, to the regret and relief of both of them. "I guess this ties it up, Steve," she said one night as they sat eating scrambled eggs. "The show goes on the road next week and I'll be knocking around the sticks for a year probably. Charlie will be out by that time; not that that would make any difference! Charlie'd like you. No. It ain't that," she sighed. "We get along too well; like a pair of old slippers, just too darn comfortable. Know what I mean?" Steve said yes, he did. "Sure, you do," she went on. "There ain't nothing like being real good friends to take the kick out of a thing like this." She twisted around in his arms and looked up at him. "Take right now. Do you feel like going to bed?" Steve said no, he didn't. "Well, there you are." She nodded. "Neither do I. Let's have a beer and forget it."

Charlie got out after Florette had gone, and while he was getting rid of his prison pallor in the little flat on Riverside Drive, Steve sometimes went up there to listen to Charlie talk. Oddly enough, Charlie looked a good deal like Curtis, the only really honest man Steve had ever known. He had the same fine, sensitive features and high, intellectual brow and his mild brown eyes gazed at Steve with the same innocent expression.

One night when they had been talking about Charlie's methods of crime and his years up the river, Steve told him bluntly he looked less like a crook than most men he knew. Charlie, slouched low in his chair, his thin ankles crossed, his hands in the pockets of his cheap new suit, nodded without offense. "That's right," he said. "They look like crooks because they are crooks. I don't look like a crook because I ain't one."

"How do you figure that, Charlie?"

"Don't have to figure. My old man gave me a pretty good education," he went on, "and he was mighty proud when I got in a bank—thought I'd be president inside a year, but I hadn't been there six weeks before I knew I'd never get off that stool."

"Why not?"

"They keep honest men on those stools. Funny thing"—he paused reflectively—"a crook will cheat an honest man every chance he gets but a crook never thinks an honest man will cheat him. That's about the only advantage an honest man has."

Steve shook his head. "Even your thinking's crooked, Charlie."

"Show me where," demanded Charlie with spirit. "Show me where. See here, Steve. You figure out how to make money, don't you? Right. That's what I did. Figured it out. And I find that three quarters of the money that goes through that bank got there through fraud of some kind. Legal fraud? What's legal about fraud? Tell me that. I see an opportunity to make money and I take it, same as you do. What's the difference?"

Steve grinned at him. "You get pinched."

"Sure, that's right. I get pinched and you don't. A hell of a thing!"

But it was Charlie's way with figures that fascinated Steve. He was pretty good at figures himself but Charlie was a mathematical genius. As he listened to Charlie's astonishing manipulations, he developed a warm admiration for the man who had caught up with him.

"Hell!" said Charlie with scorn. "Half a dozen of 'em were at it for six months and then they didn't get anywhere near it. They got enough to send me up but I'm out now and I've still got plenty to see me and Florette through the rest of our lives."

"How well would you do if you worked for me, Charlie?"

Charlie thought a moment. "Oh, I could probably take you for around fifty thousand a year for a couple of years. Maybe more. Depends. I'd have to know your layout. But I ain't working for you," he added.

"You're dead-right you're not," agreed Steve emphatically. "But I'd like to see you go straight, Charlie. Like to see what you could do to the Street."

Charlie looked at him with those brown eyes. "Straight! Who? Me? I'm telling you. I'm straight. I take my chances, don't I? It's them that don't that ain't straight."

And sometimes, talking with his friends in finance, Steve wondered if Charlie wasn't right.

But it was the theater that gave Steve his real diversion. Over the years his interest in it had grown until now it embraced every angle of the fascinating, unpredictable profession of selling fairy tales to the public. He backed shows the way another man backs race horses, and with about the same results, but win or lose, he found satisfaction for his restlessness in the constant change, excitement, and confusion of the theater world. He liked the people who took this gamble with him; the nervous man who wrote the show, the caustic manager who promoted it, the feverish and voluble director who staged it, the artists who designed the costumes and the sets, and above all, the actors who came to focus on the stage to place their bets, as he did, on a new show.

A new show was opening that night, a musical comedy with a large cast. The first act was set, the orchestra tuning up, and behind the curtain the actors were clustered around the peephole sizing up the "house" that would make or break their efforts. "Bradway's out there." "Yeah, that big fellow, second row left on the aisle. He's got a bunch with him."

Steve had; one of them, an art dealer by the name of Mayo, was giving a party after the show. He didn't think much of Mayo but it amused him to watch the merchant's manipulations in turning wealthy guests into potential clients. This was done with the help of excellent food, vintage wines, pretty girls—and Mayo's famous swing.

This shrewdly contrived advertising medium, made of pink satin garlanded with fresh roses, hung from the ceiling of an exquisite little room paneled with Fragonard paintings. Girls did not swing in this swing stark-naked, as scandal insisted they did, but it was a fact that as the evening progressed, impeding outer garments were sometimes shed as the competing girls, curls flying, pretty legs outstretched, earnestly endeavored to touch with their toes the twenty-dollar gold piece represented by a certain cupid on the ceiling.

But that entertainment was coming later. Now the curtain went up and Steve leaned back, watching with interest how the show would shape up. He was idly deciding which of the cavorting blondes he would take to Mayo's when he caught sight of a black head in the midst of the swirling dance. It disappeared into the back row. Toward the end of the act the black-haired girl came forward again for a moment, but long enough to see that she was flat as a lath, her long legs thin as those of a young doe, and that she gave him a glance of sullen contempt as she whirled past. She looked like a thistle in a bunch of poppies. Steve grinned. That was the girl he'd take to Mayo's party!

At the end of the act he went backstage to find the stage-doorman. "What's the name of that skinny black-haired girl?" he asked.

The potbellied old fellow tilted back in his chair, looked up without interest. "How do I know? There's a dozen of 'em in the show."

"Not like this one," protested Steve. "She's got her hair cut like this." He drew his hand straight across his brow, but the old man shook his head.

230

"Can't tell you, mister. They all look alike to me."

Steve took out his notebook, scribbled, and handed the sheet with a five-dollar bill to the doorman. "See that she gets this," he said. "You can't miss her. Kind of a sulky face. Not another one like her in the show."

"Well"—the doorman fingered the bill—"I'll try to pick her up for you but I ain't makin' no promises."

During the rest of the show Steve watched for the black-haired girl, expecting to see some sign that she had received his note. Once she came forward in a fluffy dress, her thin arms waving two sticks covered with yellow silk. Steve made a move to attract her attention but she passed and disappeared without a glance.

The men with him had seen abundant acknowledgment of their notes, and after the show they all made their way backstage to pick up their girls. There was, at first, some confusion about who belonged to whom but finally a plump, lively little blonde sidled up to Steve and showed him his note. "I guess you're mine," said she coyly. "My name's Gloria. What's yours?"

Steve looked at the doorman, who shrugged and raised his hands. "I seen her but she run out so I give it to that one. Don't make no difference—they're all alike."

Steve was annoyed that his joke on the boys hadn't worked but Gloria was a good-natured little bundle already familiar with Mayo's swing. "That's a cute idea, ain't it?" she said as they drove to the party. "Lots of fun and gives Mayo a chance to look for his legs."

"His what?"

"Legs. Mayo's crazy about legs. Didn't you know that? He had a girl once. She told me. He'd give her new slippers every night and make her walk up and down for hours. You know—pose, like. Then he'd close his eyes and tell her to go home. She swore to God that's all there was to it but it got her so nervous she had to quit. Now, I ain't the nervous kind," she went on reasonably. "I'd walk up and down all night for the money he give her but I guess I ain't his type. I been in that swing a lot of times but he never takes a squint at my legs."

Steve laughed. "I'll take a squint at 'em," he promised.

He had plenty of chance. Plump little Gloria's efforts to kick the cupid were the high spot of the evening, and when he lifted her from the swing and led her to a divan against the wall, she snuggled against his shoulder, panting with her exertions and turning the gold piece in her hand. "Well, I made it this time," she said. "How do you like my legs?"

"Fine." He yawned as he fed her champagne. He didn't pursue the subject; he was bored with the party. Another girl was in the swing. She wasn't going to make it. He'd bet that if the black-haired girl was up there she'd stand up and punch that cupid in the face with her fist.

"What's so funny?" demanded Gloria petulantly. "What you laughing at? Me?"

"No." Another yawn. A pause. "What's the name of that black-haired girl in the show—the tall, thin one with bangs?"

"I don't know. I don't make friends with people like that."

"Why not? What's the matter with her?"

"She's just a hick come in from the sticks somewhere. I don't mix up with that kind of people. I come from Brooklyn, and if you're so sleepy you got to yawn in my face, you better go home."

Steve eyed her with owlish solemnity. "Gloria," he mumbled, "you're a wonderful girl. That's the most intelligent remark I've heard in a long time. It's worth another gold piece."

CHAPTER 9

A show, like a cake, can fall flat. In spite of experienced blending of materials and a long, hard beating to whip them together a producer can be, and often is, left with a sticky, soggy mess on his hands that no amount of frosting can induce the public to swallow. It was so with this show and Gresham, standing on the stage one night after the curtain had thumped down with no ripple of excuse to raise it again, turned to Steve with baffled exasperation. "Listen to that, will you? Not a hand. You'd think they were dead out there. What's the matter with this show? Music's good. Kelly's good. We get a good house every night; just short, that's all, but it don't pick up. Damned if show business ain't worse than the track. Anyhow, a horse can't yap at you if he's short on speed."

Steve agreed with him. "I don't like it any more than you do, Herb," he said, "but this show isn't pulling. We might as well face it."

"Hell!" the stage manager exploded. "I'm telling you. If we could run another month we'd make money on the road. Sure thing. If we fold now everybody loses." A group of girls went by on the way to the stage door. "All those poor kids out of work in the middle of the season," he added sentimentally. "It's tough." He hitched his belt and eyed Steve. "Why don't you talk to Rathburg? He'd listen to you."

Steve grinned. "Rathburg's been talking to me for a week."

"No dice?"

"No dice, Herb."

Gresham shrugged. "Well, I guess you're right at that. You can't back a plater into a winner. Sometimes you get a break through," he insisted, still strumming on the subject of keeping the show going. "Take *Snowballs* last season. Notice up—and they hit the jackpot. Going yet. Got a company on the road. You can't tell."

Another girl clattered down the iron stairs, pulling on her coat that flapped like a scarecrow in the wind as she hurried by. As she passed, her dark eyes swept both men with a venomous glance.

"There goes one of your poor little kids," Steve commented. "She looks about as helpless as a fish hawk."

"That one?" The stage manager's eyes followed the slight figure. "That's one I could do without. I'd like to bet she's the one put the jinx on us. Wish I'd fired her."

"Why didn't you?"

"I dunno. Quick, for one thing. Show her something and she had it. That's something when you're working with a bunch like I got here. But she's a bad actor. Can't handle her any more than you could a rattlesnake." He shoved back his cap and scratched his head. "Well—the hell with all of 'em. We close Saturday night. Right?"

"Right. I'm out from now on."

"If you're out we're all out," said Gresham philosophically. "I don't blame you. What makes you play around with show business, anyhow? You must like losing money."

"I don't like a poor bet any better than the next man," said Steve, "but that's not the point. Right now I feel the way you do about the track. A horse gets his oats, win or lose. You people don't. I don't like that angle of it."

"Forget it." Gresham wagged his head. "We're used to it. Anybody looking for oats wouldn't be in show business. We've had a couple months off you, ain't we? That's something." He stuck out his hand and Steve grasped it. He liked Gresham.

This was Tuesday night. Steve didn't see the show again. The theater was made ground for him. He didn't belong in it but he was willing to pay a good price for intruding on it. He liked to watch a show take shape, liked his share in the excitement of opening night, but there was no pleasure in watching a show die. It hurt to see those light feet dancing with lead in the heels. He stayed away.

But there are always certain details to be cleaned up after the dead. On Saturday night when he knew the disbanded company had cleared out for the last time he cashed in his chips at the club and drove to the theater to keep his appointment with Rathburg and Gresham. He found them on the empty stage at a deal table under the glare of a single light discussing back salaries and the disposal of scenery and costumes. The back of a theater curtain is not gay; stacked scenery casts ugly shadows, and there is no spot on earth where gloom can settle more quickly than on an abandoned stage. The worried men greeted him with obvious relief, and after disposing of the back-salary problem Steve shoved a check across

234

the table to Rathburg. The producer seized the check with one hand and grabbed Steve with the other. "Mr. Bradway," he said, his dark eyes moist with emotion, "I hate to take it." Steve grinned. "I do—and so help me God, I'll make it up to you. Take it from me. The next time I get a hit you're the first man I'll see."

"I can bet on that, Eddie," said Steve. "Now, about this rental contract. I don't think you'll be sued, but if you are, get in touch with me." He stood up and shook hands with both men. "So long. Better luck next time."

A light was still burning over the stage door but the alley was dark. As he stepped forward, a figure moved out of the shadows, blocking his way. It was snowing and she must have been standing there a long time for the battered felt hat was filled with snow and the big flakes had caught on the coat she clutched beneath her chin. There was no mistaking the small face, dead white in the gloom, or the dark eyes raised defiantly to his.

"What are you doing here?" he asked harshly.

"I thought you was Gresham," she said. "I got to see him. The show's closed."

"Why are you standing out here? Why don't you wait inside?"

"I don't know," she said uncertainly. "I got to see him."

Steve stared down at her. She wasn't as tall as she looked on the stage. The snow was falling, swirling between them, and she kept her eyes fixed on his face. He wanted to brush her aside. Go home. Forget these people out of work tonight. Like this one. "You won't see Gresham," he said. "He's busy in there with Rathburg. Come along. I'll get you something to eat."

She hesitated for a moment; then he saw her shoulders sag a little. "All right," she said.

Steve took her to Shanley's and got a table in a booth. She took off her coat, slipped into the seat, and picked up the menu. "Have anything you want," said Steve. He leaned back, lit a cigar, crossed his legs, and watched her through the smoke of his cigar. She wasn't much to look at. The black hair was twisted in a tumble-down knot at the back of her head, and smeared traces of make-up were in the roots of it around her ears; the cheap red wool dress she wore was too big for her, the white collar was soiled around the neck, and the finger tracing the menu was as dirty as the collar. She shoved the menu aside and looked up. "I want a steak with fried onions and a baked potato and a cup of coffee," she said.

Steve gave the order and turned to her. "You seem to know what you want," he smiled. "Why were you waiting to see Gresham?"

"I got to have a job, ain't I? The show's closed. He's the only one I know in New York."

"That so? How did you get here?"

"On the Erie Railroad."

Steve laughed. "All right," he said. "Keep it to yourself if you want to."

The steak came and she pitched into it with the energy of a lumberjack. Steve tried to attract her attention at one point. "How's the steak?" he asked. She shrugged without looking up. When the steak was finished, she mopped up the gravy with a piece of bread, shoved back the empty dishes, leaned back, and gave him a bold, straight look. "That was good," she said.

This was the first time Steve had seen her eyes clearly. They were wide set, heavily fringed with long black lashes, deep violet in color, startling in the direct intensity of their gaze. "How about some ice cream?"

"All right. Chocolate."

She was halfway through the ice cream when she looked up again. "Say," she said, "I bet I could get a job right here if you talked to that man. It's a good place to eat and lots of show people come here."

Steve frowned. "What are you talking about? You can't get a job at Shanley's."

"Yes, I can," she insisted, leaning forward. "Didn't you see that old woman out there where you left your hat? Her glasses fell off . . . I bet she gets those hats all mixed up. I bet I could get that job if you spoke to that man."

"You mean you want me to put that woman out of her job so you can have it?"

"I need a job, don't I?"

Steve leaned back. That shabby female across the table was as unscrupulous as any pirate he had ever encountered in his life. She disgusted him. "What makes you think I'd do a dirty trick like that?" He scowled.

"I guess you done plenty," she said coolly. "You was the one let the show close. I heard you talking to Gresham that night. I just remembered that. It's a good thing you come out instead of Gresham. You owe me a job."

Steve's anger boiled up. His face hardened. "You're as tough a little

236

piece as I ever ran into," he said, "but if you think I owe you a job you've got another guess coming. Put on your coat. You're getting out of here."

She threw back her head, raised her hands to the untidy black mass at the back of her neck and began twisting it. "What's your hurry?" she said coolly. "I got to fix my hair." Her pose and the movement of her arms spread the wings of the white collar and Steve caught a glint of gold beneath her chin. She had on a gold pin. A good-looking gold pin. Steve looked at it. Looked again, hard. Funny! "Let's see that pin you've got on."

One hand flew to cover it. "What you want to see it for? It's mine."

"It's yours unless you picked it up somewhere." He stretched out his hand, palm up. "Let me see it."

She drew back against the wall. "What do you want it for?" she repeated. "You said you was in a hurry."

"Hand it over."

The black coil loosened again as both hands fumbled with the pin. "You can see it," she said sullenly. "It's hard to get off is all I meant." And in a moment the pin lay in his hand.

Now that he had it Steve didn't look at it. He didn't have to. He knew what he held in his fist as certainly as he knew that his heart had lurched to a stop and then plunged on again. He stared at the girl. After a long time and from a great distance her voice came to him. "What's the matter? You sick?"

"No. No." He roused. "Nothing the matter. Where did you get this pin?"

"It's none of your business where I got it," she flared. "It's mine. Give it back."

His fist opened and the pin lay in his palm, glittering in the light. There were thousands of pins like this in the world, lover's knots. But he knew this one. There was the crack across the blue stone that he had used to force a bargain with the jeweler in Chicago twenty years ago. No question about it. He shoved the pin across the table. She fastened it in her dress and her hands went back to her hair—that thick black thatch! "I don't see why you act so funny about it," she said resentfully. "You act like I stole it. Can't a girl have a pin without you think she got it somewhere?"

"No—no . . ." he repeated. "Nothing like that. It's a pretty pin, that's all." He stood up. "Come along—it's late."

They were halfway across the crowded room when he felt her

pluck his sleeve. "Here comes that man. You said you'd get me a job."

Steve stopped. He wanted, as he had never wanted anything in his life, to get rid of this girl at his heels. He felt as if he had a wolf on his trail and it was following—following—the way Kit had followed him that morning through the woods. He shook his head. Nonsense! The headwaiter hurried to him, zigzag through the tables, a smile on his face, a worried look in his eyes. "Yes, Mr. Bradway. Can I do something for you?"

Steve took his wallet from his pocket and handed him a large bill. "Everything's all right, Gus. But you can do me a favor. This young woman needs a job. She'd like to work in your coatroom."

The man hesitated, embarrassed, eying the bill. "I'm sorry, Mr. Bradway," he began, "but we've got a good girl there. We——"

"I know you have," Steve interrupted. "Marie's all right. This girl won't interfere with her. I'll speak to Marie. If she wants her in there, you take it up with Shanley. Tell him I told you to."

"Yes, sir. Thank you, sir."

Marie produced Steve's coat and hat before he could find his check. He had trouble with his coat, too, fumbling for the sleeves before she helped him into it. "There you are, Mr. Bradway." She smiled, her tired face resolutely cheerful.

Steve looked at her. "You're a good girl, Marie," he said soberly. "I want you to do something for me. This girl is out of a job. I want you to take her in here with you."

"Oh, I couldn't do that, Mr. Bradway." The check girl flushed when she saw the bill he offered her. "You don't have to do that," she protested. "I'd do anything I could but I can't do that. Customers are awful particular about their checks. You don't know how they carry on when they get the wrong hat. I couldn't."

Steve pressed the bill into her hand. "She wouldn't have anything to do with the checks," he urged. "She could hang up the coats; help you out that way, couldn't she? You must be rushed here at times."

"She might. I do get piled up here sometimes." She turned to the girl, whose eyes were fixed on the bill. "What's your name?"

"Carla."

"Carla. That's a cute name. You're on the stage, ain't you? I thought so. I was, too, a long time ago. I know what it's like to be out of a job. I guess we'll get along all right." She held out the bill. "But I don't want this, Mr. Bradway. I'd do it anyway."

"Keep it," said Steve bluntly. "It's worth it to me. And if she

238

makes any trouble for you, get rid of her. I'm not asking you to put up with her. It's nothing to me. She's got a job. It's up to her to keep it."

Marie surprised him. "Don't be so hard on her, the poor little thing," she said. "She'll be all right." She swung back the counter and laid her hand defensively on the girl's arm. "You can start right now, Carla, if you want to; help me with the last customers so you'll get the hang of it. They ain't so particular late at night."

The last Steve saw of Carla she was taking off her coat and glaring at him from under the old felt hat. He knew as well as if she had shouted after him what was in her mind: "You mean, stingy old man! You didn't give me no bill!"

CHAPTER 10

When the door of Shanley's Restaurant closed behind him, Steve's mind closed with it. There wasn't a thought in his head as he crossed to the curb and stood there, frowning, drawing the cold night air deep into his lungs. He noticed that it had stopped snowing. That was good. It was a relief to a man as tired as he was not to have to battle with the snow on a dim trail. Confusing. He was glad it had stopped snowing. He'd get his bearings in a minute now. A cab came along, its approach muffled in the snow. It passed before he roused with an effort, hailed it. Back at his club, Steve walked straight through to his room, went to bed, and slept like a man felled with an ax. No dreams disturbed him.

The next morning he woke up feeling fine, his mind alert and ready for the day's work; all but one small corner of it. This was not the first time, by many, that Steve had sealed out of his mind certain thoughts he didn't care to face. He did it thoroughly and they ceased to trouble him. He did it thoroughly now, and for the next two weeks went on with his life as if his heart had never jolted to a stop.

Then one day, seated in one of the club's seductive easy chairs, he was tempted to open the door a crack and the hidden thoughts swarmed out. Well, let them come; take a look at them. Might as well face it and be done with it. He settled back, smoke drifting from his big cigar, to examine the extraordinary coincidence that had thrown that girl across his path. Not so extraordinary, come to think of it. A good deal of that flotsam drifted onto the stage, and once in those shallows, was bound to drift to New York sooner or later. He'd seen longer shots than that come off.

And she was his; no getting around that. It stuck out all over her. Not so much in her looks; any man might have sired that black hair, those high cheekbones; and there was no trace of her mother in her except, perhaps, in her wide blue eyes, darkened by some alchemy with his own. It wasn't her looks that convinced him, or the fact that she had that pin; it was her character. It galled him to his soul to admit that in this female he saw himself reflected, blurred and distorted, as in a cheap boardinghouse mirror. But there was no getting around it. Her greed, the way she seized an opportunity and hung on to it until she got what she was after were traits too familiar to be denied. There he was in all his pride reduced in size to a petty chiseler after a job in a coatroom. He squirmed in his chair. Damned if he'd admit, even to himself, that this sloven with the dirty neck, kicking the backdrop in the chorus, was any part of himself. She had survived without him for twenty years. Let her go on surviving. She was nothing to him. Nothing at all. A man wasn't obliged to open up a thing like that after twenty years. Be tough on him if he had to; tough on his family, too. For the first time in months his thoughts flew to Amelia and his uneasy conscience rushed to her like a man arriving at sanctuary. What was he thinking about? He couldn't rake up the past now even if he wanted to. Certainly not. A man's first duty was to protect his wife. The girl had given him a jolt; no question about that, but a man kept such jolts to himself. Thing to do was take it, get over it, forget it. That was it. Forget it.

Satisfied at last with this virtuous disposal of the past, Steve shoved Carla back into the corner of his mind, slammed the door, sighed, leaned back in his chair, and lit a fresh cigar.

Twenty-four hours later the past caught up with him again. It was raining hard that night, the cold driving rain that in the forest washed away the remaining patches of snow from beneath the trees in preparation for spring. Steve, whose thoughts lately were alive to such suggestions, was standing at the window thinking he was lucky to have a thick carpet beneath his feet that night instead of a soggy trail when the callboy, gliding across the room like Mercury on skates, slid up to him. "Sorry to disturb you, sir, but somebody wants to speak to you."

Steve turned with a start. "Who is it? What's his name?" he snapped.

"It isn't a gentleman, sir. It's a young woman. She's out there. She wants to speak to you. She won't give her name, sir."

"Nonsense!" Steve glared. "You know better than to come to me with a thing like that. Get rid of her."

"Beavers tried to, sir, but she got past him. She's sitting there. She says she'll stay until she sees you. Beavers wants to know what to do, sir. Several gentlemen are complaining."

Steve, boiling-mad, launched himself across the big reading room.

241

Heads behind newspapers turned as he passed. She was there all right, sitting in the entrance hall looking like a drowned rat, the battered hat dripping, soggy with rain. He strode up and faced her. "What's the meaning of this?" he demanded harshly. "What are you doing here?"

She sat there as if screwed to the chair, her pale face, drenched with rain, raised to his. "I quit," she said. "She kept me in back there and wouldn't give me no tips, so I quit."

"What's that to me? It's none of my business."

"Yes it is," she said, her eyes on his. "You know it is. You got to get me another job."

Got to! Steve stared at her, the door in the back of his mind wide open again. Got to! What did she mean by that? What was she up to? A good many ears were listening for the answer to that. A man Steve knew came in, stopped as if to speak, passed with an amused grin. Steve, furious, turned to the doorman. "You'll hear from this, Beavers," he declared. "Get my coat and call a cab."

In the cab with that girl beside him, filling the air with the rank smell of wet wool, he sat silent, trying to control his anger. Emotion out of control had seldom been a handicap to Steve but it was now, and he knew it. This was no time for a snap decision. It wouldn't do, for instance, to stop the cab and pitch her out of it. If this woman had guessed his relationship to her, he was in for a bad time. If she had proof of it and had come to New York to engineer that "chance" encounter with him, he was in for worse than a bad time; he was in a hell of a fix, and it looked damn likely. Well, he wasn't the first man to face that problem. Come to think of it, females out of the past seemed to dangle around the necks of most prominent men with big bank accounts. He knew a dozen of them himself. They were all surviving. Looked at that way, this affair lost some of its sinister aspect. Steve felt better. He could handle this. Thing to do was find out where he stood and carry on from there.

As if she sensed his change of mood, he heard the girl speak. "Where are we going? Ain't we going anywhere?"

For some time the cab, driven by a bent figure shrouded in black oilcloth, had been rolling along at the pace of a hearse. Where they were going lay in the clouded future, but it occurred to Steve that he could at least control their immediate destination. He opened the door a crack and shouted to the jehu on the box, "Go to Manetti's on West Thirty-seventh and get a move on."

Manetti's was a small Italian restaurant patronized by those customers who read a menu from right to left. Steve had been there with Gresham, and Gresham was in his mind at the moment. Help might lie in that direction. Not many patrons were seeking nourishment on that stormy night and none paid any attention to the well-dressed man and the shabby girl who made their way to a table in a far corner. Carla took off her coat. "It's always bad weather when you take me out," she remarked as she shook the rain from her hat. Steve agreed with her on that point.

She sat down, put her elbows on the table, and ordered spaghetti. She had on a cheap new dress—a black and white check with a red belt around her slender waist, the pin conspicuous in a red bow beneath her chin, and the wide red slash of her lips brought out the delicate structure of her small pointed face. She looked clean; well fed, too, as if she had made the most of her stay at Shanley's. Steve was surprised at the change in her. She wouldn't be bad-looking if she got rid of that sullen expression.

He crossed his arms on the table and leaned forward. "That's a nice dress you've got on," he began. "Where did you get it?"

"Marie gave it to me. She wanted me to look nice. She was good to me at first."

"Why didn't you stay with her?"

She shrugged, turning the spaghetti on her fork. Thick lashes fanned the faint blue shadow under her eyes. "That wasn't any kind of a job," she said. "I want a better job than that. You'll have to get it for me."

"Have to?" Steve frowned. "What do you mean by that? Can't you get one for yourself?"

She shook her head. "I don't have to," she mumbled through dangling spaghetti. "You'll get it for me. I found out where you was so you could get it for me."

Steve sat back. So that was the way of it! But if she knew the truth why didn't she come out with it? She'd been in New York for three months with that show. What was she waiting for? Not sure? Feeling her way as he was? He was certain she had some suspicion of the truth—he had practically handed it to her by his fool behavior over that pin. But how much did she know? That was the point—how much? He watched her face for some trace of expression. He might as well have been looking at an egg. The only thing he could be positive about was that pin under her chin. It glittered in the light like a malevolent eye.

He was in a tight spot, but in spite of himself Steve felt his anger

243

rise again. Damned if he'd put up with this cat-and-mouse game any longer. "Found out where I was, did you?" he said harshly. "Tracked me down. What was the idea behind that? What makes you think I've got to get you a job? Out with it."

The wide eyes, blank as an idol's beneath the straight black fringe across her brow, gazed at him. "What are you so mad about? You got me that other job."

So! Steve shifted his attack. "All right, Carla," he said, his manner easing. "You want a job and I've got to get it for you. That's it, isn't it?" She nodded. "All right," he went on. "I got you one job and you threw it away. I'm not going to put up with that again." She gave him an odd disquieting glance and lowered her eyes. "I mean it," he said firmly. "I don't want you coming to me again. Now! What kind of a job do you think you can hold down?"

"On the stage."

Steve shook his head. "That's out. You wouldn't last a week on the stage. You haven't got the looks, for one thing, and Gresham told me you were no good. He wanted to fire you."

That touched her up. A faint red ran up her cheeks. "Him!" she flared. "A lot he knows. Him and his dumb blondes. I know every step he knows and a lot more. That's why he kept me back."

This was better. Steve crossed his arms and leaned forward. He smiled. "Nonsense. Gresham knows his business. He's the best stage manager in New York. You'd better give up this stage idea and go back home. You ran away from home to go on the stage, didn't you?"

"Me?" She retorted hotly. "I been on the stage all my life. I was born on the stage. That's more than that Irish mick can say."

Kit on the stage? Something wrong there. "So your mother's an actress, is she? Why aren't you with her?"

Her face settled into its habitual sullen mask. "I don't see why you've got to ask all these questions for. All I want is a job."

"I'm not so sure about that. I don't know what kind of a girl you are—don't know anything about you. Before I get you a job, I've got to be sure I'm not running into trouble with you." He hesitated. Decided. "Now, you take that pin you've got on," he went on carefully. "You wouldn't let me see it the other night. Wouldn't tell me where you got it. You say you quit Shanley's." He moved as if he meant to get up. "I think I'd better go around there and find out why you quit."

She reacted again with violence. What was it Gresham had called

244

her? A rattlesnake. She looked it as she thrust her chin forward and blazed at him. "Don't say things like that to me. I quit like I said I did and it's none of your business what kind of a girl I am." She jumped up and grabbed her coat. "I can take care of myself like I always done. I don't need no sneaky old man to help me."

Steve's heart bounded with relief. She was halfway across the room before he caught her arm. "Don't be a fool, Carla," he said. "Come back here. Let's have this out. I've got something to tell you." She gave him a long, level look and went back to the table. He asked her if she'd like some ice cream and she said she would. He ordered it, and coffee for himself. He lit a cigar and they settled down. "I'm going to tell you something that will surprise you, Carla," he said after a time. "I know where you got that pin."

The surprise boomeranged. It came back and hit him a wallop that knocked his breath out. "I know you do," she said calmly, the spoon halfway to her mouth, loaded with ice cream. "You was the one acted funny about it—not me. That's why I found you again. I guessed perhaps you was the one gave it to my ma. She said he was a rich man from New York."

"Yes, Carla," Steve admitted cautiously, after a moment. "I recognized that pin. I gave it to your mother a long time ago—long before you were born. She was a little girl then with yellow hair. Where is she now? I'd like to see her again."

"She's dead," she said, scraping her plate for the last of the ice cream.

"That's too bad, Carla. Is your father dead, too?"

"No," she said darkly. "He's around someplace, I guess."

"What was his name?"

"D'Angelo."

"Carla d'Angelo. That's a good stage name. Sounds Italian."

"That's right," she nodded. "He was a juggler in a show and Ma was wardrobe woman. That's what I mean I was born on the stage. That Gresham don't know what he's talking about."

"Do you remember your father?"

"I remember one thing," she said savagely, her hand over the pin beneath her chin. "He tried to take this pin from Ma so he could hock it, and she wouldn't let him, so he beat her up awful and walked out on her. He never come back. She was sick after that, but she was a long time dying. She had to keep going to take care of me. First job I got, she died."

Poor Kit. Poor little Kit! Steve had never known shame before in his life but now shame flooded through him, a deep and bitter draft of long standing. He heard the girl across the table speak to him. "You don't have to feel bad about it. It was a long time ago."

A long time ago! He stood up. "Come along, Carla," he said brusquely. "I'll take you home."

CHAPTER 11

At the time Carla crossed his path, Steve was almost fifty years old. His tall frame had filled out and the deep satisfaction of positive wealth had toned down his aggressive behavior and softened the impact of his glance. He enjoyed good food and was inclined to like large diamonds for shirt studs. A gold nugget the size of a walnut hung from his watch chain. Wrinkles, etched there by a lively sense of humor, now crisped the corners of his eyes but the mouth beneath the drooping black mustache was firm and grim.

A man of this appearance is not apt to be lost in the crowd. This man was not. Except for old Morrison himself, no man in New York at that time was more conspicuous than Steve Bradway. He loomed like a granite crag, a fine target for envious gossip.

The night he drove Carla home in the rain to her sordid boarding-house he gave her all the bills in his wallet. She took them without comment. "This will hold you for a while," he said. "Do you know any decent hotel around here?"

"Some of the principals lived at the Rockland. I know that."

"Right. Get a room and stay there until you hear from me. And don't come to my club again. You understand?"

"That made you mad, didn't it?"

"That, and a few other things. You do it again and it's the end of you. From now on you take it my way or not at all. Don't get any idea you can crowd me. I'll get you a job for the sake of"—he hesitated—"for the sake of old times, but I'm not putting up with any nonsense from you. Is that clear?"

He couldn't see her in the dark corner of the cab. "I guess I know how to act," she said.

When the cab drew up, she jumped out, ran across the pavement, up the rickety steps, and slammed the door. No upsurge of paternal emotion filled Steve's breast as he watched her go.

And none was there when he tried to get in touch with Gresham the next morning. A good deal of time that might have been more profitably spent on lucrative financial problems was wasted before the stage manager's voice came over the telephone in a loud yawn. "Yeah? Who is it? Oh, hello, Steve. Sure, I'm awake." Another yawn. "What's that? Not today, I can't. Got to get to the track and I'm late now."

"You're meeting me at Lüchow's at five o'clock," Steve snapped into the box on the wall. "Got that?"

"All right, all right. Don't bust my eardrums. What's on your mind? Got a new show?"

What was on Steve's mind, and remained there the rest of the day, was how to approach Gresham on the subject of a job for that girl without revealing his real reason for doing it. Nothing short of the truth would keep Gresham from leaping to the obvious conclusion and his pride, already badly damaged, rebelled against any such unfair assault upon his record. On the other hand, the immediate problem was to get the girl off his hands and into a job. He was willing to put up with a good deal to accomplish that. Once rid of her he could keep an eye on her from a distance, see that she had funds from time to time, and so dismiss the whole matter from his conscience.

But as he walked from Wall Street to Fourteenth that spring evening, the persistent, nagging obligation imposed on him by that girl galled him like a yoke around his neck, and he still could see no way of enlisting Gresham's help without looking like a damn fool.

He found him in a gloomy corner of the Tyrolese interior of the Hofbrau bent over a tall stein of beer in an attitude of extreme dejection. Steve had never seen Gresham in any apparel but the sagging trousers and tattered tan sweater he wore at work on the stage. The new spring suit he had on now, a bold brown and white check, set off by a green silk shirt of glossy texture, should have lifted the spirit of any man behind it, but there was less than no spirit in the face raised to greet Steve.

"What's the matter?" asked Steve. "Wouldn't they run for you?"

Gresham swore. "Run? Sure they run. They run me out of every dollar I got. Take the seventh," he went on, warming to the subject. "Had it cold all the way to the stretch. Length and a half in front. All he has to do is keep going and that bastard, Ismay, has to give him a crack with a whip. He rears, ditches Ismay—I wish to God he'd broke his neck—and goes on to win. I ask you. Can you beat it? I'm at the window ready to cash in twenty to one when I hear it."

248

Steve sat down and sympathized at some length and over several beers before he got around to his own hard luck. "Don't worry about the money angle of it," he said finally. "I've got a job that may pay you something."

"Yeah? What is it?"

Steve shifted, crossed his legs. "You remember that girl in the show, the one you wanted to fire?"

"Yeah. What of it?"

"I want a job for her."

Gresham looked up. "That so? How come?"

"She's been pestering me. Seems to think I owe her a job. Came to my club and made a nuisance of herself."

"She would. Why don't you throw her out? You don't owe her anything."

"I know that but she's out of work and I feel mean about it. The easiest way out is to get her a job. I want you to get it for me."

Gresham wagged his head. "You're an easy touch, Steve," he said. "You better drop it while you can—unless you're stuck on her. Even then," he added sagely.

Steve flared up. "Don't be a damn fool, Herb. You know me better than that. That cheap piece of goods? She's the last female on earth I'd look at from that angle. The long and short of it is I want a job for her."

"I believe you. I believe you," protested Gresham. He leaned forward, considerably more mellow, his hand around his beer mug. "I think I know what you mean. To tell the truth, that girl interested me. Same as you. Nothing personal, you understand, but you know me—always looking for talent. Well, I thought for a while that she had something. Personality. That's what it takes in show business. Fay was the same kind of a hellion when she was a kid and I had a tough time breaking her—but she's Fay Templeton today."

"You think this one's another Fay Templeton?"

"Hell, no!" The heavy shoulders swayed, rejecting any such idea. "There'll never be another Fay, not in a hundred years. I'm telling you she interested me, same as she does you, trying to get her a job. That's all. She's a good hoofer, I'll say that for her. Know anything about her?"

"Not much. She says she's been on the stage all her life. Her father was some kind of an acrobat named D'Angelo. Ever hear of him?"

"No." Gresham shook his head. "But that accounts for some of it. Probably in his act when she was a kid. I always feel sorry for the little kids those fellows throw around, but it's good training." He gazed for a moment at the black beams above his head. "There's nothing doing right now," he said, "but I'll tell you what I'll do. I've got a new show coming on this fall. Start rehearsals in August. If you can stall her along until then, I'll take her on."

Steve was enormously relieved by the slant the conversation had taken and it was an effort not to show it. "That's fine of you, Herb," he said casually. "What's the new show?"

"New piece. I haven't seen it yet but they say it's a dandy. They're starring Florette. Say!" His head jerked up. "You used to run around with Florette, didn't you? Sure. She a friend of yours?" Steve nodded, and the showman's eyes lit up like a prospector's at the glint of gold. "It's a natural," he exclaimed. "On a platter. Plain as print. Florette's a good sport. Get her interested in this girl. Get her to tame her down a little before I tackle her in August. Think you can do that?"

"Yes. Florette's a good friend of mine. Sounds like a fine idea."

"Fine idea? It's a handout. That's the way they come." Gresham shoved forward in his chair. "You got to recognize those things," he said earnestly. "I got a hunch as big as a house that if we can break that filly right, we've got something. Why not? New ones coming up all the time. This black one's got temper and speed. What more do you want for a start? By God," he swaggered, downing his beer and wiping his mouth with the back of his hand, "it won't be the first time I've picked a winner."

Steve grinned. "You picked several this afternoon, didn't you, Herb?"

The showman looked across at him. "What you talking about? This ain't the track. This is show business."

But the more Steve turned over in his mind Gresham's high-flown solution to his problem, the less he liked it. Whether the girl had talent was of no interest to him one way or the other and there was a feeling of undertow in the scheme that made him uneasy. He had experienced this warning of pull in the wrong direction many times and had learned to heed it, but it began to look as if this was one investment he couldn't write off. And yet it was simple enough on the surface. All he wanted was a job that would take the girl off his hands. It already seemed a long time since he'd been burdened with her, and if he went into this scheme of Gresham's, four months more of it lay ahead. No use giving her money to clear out. She was smart, hard, and unscrupulous, and he was certain she had sensed her hold on him. Crowd her too far and she'd search out that acrobat, and between the pair of them, there'd be hell to pay.

Behind closed doors in his office, "in conference" with his thoughts, Steve wrestled like a lion in a net, trapped and indignant. Well, there was nothing for it but to go with it and watch for a chance to get out.

Florette might be the answer. She was a smart one, too, and this was women business. To his relief he learned that the little star was back, "resting" on a farm on Long Island. He got into his new motor vehicle and drove down there. It took him most of the day but finally, covered thick with dust and sweating like a dock hand, he pulled up before an old weather-beaten shingled house with lilacs in bloom around it. Florette, in a pink dress, was in the yard feeding chickens. She jumped at the blat from the rubber horn and stared at the wicker brackets, the glittering brass, the red morocco. She didn't recognize the figure on the seat, disguised in a long tan dust coat and a checked cap with a visor as long as a shovel on his head, until he whipped off his goggles and vaulted out. "Steve!" she cried, hurling the pan at the hens and running to him. "What are you doing in that thing?"

Steve took her in his arms. "Making thirty miles an hour when we move." He laughed, kissing her. "Come on. Take a ride in it."

"Not me." She shook her head, holding close to him. "I ain't been in one of them things and I ain't going to. It's too dangerous. I got to think of my legs."

"Oh, come on," he urged. "I'll take it easy. I want to talk something over with you."

She gave him a quick look. "All right then," she said. "Let's go to the beach. It's nice there."

Steve escaped a smashed wrist by a split second when he cranked the machine, leaped in, and they drove for three miles without having to stop, through the sweet-smelling jack pines to the beach. Florette found a sheltered spot on the dunes and they sat for a while on the warm sand, looking at the sea. "How's Charlie?" Steve asked.

Florette sighed, her arms around her knees, her gaze far in the distance. "He's all right," she said. "You were awful good to him when he got out. I don't know what he'd done without you—me way off in California like that. I know you did it for the best, but he ain't the man he was."

"What do you mean? He's working, isn't he?"

251

"Yes. In a way. But the trouble is those people you sent him to are honest, decent men. They like him and he likes them. He sees the mistakes they make but he can't take advantage of 'em. I keep telling him he ought to get a job where he can have a free conscience. He'd be all right then."

"If he gets picked up again he'd be in for keeps, Florette," said Steve gravely.

"I know he would and so does he. But he'd better be in, feeling proud, than out, feeling the way he does now. A man can't be happy with a bad conscience like he's got. He feels like he's cheating every time he passes it up."

Steve, too, sat with his arms around his knees, his gaze on the distant horizon. He had no intention of doing more than ask Florette's advice on an abstract question; what he did was to tell her the entire story from beginning to end. He told it soberly, honestly, and she listened without a word until he finished. "You poor nut," she murmured then, her hand on his knee. "You poor nut."

After a moment she turned around and faced him. "You ain't in such a fix as all that, Steve," she said briskly. "There's plenty of bastards turning up every day and I'll bet she don't know where she come from any more than a rabbit. She's been kicked around so long she can't understand why you're good to her, that's all. I bet she's just a scared kid. That's the way she would act if she was scared; cautious-like, and watching her step. I think you got it sized up wrong because of what's on your mind. Anyhow, that's what I'm going to think till I see her." A cold wind had sprung up now that the light was fading. She jumped up and shook the sand from her skirts. "Come on," she said. "I got to get back to my hens."

Nothing more was said as they drove back until the little house came in sight. "Now you do like I tell you, Steve," she said then. "Drive her down here in this thing in a couple of days and I'll see what I can do. She won't fool me and push me around, if that's what she's up to. But I don't believe it. Right now I feel sorry for her—sorrier than I do for you. But don't tell her you've got a job for her. Just bring her down here, and we'll see."

When Steve lifted her down, he did so with more tenderness than he had ever felt for a woman in his life; more than he had ever felt for all of them put together. He thought the world of her. "Now, now," she laughed, pulling away from him. "None of that. Get back in that thing and go home. I'm resting."

CHAPTER 12

Steve drove back to New York feeling better. He had another puncture before he'd gone a mile, and two more before he reached the city, but the tires seemed to go on easier than they had on the way down and he sat on the high seat like a king on his throne while people and horses scattered like leaves at his approach. He felt optimistic enough to go home, but when he got there Amelia and Victor had gone out to dinner so he washed up, put on a dressing gown, and too restless to read, wandered through the empty house for a while looking for something to do. Finally he went to bed. There was nothing to do there, either. He thought about Florette. Fine woman. He was glad he'd talked to her, got it off his mind. She'd know how to handle it. Perhaps she was right. Perhaps the girl was all right. Well . . . He fell asleep.

The next morning, still feeling that after all the world was a pretty good place to be in, he walked down the hall to his wife's room. Amelia was sitting up in bed with her breakfast tray in her lap, reading her mail, envelopes and papers scattered on the satin coverlet. "Steve!" she exclaimed, whipping off her glasses and clutching her bed jacket to her breast. "Oh, how you startled me! Won't you ever learn to tap on my door?"

"No." He lifted a delicate satinwood chair and started to sit on it. She stopped him with a shrill cry. "No, no, Steve—not that one. You'll break it." So he let himself down on a tufted upholstered one that squashed under him like a cream puff. He looked at his wife. Her tiny figure, framed in the graceful folds of peach-colored taffeta hung from a gilt crown above her head, looked thin and old, almost lost in the lacy pillows at her back, and the morning sun, filtering through the same peach silk at the windows failed to soften the dry pallor of her skin. It had been a long time since Steve had been in his wife's bedroom and she had not improved during his absence.

"Well, Amelia," he said genially. "How long have you been wearing glasses?"

She gave him an angry glance, then her face wilted into the

253

familiar lines of martyrdom. Something was coming. He wished now he'd gone to the office. "I don't wear glasses," she protested fretfully, "but if I'd gone stone-blind you wouldn't know it. You don't care what happens to me. You take no interest in your family. I don't suppose you even know that Victor's getting married this fall."

"That's fine. Who to?"

"To the Schultz girl. Her father makes those soups. They have a magnificent place on Long Island."

"I know Schultz. Nice old fellow. We make his cans for him."

"He is not nice," she protested. "He's acting abominably. He hates Victor. He says he'd rather see his daughter dead than married to him. His only child, too. Can you imagine a father acting like that? He's horrible. Why, he actually tried to hit Victor one night."

"Did he?"

"Hit him? Of course he didn't. You don't suppose Victor would let a man like that hit him, do you?"

Steve remembered the yellow lump on Victor's jaw. "Not if he could help it," he said dryly.

But Amelia was too busy getting to her point to hear him. "But he can't stop it," she went on. "It's been announced. Her mother and I saw to that. They're going to be married. The only thing is"—she hesitated—"the only thing is that horrible man says he won't give them a penny."

"I see." Steve stood up and the pouf rose under him with a sigh of relief. "If you think I'm going to let Schultz pass the buck to me you're mistaken. You'll have to thrash this out yourself."

"Oh, Steve, wait a minute," she cried. "I didn't mean that we'd support them. I wouldn't think of it. Of course not. She's a common little thing without her money. But I thought if we made a gesture, perhaps gave them a house for a wedding present, he'd be shamed into keeping them in it. He ought to be delighted to see his daughter married to a man like Victor. It's worth every penny he's got and she'll never get another chance like it. She's a homely little thing but she adores Victor, absolutely adores him. I think she'll die if that old man goes on behaving like this. He won't listen to me but perhaps if you told him . . ."

Steve shook his head. "Schultz knows what he's doing. Let him take care of her."

Amelia threw her head back against the pillows and began to cry. "Oh, Steve," she wailed, "I'm not thinking of her. I'm thinking of Victor. My poor child. Robbed of his inheritance. It's been too, too

254

tragic for him. You've no idea how I've suffered over it. For years and years. I've done all I can for him. I worked so hard over this, and she's perfect for him. All I ask is a little help. Oh," she sobbed, "how can you be so unkind after all I've done for you?"

Steve felt stifled in this pink room. Pink! Florette's pink dress crossed his mind. How fresh and clean it had smelled! He wanted to get out. Let Schultz take care of his own daughter-troubles. He had enough of his own. "All right," he said bluntly. "If it's that Fifty-second Street house you're after you can have it, but that's as far as I'll go, now or in the future."

Amelia's grief disappeared. She smiled, mopping her eyes. "How wonderful you are, Steve. How did you guess it? It's just what I want, but I had to be sure. Now Victor and I can go abroad next week to buy the furnishings for it. The poor girl has atrocious taste, so I'll have to do it for her. I dread it. It's too much for me, really. Another house! But when they're married and moved in, that awful man will have to change his mind. His wife is sure he will. He pretends he's not ambitious socially but she is, and when he sees what Victor can do for his daughter——"

"I hope to God he fools you," declared Steve as he walked out.

Thus two events of interest to society would take place the following October—the Schultz-Hamilton wedding, and the opening of the new musical extravaganza starring Florette. Both spectacles had much in common; the selection of the minor members of the cast, their costumes, the setting, the rehearsals. Large sums of money would be poured into hazardous ventures, with no assurance of success. As a gamble there was nothing to choose between them.

Early in the summer Steve took Carla in his "buzz-wagon" to see Florette. The girl was sullen and frightened. "What are you taking me to see her for?" she asked, clinging to her big hat with one hand and the brass rail with the other.

"Florette's an old friend of mine. Perhaps if you behave right, she'll give you a job in her new show."

"She don't have nothing to do with that," Carla replied scornfully. "She's the star. She won't pay no attention to me. I wish I hadn't come."

Dust rolled up in clouds, settling on the black and white check dress with the red belt. "Here." Steve tossed her the lap robe. "Take off your hat and wrap this around you." She did, and for the rest of the long, hot trip to the North Shore, sat beside him, stiff and silent as a mummy. When they pulled up at the little farmhouse, her lips fell open. "Ain't you in the wrong place?" And with that, Florette came running out like a girl of sixteen. She smiled at Carla and held out both hands.

"Why, you must be hot and tired, riding in that fool thing," she said. "Come on in and we'll get rid of that dust." She turned to Steve. "Go on around to the back porch. It's nice and shady, and there's some lemonade there. We won't be long."

Steve could hear her chattering and laughing inside the house and in a few moments she came out, pushing the girl ahead of her. "There," she said. "Don't she look cute?"

Carla had on a blue muslin dress with a ruffle around the skirt and neck, and her black hair, loose on her shoulders, was tied back with a blue ribbon. Her eyes were lowered, their dark gleam directed sideways at the floor. She looked grave, hesitant, and young. "Here." Florette whisked an apron around her waist and handed her a pan filled with green peas. "Shuck these for me. I picked 'em this morning. My, don't they look good? We'll have them with lamb chops for supper."

Carla retreated to a chair in the shadow of the vines that draped the lattice, and the popping of pea pods punctuated Florette's chatter about her year on the road. "God, I'm glad to be back," she said. "Being out there in the sticks again got me scared I'd never get back. When we went through them tank towns, I'd pull down the shade. We didn't stop at 'em this time but I kept being afraid we would. All them towns! I know every one of 'em like I know my hand. Crisscross, back and forth. A person don't forget the road in a hurry, do they, Carla? Anyhow, I don't."

Steve, munching cookies and drinking lemonade, glanced at the girl in the corner, her head bent over the fresh green in her lap. She didn't appear to be listening.

The cool shadow on the porch deepened as the sun traveled toward those tank towns in the west. After a while Carla spoke. "These are done," she said, and Florette jumped up.

"My God, the stars will be out before I get them chops done!" she exclaimed. "I'd better hurry if you're going to get back to New York tonight." She stopped in the door as if struck with a sudden idea. "Look, Carla. Why don't you stay here with me? Charlie's in Chicago and I hate being alone. It would be a real favor to me and we'd have lots of fun on the beach. And I tell you what," she went on enthusiastically, "you can hear me in my new part. I can't learn a line unless I got somebody to listen, and for once in my life I'd like to go into rehearsal knowing my lines. Come on. Be a good sport and help me out. Let Steve go back in that thing. I hear they blow up at night anyhow."

Steve drove back to New York alone, and for the next two months saw no more of Florette or Carla. He was satisfied with that. He'd done all he could for the girl. Florette would see that she got a chance in the show and after that he could let her go her own gait. Nevertheless, he felt depressed. He missed the prod that had agitated him these past months. The city was hot, stale, the market stagnant, and most of the men he knew were out of town with their families. Curtis was in Maine with his boys—four of them—and half the office staff was on vacation. His house, shrouded in ghostly dust sheets, repelled him. He moved to the club. Most of the easy chairs in the big rooms were empty, but old Bert Babcock was in one of them.

Bert had aged rapidly since his wife's death six months previously. He said little about his loss until one night when they were sitting alone in the shadowed room. "I've sold my house," he announced abruptly. "I can't live there alone." He lifted an oblong package from beside his chair. "This used to hang beside the fireplace where she sat. She told me she wanted you to have it."

It was a small painting of a hill with a temple on its crest. A tiny figure with a staff was plodding up the hill. Steve had driven to the house with Bert once or twice a week to call on Mrs. Babcock while she was still able to be downstairs. He remembered the picture and held the gilt frame in his hands for a long moment before he spoke. "She used to tell me about these temples in Greece," he said, "I think she was trying to get my mind off the market."

Bert's moist gray eyes rested on him. "She tried it with me all her life, but she never got anywhere. We miss a good deal down there on the Street."

"I guess we do," said Steve, "but damned if I know what it is. We get going and keep going, that's all."

Bert shook his head. His flabby jowls, once so ruddy, quivered against his collar. "That's the point. We don't keep going, and the end comes faster than you think," he protested. "Those young rascals down there won't listen to an old man. They want him to get out. You've seen it yourself; done it yourself. Unless a man develops some other interest, he's through. Look at them down there—even Morrison—trying to dodge it with their art collections and libraries and all the rest of it. Poppycock! They're on the dust heap, same as I am. Ring for the chessboard and we'll have a game."

By the middle of August, Gresham, who had been away all summer following the horses from one track to the next, came back to begin rehearsals for the new show, and in the presence of that dynamic gentleman the sluggish current began to move again.

"You don't say," he said to Steve, hitching forward in his chair and planting his elbows on the table. "Been with Florette all summer, has she? What did I tell you? Florette's smart as they come. She sees something there, same as I do. Talent. No other reason for her to waste her time. Think she's been training her for understudy? No." He shook his head. "Can't be that. The girl's not the type. Maybe she'll give her a small spot in the show; see how she works out. Solo dance, maybe. Something like that. Anyhow, she's interested, and you can bet Florette knows what she's doing." His small, shrewd eyes glittered. "Looks like we got a winner at the post, Steve."

Steve laughed. "I think you're all wet, Herb," he said. "Don't get your hopes up. Florette took her in out of kindness. She was down there alone——"

"Kindness, my hat!" interrupted the showman. "Florette is no soft touch. I know her. I've worked with her. She looks soft but you try to get her to do something she don't want to do! She wouldn't take in that hellion without some damn good reason for it. I know it. Well"—he shoved back—"rehearsals begin tomorrow, and we'll see."

After that Steve often joined the silent, or brooding, or savagely gesticulating group in the dark auditorium to watch Gresham's efforts with the heterogeneous mass of humanity on the stage. Time after time angry disputes erased all sign of progress, but gradually the principals ceased sparring and accepted their roles, the chorus got into line, kicks were co-ordinated, and the show got under way.

Florette, when she wasn't on the stage, often came to sit with Steve and watch what was going on. "There she is," she said one day, and Steve saw Carla in the row of chorus girls Gresham was directing with more energy than temperance. She looked as she always did, dark, scornful, her face set, but she was working hard and with an exquisite precision that made her stand out like a polished gem in a row of paste.

"I don't know," Florette whispered. "She's a funny girl. Broody—like my hens. But it ain't what you think. She never mentioned you all summer, and she would of if she'd had it in for you. It's that acrobat she's after. If she ever meets up with him—well, I never thought I'd feel sorry for an acrobat. Funny thing. When she talked about him, I seemed to remember that wop out there on the circuit, too, fifteen years ago when I was just beginning. Seems to me he was knocking a child around. Maybe I'm wrong. Naturally I didn't say anything to her, but it's him she hates."

They watched the show for a few minutes. "Look at her," Florette went on. "She'd be good, Steve, if she wasn't as hard as nails. She's like you that way but she hasn't got your nice streak with it. And yet"—she shook her head—"somehow she makes you want to help her. What can you do with a girl like that?"

"Nothing," replied Steve promptly. "Don't worry about her. She's not a child. She's all right where she is. She's got a good job. She can take care of herself."

Florette turned on him. "My God, Steve, you're worse than she is. She's yours, ain't she? Your own flesh and blood? You've got to see to her, ain't you?"

"No," said Steve. "I don't look at it that way. I'll take care of her financially if she needs it but that's as far as I'll go. Fact is, she's damn lucky. What are you trying to do? Hang her around my neck? No. I'm through. And you keep out of it too. You've done enough—more than enough. Let her go her own gait from now on. She's all right."

CHAPTER 13

The new musical comedy opened in New York the first week
in October after a week's tryout in Boston, where the press
and public enthusiastically declared the show was a smash hit. Thus
encouraged by an opinion they secretly respected, New Yorkers
rushed to the ticket office and the house was sold out for a month
in advance. It looked as if Florette was in for another of her spectacular runs on Broadway.

The curtain went up to a full house, and as it did, several customers were annoyed by a fashionable couple who wedged their
way without apology to seats in the middle of the row. They were
recognized in whispers as Mrs. Stephen Bradway and that son of
hers who was to be married the following week to the Schultz girl.
"You mean that homely, shy little thing? That good-looking man?
Why do you suppose he's doing it?" "Money, of course." "Nonsense,
his mother's got millions."

"P-s-s-t!"

Steve, in the second row, was unaware of the arrival of his wife.
His eyes were fixed on the galloping chorus, dressed to look like
Spanish peasants gone mad in some hill town. He caught sight of
Carla several times, and once, as she whirled past, she gave him a
fleeting glance. She was the best-looking Spanish peasant in the lot,
in his opinion. Red and yellow made her black hair look all right.
After blasting the way for the entrance of the star, the chorus parted
and Florette rode in on a donkey, a very superior peasant in yards
of spangled silks, with red and yellow puffballs dangling from the
brim of her wide sombrero. "Hu-la!" she cried, leaping from the
donkey. With a roar of applause the show was off to a lively start.

But the second act began with a quiet interlude, checking the pace
of the musical comedy. The curtain rose on an empty stage, moonlight falling on the white façade of a villa on the right and sparkling
on a fountain in the center. Flowers spilled over the balustrade of
the terrace around the fountain and a glimpse of the sea could be
seen through the dark cypress trees in the background. Soft music

260

came from the villa as a slender figure stepped out and stood for a moment looking at the moonlit garden. She was dressed in black lace that foamed in a train in the back, short in front, showing slim ankles and the sparkle of buckles on satin shoes. A long black mantilla sewn with silver paillettes hung from a high comb in her black hair, the delicate lace etched across the white brow. Except for the somber shadow of the eyes and the wide red slash of the lips, there was no color in the face, and the arms hung white and motionless against the black of her dress. Slowly the figure moved down the steps into the moonlight. Slowly she began to dance, drifting with exquisite grace around the fountain. The pace gradually picked up until the airy grace gave way to a whirling fandango, a passionate defiance that mounted like a shriek in the night. Suddenly it was over. The white arms dropped. The figure paused, one white hand on the rim of the fountain, then sank down, and with an almost audible sob of defeat, the proud head drooped forward. She held this lovely, significant pose for a long moment; then on a burst of lively music from the villa, she started—looked around; a bitter smile bent the red lips. She rose slowly to her full height and with little gestures arranged her dress. Then she walked slowly, with extraordinary deliberation, across the stage and disappeared into the villa.

It was no dance for a musical comedy. The audience sat in stunned silence while the orchestra leader, stunned himself, stood with raised baton ready to let forth the blast that would bring the merry throng pouring from the villa. There was a faint ripple of applause but not enough to keep the baton inactive. The show went on.

Steve, sitting in the second row, was as astonished as the rest of the audience at this brief intrusion of tragedy into the froth of the show. He had seen Carla rehearse the dance a dozen times; a simple little number that involved nothing more than skipping around a fountain. Except in pace, she had changed the dance very little, but the interpretation she had put into it now was bold and entirely her own. Deeply stirred by emotion he didn't stop to analyze, Steve stood up, and as soon as Carla left the stage, he hurried up the aisle. Victor turned his head and watched him go.

"Why is he making such a spectacle of himself?" complained Amelia. "Rushing out like that."

"I don't know," murmured Victor thoughtfully. "That girl was rather lovely."

"Lovely! I never was so bored in my life. I hoped with Florette in it we'd see a good show—perhaps our last together, darling. I mean alone. But if it isn't any better than that——"

"You'd do well to keep your opinion to yourself, Mater," whispered Victor impatiently—his impatience with his mother had increased lately. "That dance is the only good thing in the show. I'm surprised Florette allowed it. I say, if you've had enough, let's leave." And again they wedged past the indignant patrons.

In the meantime, Steve was backstage. Florette was standing in the wings ready to go on. "Where is she?" he asked.

"Oh, let her alone—and let me alone, too. I'm nervous. Go on back where you belong." The music gave her cue, her face lit up with its professional smile. "Come around after," she threw at him over her shoulder as she bounced out onto the stage.

The final curtain went up and down a dozen times while the audience, standing in the congested aisles, clapped and clapped and the little star smiled and blew kisses to her enthusiastic admirers. As the curtain went up for the last time, she turned and pulled to her side a girl from the chorus behind her and the crowd, recognizing the generous gesture, clapped louder than ever. The curtain came down and the show was over.

Florette was in her dressing room, in the same old kimono, getting the make-up off her face, when Steve gave his double knock and went in. Gresham was with her, raging-mad. "I tell you I'm going to fire her," he shouted. "I'm going out and do it now. She can't go out there and make a monkey of me again. I gave her a nice little spot—and look what she did with it. She damn near put the blitz on the whole second act. We couldn't get going again for over ten minutes."

"Oh, shut up!" snapped Florette. "Don't you know a hit when you see it? In another week, when it gets around, that spot will stop the show."

"She damn near killed it dead in its tracks tonight," protested Gresham, "but if you don't want her fired I can't fire her. I'll put the whole chorus on with her tomorrow night," he added belligerently. "That'll fix her."

Florette swung around in her chair, pawing savagely at large globs of discolored cold cream clinging to her face. "Herb, for God's sake, show some sense. Maybe you're right. Maybe she does belong with the Greeks, like you say. I don't know. But you let her work out that spot the way she wants. She can't hurt your show. Let her alone; don't pick on her. I mean it, Herb. Now go and cool off.

Get rid of that gang out there. I ain't seeing anybody tonight. Not anybody—you understand? I'm tired as a worn-out shoe."

Gresham went off, muttering, and Steve sat down to wait for Florette. She didn't speak, and after a while he asked her if there was anything in what Gresham said. "Yes, there is," she said. "She nearly put a crimp in us, going off half-cocked like that. She's got no right to do it but"—she turned and looked at him—"the point is, Steve, she had the nerve to do it and she got away with it. Herb talks about firing her! Inside a month he can't hold her. Maybe I can't. Some snide will come along with a contract, she'll sign and be through before she knows where she is. Being on the stage all her life ain't going to help her. That's hack work. She's got to learn the business, get on to herself, and we got to help her—not slam her down like Herb wants. Trouble is the poor kid's got the big head. Well, maybe that can be cured. I had it myself once and I guess you did, too. Maybe that's where she gets it." She smiled, a weary little smile. "Funny you ain't proud of her like you ought to be. Nobody but a chip off the old block would do what she did tonight. Come on. Let's take her out and give her a steak. She needs a break same as I do."

"What makes you think I'm not proud of her?" protested Steve. "I am proud of her—damn proud."

"Aw, go on." Florette got into her coat. "You don't know the meaning of the word."

CHAPTER 14

The next morning on the way to the office Steve read the reviews of the new show. It was a hit. Florette was welcomed back to Broadway with affectionate praise, and Gresham was applauded for opening his second act with a dramatic dance by a Miss d'Angelo—a welcome departure from the usual hurly-burly of the conventional musical show. The cab was passing a florist's shop when Steve read this. He shouted to the driver and jumped out to send a large bunch of red roses to Carla. He had some difficulty in writing the card that went with them. He wrote several, tore them up. "Congratulations—Steve" was as close as he could get to it. He was out on the street before he thought of Florette and went back to send flowers to her. He acted, thought the florist, like a man in love.

Steve wasn't in love. He was excited. That girl, that chip off the old block, in the New York papers! His satisfaction clung to him all day and still radiated from him when he saw Florette that night. "She's good," he told her. "Damn good. Did you hear the hand she got tonight?"

Florette laughed. "You're a funny fellow, Steve. Sure I heard it. She's made a nice little hit, and we've got to push it. Get her name on the program for one thing. And you better buy her some clothes so you can take her around places—show her off. It won't hurt you and the poor kid needs it."

"Hurt me!" protested Steve indignantly. "I'm proud of her."

To solve the clothes problem he took Carla to Suzanne. For the past ten years he had poured thousands of dollars into her establishment and, not yet beyond caution, he decided that on that basis he might make a deal with the Frenchwoman. He made an appointment with her at an early hour, when the shop was free of customers and Suzanne, already convinced of the character of the meeting, led him into her private office with the air of a conspirator. "Ah, Monsieur Bradway, it is so much a pleasure for me to meet you," she cooed. "I have so many good checks from you."

264

"You come to the point fast, don't you?" Steve remarked with appreciation. "But there will be no more of those good checks if you make the mistake of revealing my reason for coming here. If you are as smart as you look, you'll get more of them. I want some dresses for a girl."

Suzanne pressed her hand to her bosom. "Ah, monsieur, I comprehend. Do not be alarm. Monsieur can trust me. This is not the first time. *Ah, non.* This is business for me. All is secret. No trouble comes. These thing are not my affair except"—she gave him a coy, significant look—"except the good check, *n'est-ce pas?*"

Steve was satisfied. "She's outside in a cab," he said. "I'll bring her in."

In a moment he was back, followed by a tall, long-legged, shabby girl. Suzanne's bead-black eyes swept over the battered hat, the clumsy dress, and worn shoes. Her eyebrows arched. She glanced at Steve. He was looking at his watch. "I'm late." He frowned. "See that she gets what she needs and don't overdo it." He hurried out to the cab. Hein! What was here? Monsieur not waiting to see the pretty pose, to receive the arms around the neck? With the eloquent shrug of one who has seen many things and now sees another, Suzanne led her new client into the salon. "*Eh, bien,*" she said. "Now we shall try what we shall do. Will Mademoiselle remove the dress and stand before me?"

Carla, in her petticoat and corset cover, stood and turned and moved while the dressmaker, her chin on her hand, peered at her with mounting interest. "*C'est une originale, un vrai type,*" she murmured to herself. "Oui—the long line, very fine—the pose, the eye, the calm—thin like a child. But not the child. *Ah, non.* Inside is very old, very strong. If she is smart to learn she can go far, this little one. *Eh, bien,*" she said aloud. "Come sit by me, mademoiselle." She laid her hand on Carla's knee. "Now tell Suzanne; she must know. You are the dancer? You wish always to be the dancer?"

Carla, her head bent in an exquisite pose not lost on Suzanne, was silent for a moment. "No," she said then, slowly. "Not always. I want to be an actress. I've always wanted to be in plays. I'm going to be, too, someday, but I've got to go on dancing till I get there. It's the only way."

"The only way? *Ah, non.*" Suzanne moved closer. "Now we make what is here come out." She tapped her brow. "Is nothing there, we finish. *Attendez!* To dance on the stage is not enough. The actress must be more. She must create herself; she must make the style, the type. In her life she is every hour on the stage. Always the eye is on her. When she enter the restaurant, when she eat, when she look, when she speak—always she is on the stage. Always she make the style. Always. . . . You comprehend?"

Carla's dark eyes lifted, dropped. "I know what you mean," she said. "You want me to have lots of clothes and wear them around the way Florette does."

Suzanne clapped her hands on her bony knees. "Ah, you are a smart girl!" she exclaimed. "Come. Now we measure for the little dress to please Monsieur."

When the tape measure had finished its travels and Carla was dressed to depart, Suzanne flipped with her finger a little gold pin the girl wore. "What is this?" She shrugged. "You must not wear this thing. It ruin the style. Someday, the jewel but now—nothing."

"I want my pin." Carla's face set. "I always wear it."

"You do not permit Suzanne to advise?" The designer's hands, shoulders, eyebrows went up. "*Bien*. Now we come to understand. Listen to me. I do not allow you shall wear such a trash on the costume create by Suzanne. I will not be ruin by you. Never. Remove this pin so I shall see you understand or you do not come back to Chez Suzanne."

Carla was halfway to the door before she hesitated; then slowly she took off the little gold lover's knot, dropped it in her purse, and closed the clasp with a decisive snap. "*Bien*." The dressmaker nodded with cool authority. "It is understand, *n'est-ce pas*, that in the costume you obey Suzanne? Regard in the glass, mademoiselle. You are not the pretty girl. Without Suzanne you are nothing, but if you obey, we create the style unique for you. You become the beauty original. If you wish this, return in two days to fit the costume. *Au revoir, mademoiselle*."

This was the beginning of the long and profitable association between Carla and her designer. If, in later years, Carla's public wondered why the young star tolerated the abusive old Frenchwoman who clung to her like a leech, it was because the star was well aware that, without her, the brilliant career would collapse like a pricked balloon. It was Suzanne who created the famous "D'Angelo silhouette" that sent hordes of diet-haunted women to the Turkish bath and massage table. It was Suzanne who, screaming like a maniac, taught her the willowy, drifting carriage, the elusive haunting grace that became the stock in trade of the slant-eyed siren. "Imbecile! Let go the knee, the hip! Let go the hand to wilt, *comme*

266

ça, on the arm. *Non, non, mon Dieu! Comme ça! Comme ça!*"
Suzanne created the actress as surely as she created exquisite costumes for her from a shapeless bale of beautiful goods—and the
actress knew it.

But this was far in the future and only Suzanne's experienced eye
caught the glimmer of it when she saw Carla's dance. In bed that
night the tired, withered old woman, looking like a mummy without
her wig, lay for a long time thinking of Monsieur, the good checks,
and the dancing figure of the ambitious girl. "*On arrive*," she sighed
as she put out the light. "*On arrive enfin. Peut-être.*"

One night soon after her first visit to Suzanne, Carla went into
Florette's dressing room wearing her new dress, a plain, dark blue
serge with immaculate white collar and cuffs. Her hair, brushed
back from her wide, white brow, was tied at the neck with a black
taffeta bow. "Carla!" exclaimed Florette. "My God, I never would
have known you. What have you been doing to yourself? You look
about sixteen. Where did you get that dress?"

Carla told her. "She wants me to model down there so I'll get to
know how to wear clothes. Like this." She swayed forward with
the elegance of Suzanne herself. Florette sat back and laughed.
"Making a Frenchy out of you, is she? Well, they've got something.
I'll say that for 'em. She's right about your hair. It's your style. Different. And you certainly look good in that dress." She turned back
to her make-up table. "I see what she's up to," she went on after
a while. "Maybe it's a good thing, Carla. Maybe it's what you need."
The puff scattered powder for another moment, then the good-
hearted little star turned around again. "I've been thinking a lot
about you lately," she said, "and we got to face it, honey. You don't
belong in this end of show business. You ain't the type. I know you're
doing all right in your dance," she went on, "and you better stay with
it for a while. This season, anyhow. You've got a lot to learn. You
can't bust in on the legitimate like you can in this business. You got
to be educated." She turned back to her mirror. "I'll tell Steve to
get you one of them tooters right away."

"What's that?" asked Carla suspiciously.

"One of them fellows teach you to read out of a book; fix your
voice right; all those things. Legits don't want people like us around
any more than we want them." The callboy rapped on the door.
"Fifteen minutes. Fifteen minutes." Florette grabbed the mascara
brush. "Say! You better run along, honey—if you can run in that
dress."

267

Steve, with the bill for it in his pocket, didn't think much of the new dress. "Make her put some trimming on it," he said. "Where's your pin? Why don't you wear that?"

"She won't let me. She says it's too cheap."

"Cheap?" Steve growled. "I'll get you one she won't call cheap." And a few days later Carla showed Suzanne a diamond lover's knot with a good-sized ruby in the center. Suzanne gave it a moment's hawk-eyed appraisal. "Very nice," she said coolly, "but one small jewel show we have no big one. Tell Monsieur you cannot wear this until you have the ruby for the ear."

Florette's reaction to Carla's first diamonds was different. "Steve," she said, her candid blue eyes on his, "I don't like it. I know how you feel and I know why. Keep her going like you said—that's only fair —but lay off giving her rocks. She's hard and she's greedy, and if she once gets started, she'll give you an awful beating. I see it coming and it worries me."

Steve put his arm around her with casual affection. "Nothing to worry about," he smiled. "She's an investment in a piece of myself, that's all. I want to build her up, see what I can make of her. She's doing fine so far."

"All right, Steve." Florette sighed and pulled out of his arm. "Go ahead. It's your funeral, and nobody can stop a funeral."

Steve went ahead with his investment. At first Carla's wants were modest. She had her tutor, a palsied old actor who relieved the frustration of a lifetime by teaching her Shakespeare. She liked it. She studied hard and developed a low, husky, resonant speech expressive of her dark personality. When she read for a small part in Daly's company the following fall and got it, she stayed with it for two seasons, steadily advancing until she became the understudy for the leading lady, another dark beauty, who watched her progress with flattering alarm.

During this time Steve Bradway was seen more and more frequently in restaurants with the young actress, but it was not until Carla appeared with him in Delmonico's one night that the storm began to gather. She came in on his arm in a ruby-red velvet dress that clung to her slender figure in a shocking revelation of seductive curves that, in that period of flounces and furbelows, was a sensation in itself. But it was the strange, elusive beauty of the woman that turned every head in the crowded room. She stood, composed and grave, her black hair framing the delicate contour of her pale, oval face, the thin arch of her black brows, the oddly elongated, luminous eyes shadowed by remarkably long black lashes. Steve, handsome, proud as a king, guided her across the room. Subdued but excited chatter broke out over the candlelit tables.

"Who's that Bradway's got with him this time? Extraordinary-looking, isn't she?" . . . "Where do you suppose she got that dress? Heavens! I hope Worth isn't putting us into that sort of thing. I wouldn't think of wearing it." . . . "You couldn't, my dear." . . . "Poor Mrs. Bradway! How dare he bring such a woman to Delmonico's? Anyone can see what she is. They ought to be put out. I declare I don't see what the world is coming to. One isn't safe anywhere any more."

So the storm began to gather, in light gusts at first, like this in Delmonico's, but it had to rise to a buffeting fury before Steve became aware of it. For three years he behaved like an infatuated lunatic and his world, ignorant of his reason for it, took it for what it looked like—the silly folly of a middle-aged man in love with a young and beautiful woman. Well, he was in love by this time—deeply, proudly in love. Steve was a strong, lusty man who never before had felt more than a passing emotion for any woman. Now a tide of possessive passion for this one completely obliterated every other interest in his life. He dressed her. He paraded her. He loaded her with jewels until she glittered like a Christmas tree. A Christmas tree! ("Steve, can you make a star? A big star to go on top?")

Carla was genuinely indifferent to jewels. She wore them because she had them, and Suzanne now insisted on it. What she did want with a passionate ambition that matched Steve's own was success on the stage. "I've got to get somewhere," she declared, pacing dramatically before him, letting go with "the knee, the hip." "That woman hasn't given me a chance in two years, and she never will. I can't go on waiting forever, I can't. I won't."

"Seems to me you've done pretty well for a girl in the chorus three years ago," said Steve dryly. "You're getting along all right." With that, she wheeled on him in one of her imperious rages that, in later years, were the delight of her press agent.

"Getting along all right? Walking on at Daly's night after night?" she cried. "I was better off with Florette. I'm twenty-two years old. I've been on the stage all my life. I know what I can do. I'm not going on like this. I want a real chance, a big chance this season. Oh! You give me these clothes, these diamonds. What do they amount to? I'm nothing but a showpiece for you. I'm sick of it. Sick and tired of it. Why don't you DO something for me?"

269

That season, in England, a great Shakespearean actor, long on laurels but short on cash, had decided on one more final tour of the American provinces. On his arrival he was met by his backers, one of whom presently approached him with an extraordinary proposal. "But, my dear fellow," protested the astonished star, "I have a quite adequate Ophelia engaged for the tour. Sorry, but it is quite impossible to consider your suggestion."

"What would it be worth to you to risk a change in your cast?" asked Steve bluntly.

"Risk?" The great man drew himself up. "It is not a question of risk. My dear fellow, my public would follow me if I played with a cast of idiots—which I may say I do—but that sort of thing isn't done. It's quite unthinkable."

"Think again," suggested Steve. "Would twenty-five thousand, cold cash, assist you? It's possible your actress may be too ill to play. She may prefer returning to England with her season's salary. The young lady who would replace her is an accomplished actress, and the ambition of her life is to play with you."

The noble pose relaxed. The Hyperion countenance smiled. "Not an unusual ambition, I may say. I have experienced it ere this—but never quite in this form. Extraordinary people, you Americans," the resonant voice went on. "If you will allow me to say so, in a civilized society your—ah—preoccupation with the sum you mention would be regarded as an insult to my honor. I should be obliged to challenge you."

Steve's grin broadened. "Go ahead."

"I do—with pleasure . . . When can I see the young lady?"

On the opening night, before a house crowded with a fashionable and sophisticated audience, Carla played Ophelia to the great star's Hamlet. She wasn't great in the role, but she gave a remarkable interpretation of it. Pitifully young, bewildered, as she tried to stem Hamlet's brutal dismissal of her, she made it abundantly clear to everyone but Hamlet that a nunnery was not the refuge she needed. Fright mounted to terror in the following scenes until finally the tension snapped and she drifted across the stage, errant as a leaf at the mercy of the wind, the dark, oblique eyes vacant and smiling now as she sang her revealing little rhymes in a heart-breaking whisper that crept into every ear in the hushed house. " 'Let in the maid, that out a maid, Never departed more. . . . I hope all will be well,' " she faltered. " 'We must be patient . . . good night, sweet ladies; good night, good night.' "

270

As she slipped from the stage, Hamlet, watching from the wings, heard with annoyance a burst of applause from the audience. An outrageous performance, really. Poor Ophelia! No sweet maiden this time, grieving for her father. However, it was evidently good box office. These Americans! Listen to that hand! He shrugged.

When Carla left the stage, Steve, sitting alone in the front of the house, got up abruptly and went out. Another man, also alone, turned his head and watched him go, an amused smile on his handsome face. It was a cold, clear night, and for a time Steve stood bareheaded on the street looking up at the stars. They seemed unusually brilliant that night and his spirit soared to meet them. Steve seldom indulged in sentimental satisfaction, but he did to the full that night. He was a proud and happy man as he made his way backstage to see his daughter, secure in the future for her—and for himself in her.

He found Carla seated before her dressing table, still in her white costume, absorbed in reading a letter. Suzanne was with her, lifting a huge bunch of white roses from a box as he entered. "You make the big mistake, *chérie*," he heard her say. "It is not yet you can——" Carla looked up, her expression changed, and she slipped the note into her dress. Steve went to her and laid his hand on her shoulder. She was rigid and trembling. "There, there." He patted her. "Everything's all right now. You were great. Great! Nothing to do from now on but go ahead. I'm proud of you." He reached in his pocket and pulled out a box. "Here's a little present to celebrate."

She didn't touch the box, but Suzanne did, and a magnificent diamond bracelet flashed in the light. The Frenchwoman gave a little gasp. "*Regardez!*" she said sharply, thrusting the box at Carla. "*Regardez!* It is as I say, *n'est-ce pas?*"

Carla turned on her. "You keep out of this, Suzanne," she said in a harsh, low voice. "I know what I'm doing." She turned to Steve. "I don't want it," she said. "I don't want anything ever again from you." She tried to meet his eyes. Couldn't. Tears began to roll down her cheeks, her hands twisted in her lap. "Don't look at me like that," she cried. "Haven't you seen? Don't you know?" With a gesture more dramatic than anything she had done on the stage she jumped up, seized the white roses, and buried her face in them. "This is what I want. This! This!"

Steve frowned but he was not too disturbed. "Somebody else, eh? Well, it was to be expected sooner or later. That's all right. It'll be

271

good for you if you keep your head. It won't make any difference to me, Carla, if that's what's worrying you."

"Yes, it will," she said, her voice smothered in the flowers. "Yes, it will. I want it to."

"Want it to? Why? Speak up. I'm no child."

She lifted her head and looked at him. The tears were gone, her face hard and white as marble. "It will make a difference," she said steadily. "I'm in love with Victor Hamilton, your stepson. I've been living with him for some time. I'm going on living with him. I promised him I'd tell you so tonight."

Steve sat down on the first chair he could see. "Well, I'll be damned," he said after a moment. "Victor! So that's what he's been up to, is it? You know he's got a nice wife and two babies, don't you?"

"Of course I do. What difference does that make? She's nothing to him," she said scornfully. "We love each other."

"Bosh!" Steve exploded. "Nothing to him? She's his bankbook. He'll drop you in two seconds as soon as he's even with me. Don't be a fool, Carla. He's no good, never has been. I know what's behind this."

She put aside the roses and sat down, deadly calm. "I know better than you do what's behind it. I know all about it," she said. "Victor told me. It was you who ruined him, forced him into this stupid marriage." She gave the bracelet a contemptuous glance. "Now that you've got his money you're looking for something else to satisfy your greed. You think you can parade me, buy your way into my career so you can swell around and take the credit for it. There's been something funny about you from the start. I've always felt it but I didn't understand it. I do now, and I'm through with you. I never want to see you or hear from you again. I despise you."

Steve saw his own image in her eyes, heard his own ruthless decision in her voice. "You mean that, don't you, Carla?" he said quietly.

"Mean it? Mean it? I mean it with every fiber in my body."

Steve smiled at that. "Every fiber in your body, eh? That's saying a lot. So you believe this yarn of Victor's—think he'll marry you, do you?" His smile broadened. "I'd like to see that. Do you know his mother? She's my wife."

"That has nothing to do with it." She defied him, but his head was bent and he seemed not to hear her.

"Yes," he repeated, "I'd like to see it. I'd give a good deal to see

272

you marry Victor." He began to laugh, his big shoulders shaking. "That's a draw I didn't count on. Too bad there's no stake in it." He stood up. The chair was a low one and he was clumsy, slow in getting out of it. "Well, I'd better be getting along," he said.

His eyes had never frightened Carla but they did now. She shivered and turned away quickly, picked up the bracelet and held it out to him. He took it, glanced at it, and tossed it into the box the roses had come in. "Better keep it for her, Suzanne," he said. "It'll last longer than those roses."

As he turned away, a rap came on the door. "You're wanted on stage for curtain call, Miss d'Angelo. The show's over."

CHAPTER 15

After he walked out of the theater that night, Steve never saw Carla again. He made no conscious effort not to see her but the current of his life swung away from her and he let it take him. It began the next morning. He woke up feeling dull, heavy. He ran his hand over his face, got up, and went in to shave. He remembered clearly enough what had happened the night before but he couldn't seem to care about it, couldn't get his mind on Carla, somehow. Like a dream she had slipped away, leaving only a nagging, uneasy impression of something forgotten, something lost. He frowned, staring at himself in the glass, vaguely disappointed at his lack of emotion. He ought to feel like cutting his throat and here he was, shaving. Funny! It didn't occur to him that a mortal wound is numb sometimes, for a while.

He went to his office that morning like a man returning from a long voyage, fully confident of plunging back into the activities of his normal business life. The staff greeted him with more surprise than warmth and there was no rush to his office for discussion or decision. The departments were rolling along with the smooth coordination of a powerful machine, detached and indifferent to his strolling inspection of its parts. He asked questions and got answers. Only Curtis, the actual working head of the business now, welcomed him with the joyful relief of a devoted nurse who sees, at last, a normal temperature in a fever patient who has been desperately ill for a long while. "You mean it, Steve? You're back?"

"Yes. I'm back, John. I haven't been around much lately but things are in fine shape." Steve hesitated. "I appreciate it."

"Nothing to appreciate." Curtis' glasses shone with the affection behind them. "We've done the best we could, but things will begin to hum now that you're here."

Things were humming at top speed as it was, and Steve's presence made little, if any, difference in the tune. However, he went to the office every day and sat behind his big, flat-topped desk mak-

274

ing gestures; the handsome, impressive figurehead of a huge organization that no longer needed him.

One morning a week or two after his return to Wall Street, he walked up Fifth Avenue to see Amelia. He had seen less of Amelia than he had of his office during the past three years and she was bitterly hostile to him, but he had decided that there were some things he wanted to discuss with her before he sealed up the dark chamber in the bottom of his mind for good. He found her sitting up in bed, her writing pad on her knees—a withered, sharp-featured little body scribbling as if the fate of the world depended on what she did. She looked up and gave him a quick, darting frown. "Steve! What brings you here? Is anything the matter?"

"No. Nothing the matter." He walked to the window, parted the curtains, and stood for a moment looking out over the park. "Nothing the matter," he repeated. "I came to talk to you about a divorce."

"A divorce!" Amelia threw herself back on the pillows and the familiar red rage swept over her face. "A divorce! So that's what you want now. I might have known it. A divorce so you can marry that creature. As if I hadn't been through enough with you!" She sat up, her tiny fists clinched. "Let me tell you something, Steve Bradway. Nothing in this world would give me more pleasure than to be rid of you. Rid of you, do you hear? But I won't go through a divorce even for that. Never! Never—as long as I live. I wouldn't think of it. Decent women don't divorce their husbands. It's insulting to suggest such a thing. If you think I'd go through——"

"Just a minute, Amelia." Steve turned wearily and sat down facing her. "You haven't lost your speed in jumping to the wrong conclusion, have you? I'm not asking you to divorce me. It wouldn't interest me. I haven't, and never have had, any intention of marrying Miss d'Angelo. But Victor has."

"Victor!"

"Yes, Victor. He's living with her. Has been for some time. Schultz has found out about it and is getting a divorce for his daughter. That's the divorce I'm talking about."

"Victor! Living with that woman?"

"Yes. You'll have him back on your hands inside of three months without a nickel."

"I don't believe it. I don't believe a word of this. You're trying to frighten me. Why, it's impossible. He's married. He has two children."

"He won't be married when Schultz gets through with him. He'll

275

be back here with you." A grim smile touched his lips but didn't reach his eyes. "He may bring the girl with him. I'd give a great deal to see that."

"Victor? Bring a woman like that into my house?" Amelia gasped. "You must be out of your mind. Victor wouldn't do a thing like that. It's impossible. I don't believe he even knows the woman."

"He knows her all right and he'll be along in a few days to tell you so. That's what I'm here to discuss." He gave her a straight, steady look. "Get your mind on what I'm telling you, Amelia. Victor is out with Schultz. No question about that. Now. If he marries the girl and brings her here, I want you to tell him I'll give him fifty thousand a year as long as she stays in this house. If she doesn't come with him, you'll have to support him without help from me—or kick him out. Is that clear?" He began to laugh, the heavy, silent laughter that so often shook him lately. "You can also tell him that if he has a baby by her I'll see that he gets every cent Horace took away from him, plus interest at five per cent."

Amelia stared at him, her mouth open. "Oh," she breathed at last. "Oh, how awful. Unless you're mad there's something monstrous behind this. Horrible. I feel it. You've done this deliberately, you and that wicked woman. She's broken up my poor boy's marriage so she can force herself on me. You've planned it, helped her with it. Oh, how monstrous! How wicked!"

"Nothing monstrous about it," said Steve evenly. "She's not having a baby by me, if that's on your mind. No. Taking all things into account, it's a fair proposition all around. There's a nice bunch of money in it for Victor; couple of millions if he works it right. You'll see it that way—both of you—as soon as you've had a chance to figure it out. You'll work it. I can bank on that." He stood up and moved to the door. "Trouble is"—he shook his head—"that girl is likely to throw Victor overboard faster than you will when she hears of this. You'd better figure on that, too." He took the key of his house from his pocket and tossed it on the coverlet. "You won't need a divorce to be rid of me," he said. "No change financially. I owe that to old Cyrus. But I'm not supporting Victor except under the conditions I've given you. Work it out to suit yourselves, the three of you. Win or lose, I'm out of it. Debts past due cleaned up and the books closed." Amelia was still staring at him, speechless, her mouth open, as he went out.

On the street, Steve looked at his watch. He had a directors' meeting at eleven o'clock. It was that now. Well, what of it? He'd done a good morning's work; squared away at last all along the line; the door to the past shut tight and sealed to stay. He was free again, free of that pack on his back for the first time in over twenty years. It felt good. He drew a long, deep breath, squared his shoulders, hailed a cab, and drove rapidly to Wall Street.

At the beginning of his erratic behavior Steve's business associates had been tolerant enough, but as time went on, his supposed guilty infatuation ceased to be a joke among them. He seldom attended meetings during that time, and when he did, his impatient lack of interest in the proceedings at first annoyed, then finally disgusted every man around the table. There was ugly talk, some of it the gossip of indignant wives, most of it born of an active desire to carve up Steve and be rid of his hampering presence on the board.

"That watchdog he's got over there—what's his name?—Curtis?— is a damn nuisance."

"Wish I had one like him. The damn fool is as strong as Gibraltar with that fellow behind him. Think he'll ever get down to work again?"

Steve got down to work that morning. He strode in to the meeting twenty minutes late, relieved to be there, confident in himself and in his relations with these men. His sins of omission were over. He was ready to play ball. Nobody seemed ready to play with him. After the brief interruption of shoving chairs to make a place for him, the meeting droned on. Details he had never heard of were discussed. The eyes that met his were cold and hostile, not the familiar hostility of businessmen jockeying for position, but hostile to him as a man. It puzzled Steve. When the meeting was over, he crossed the street to his own office deeply disturbed. "What's the matter with that bunch over there?" he asked Curtis. "They act as if I'd been stealing pennies off dead men's eyes."

Curtis flushed. "You haven't been following the business very closely, Steve. They want to reorganize but can't do it without the vote of your stock."

"Why didn't they take it up with you?"

"They did." Curtis' embarrassment deepened. "It's a good company. They're making money fast. What they're after is your stock. They think you've got too much of it. They want to buy you out— get you off the board."

There was nothing numb about Steve's reaction to that. His eyes blazed. "Why the hell didn't you pull out?" he snapped.

"I couldn't go as far as that without your consent," replied Curtis with considerable dignity. "I tried several times to get your attention on it."

"I know. I know, John. I couldn't expect it. But we'll pull out now. Pull out fast and see what happens to their damn stock."

Curtis shook his head. "We'll get out if you say so," he said, "but not too fast. You don't want to pull the market from under it, do you?"

"No. No. I suppose not. But get me out. If they want a fight I'll give it to them."

Other organizations, several of those he'd built up himself, seemed to want a fight, and Steve became aware of a marked change in the weather. There was the nip of frost in the air. Gusts of surprising force swept around him at more than one directors' meeting. His interests were too strong a shield for these antagonisms to affect him financially to any extent, but he resented being forced to use that shield to protect himself. He no longer found any pleasure in these meetings, none of the old fraternal intimacy of pirates below deck, gleefully sharpening their knives. They were down there—but he wasn't. He was on deck, waiting, in the wind.

But there was a certain amount of stimulus in these buffetings; a grim satisfaction in whipping the devil around the stump that helped pass those hours spent in his office. It was in his club, after office hours, that the deadly calm set in. There was no nip in the air there, no nip of any kind in the deep hush of thick carpets, shaded lights, and easy chairs. It must always have been so, but in the early days of his ambitious activities a chance to read his newspaper in peace had been a welcome respite. Now it was not. Entering the quiet room was like dropping to the bottom of a well, where the air was stagnant and the only sound an echo. He missed old Bertie. Bert had died more than a year ago. Steve, absorbed in Carla, had given little thought to it at the time, but he did now as he sat in Bert's old chair, smoking, looking out of the window at the passing traffic.

But he was no Bert Babcock sitting there, beaten, spent, on the ash heap. Damn it, he was in better shape than he'd ever been in his life, his mind as alert and as eager for action. Nothing the matter with him, nothing to account for this fog that hung over him, heavy as lead. Thing to do was get rid of it, shake it off. He did for a while. Dressed up, his diamond studs flashing in his stiff shirt bosom, he went back to the theaters and pretty girls. Plenty of friends there. Chatter. Sparkling eyes.

One night he ran into Gresham, who greeted him with enthusiasm.

278

"Hi'ya, Steve? You're looking fine. Let's go someplace and find a drink. Where you been?" the stage manager went on as he settled in his chair, his hand around his drink. "Haven't seen hide nor hair of you for a couple of years. Lost your interest in show business, did you? Sure. They all do after they been stung a few times. I told you you would."

"That's probably it," admitted Steve. "How've you been doing?"

"Me?" Gresham went off into a long account of his hard luck at the tracks and in the theater. "Haven't had a break since *Fiesta* closed. You know Florette's retired, don't you?"

Steve nodded. He knew all about it. Under the strain of honest employment Charlie's conscience had again broken down and Florette had hastened with him to a ranch in Canada, where his genius in rapid multiplication was showing remarkable results in the cattle business. Steve had recently received a letter with a snapshot in it of Florette jauntily perched on a cow pony, surrounded by a bevy of calves. "Look at 'em," she wrote. "Ain't they grand? And not a mark on 'em when we get 'em. This is the life. We sure wish you'd come out here. Don't forget the name when you write. Frank Cooper. F.C. Get it? Makes a swell brand but I don't like putting it on. They bawl worse than Gresham used to. I'd like to put it on that old maverick, though. Tell him so when you see him."

Steve didn't, and Gresham rambled on about the theater world, Steve scarcely listening until his ear caught Carla's name. "That's what I mean," the showman was saying. "You build 'em up, give 'em the breaks, give 'em everything you've got, and what does it get you? Buckwheats! She threw you down, same as she did the rest of us. Sure she did. Don't kid yourself. You know she went to England with that highbrow troupe, don't you?" Steve shook his head. "No? Well, she's playing in London right now. Say! The fellow that chucked his wife for her was some relative of yours, wasn't he?" Steve shook his head again. "Funny. I thought I read something in the papers had you in it. Sure I did. I remember thinking——" He caught Steve's eye and stopped so fast he strangled over his beer. "All right. All right . . ." he choked, coughing. "If that's the way you feel about it . . ."

It was late when Steve finally parted from Gresham, and as he walked across the silent city to his club, he faced the fact that there was no more release for his spirit in show people than there was in the office. The showman had bored him. He realized with dull surprise that even Carla's name had failed to fan a spark of interest in his breast. That fire was out. Over. Dead and buried in its own ashes, and with it went the rest of it. Why? He knew why. It wasn't only Carla. The long climb was over. He had reached the summit and there was nothing further to head for. No place to go. Money? He was glutted with money. Everything he touched turned to more of it. Power? There was no satisfaction in packing a wallop when the fight was over. That was it! The fight was over. He was on top and it was a damned uncomfortable spot to be in, lonely and bitter-cold.

When he reached the club, the old nightwatchman let him in. "How you making out, Collins?"

"Fine, sir. Thank you, sir. Couldn't ask for anything better."

"Satisfied, are you? Don't you find it lonely through the night?"

"Well, yes, sir. Sometimes. But the morning always comes. A man can count on that."

"He can, eh?"

Most of the lamps were out in the big reading room, but a cone of light shone down on old Bert's chair. Steve started toward it. An old man was sitting in it, sound asleep, his gray head slumped forward on his chest, his palid hands feebly clasped in his lap. The book that had slipped from his knees lay on the floor. Steve pulled up short at sight of him. A wave of profound revulsion swept over him, scattering the ashes, lighting a new flame that roared through his heart and burst in his head. His face turned scarlet. "So that's what you're headed for, is it?" he shouted above the rush of his spirit. "That's what it's come to, is it? Like hell it is! What makes you think so? Get out of that chair and stay out. Get out! Get out!"

The sleeper didn't stir, didn't hear him, for there had been no sound in that hushed room. It didn't matter. Steve wasn't addressing the sleeper.

CHAPTER 16

Steve's outer offices were now large and impressive, but his own office was still the modest little room in which he had begun his life on Wall Street. It was considerably more comfortable, now that he had brought in most of the furnishings from his bedroom on Fifth Avenue. A couch was against the wall beneath the photograph of the Iron Queen and a cabinet filled with books stood under the *Cyrus*, still bucking the heavy sea. On the wall facing Steve's swivel chair the worn old antlered buck kept a steady gaze on the bookshelves, and on the wall space between the windows at the end of his desk hung a small painting of a temple on a hill.

On the morning after his encounter with the specter in Bert's old chair, Steve strode through the outer office without a glance at the startled staff just settling down to work, closed the door to his room, and rang for Curtis. Curtis' narrow shoulders in his neat gray suit were stooped now but his step was brisk as he came in.

"Sit down, John." Steve motioned to the chair opposite his own. "I've got something to talk over with you." He lit a cigar, leaned back, crossed his legs, and for a moment his eyes rested on the old buck above Curtis' head. "I might as well start off by telling you now that I knew the first minute I clapped eyes on you away back there in Haley that I needed you more than I did my right arm. I've sucked you dry, John, for twenty-five years. This is the end of it."

"End of it?" Curtis' glasses fell off and he fumbled for them, helpless without them. "End of it? You mean you're retiring me, Steve?"

"Retiring you?" The smile that was so winning and so rare bent Steve's mouth. "That's the last thing I want. I'm doing the retiring. You're on your own here from now on without further interference from me. I'm pulling out, John. For good."

"Pulling out!" Curtis stuttered. "What are you talking about? You can't pull out. You mean you want to liquidate the business?"

"No. Nothing like that." Steve's mouth set again. "You know as well as I do I'm of no further use around here—to myself or anyone else. This game is played out for me. I'm through. I'm getting out, starting over again. There's nothing in having the chips. I've found that out. It's playing the game, win or lose, that counts."

Curtis shook his head. "I can't understand you, Steve. You've got everything you want, everything you started for. What more do you want?"

Steve didn't answer for a moment. "Yes," he said finally. "I suppose most men would see it that way. I don't." He got up and began pacing the room. Curtis, watching, saw the same gleam in his eyes, the same resolute set in his shoulders that he'd seen that night, long ago, in the cabin with Cramer. "What do you expect me to do?" Steve went on. "Warm this chair, push that button the rest of my life? I'm in as good shape as I ever was. Better. I want to hit a new trail, feel a pack on my back again. Damn it, John, a man bossing a construction gang gets more out of life than I do. I'm pulling out. Going back to work while I've still got the sense to do it."

"I don't understand you, Steve," Curtis protested again. "These aren't the old days. You've built up responsibilities. Heavy ones. You can't walk out on them."

"Why not?" Steve wheeled on him. "I built this thing up, didn't I? You mean to tell me I've got to stay with it till I rot? No! I made it and I'm getting rid of it." He sat down, crossed his arms on the desk, and leaned forward. "No use beating around the bush, John. I'm pulling out. There's no great rush about it—but this is no fishing trip. I won't be back."

For a moment the eyes of the two men held, locked across the desk in a look that spanned the past with deep affection. Curtis' bent shoulders straightened. "All right, Steve. If that's the way you want it. If it was any man but you I'd say he was crazy, but you're different. Always have been." He flushed a little. "To tell the truth, I've been afraid of some kind of a break for the past three years, but I didn't expect this. Well, if it's come we'll go through with it. Have you got any plan—know where you're going?"

"No. Anywhere. That will take care of itself when I get loose. I need your advice on that. I want to get out of the market, clean out for cash, without throwing a monkey wrench into the works."

Curtis, nervous, shaken, cleared his throat. "I think it can be done if no one gets wind of it. Lucky those people are after your stocks. You ought to be able to unload privately without going on the market to any extent. You mean to get rid of everything, including the Iron Queen?"

Steve hesitated, shook his head. "No. Not the Queen. Not yet. Let that ride until we see how the rest of it works out. Aside from that I want you to clean me up as if you were closing the estate after my death. When we know what we've got to dispose of, we'll reorganize here. Set up some kind of a trust to take care of it. Don't look so damned upset." He grinned across the desk at Curtis' unhappy face. "It's been done before. A good many of the old customers around here feel pretty much as I do, to judge from the way they're throwing their chips on the table with their art collections and their libraries. There's no satisfaction in that to me. It's the same washed-up old game, trying to beat each other, in reverse. Not my idea of cleaning up."

"What is your idea, Steve?"

"I've told you. Clear out. Start over again from the bottom. Sit in on a new game and see what I can make of it. Why not?"

"Why not?" Curtis looked downright miserable by this time. "Steve, you're crazy. You can't get away with it. You'll lug your reputation with you wherever you go. You actually mean you're going to look for a job somewhere?"

"That's exactly what I do mean." Steve's eyes glittered. "There's a lot of world outside of New York, John, and I'm not known in every tail end of it. Plenty of places to go and no questions asked."

"That's nonsense, Steve." Curtis put in one last protest. "The newspapers will get on to it and you'll be in hot water up to your neck. You want my advice? You're stale, that's all. Take a trip around the world. That's understandable. But don't cut the guy ropes. You're not through here by any means. Inside a year you'll be glad to get back."

Steve leaned back. "All right, John," he said after a moment. "If you're crowded for an explanation, put it on the basis of a trip. It's a good idea. It doesn't alter my decision, but it will ease the take-off. In the meantime, go ahead cleaning house." He glanced at the calendar. "I'll start it myself this morning with Kendicut."

For the next three months Curtis cautiously prepared the way for Steve's withdrawal from active business on Wall Street. The market was strong. Gradually, quietly, Steve's holdings were absorbed and sizable deposits spotted in various banks, but the bulk of the great fortune, converted into bonds and cash, lay snug in the deep vaults of the bank beneath his office.

One morning during this time Steve found a letter on his desk that decided his future. He had heard from Harding from time to time, seen him once or twice over the years, but the last news of him had come from Alaska. Now Harding had written that he was back in Peru and Baker was with him in an attempt to push a railroad through the jungle to another copper deposit. The work was slow, hazardous, and with little promise of success; but both men, fascinated by the challenge of the unexplored region, were staying with it until success or disaster put an end to it. The letter was brief but Steve's blood was racing with impatience to get there before he finished it.

His plans were made and passage taken on an obscure freighter headed for Peru the following week when, one day in October, Curtis came in with a big sheaf of papers and sat down with him for a final checkup. Steve shoved the papers aside. "No use going over all this again," he said. "Just give me a rough idea of how I stand."

"That's no way to wind up a business of this size," protested Curtis with asperity. "But if that's the way you want it, I'd say you've got around sixty millions, more or less. About twenty millions in cash, the rest in negotiable bonds, plus your Iron Queen stock, which you own outright. You're out of the active market entirely."

"Fine." Steve nodded with indifference. "That ought to cover it. The next step is to make a new will and parcel it out. We've been over that but we'd better go over it again. First, the income on a trust fund of ten millions, plus the income from her personal fortune, plus the Fifth Avenue property to Amelia, the trust to revert on her death to this endowment fund you're setting up. Second, my holdings in the Iron Queen to Carla Bradway." He raised his hand impatiently as Curtis attempted to speak. "No use going into any further argument about that. I've made her my legal heir. I've told you why. She's my flesh and blood, John. There's a pull about that a man can't get around when it comes to a showdown. Furthermore, the chances are I never would have had the old Queen if her mother's savings hadn't been in my pants when I went to Boston. She's entitled to it, now she's quit Victor. I want her to know why she's entitled to it when the time comes. That's definite." He swung away and looked out of the window for a moment. Swung back. "That's about it, John. You've got the list for the rest of it. I wish you and Mary would take that million now. You've earned it twice over. It's yours. You can't avoid getting it under my will and it would mean a lot to me to see you have it. At any rate," he went on, "there's plenty left for that scholarship business of yours. That was a fine idea, John. A lot of youngsters will have you to thank for it. If he'll take it, pass the administration of it on to young Steve when you're through with it. That's that. Draw up those papers and I'll sign 'em. I'm leaving next week."

Neither man said anything more for some time. Curtis took off his glasses to wipe the moisture from them and Steve swung back to the window. "Seems to be some excitement down on the Street," he said after a while. "What's going on?"

Curtis, grateful for the change of subject, got up and joined him at the window. Men were gathered in little knots on the curb and clustered on the steps of the bank opposite. "The market's been soft for a week, Steve," he said. "It's been dropping all morning. Looks as if we're in for a slump."

"Think our getting out had anything to do with it?"

"No. We've been out for a month. Funny thing, Steve"—he tried to smile—"you can't make a move without making money. You got out at the top all along the line. If you'd go back in today you'd make millions."

Steve laughed and clapped him on the back. He let his hand linger there. "No dice, John. I'm out for good." His shoulders straightened. "Talk about millions. I haven't felt as fine as this since Harding showed up at the Iron Queen. That's the game for me. Sitting in an office, dodging in and out of the market is a poor way to gamble. What's causing this slump?"

"Lack of confidence in those banks headed by that bunch of plungers mixed up in that copper deal of Hamby's a few weeks ago. There's been quite a run on them but the clearing house has plugged it up. It'll be over in a day or two, but I hear Hamby's been cleaned out."

It wasn't over the next day, or the next. On the contrary, uneasiness spread to panic as the days went by, and people swarmed to all banks, demanding their deposits, selling stocks, calling loans. Banks, trust companies, brokerage houses went under. Private capital hesitated to come in, afraid of foundering to no purpose in the disastrous whirlpool that was sucking the financial structure of the country to the bottom. Prices on the stock market plunged, and the market wavered on the brink of closing for lack of funds to finance sales. It was a situation without parallel in the history of Wall Street.

On the day that Steve expected to sail for Peru, he was still in his office, unable to turn his back and run away from the crisis. Due to his extraordinary luck in getting out when he did, he was not deeply affected by it. Deposits, turned over to various banks for use in the

285

early stage of the trouble, were gone but the great bulk of his fortune lay in the dark vaults beneath his feet. He was safe and strong and had every intention of remaining that way.

He stood in the window that morning, his hands in his pockets, looking down at the excited crowd that jammed the street in front of Morrison's office. Men were looking for help there, as he had done years ago. He was wondering if they would get it when Curtis, pale with anxiety, hurried in. "Morrison has called a conference in his office. He's sent for you, Steve. He wants you over there. He's trying to save the market. He'll want you to chip in. I hear Stanzer's over there."

"All right." Steve swung around, his face changed—lit up. "If he needs it he can have it. No individual can save this thing, John, but if Morrison can get a big enough bunch to chip in he can save it. There's plenty of money around if he can smoke it out. Tell him I'll be over in five minutes."

Steve, bareheaded, had a hard time getting across the street. The crowd resented his big bulk forcing its way through. Faces haggard from strain, desperate faces, eyes in which madness lurked turned to watch his course. When he mounted the shallow steps to Morrison's building, an ominous murmur swept over the crowd. "That's Bradway." . . . "There goes one of the sons of bitches." . . . "Bradway? He got out a month ago, didn't he?" . . . "Sure, he did. They all did. Going in there now to clean up at the bottom. Ought to go in there and lynch the lot of 'em." . . . "I can't go home to my wife. I can't. I can't."

The heavy bronze doors clanged shut behind Steve. He strode rapidly through the outer office and he had no difficulty now in getting past the glass partition. A dozen men were sitting around the big desk, and once more Steve met the cold, penetrating stare of Morrison's black eyes. "Sit down, Mr. Bradway."

Steve didn't—he stood. His eyes swept over the faces of the men assembled at the table. "There is no necessity for me to waste your time, gentlemen," he said. "I know why we're here. I have twenty millions in cash across the street. You are welcome to all or any part of it."

A stir went around the table. Shoulders straightened. Eyes looked up. There was no change of expression in Morrison's face. "There is no need for undue generosity, Mr. Bradway," he said. "There is no security at present behind these loans, and no guarantee that our effort will succeed. That is understood?"

"Perfectly." Steve met the banker's steady gaze. "You'll pull this through if any man can, Mr. Morrison. If you fail, we all fail and I'll be back where I started—with the Iron Queen." He gave Morrison a quick smile, then his glance, resolute, kindling, went around the table again. "This is no time for talk, gentlemen. It's to our personal interests to act—and act quick. There isn't a man here who won't suffer if we don't."

Less than an hour later the immense fund from private capital that Morrison needed to steady the banks and keep the market going had been subscribed and the tired men prepared to leave. "You're the biggest man among us, Mr. Bradway," said Morrison cryptically. "Your voice may carry further than most. As you go out you might say to those people on the street that the worst is over. The market will not close, and clearing-house certificates will be in circulation tomorrow."

As Steve went through the bronze doors, the dense crowd was still milling about the street, and as he appeared, a murmur again swept through it. Steve stood on the top step and raised both arms high above his head. "Quiet!" he shouted. "Quiet. Listen to me. The panic's over. Tomorrow——"

"Over!" A voice screamed on a high-pitched laugh. "Over! You bet it's over!"

Two shots rang out in quick succession, and a guard leaped past Steve to seize a sobbing, twitching bundle of clothes sprawled at the foot of the steps. Steve spun around. His head went up as if his ear had caught an echo coming from a great distance, and a smile of surprised satisfaction spread over his face. A second guard rushed past, stopped short at the sight of that extraordinary smile. "Are you all right, Mr. Bradway?"

"All right? Sure. Sure." The shining, vivid green eyes looked down at the rapidly spreading patch of crimson on his white shirt. He shook his head, puzzled. "Sure," he repeated. "He couldn't have done better for me, Matt. He fixed it fine with that shot. I'm squared away now. Squared away. . . ."

Before the astonished guard could reach him, Steve Bradway crashed like a tall pine across the threshold to Morrison's office.